LINK + HUD

HEROES BY A HAIR

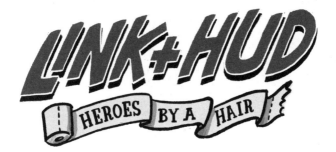

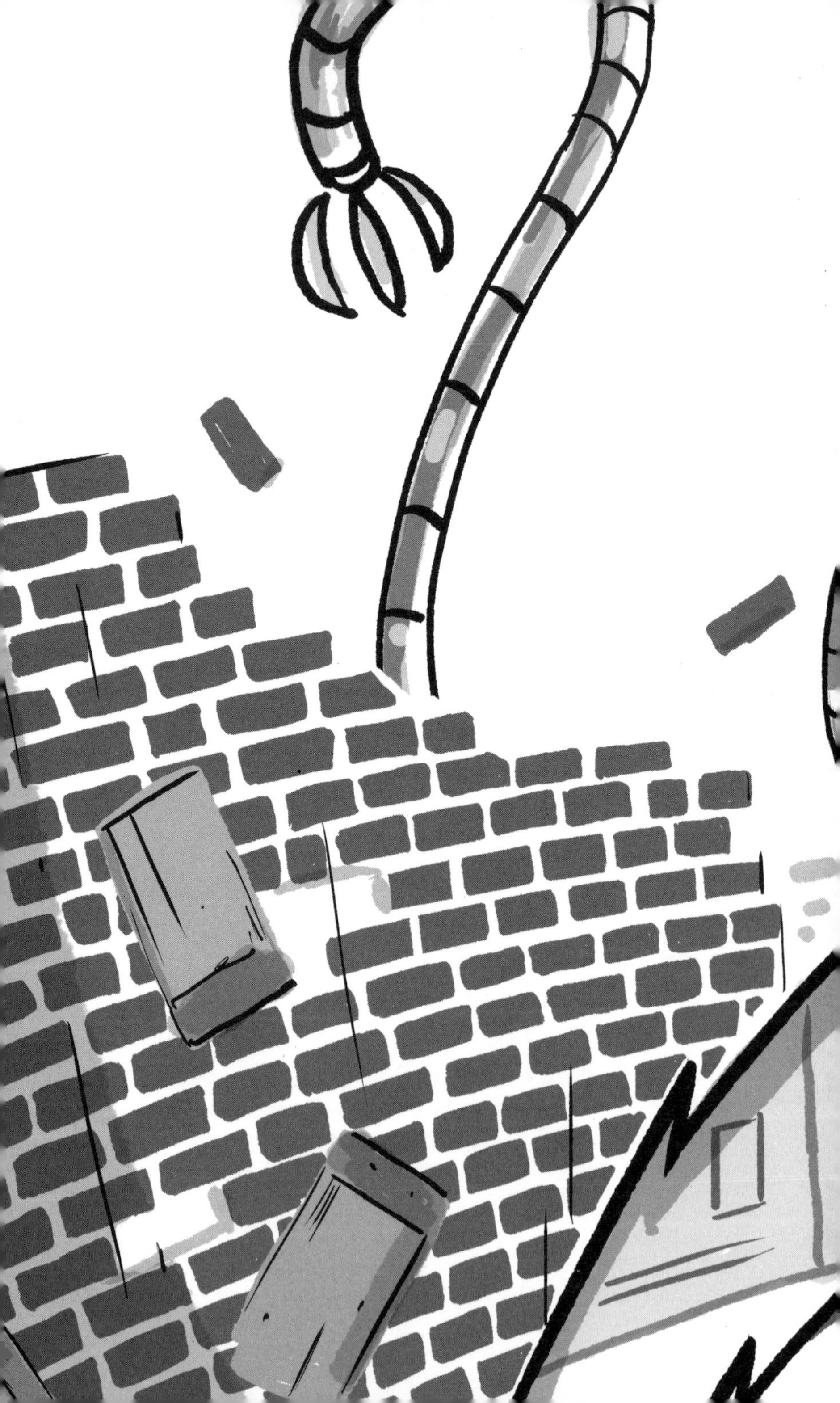

JARRETT PUMPHREY

JEROME PUMPHREY

LINK + HUD

HEROES BY A HAIR

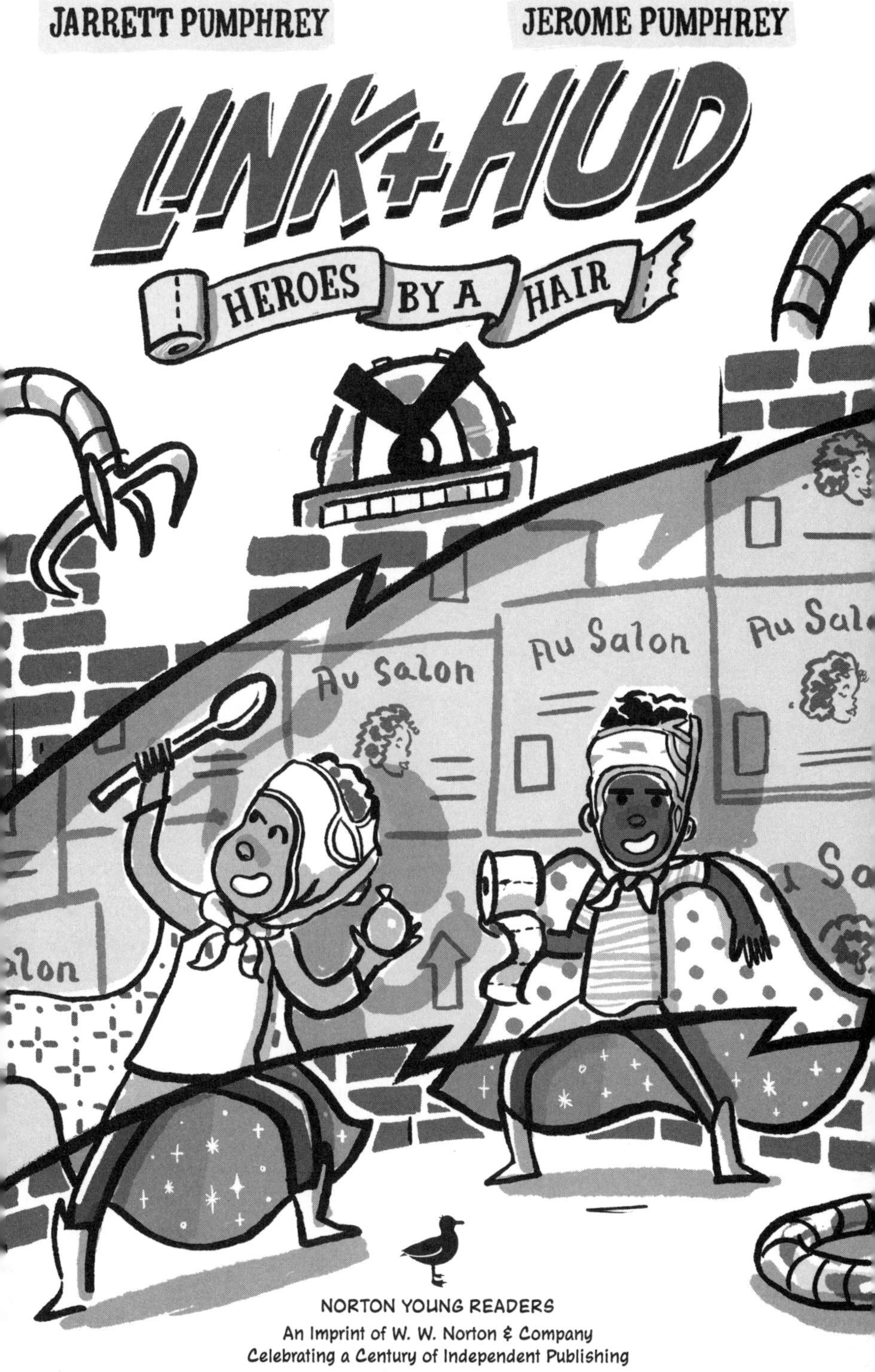
Au Salon
Au Salon
Au Sal
alon

NORTON YOUNG READERS
An Imprint of W. W. Norton & Company
Celebrating a Century of Independent Publishing

For Link and Hud

—Jarrett

For Lily, Ryden, and Effie

—Jerome

With special thanks to Simon Boughton
for asking us about brothers.

For information about permission to reproduce selections from this book, write to
Permissions, W. W. Norton & Company, Inc., 500 Fifth Avenue, New York, NY 10110

For information about special discounts for bulk purchases, please contact
W. W. Norton Special Sales at specialsales@wwnorton.com or 800-233-4830

Manufacturing by Lake Book Manufacturing
Book design by Hana Anouk Nakamura
Production managers: Anna Oler and Delaney Adams

ISBN 978-1-324-01609-0

W. W. Norton & Company, Inc., 500 Fifth Avenue, New York, N.Y. 10110
www.wwnorton.com

W. W. Norton & Company Ltd., 15 Carlisle Street, London W1D 3BS

1 2 3 4 5 6 7 8 9 0

LINK + HUD

HEROES BY A HAIR

Au Salon

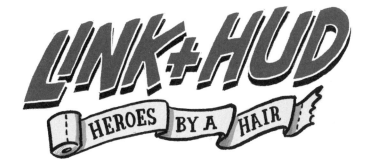

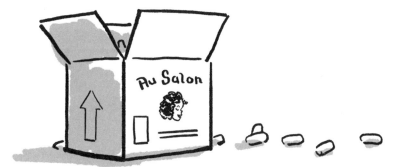

CHAPTER ONE

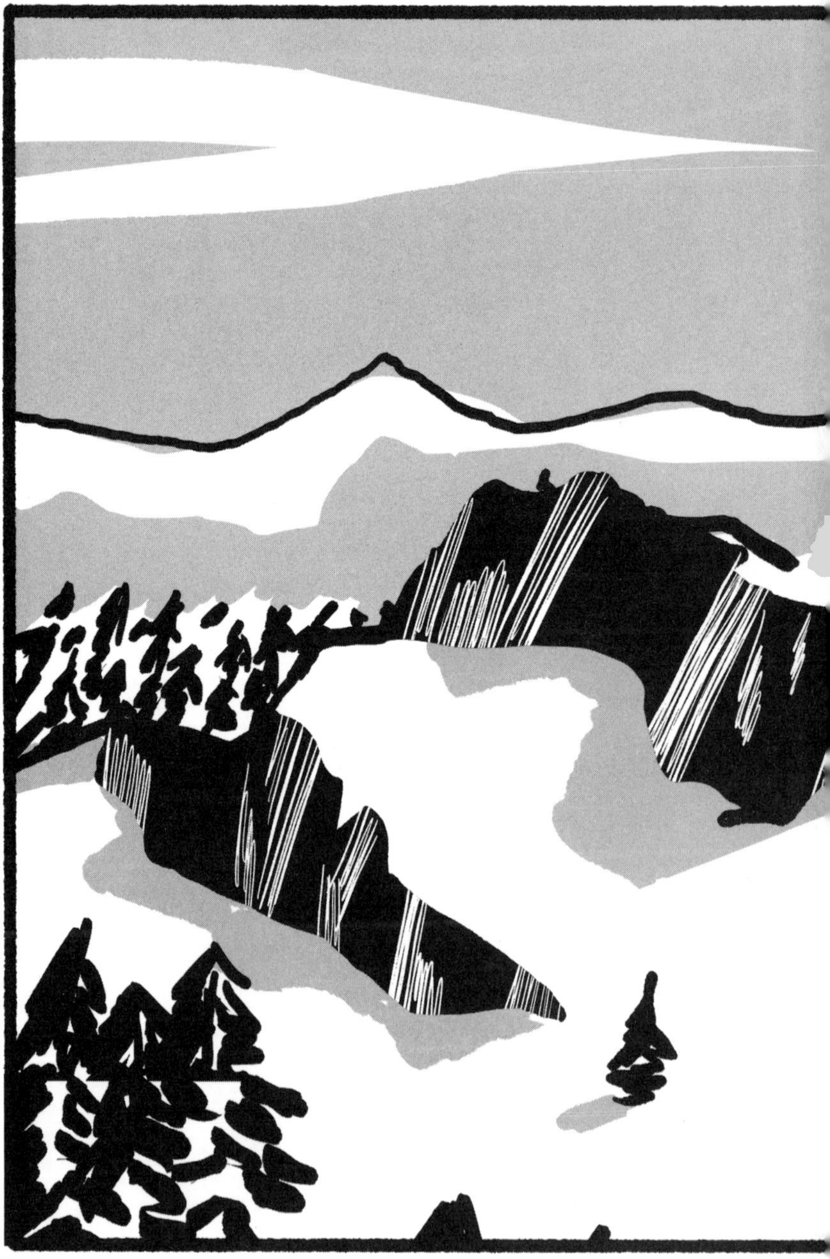

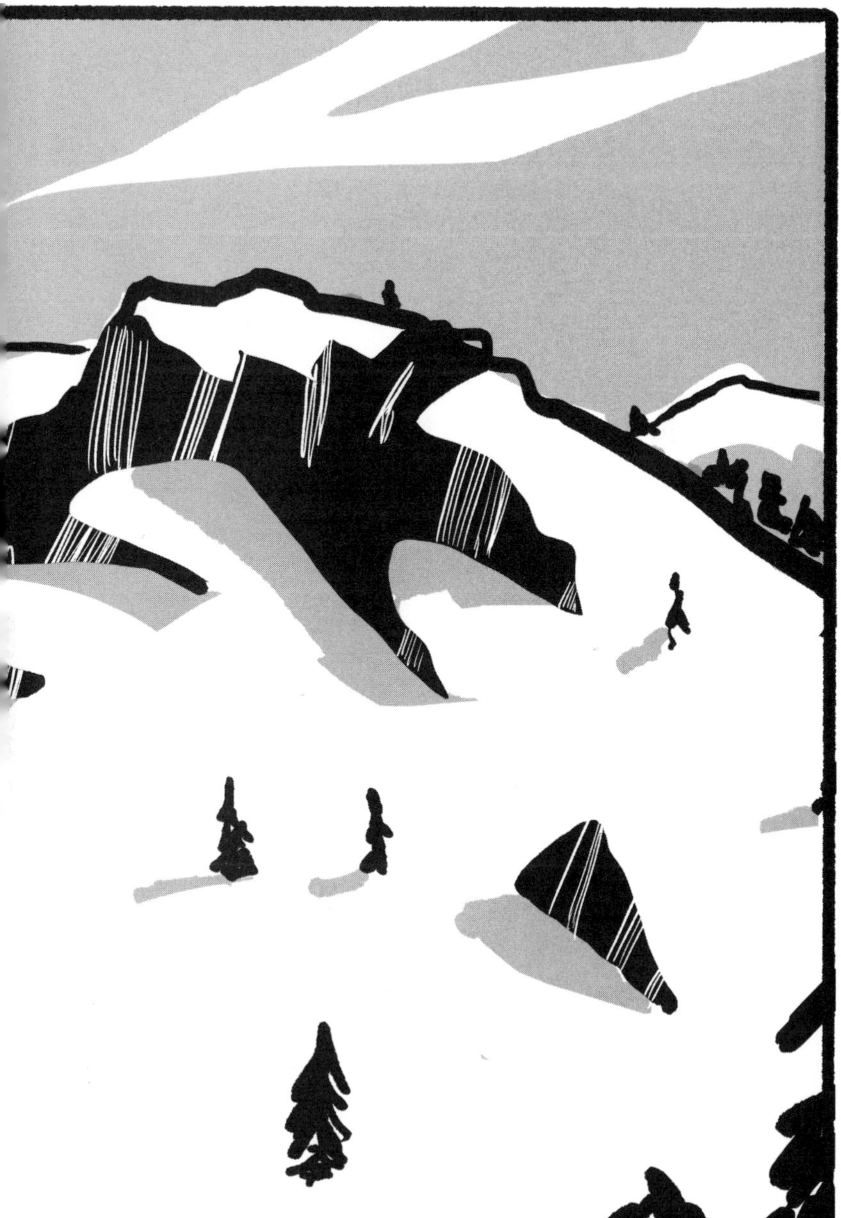

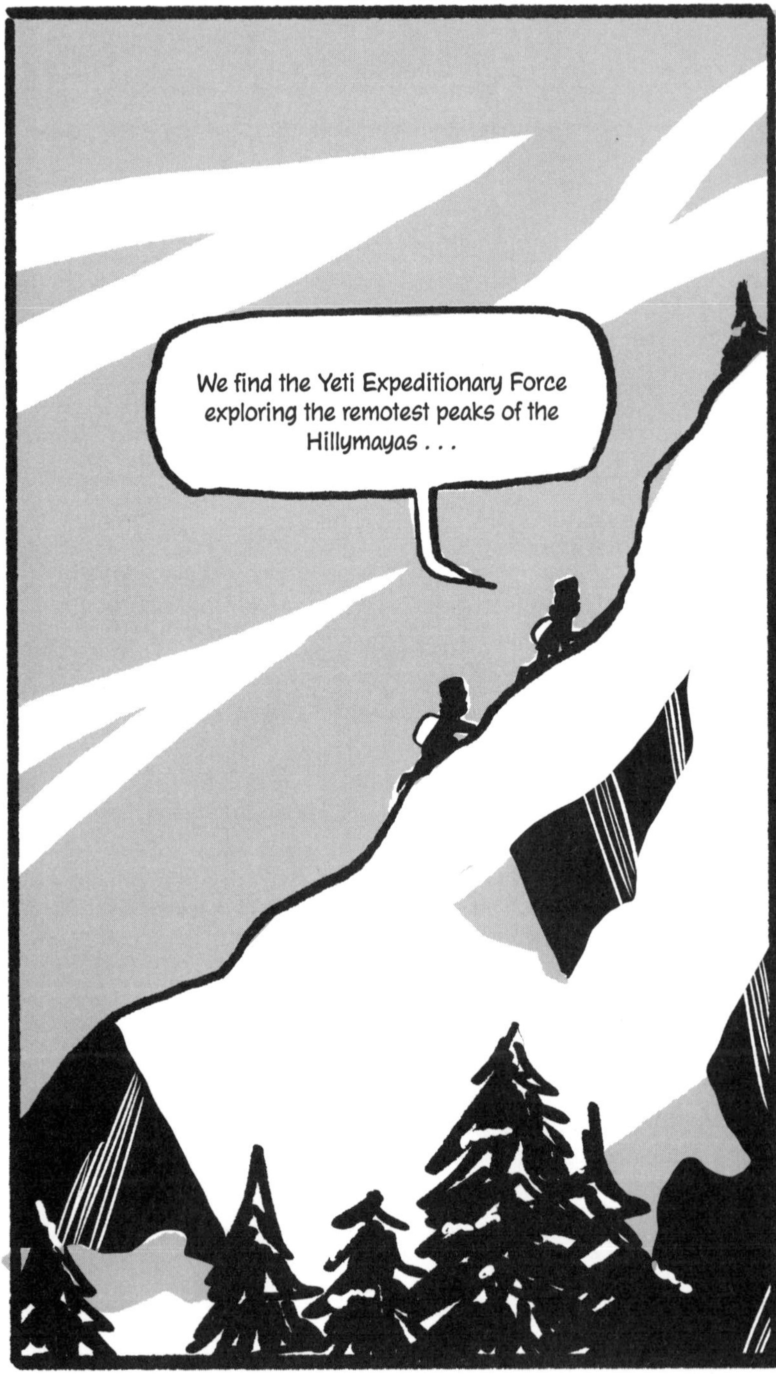
We find the Yeti Expeditionary Force exploring the remotest peaks of the Hillymayas . . .

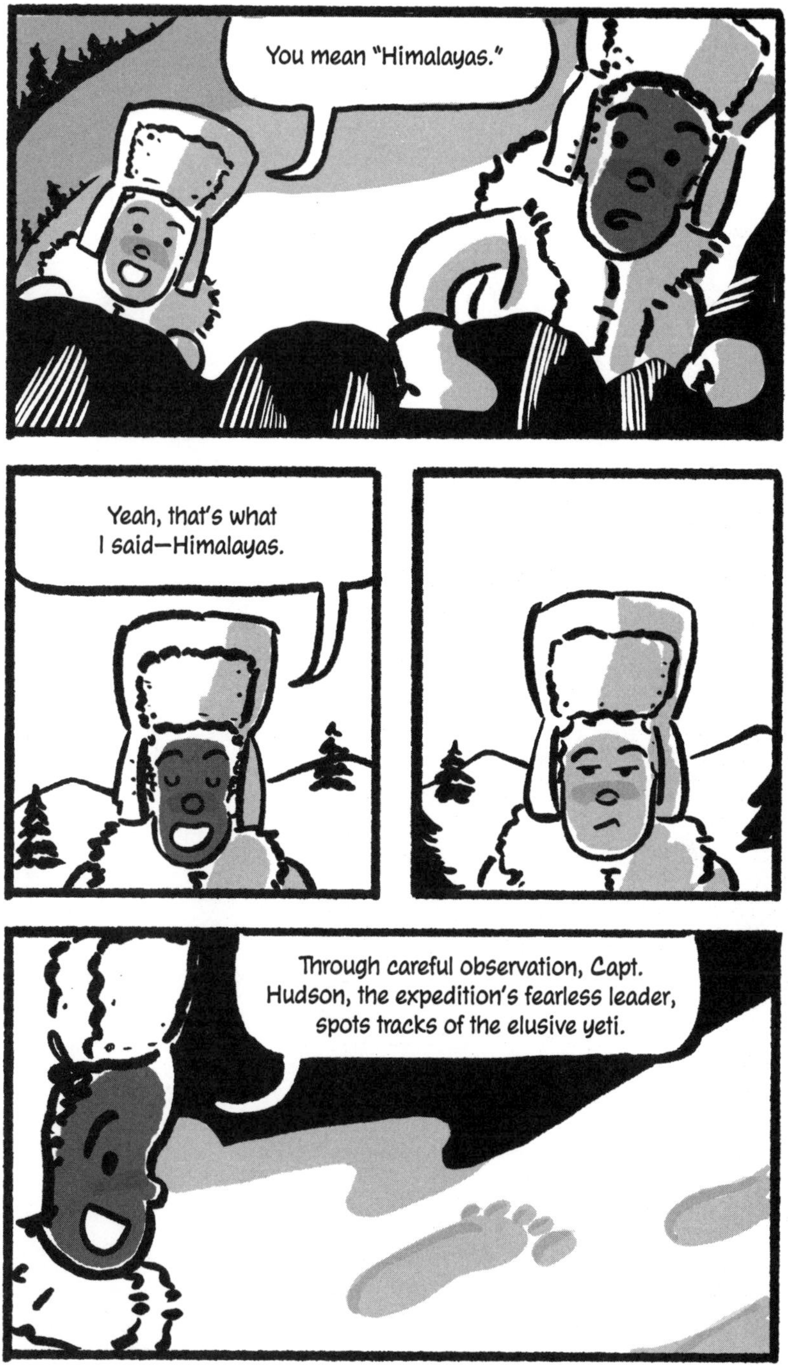
You mean "Himalayas."
Yeah, that's what I said—Himalayas.
Through careful observation, Capt. Hudson, the expedition's fearless leader, spots tracks of the elusive yeti.

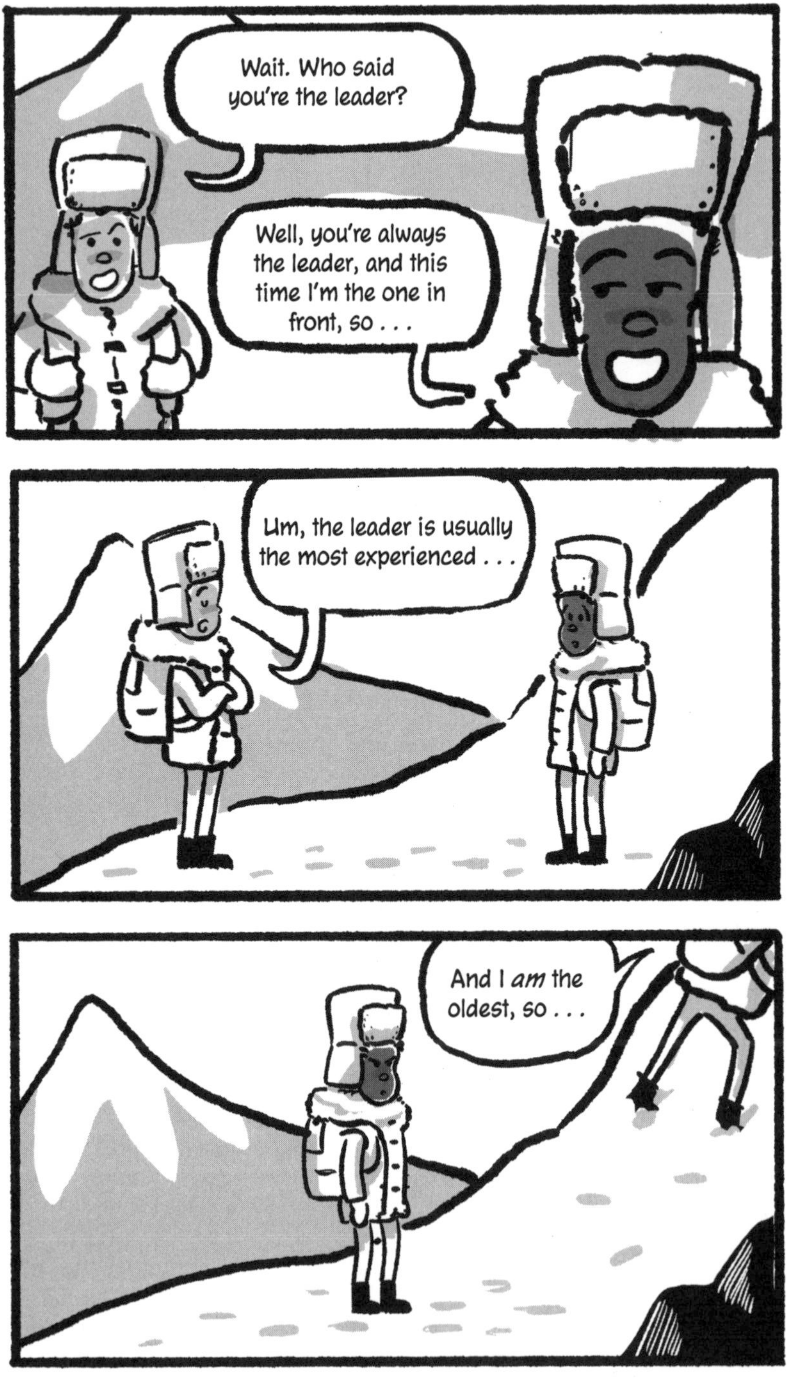
Wait. Who said you're the leader?
Well, you're always the leader, and this time I'm the one in front, so . . .
Um, the leader is usually the most experienced . . .
And I *am* the oldest, so . . .

Capt. *Lincoln*, the real leader of the expedition, climbs to a higher elevation to get a better view.

KRUNCH
KRUNCH

Mr. Hudson sits *quietly* and doesn't distract him.

KRUNCH
KRUNCH

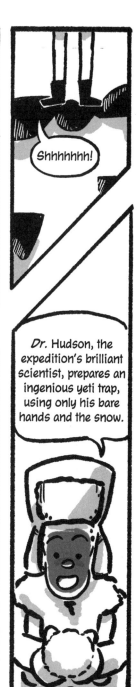

Shhhhhhh!

Dr. Hudson, the expedition's brilliant scientist, prepares an ingenious yeti trap, using only his bare hands and the snow.

5

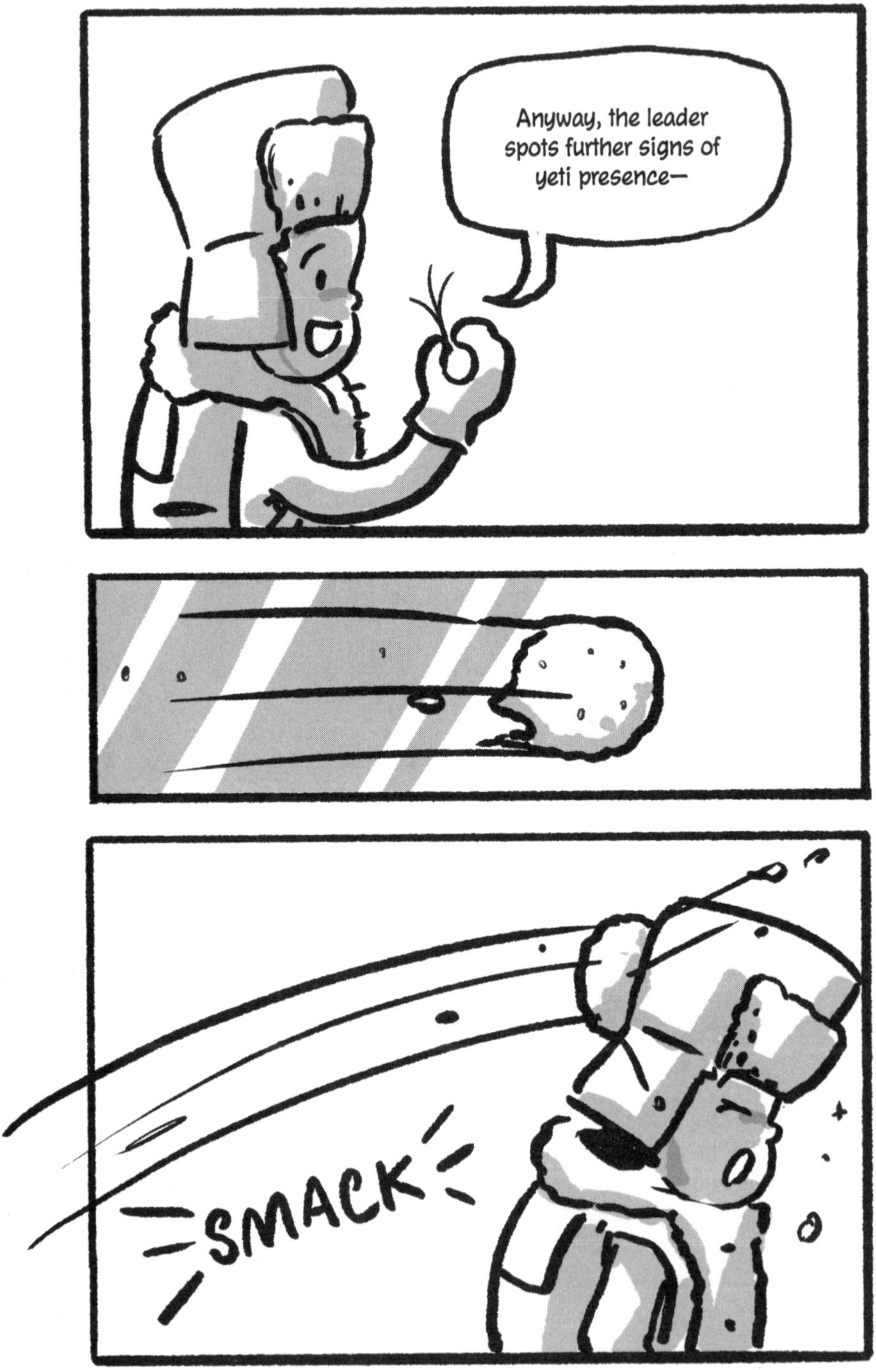
Anyway, the leader spots further signs of yeti presence—
SMACK

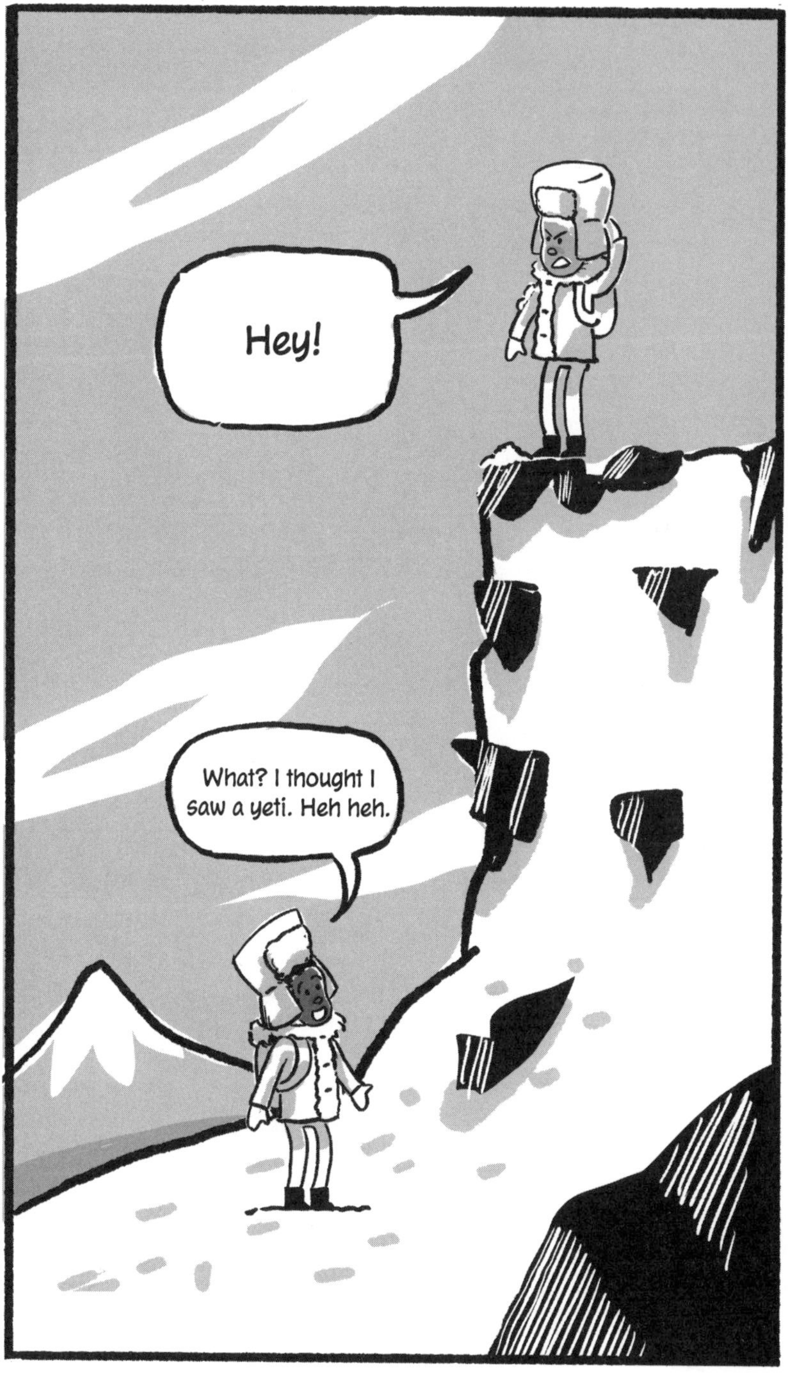
Hey!
What? I thought I saw a yeti. Heh heh.

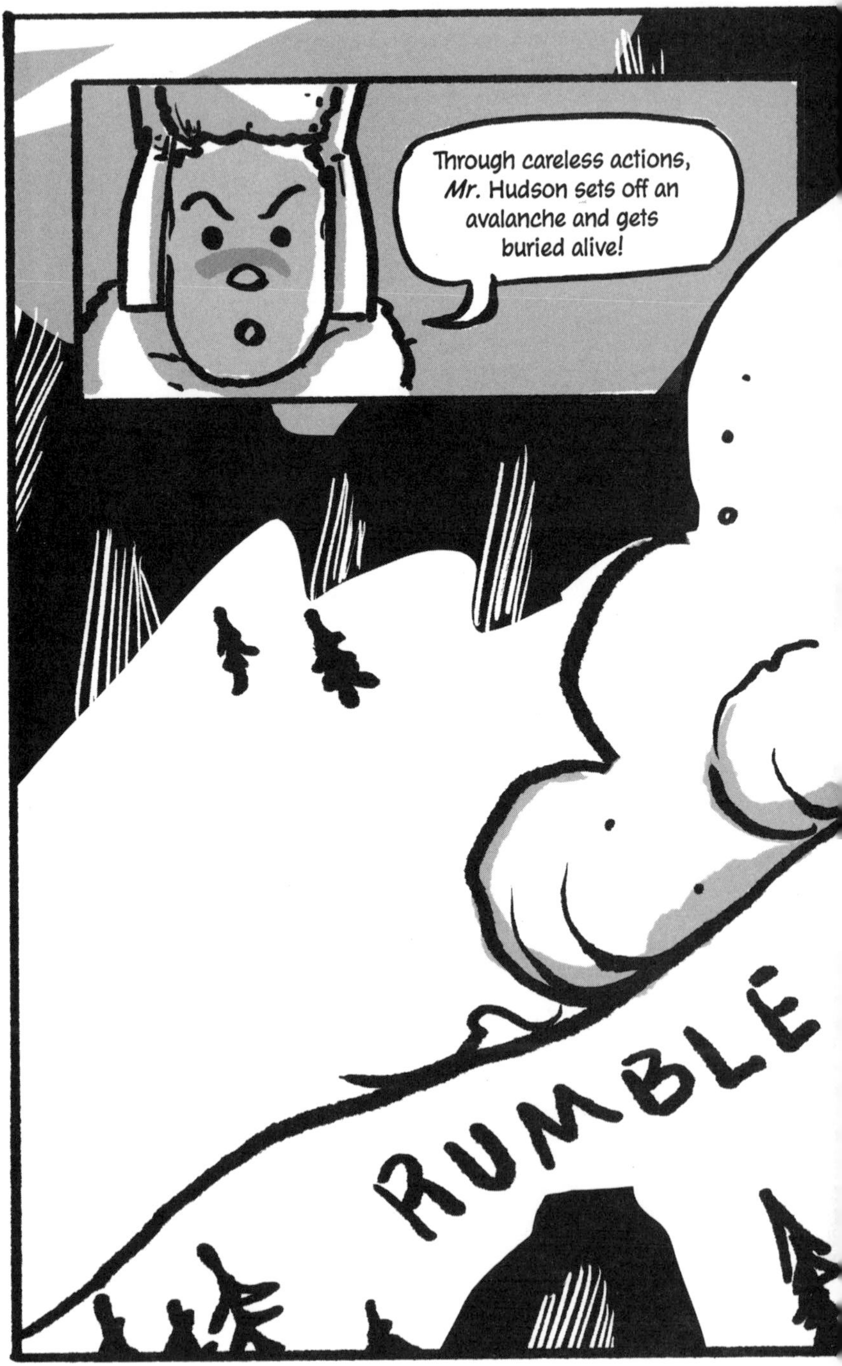
Through careless actions, *Mr.* Hudson sets off an avalanche and gets buried alive!
RUMBLE

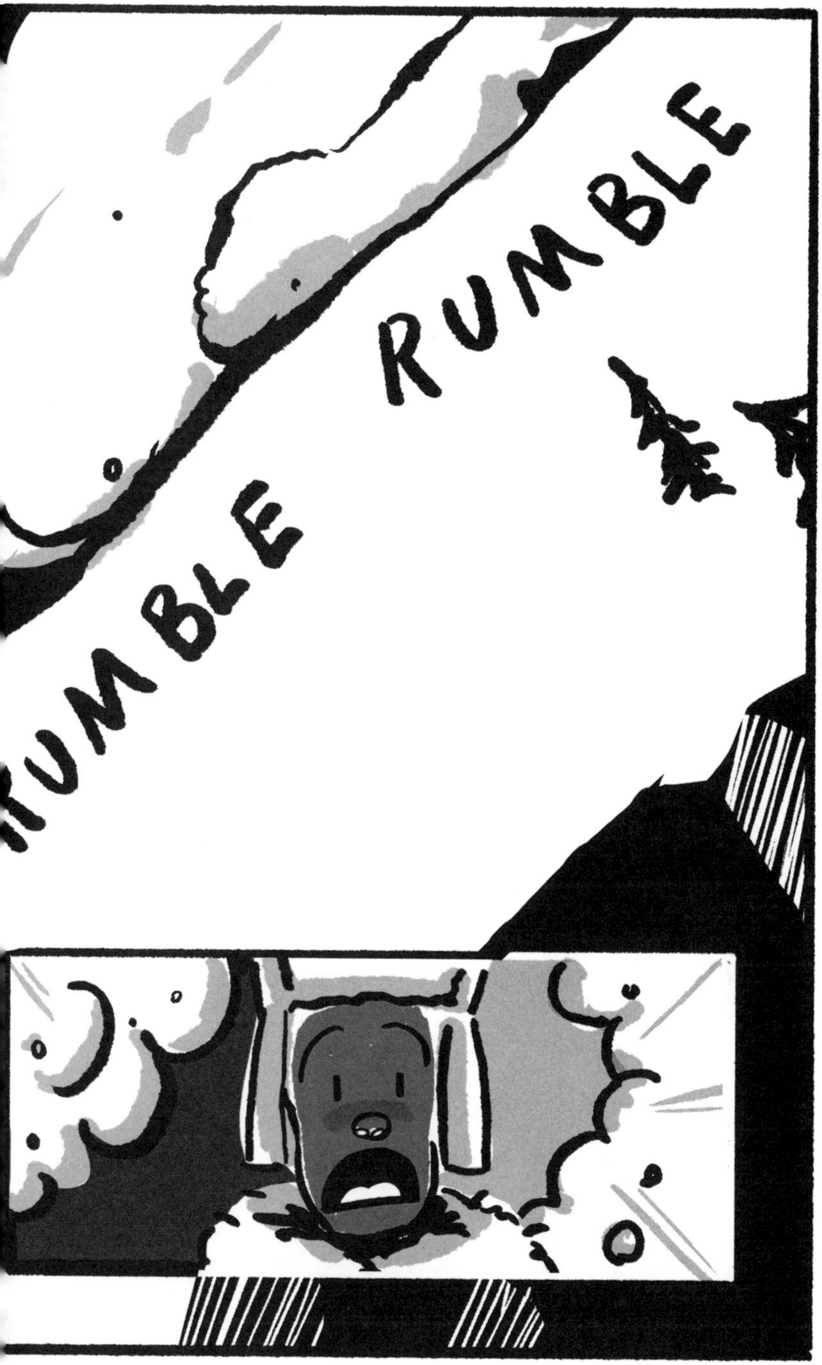
RUMBLE
RUMBLE

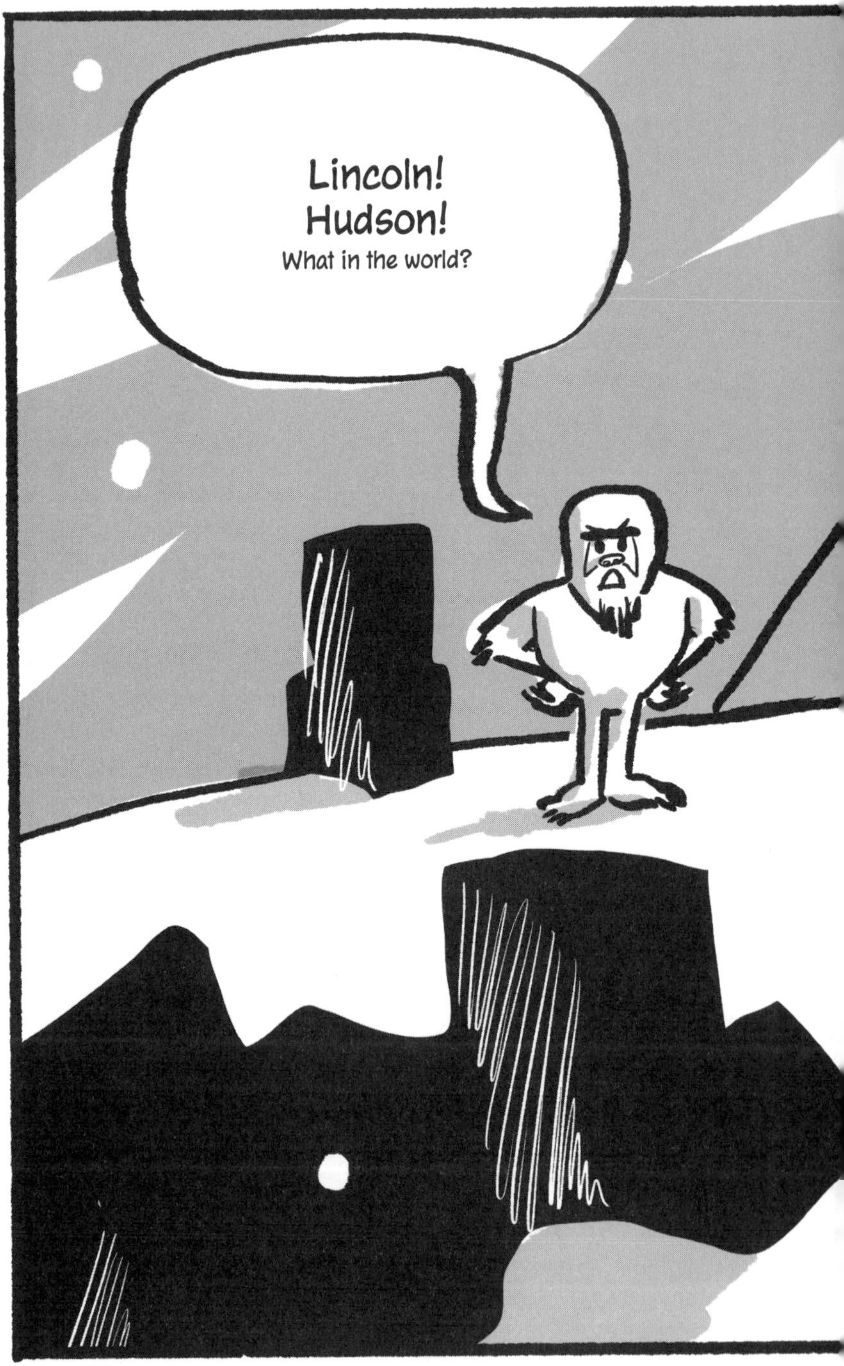
Lincoln!
Hudson!
What in the world?

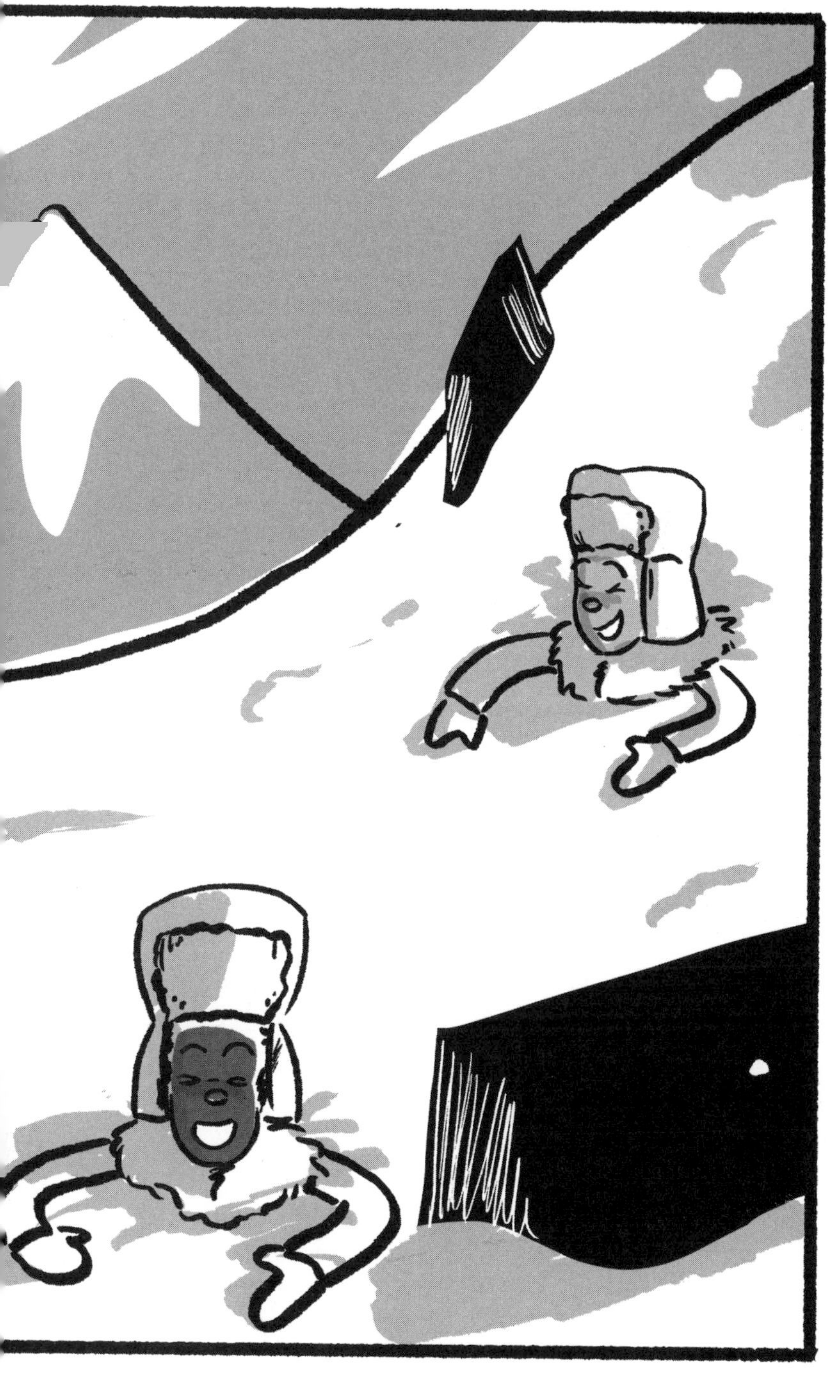

CHAPTER TWO

LINK AND HUD DUPRÉ ARE BROTHERS. THEY'RE also heroes. Well, in their heads they are, anyway.

See, Link and Hud have what some grown-ups might call "active imaginations."

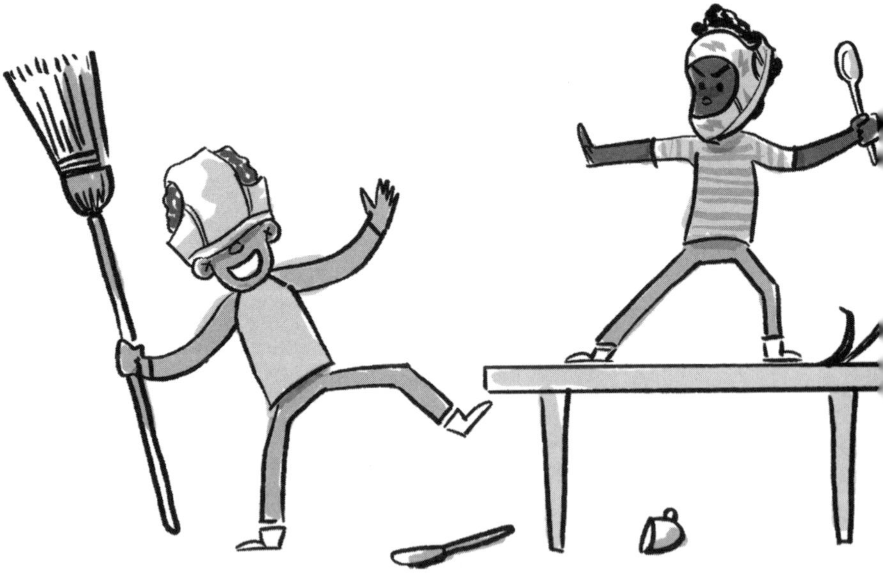

Link and Hud's imaginations are not like, say, daydreaming, an inactive sort of imagination that sits at the window, stares at the clouds, and dreams of puffy bunnies. Link and Hud's imaginations are the sort that would chase those puffy bunnies up the wall and around

Goodness me. Those boys have such active imaginations.

the ceiling while hooting and hollering and upending the furniture. All while also saving the world. Or exploring ancient tombs. Or slaying mythical monsters. Or doing any number of things heroes do.

Link and Hud's imaginations aren't just active, they run wild and free. The problem is, it's usually right out of their heads and all over the place.

Like right now.

"Lincoln! Hudson!"

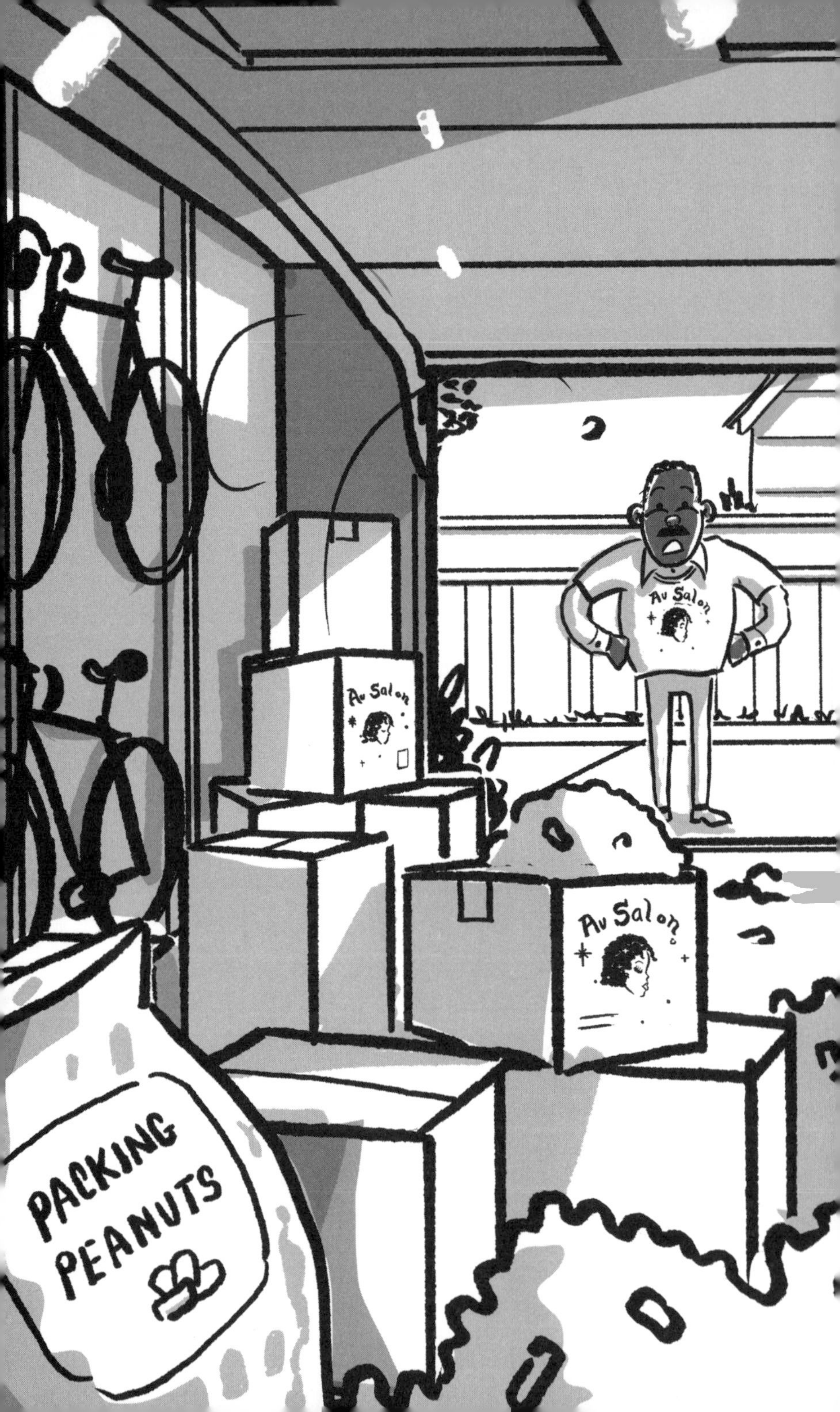
Au Salon
Au Salon
Au Salon
PACKING
PEANUTS

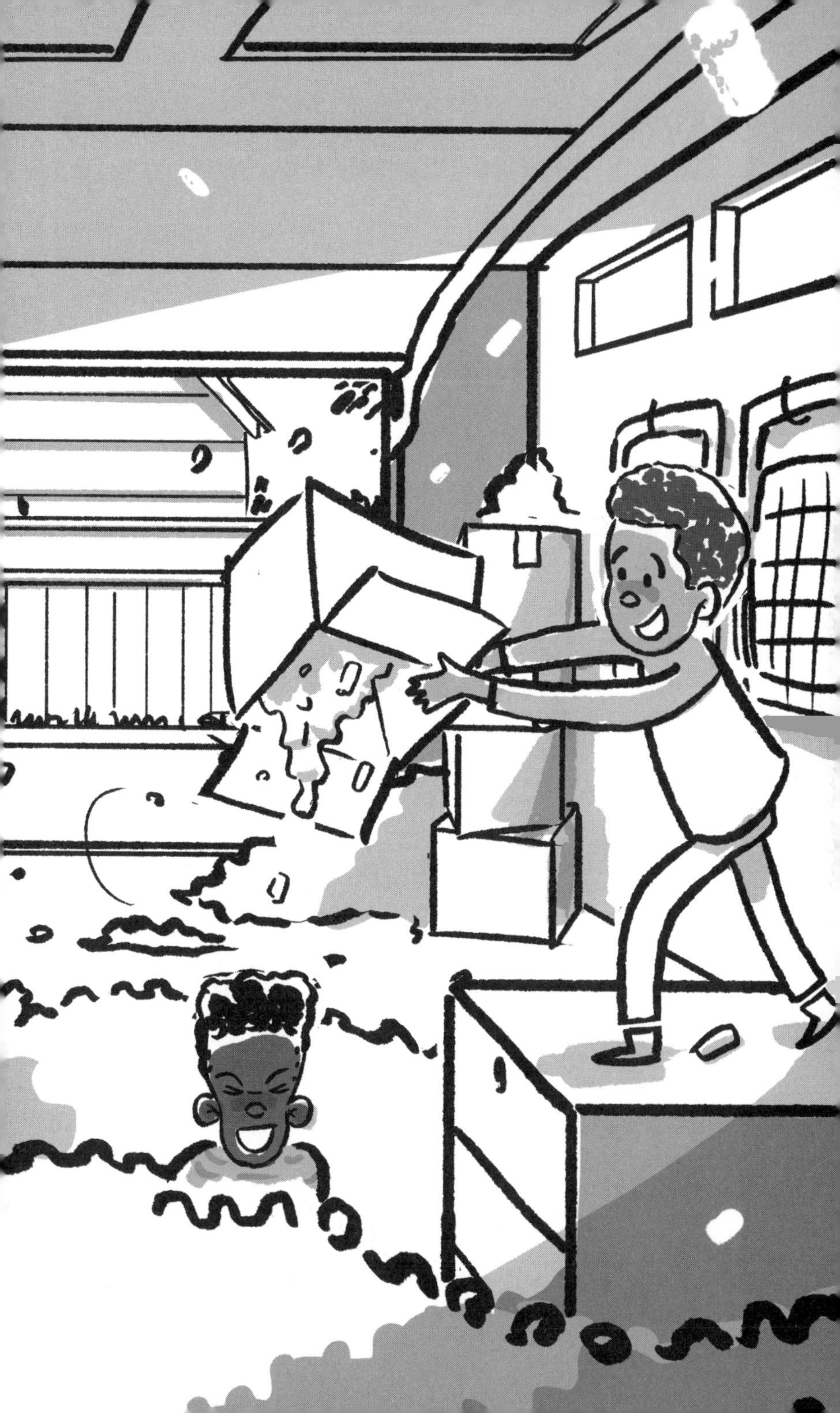

CHAPTER THREE

LINK AND HUD FROZE IN THE BLIZZARD OF Styrofoam.

"What in the world?"

That's Dr. Dupré. He's Link and Hud's dad. He's also a podiatrist, and he's just arrived home from a long day at the practice. The packing peanuts are his. Not for treating feet. That would be weird. For treating hair.

"Have y'all lost y'all's minds?"

"We were gonna clean it up," said Link quickly, as he tried unsuccessfully to shake a clingy peanut from his hand.

"Yeah, sorry, Dad," said Hud, who had started shoveling peanuts back into an empty box, though they went flitting everywhere else instead.

"You were 'gonna clean it up'?" Dr. Dupré stood there, shaking his head. "Y'all aren't even supposed to be out here. How many times have I told you two the garage is off limits? Au Salon business only."

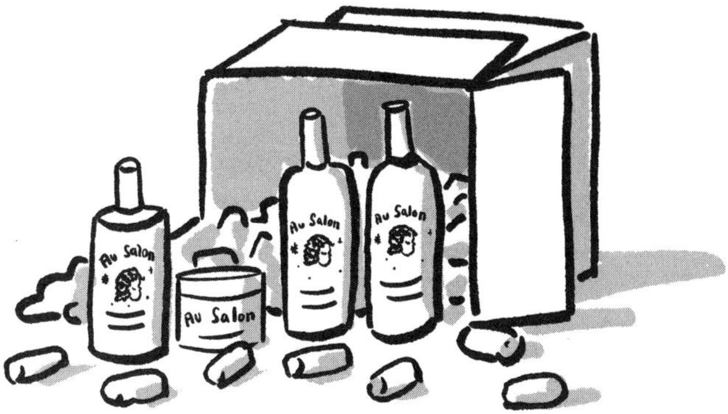
Au Salon
Au Salon
Au Salon
Au Salon

Dr. Dupré believed in a strict regimen of work and more work. During the day, he worked in his practice fixing problems with people's feet. At night, he worked in the garage fixing problems people didn't even know they had. The latest "problem" was Black hair. Au Salon, a full line of Black hair-care products he'd invented, was his solution. (Part of his "head-to-toe" business strategy.) The packing peanuts Link and Hud had been swimming in were for protecting the Au Salon orders Dr. Dupré shipped to his customers. At least, that was the plan. He hadn't actually received any orders to ship yet.

"What were y'all thinking?" said Dr. Dupré.

"Well," said Hud, "we were in the Hillymayas, and—"

"Dad," Link cut in, "we'll clean it up."

"Oh, you bet you will," said Dr. Dupré. "And after that, it's off to your room for the night."

"But, Dad—"

"Unh-unh," said Dr. Dupré. "Not a word."

Link gave up on shaking the clingy peanut from his hand as more started climbing his legs. Hud dropped the box he'd been trying to fill and—*poof!*—more peanuts went flitting.

"Tonight's an important night for me and your mama," Dr. Dupré continued. "We're hosting our first Au Salon sales meeting to hopefully get this business going, and now we gotta deal with this."

A gust of wind kicked up a flurry of peanuts.

"So, c'mon, get to it and then get to your room before our guests start arriving."

Link and Hud looked at each other and slumped their shoulders. *Aw, man.*

"Now, where's Layla? And why wasn't she watching y'all?"

CHAPTER FOUR

OH, THERE'S LAYLA.

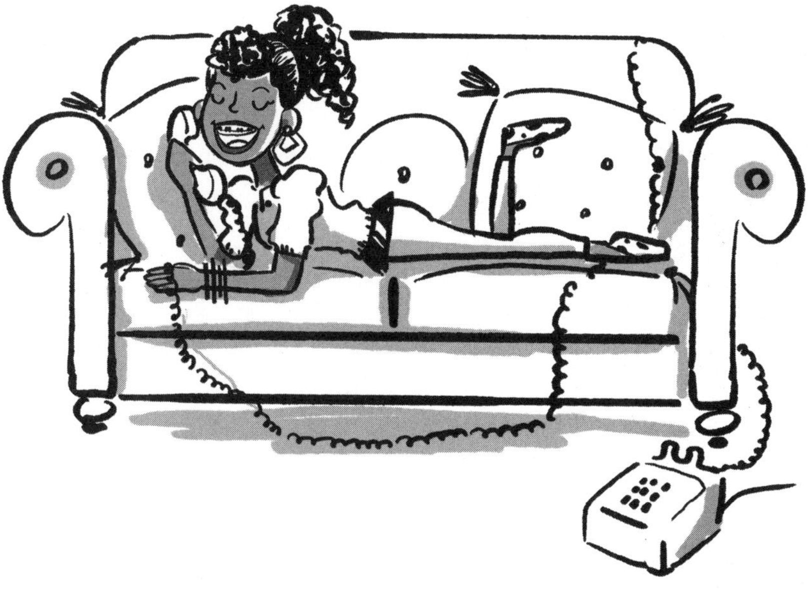
I know, right? I told Donna, like, she should just go talk to him already.

And that's why she wasn't watching Link and Hud.

Layla is Link and Hud's neighbor. She's also the babysitter Dr. and Mrs. Dupré hired to watch the boys every day after school. "Just to make sure they don't destroy the house," Dr. Dupré had joked with Layla's parents the day he offered her the job. "You know, them and their active imaginations. Ha ha."

Layla wasn't the first babysitter to watch—or not watch, as the case may be—Link and Hud. Becca, another neighbor, had tried and failed. So had Nina from down the block. And Lisa from two streets over.

Now, maybe you're thinking if Becca or Nina or Lisa had warned Layla about Link and Hud, she would have had better luck. Well, sure, that would have been nice of them. But for one, Layla didn't know Becca or Nina or Lisa. And two, she probably would have still taken her eyes off Link and Hud for what she swore was just a few minutes to take what she promised was, like, a really important phone call.

Did that make her a bad babysitter? Link didn't think so. Hud thought maybe it did a little bit.

But in any case, neither Link nor Hud felt that great when they watched from the garage as their dad walked a tearful Layla home for what was probably the last time.

"What's gonna happen now?" said Link.

"Well, Dad said he wanted us to clean up these peanuts," said Hud, as he threw a handful of peanuts in the air. "Nook, I can cash wun on ny ton!"

"No." Link rolled his eyes. "I mean, what's gonna happen if Layla can't come back?"

pffffth! Hud spit out the peanut and wiped his tongue on his shirt. "Oh, yeah. That's what I thought you meant."

"It's not like we destroyed the house," said Link.

"Yeah, it was just the garage," said Hud.

Link rolled his eyes again. Hud threw more peanuts in the air.

"Hey, hop to it, fellas." Dr. Dupré was back from Layla's. "Your mama's gon' be home soon, and y'all definitely don't want her to see this." He grabbed an Au Salon box and headed inside.

"Maybe it's not so bad if we get another babysitter," said Hud. "Maybe a new babysitter will let us do whatever we want—even more!"

"Yeah, maybe," said Link. But he wasn't so sure about that.

CHAPTER FIVE

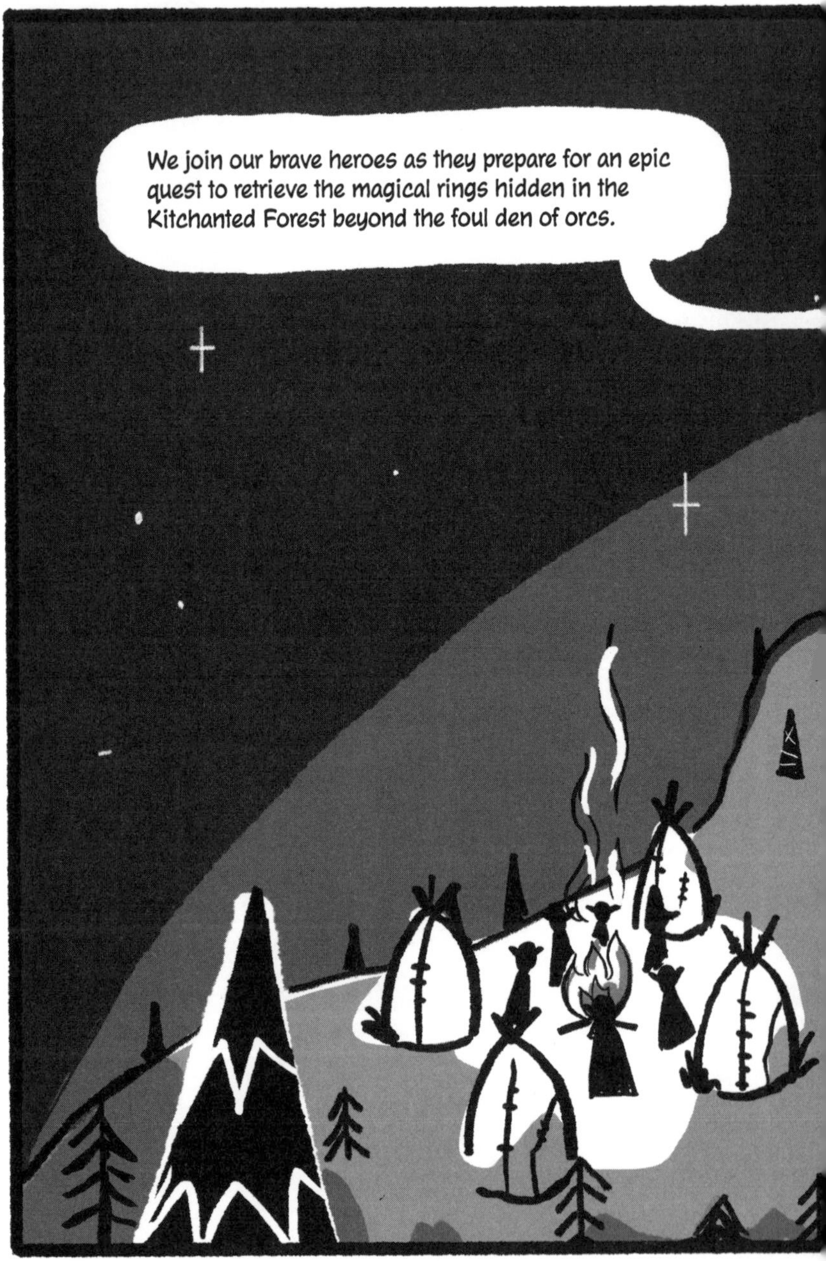
We join our brave heroes as they prepare for an epic quest to retrieve the magical rings hidden in the Kitchanted Forest beyond the foul den of orcs.

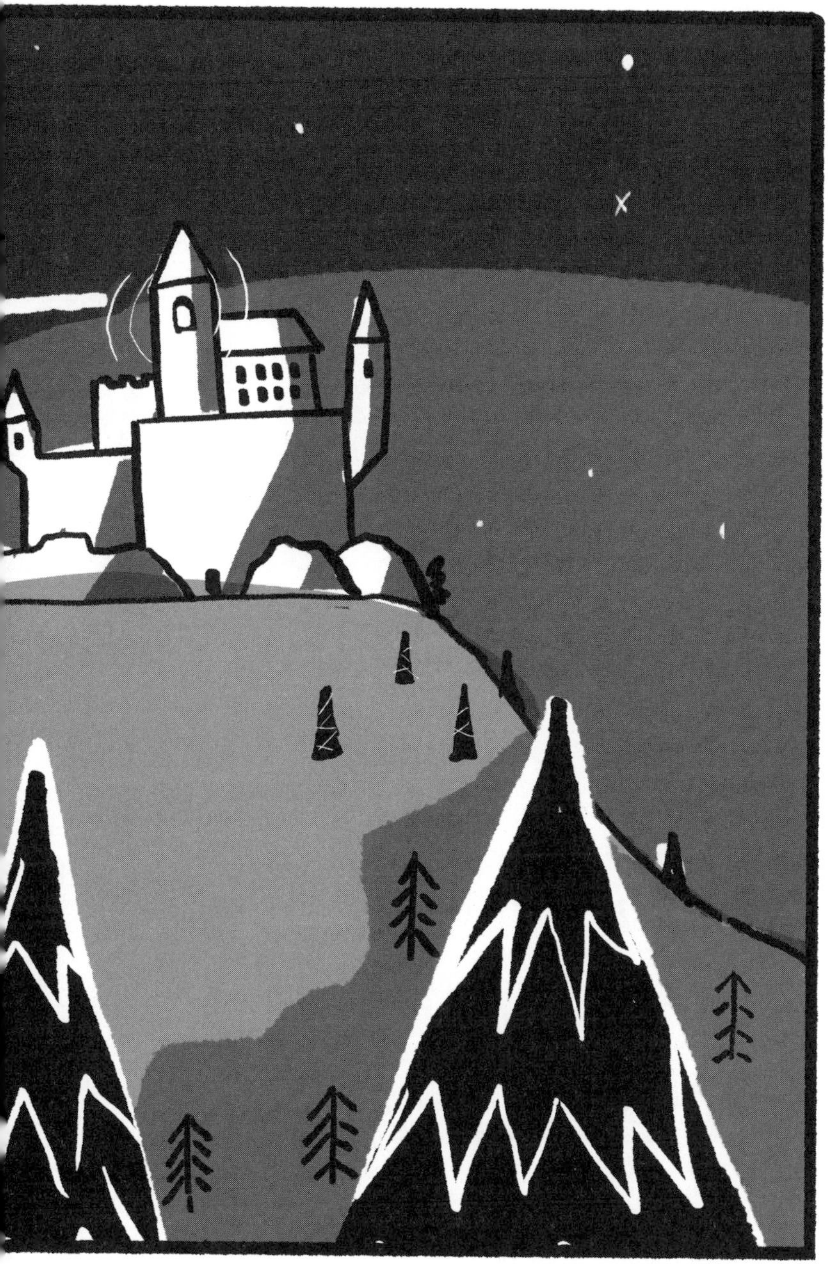

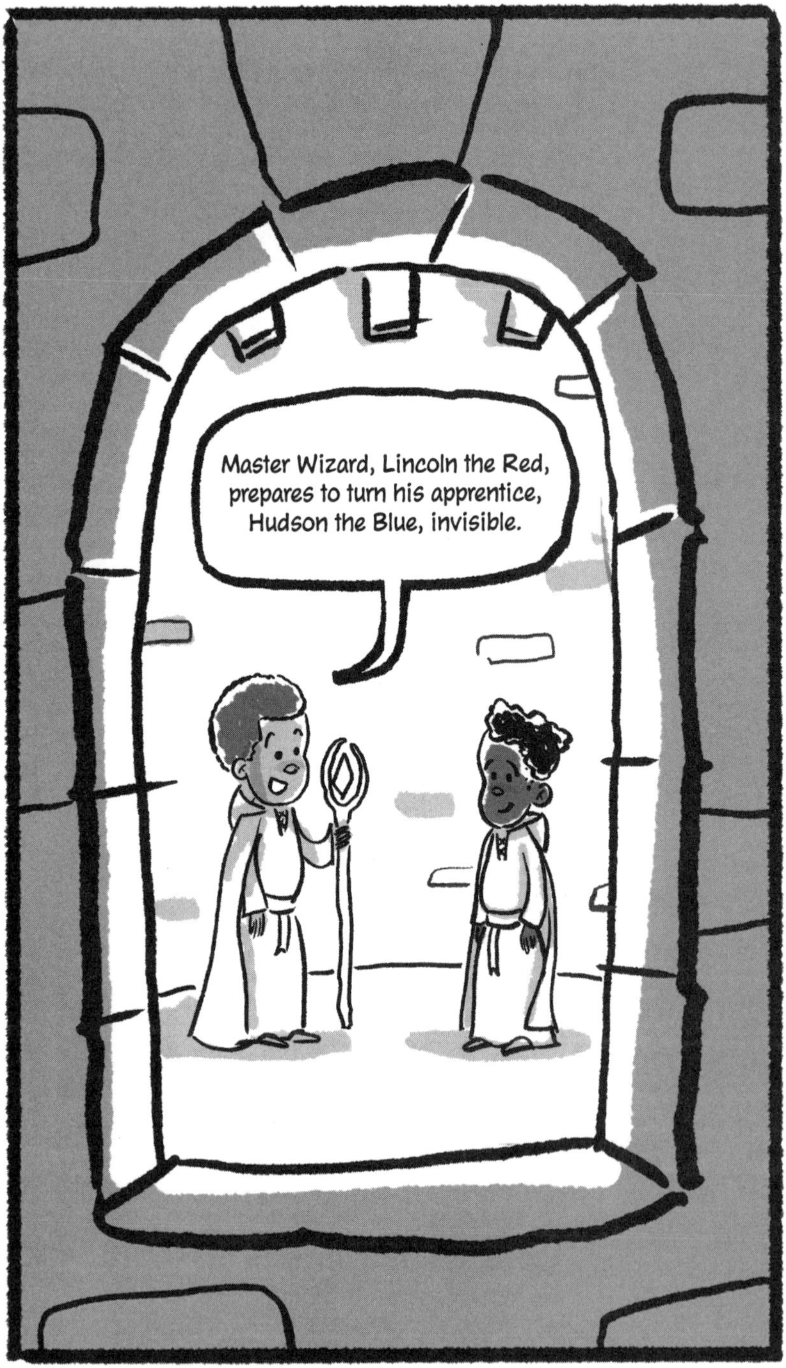
Master Wizard, Lincoln the Red, prepares to turn his apprentice, Hudson the Blue, invisible.

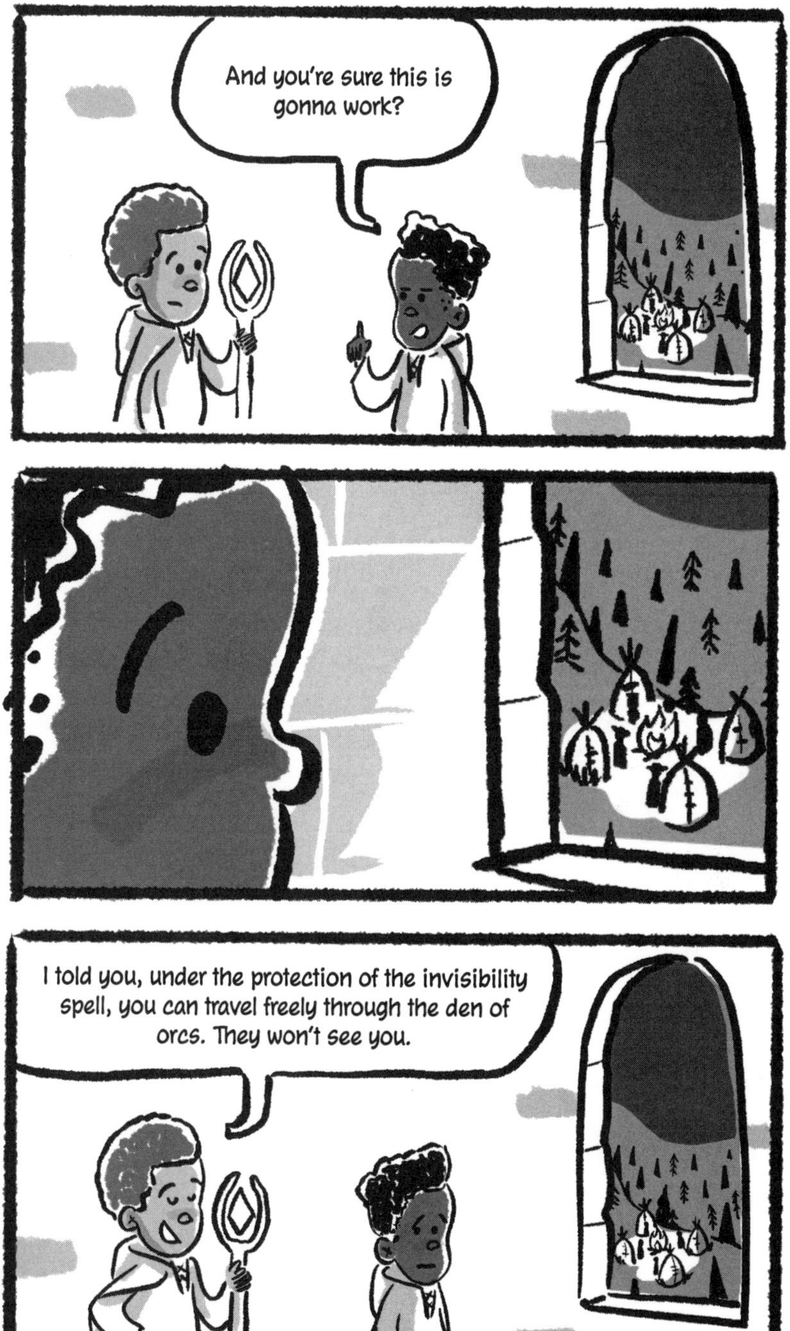
And you're sure this is gonna work?
I told you, under the protection of the invisibility spell, you can travel freely through the den of orcs. They won't see you.

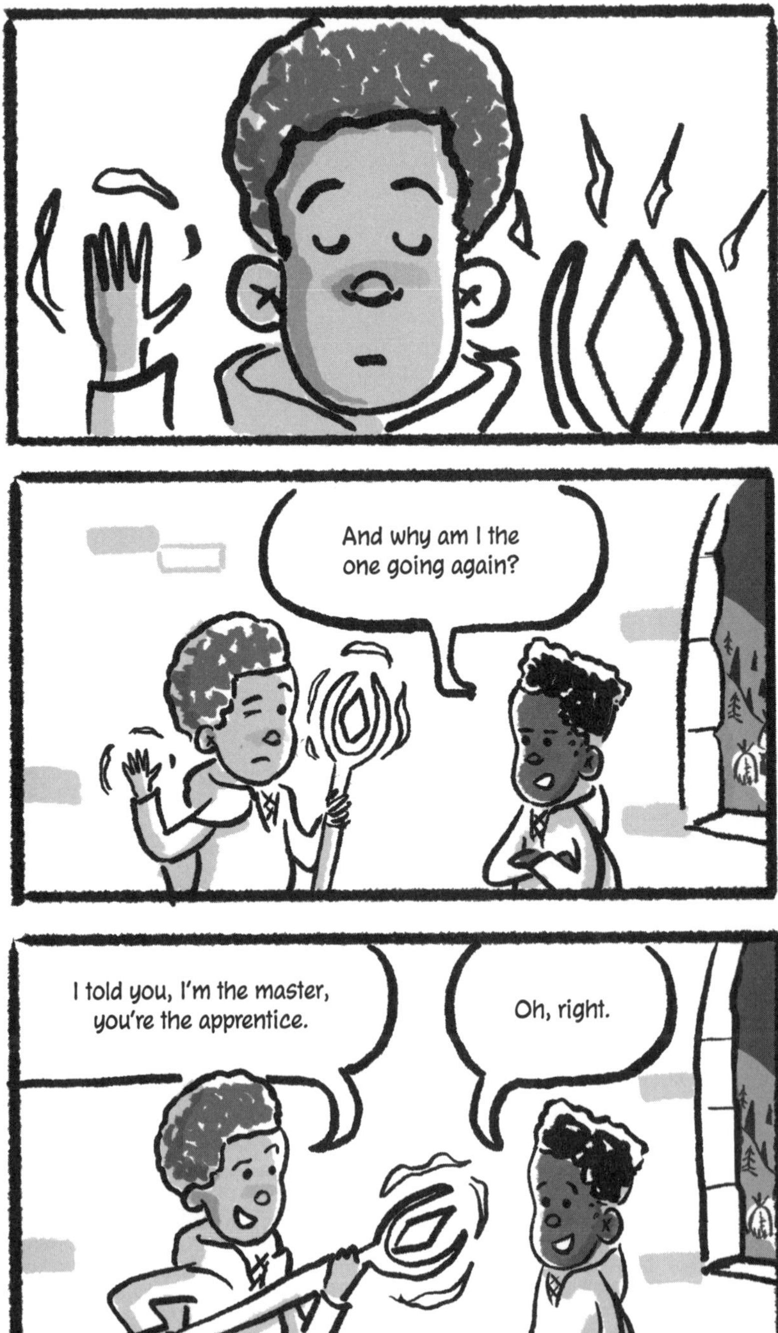
And why am I the one going again?
I told you, I'm the master, you're the apprentice.
Oh, right.

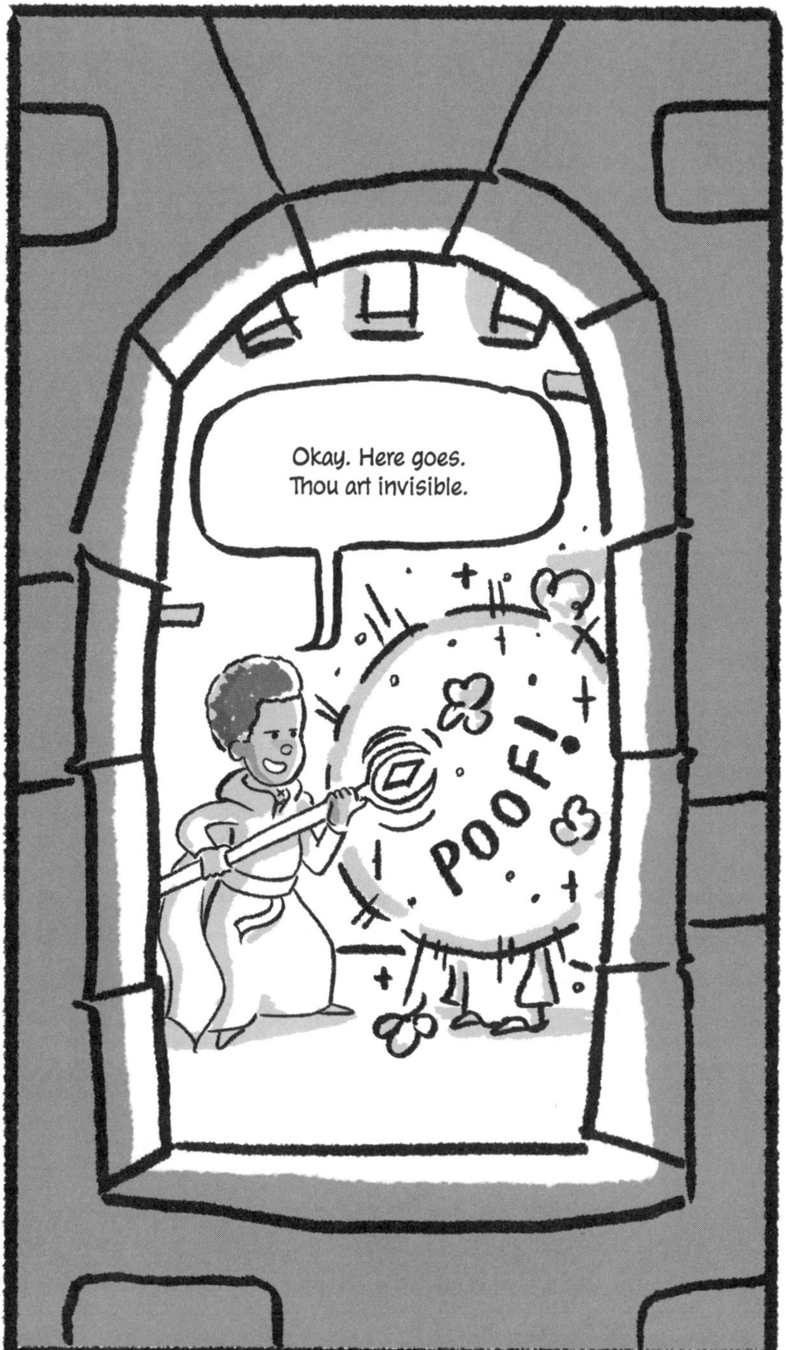
Okay. Here goes.
Thou art invisible.
POOF!

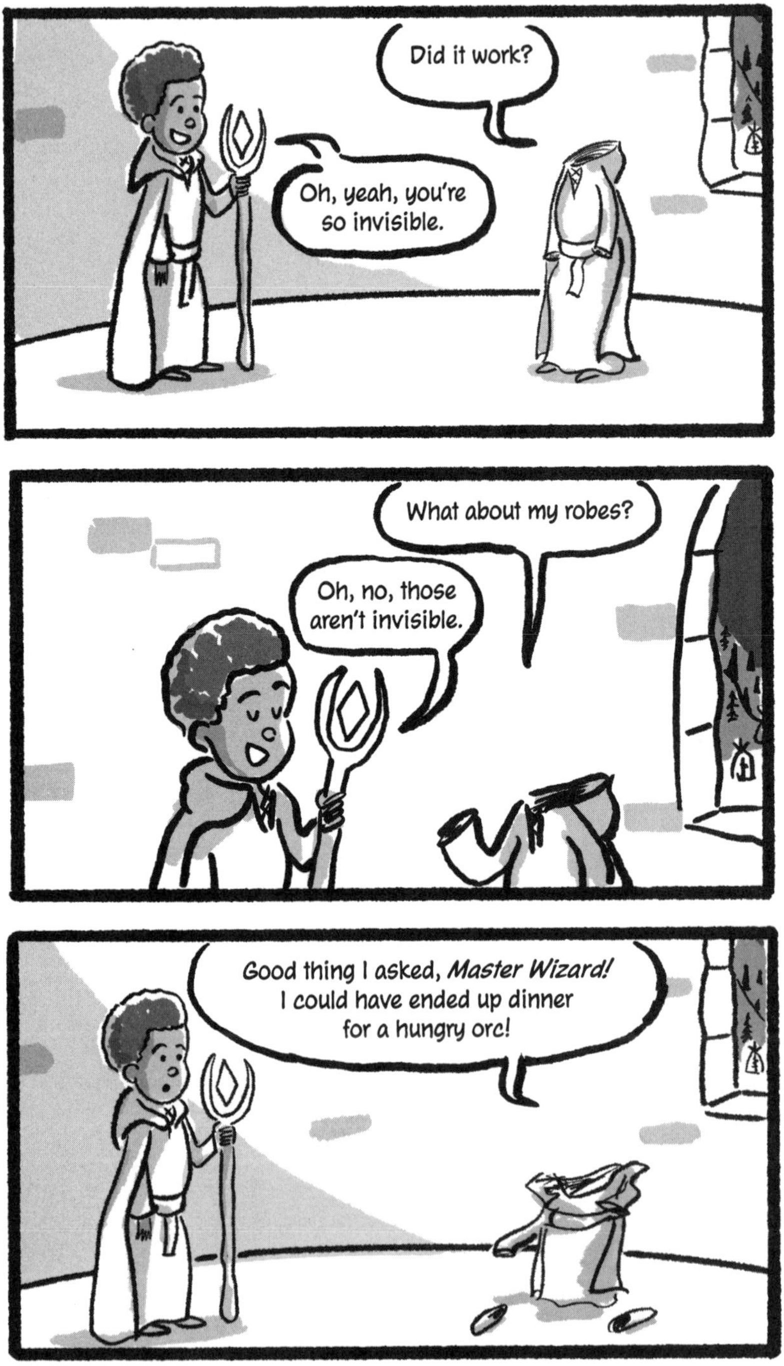
Did it work?
Oh, yeah, you're so invisible.
What about my robes?
Oh, no, those aren't invisible.
Good thing I asked, *Master Wizard!* I could have ended up dinner for a hungry orc!

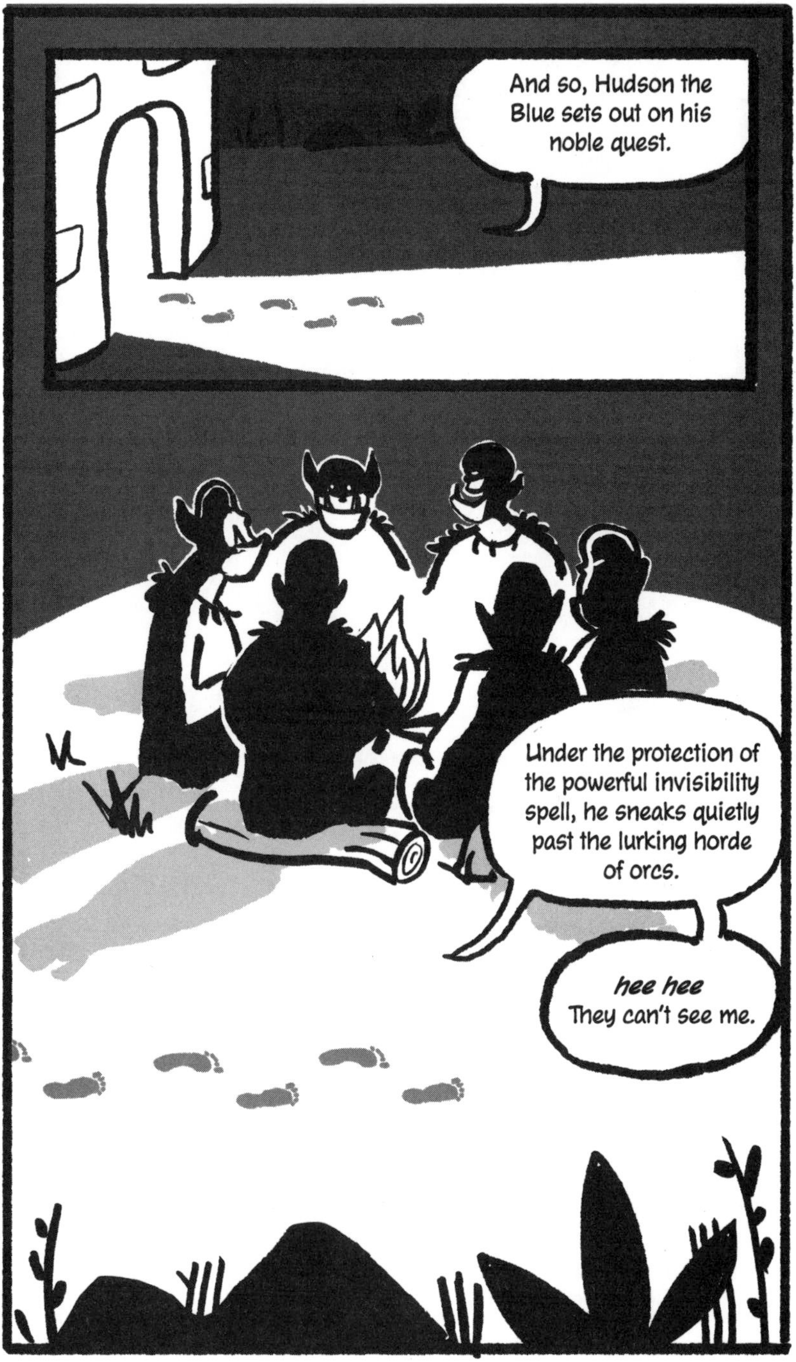
And so, Hudson the Blue sets out on his noble quest.
Under the protection of the powerful invisibility spell, he sneaks quietly past the lurking horde of orcs.
hee hee
They can't see me.

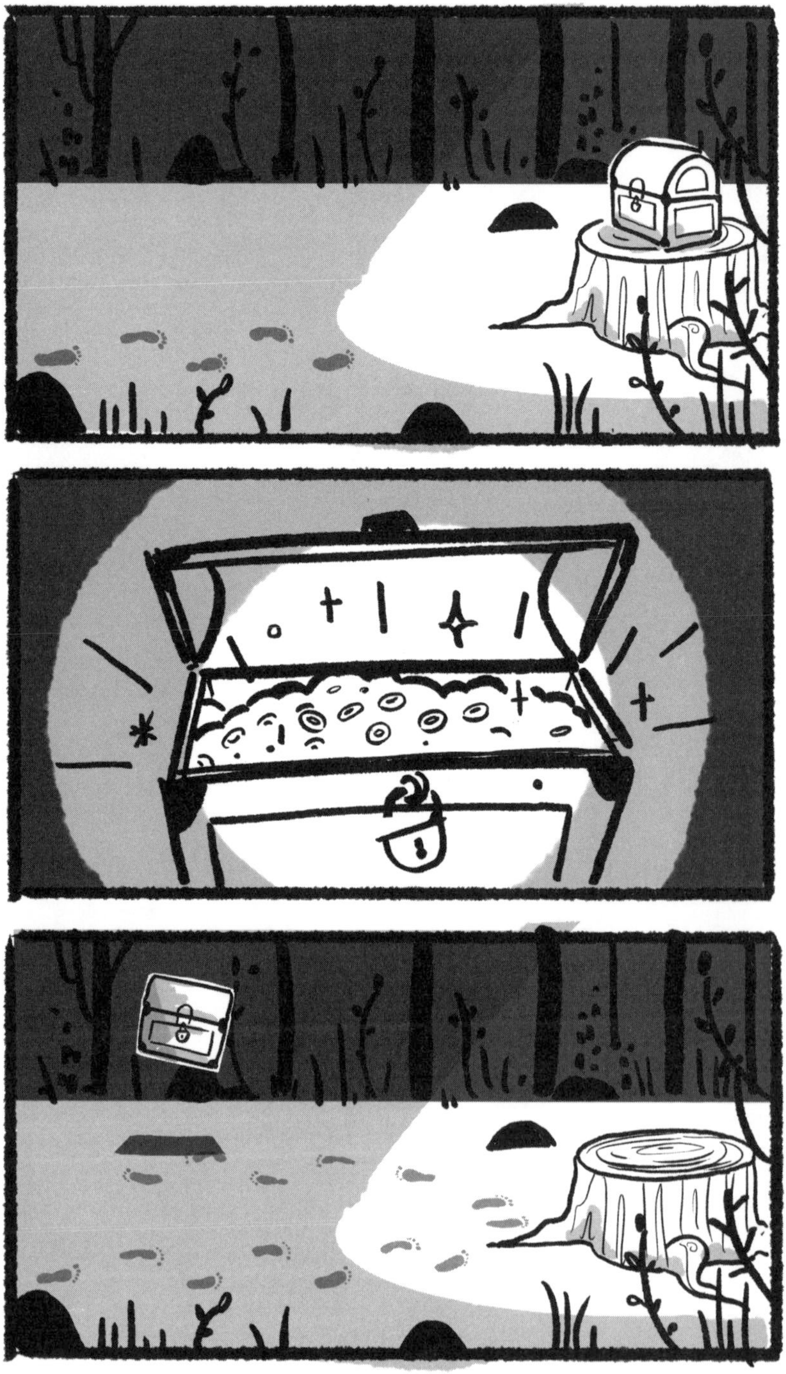

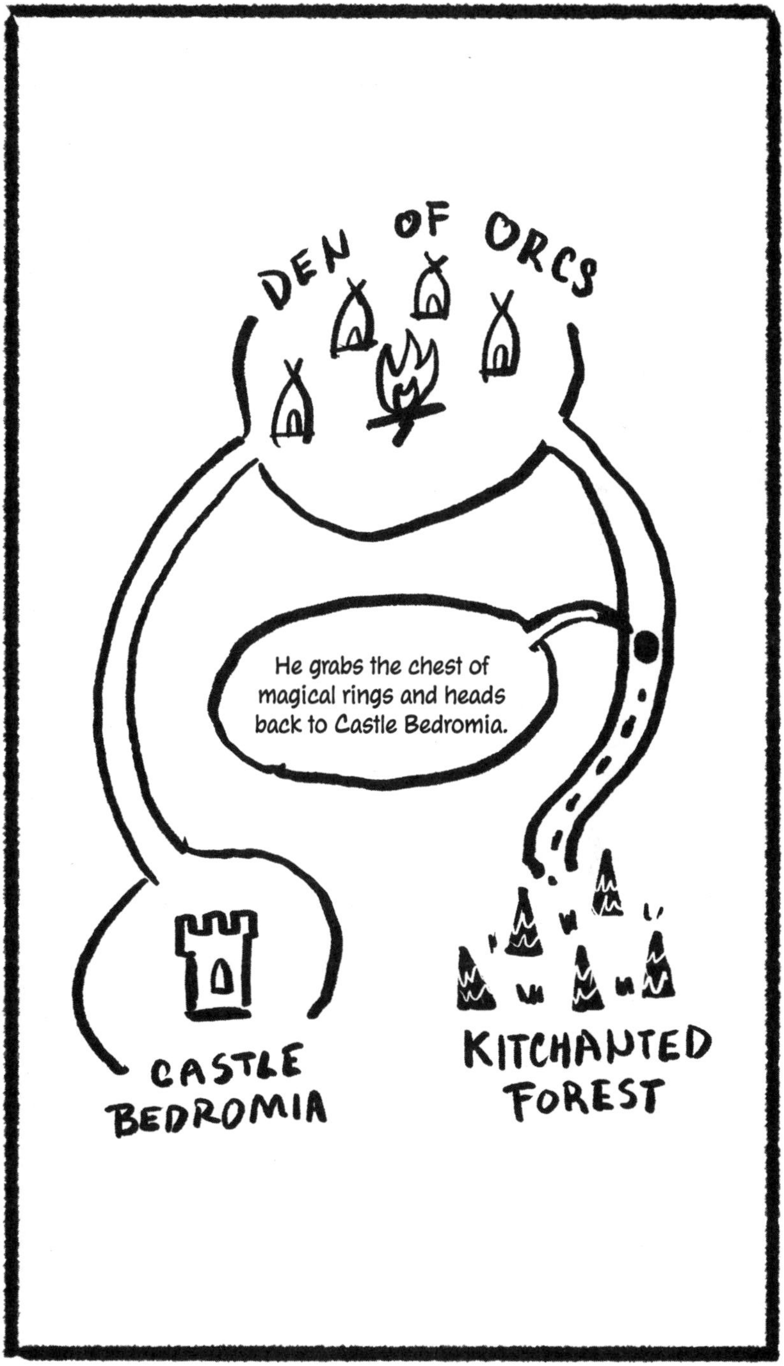
DEN OF ORCS
He grabs the chest of magical rings and heads back to Castle Bedromia.
CASTLE BEDROMIA
KITCHANTED FOREST

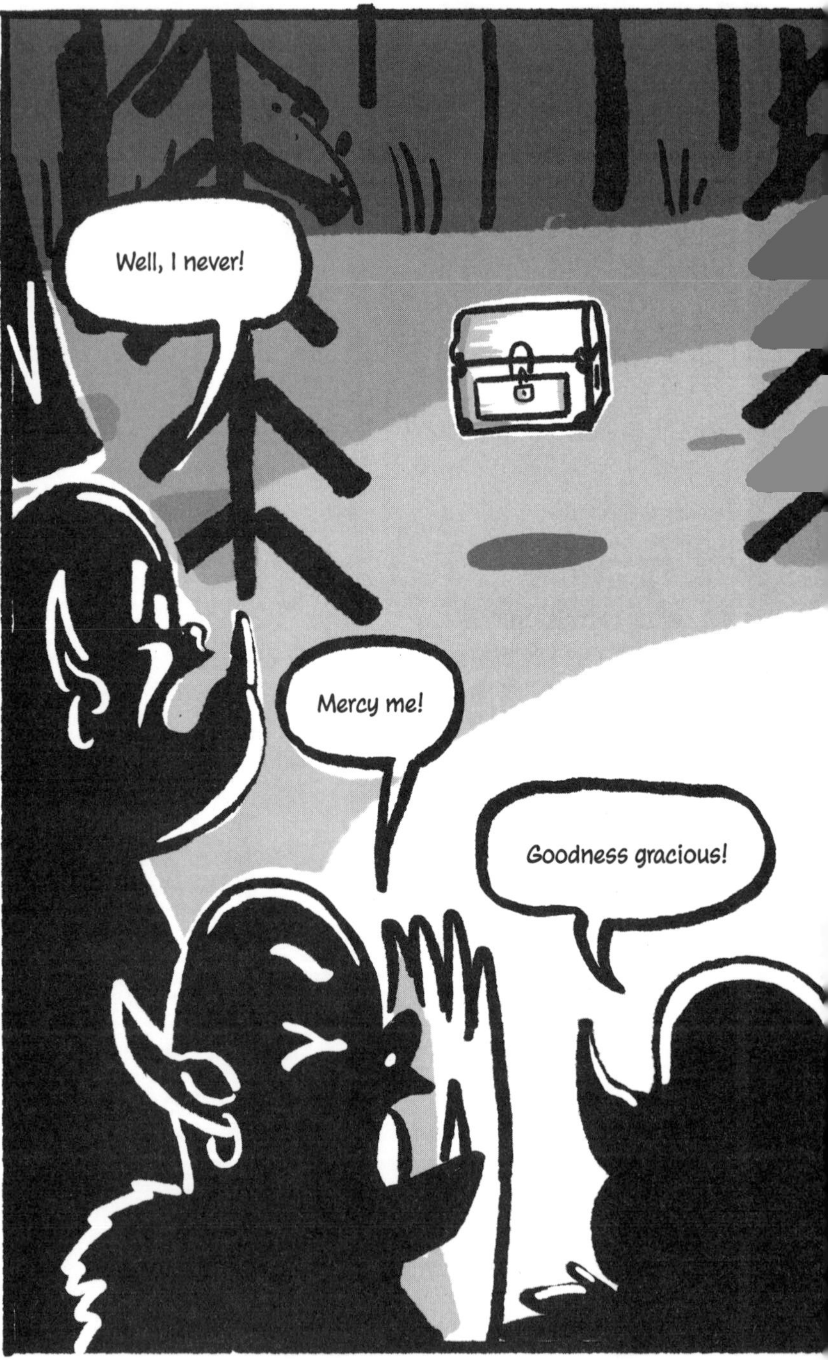
Well, I never!
Mercy me!
Goodness gracious!

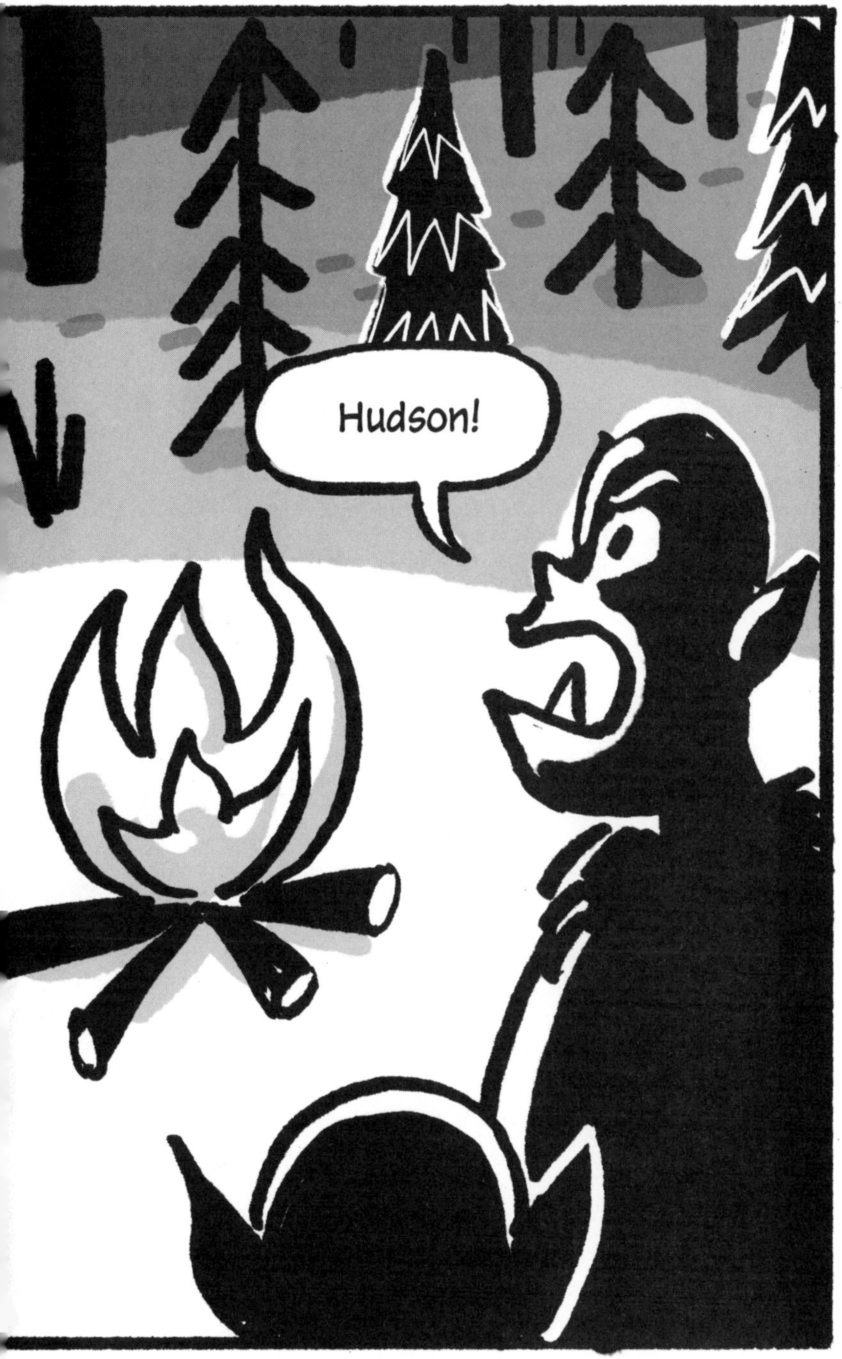
Hudson!

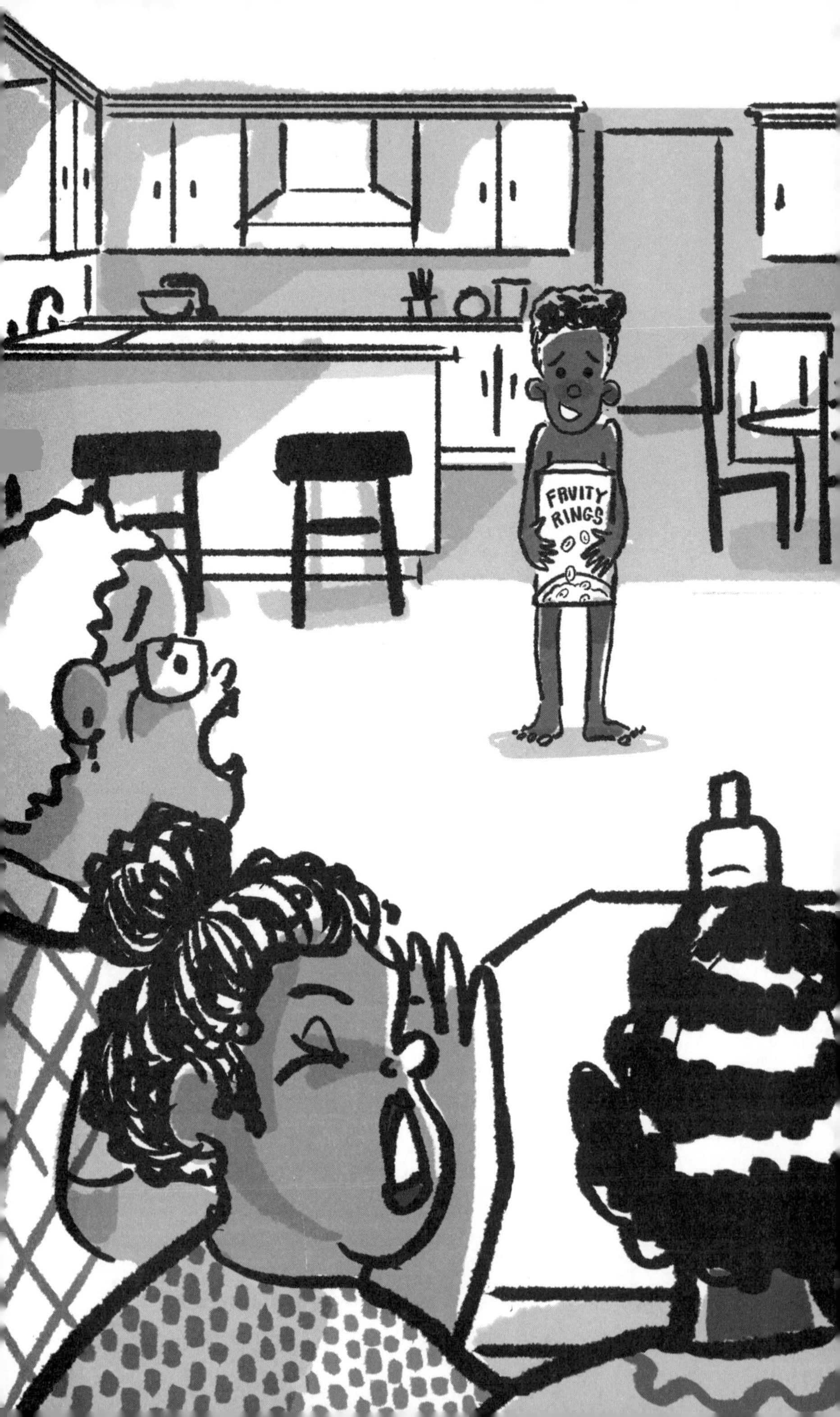
FRVITY
RINGS

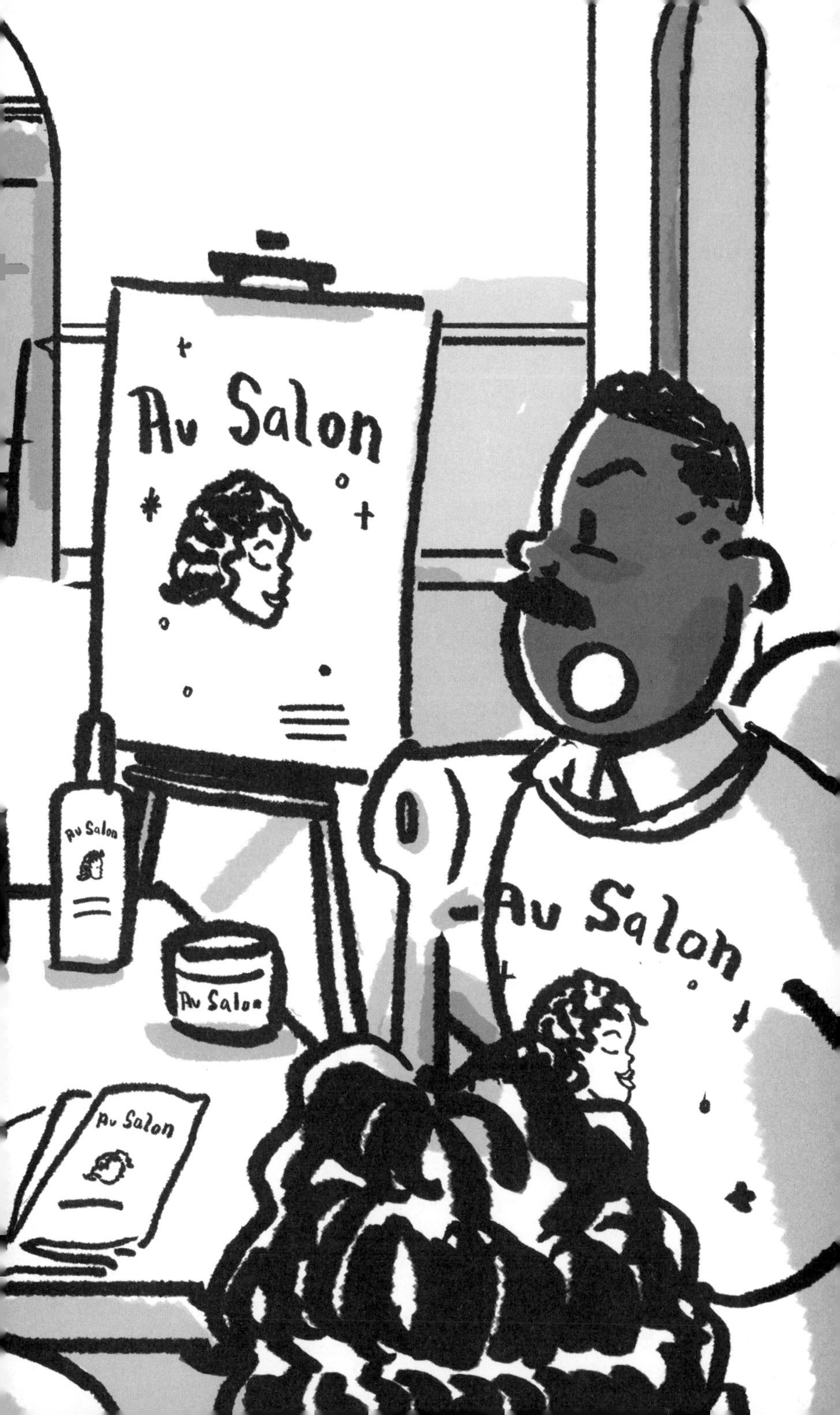
Au Salon
Au Salon
Au Salon
Au Salon
Au Salon

CHAPTER SIX

THE DEN OFF THE KITCHEN ERUPTED WITH people shouting and things dropping.

"Hudson!" shouted Dr. Dupré, who knocked over his easel and dropped the poster boards he had been presenting.

"Good heavens!" shouted a lady on the couch, who dropped the open Au Salon bottle she had been smelling, which sent cocoa butter–scented shampoo squirting across the coffee table.

"Neber in all my dears!" shouted another lady through a mouthful of Gouda, as she dropped the half-eaten cheese tray she had been enjoying.

"Oh, my nerves!" shouted yet another lady, who started fanning herself with a stack of Au Salon brochures, many of which went flying—and then dropping—everywhere.

Startled, as anyone would be by a bunch of people shouting and dropping things, Hud really couldn't be blamed for what happened next.

“Ahh!” he shouted and then he, too, dropped something: the box of Fruity Rings cereal he was holding.

“HUDSON!”

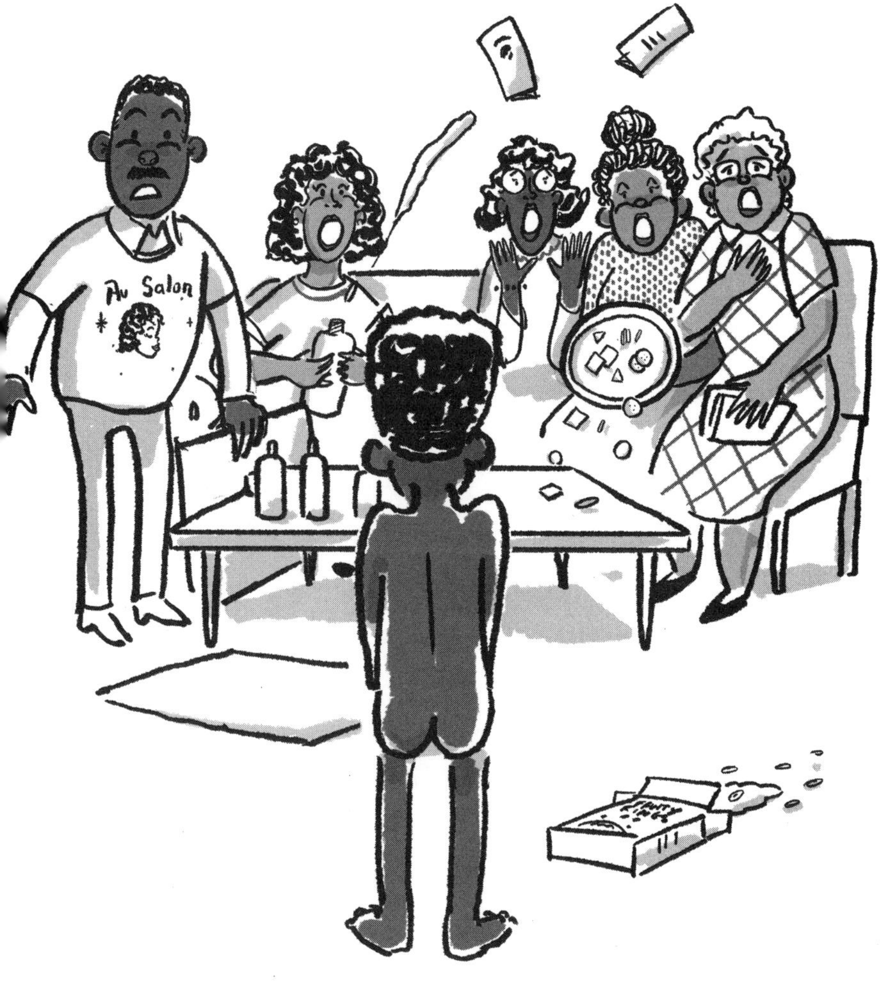
Au Salon

CHAPTER SEVEN

"HONEY, WHERE ARE YOUR CLOTHES?"

That's Mrs. Dupré. She's—you guessed it—Link and Hud's mom. She's also the only person who didn't shout or drop things at the sight of a naked little boy holding—and then dropping—a box of cereal. After years of managing Dr. Dupré at work—she ran the practice—and wrangling Link and Hud at home, there wasn't much left that shocked her. Instead, she rushed over and wrapped Hud up in a throw from the couch.

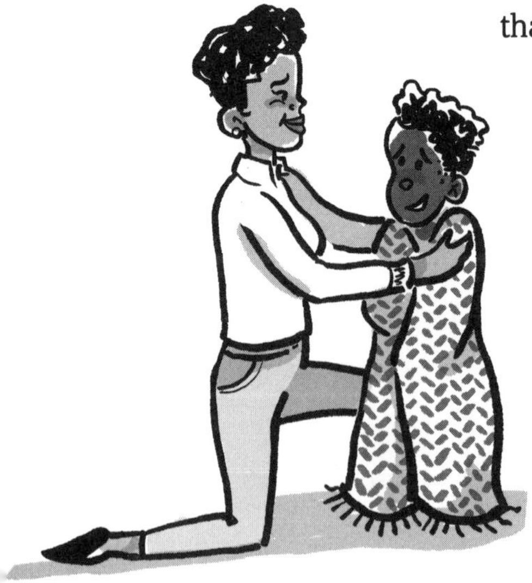

"Ladies, ladies," said Dr. Dupré, who was trying his best to restore order to his meeting, "if I could direct your attention over here to our line of activators and relaxers . . . "

"What are you doing out here, sweetie?" said Mrs. Dupré as she ushered Hud farther into the hallway. "You should be in your room."

"Well, Link said he wanted some cereal," said Hud.

"Did not!" said Link, who had poked his head out of the bedroom door. "You said *you* wanted cereal!"

"No! You said—"

"All right. All right," said Mrs. Dupré. "Just get back to your room. It's about time for bed."

"And maybe put on some britches," came a voice from the den.

Mrs. Dupré looked back at the voice. "Oh, hi there, Ms. Joyce."

A lady stood in the doorway to the den. She had a stern look on her face and a large purse under her arm.

"Boys, say hi to Ms. Joyce. She's one of your father's oldest patients and, fingers crossed,"—Mrs. Dupré crossed her fingers—"a new Au Salon customer."

She sure did look old to Link. Hud wondered if she'd come to buy *all* the Au Salon or if she just always carried around such a humongous purse.

"Hi," said the boys.

"I'll never understand why parents these days send they kids to they rooms," said Ms. Joyce. "All 'em toys and games. Ain't no place to learn a lesson, you ask me."

Link was happy they hadn't asked her. Hud decided she probably did need *all* the Au Salon to make her hair look all wet and curly like that.

Mrs. Dupré gave a polite chuckle. "Okay, boys. Off you go. No toys. No games." She picked up the cereal box. "And no *cereal*. Straight to bed." *mwah*. She gave Hud a kiss on the cheek and blew another to Link before heading back into the den.

Hud pushed past Link into the bedroom. As Link went to close the door, a glint of gold caught his eye. He looked back to see Ms. Joyce, still standing in the hallway, watching him and smiling. And there, at the corner of her otherwise white smile, flashing in the dim hall light, was a single gold tooth.

"Night night, now," she said. "Don't let them bed bugs bite you."

Link shuddered and quickly shut the door.

CHAPTER EIGHT

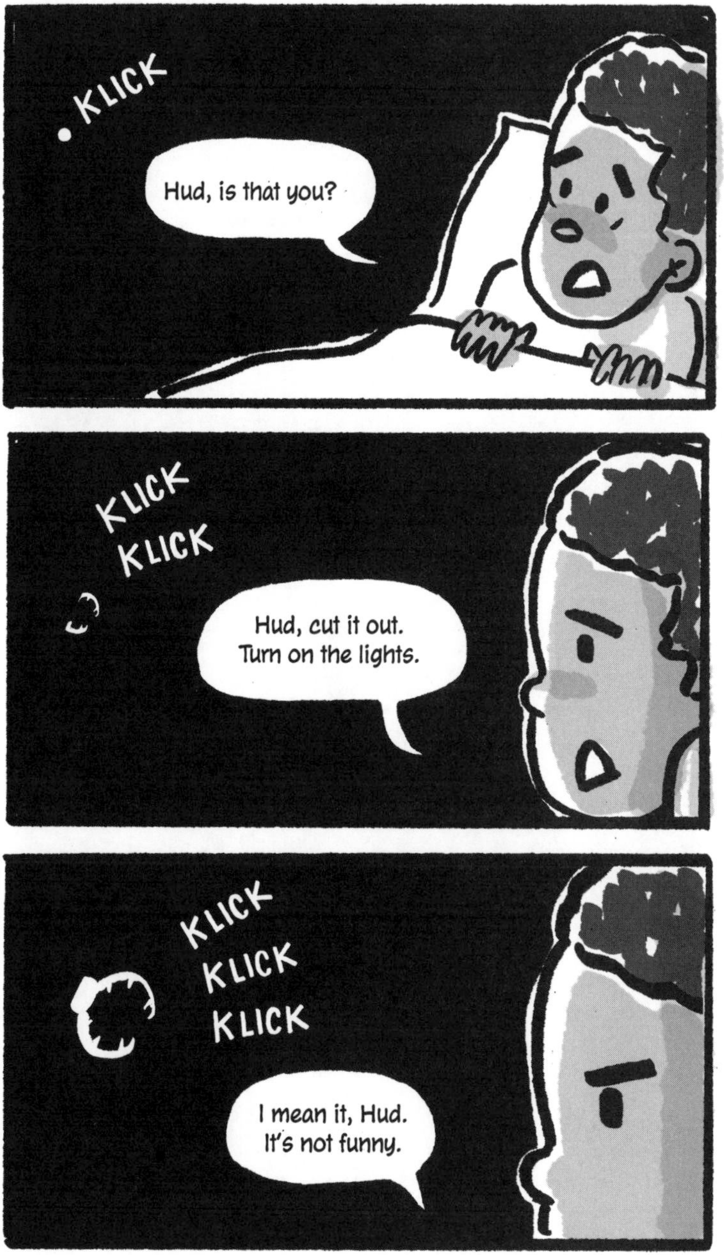
KLICK
Hud, is that you?
KLICK
KLICK
Hud, cut it out. Turn on the lights.
KLICK
KLICK
KLICK
I mean it, Hud. It's not funny.

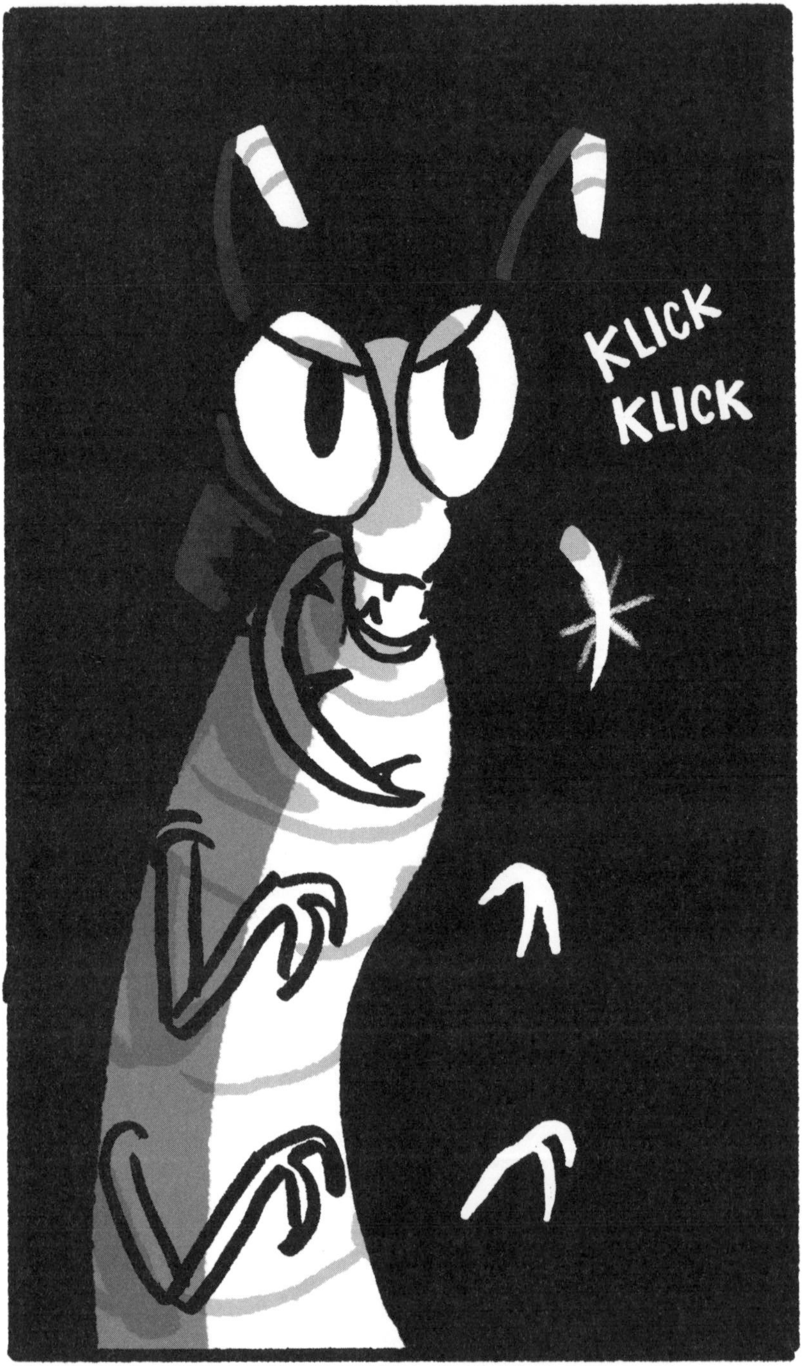
KLICK
KLICK

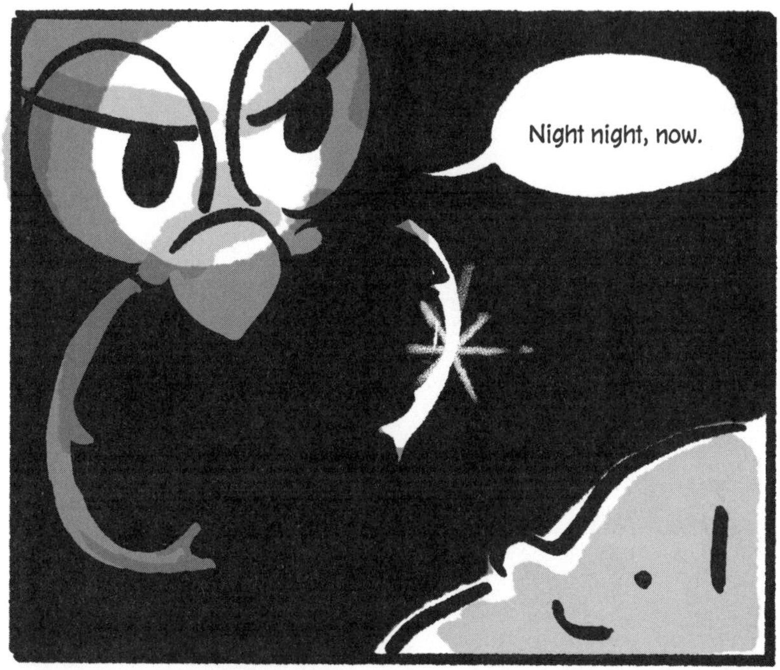
Night night, now.

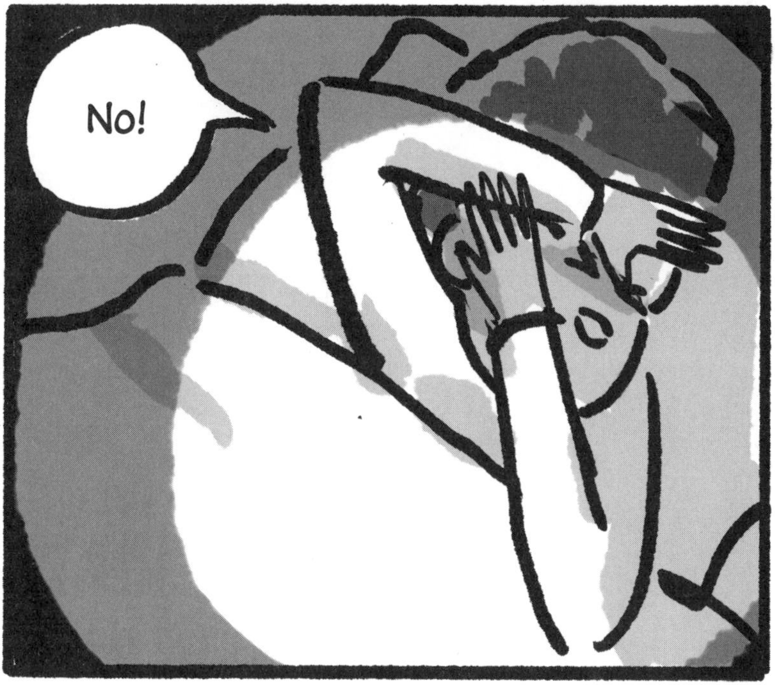
No!

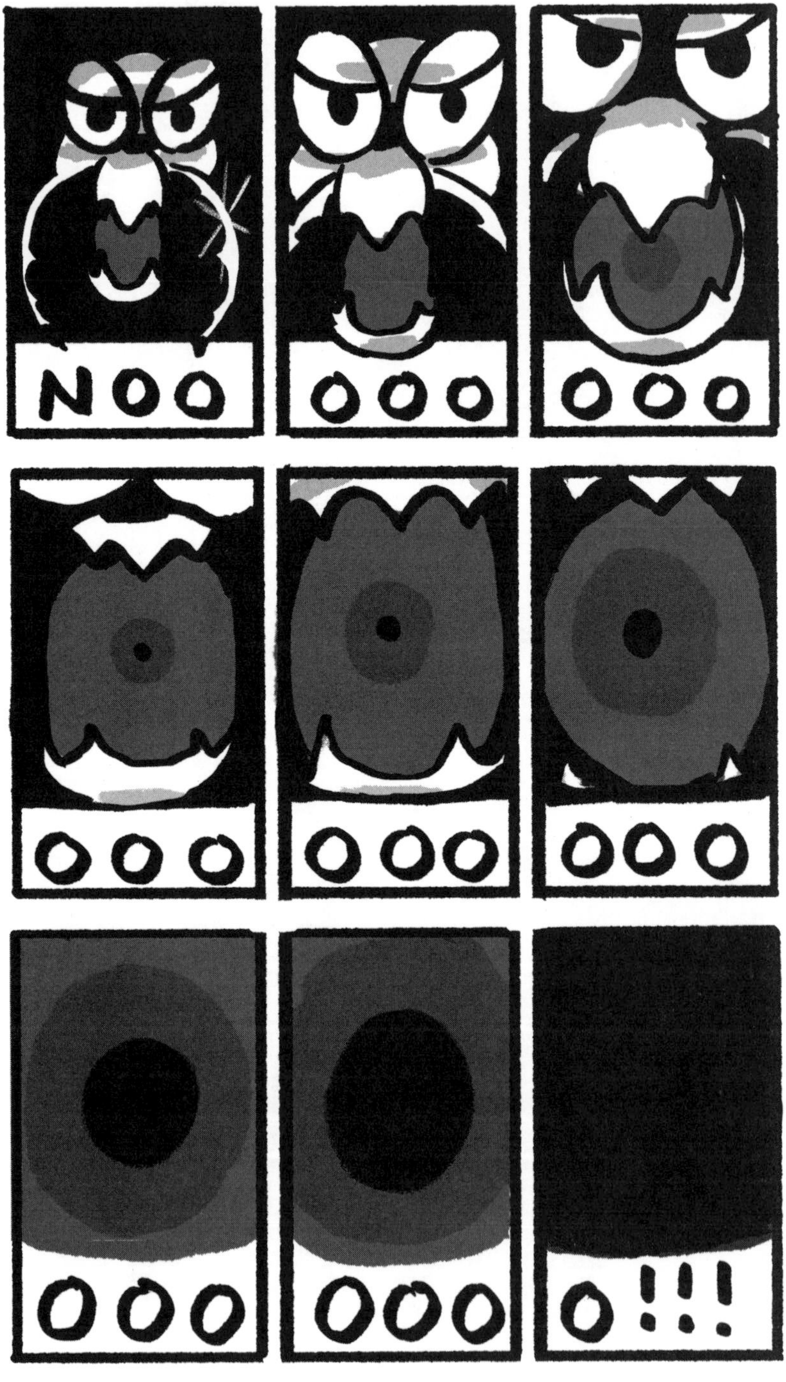
NOO
OOO
OOO
OOO
OOO
OOO
OOO
OOO
O!!!

CHAPTER NINE

"OOOOOOOOHHHHHHH!" LINK LET OUT A BIG yawn at the kitchen table, his bowl of Fruity Rings cereal untouched and getting soggy.

"Ooh, buddy," Dr. Dupré said, pouring himself a cup of coffee. "Looks like someone had a rough night."

"Hmmm," said Link, eyes heavy.

"It was a bug," said Hud as he put a spoonful of Fruity Rings into his mouth. *crunch*.

"Bugs? Where?" said Dr. Dupré. "Boss, didn't we just have the house treated?"

"Yes, dear," said Mrs. Dupré, who was cutting a grapefruit by the sink.

"Not real," said Hud before another bite. *crunch*.

"Nightmare." Then another. *crunch*. *crunch*.

"Up all night." And another. *crunch*. *crunch*. *crunch*.

"Told me—" Hud paused to wipe a dribble of milk from his chin before he continued, "all about it." Then he took another bite. *crunch*.

"Oh, sweetie," said Mrs. Dupré. She rubbed the back of Link's head as she sat down at the table. "Well, it was just a bad dream. It's over now."

"If we got bugs, it's probably all that cereal y'all eat in your room," said Dr. Dupré, shaking his head. "And son." He looked at Hud. "Next time, keep your clothes on if you gon' walk through the house for everyone to see. I couldn't sell a thing after you almost gave Mrs. Clouser a heart attack."

Hud shrugged as he sloshed more cereal and milk into his bowl (and onto the table) before loading up another spoonful of Fruity Rings and taking another bite. *crunch*.

"Speaking of last night," said Mrs. Dupré, "I'm glad you boys got to meet Ms. Joyce."

Link's eyes opened wide, and he sat up, alert. "What about Ms. Joyce?"

"Well, I happened to mention what occurred with Layla, and she kindly offered to start watching you two after school." Mrs. Dupré took a bite of her grapefruit and her lips puckered.

"Mom, no! We don't need a babysitter. You know, I'm actually old enough to watch the both of us, and Hud is old enough to do whatever I say. Isn't that right, Hud?" Link looked at Hud.

"Mm-hmm," said Hud through a mouthful of Fruity Rings.

"Mm-mmm," said Mrs. Dupré through pressed lips as she forced down the bitter grapefruit. She cleared her throat and then continued. "Your actions have proven you're not ready for that responsibility. And frankly, neither was Layla—or any of those other girls, for that matter. No, your father and I both agree it's time for someone a bit older, a bit more mature."

"But, Mom, she's ancient!" said Link.

"Yeah," said Hud, who was between bites. "Ancient."

"That's enough, now," said Mrs. Dupré, who also seemed to have had enough of her grapefruit. She put her spoon down and wiped the corners of her mouth with her napkin. "She'll be here when you get home today, so behave yourselves."

"And stay out of the garage," added Dr. Dupré, as he finished off his coffee in a final swig. "Au Salon business only."

Both parents got up from the table, placed their dishes on the counter near the sink, and then left the kitchen.

"You gonna eat that, Link?" said Hud, pointing his spoon at Link's bowl.

"No."

Hud pulled the bowl over and loaded up his spoon with soggy Fruity Rings.

"How can you eat at a time like this?" said Link.

Hud shrugged. "Anytime's a good time for cereal. Even soggy cereal." *slurp.*

CHAPTER TEN

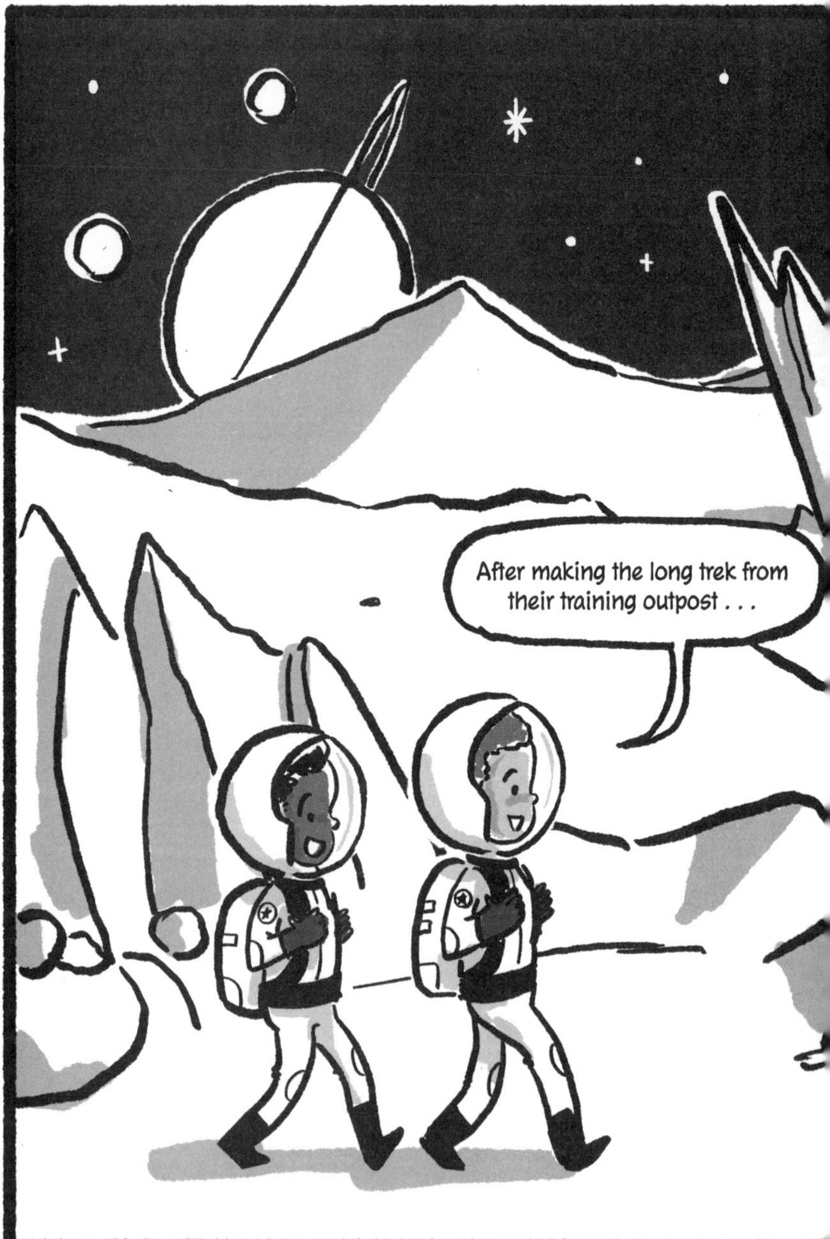
After making the long trek from their training outpost . . .

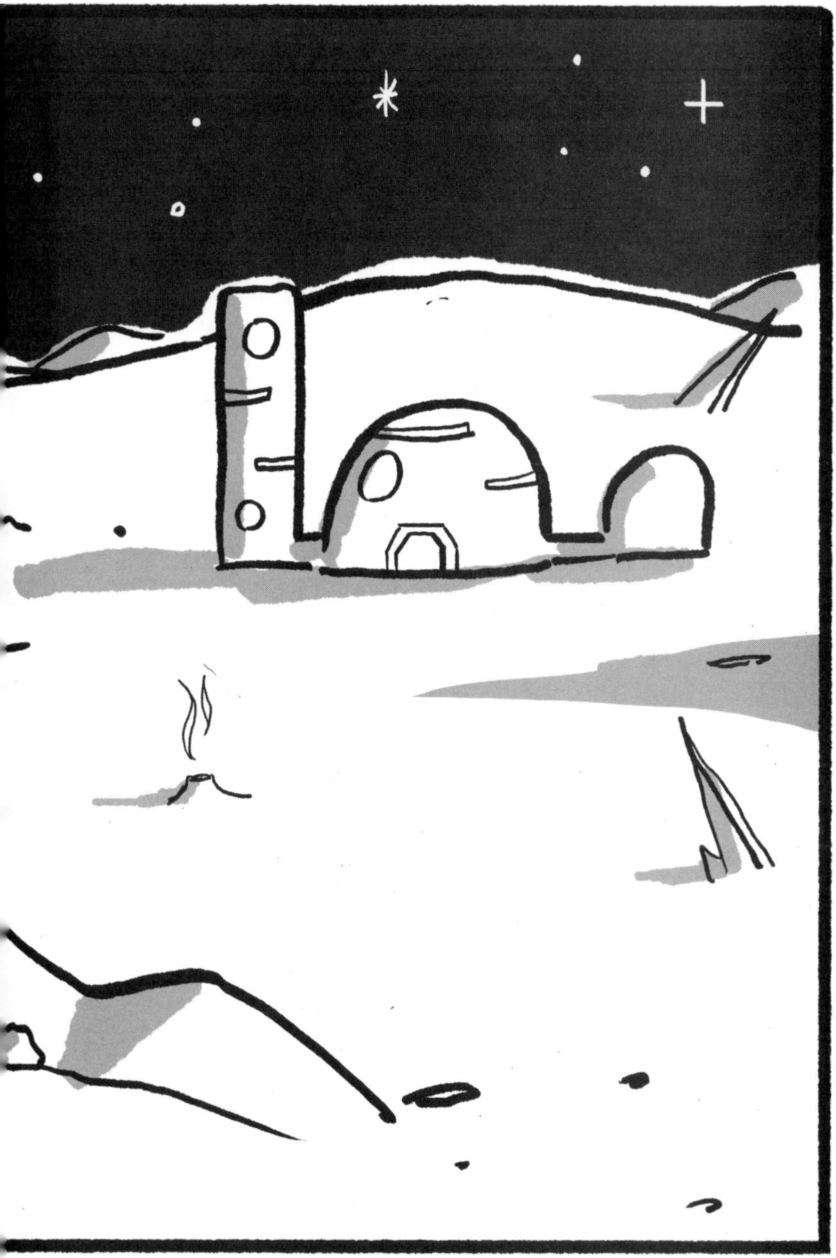

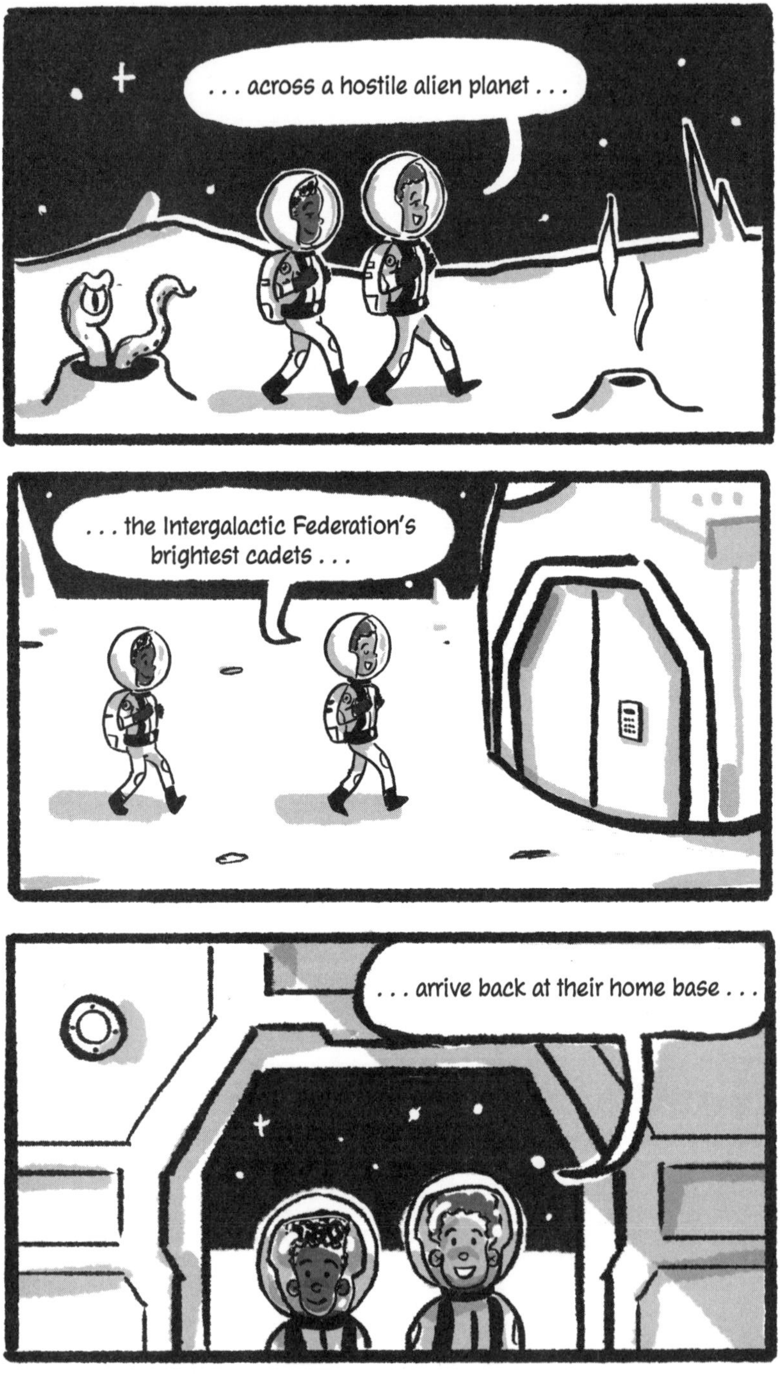
. . . across a hostile alien planet . . .
. . . the Intergalactic Federation's brightest cadets . . .
. . . arrive back at their home base . . .

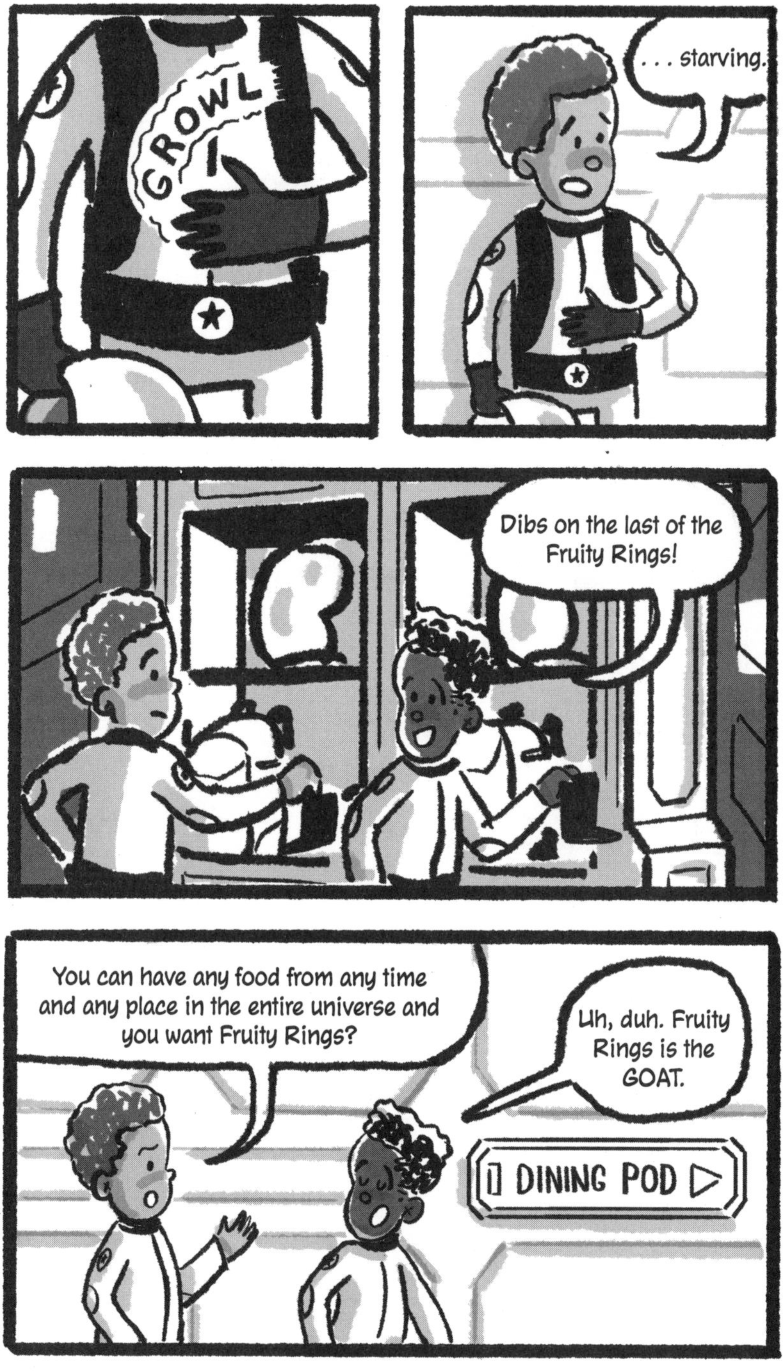
GROWL
. . . starving.
Dibs on the last of the Fruity Rings!
You can have any food from any time and any place in the entire universe and you want Fruity Rings?
Uh, duh. Fruity Rings is the GOAT.
DINING POD

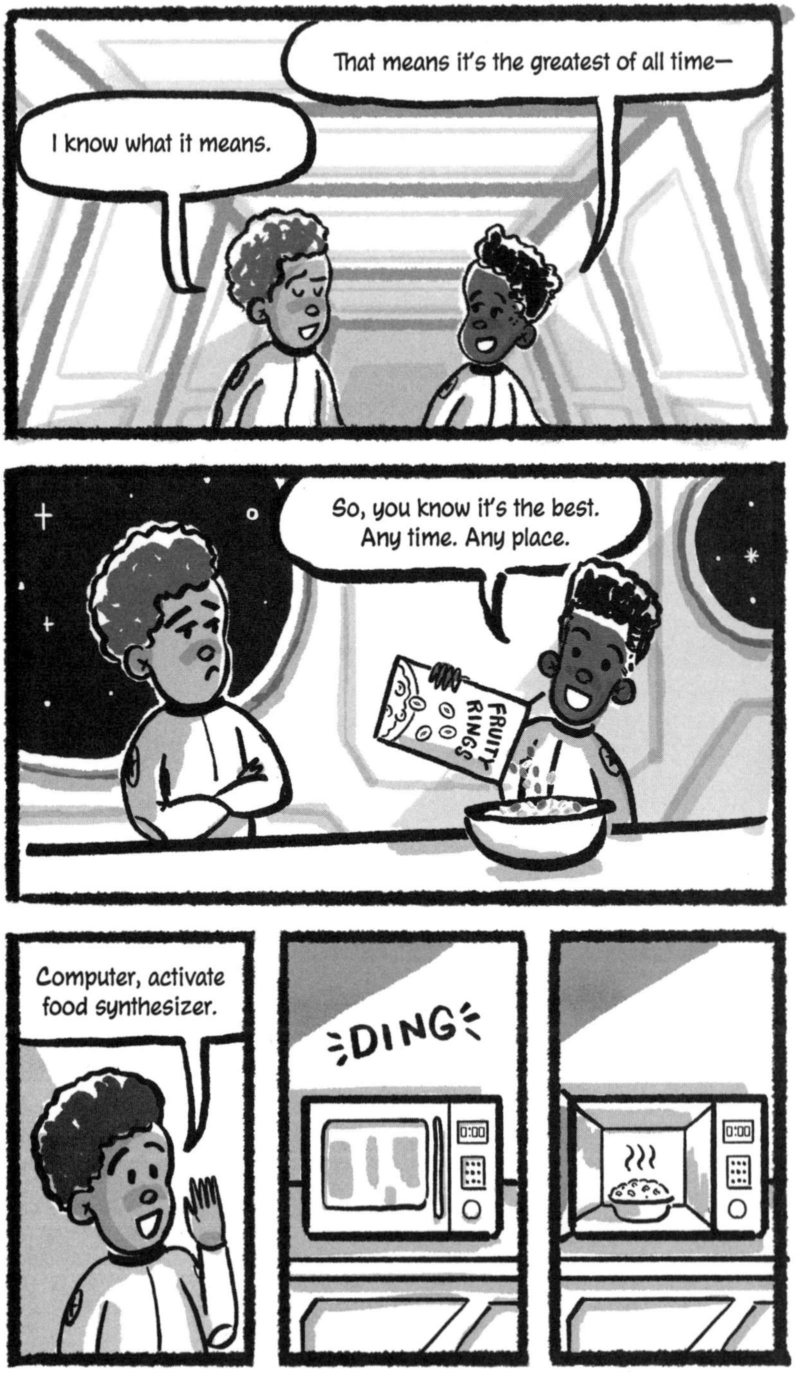

I know what it means.
That means it's the greatest of all time—
So, you know it's the best.
Any time. Any place.
FRUITY RINGS
Computer, activate food synthesizer.
DING
0:00
0:00

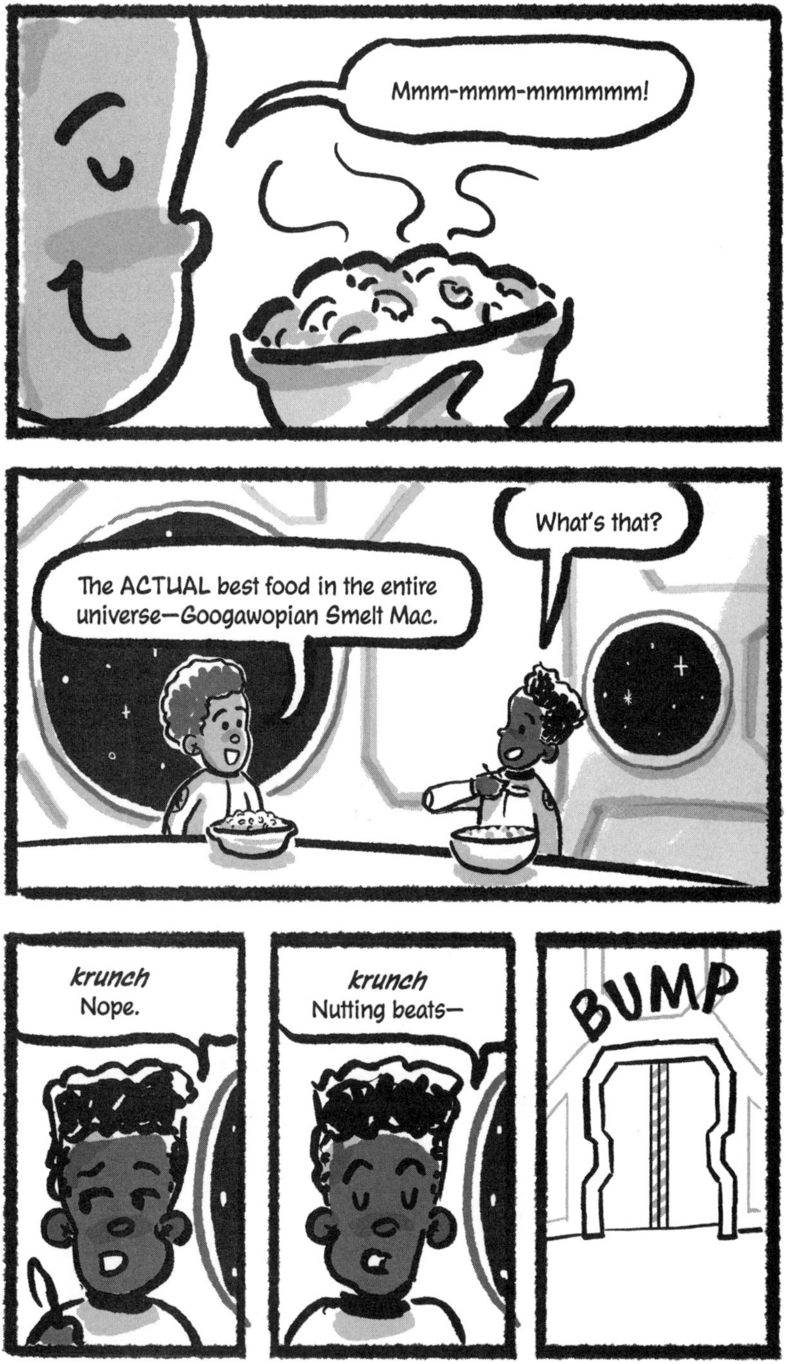
Mmm-mmm-mmmmmm!
The ACTUAL best food in the entire universe—Googawopian Smelt Mac.
What's that?
krunch
Nope.
krunch
Nutting beats—
BUMP

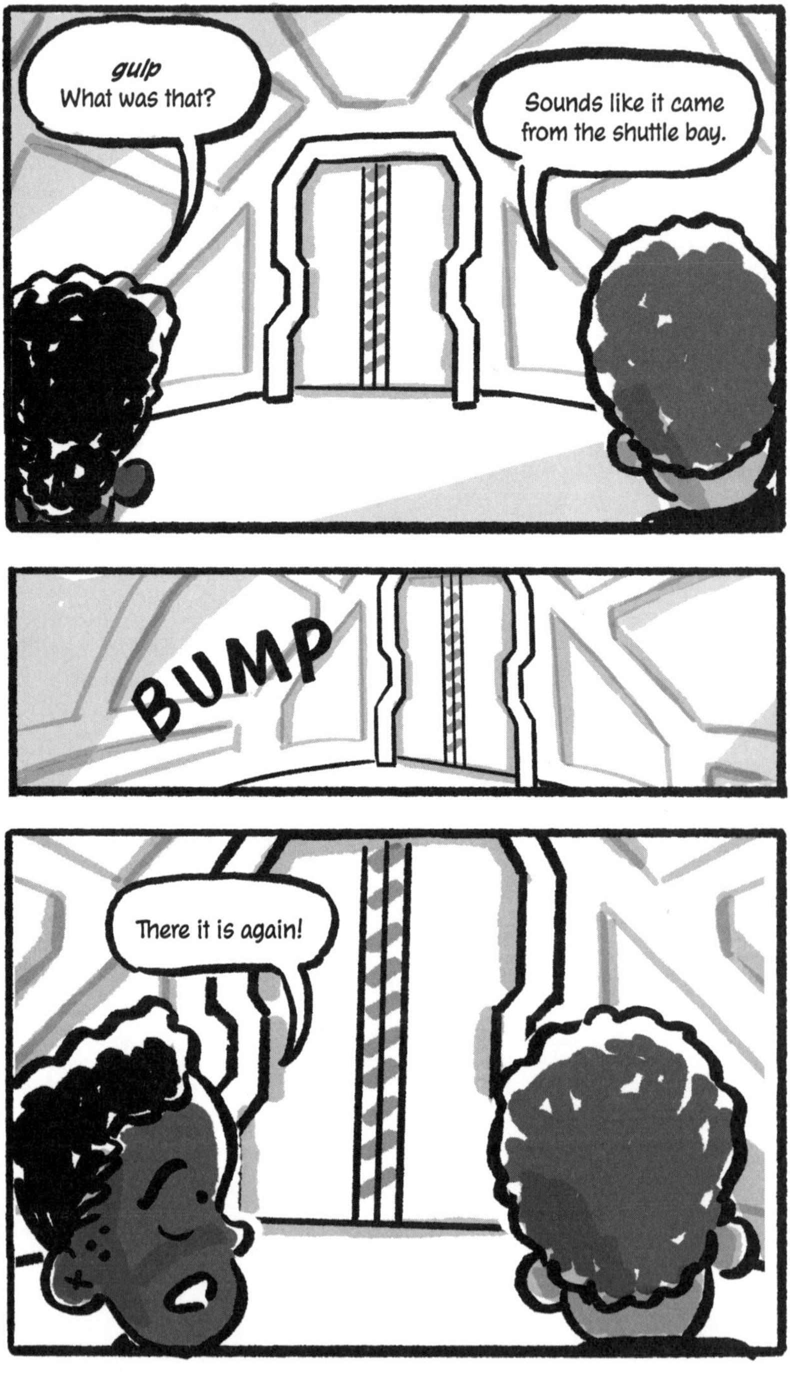
gulp
What was that?
Sounds like it came from the shuttle bay.
BUMP
There it is again!

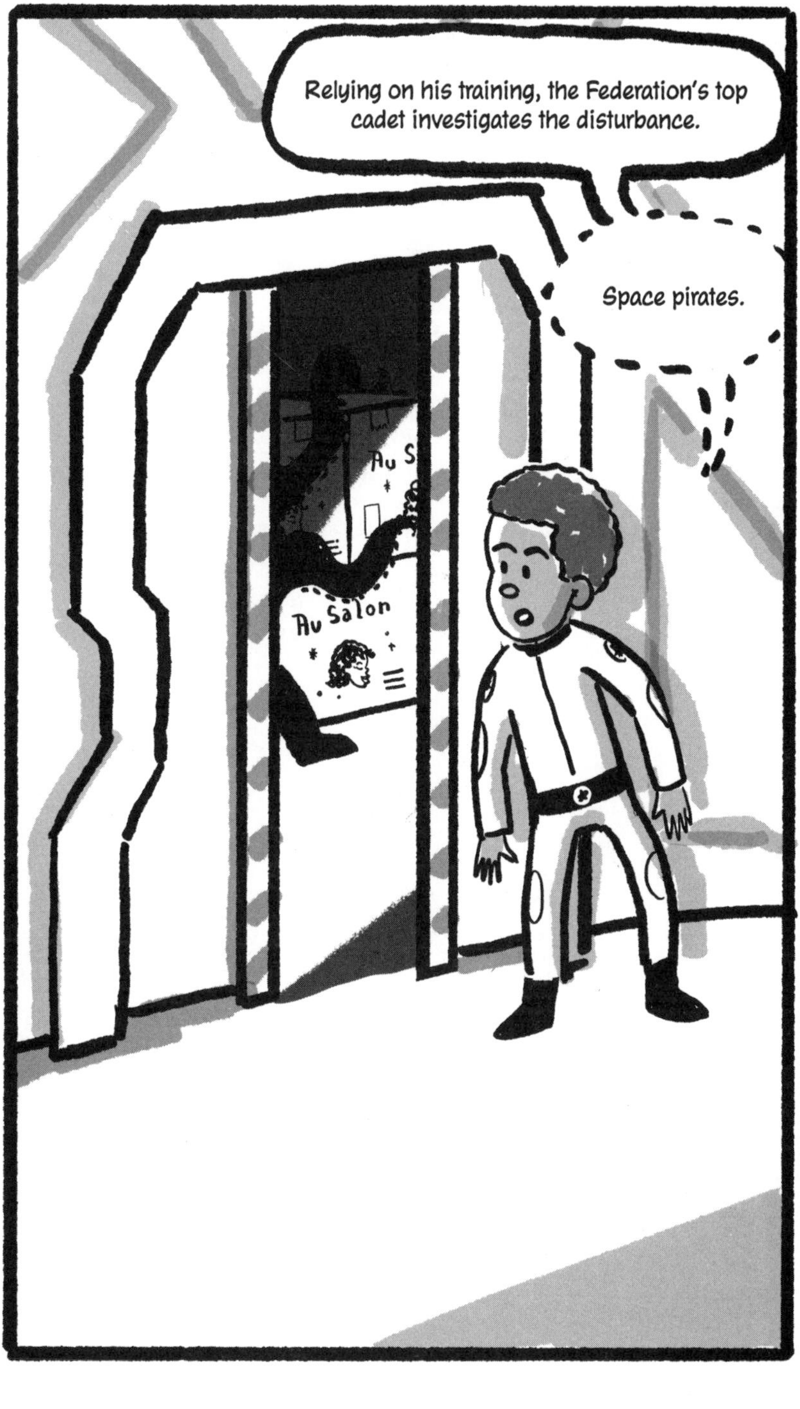
Relying on his training, the Federation's top cadet investigates the disturbance.
Space pirates.
Au Salon
Au S

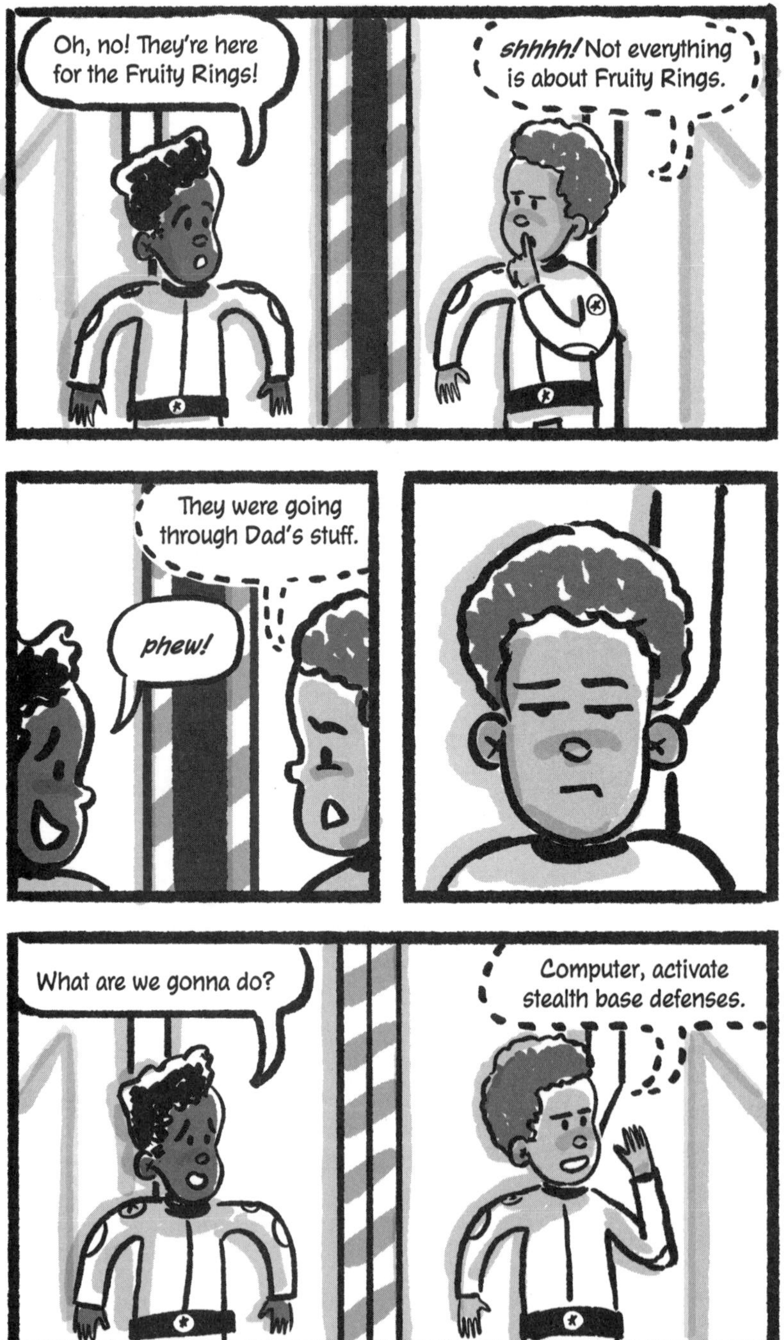
Oh, no! They're here for the Fruity Rings!
shhhh! Not everything is about Fruity Rings.
They were going through Dad's stuff.
phew!
What are we gonna do?
Computer, activate stealth base defenses.

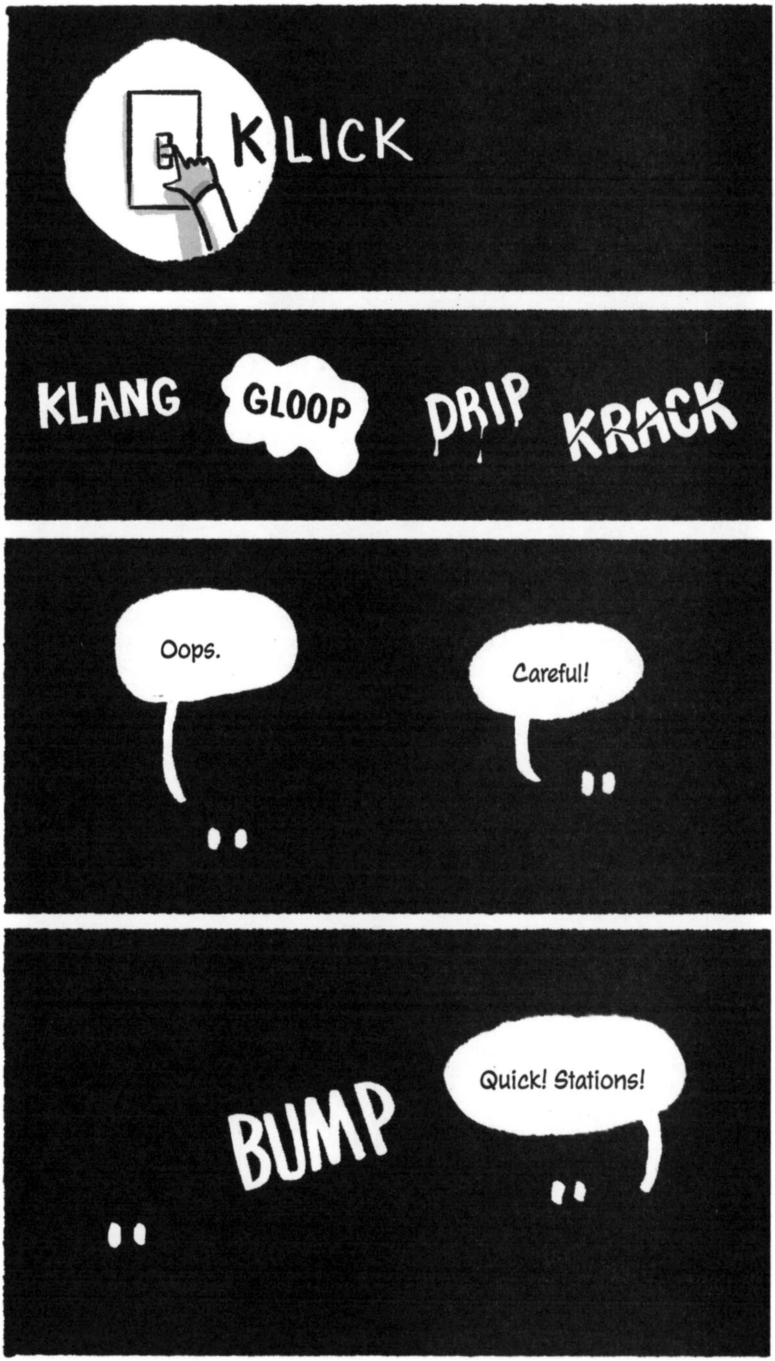
KLICK
KLANG
GLOOP
DRIP
KRACK
Oops.
Careful!
BUMP
Quick! Stations!

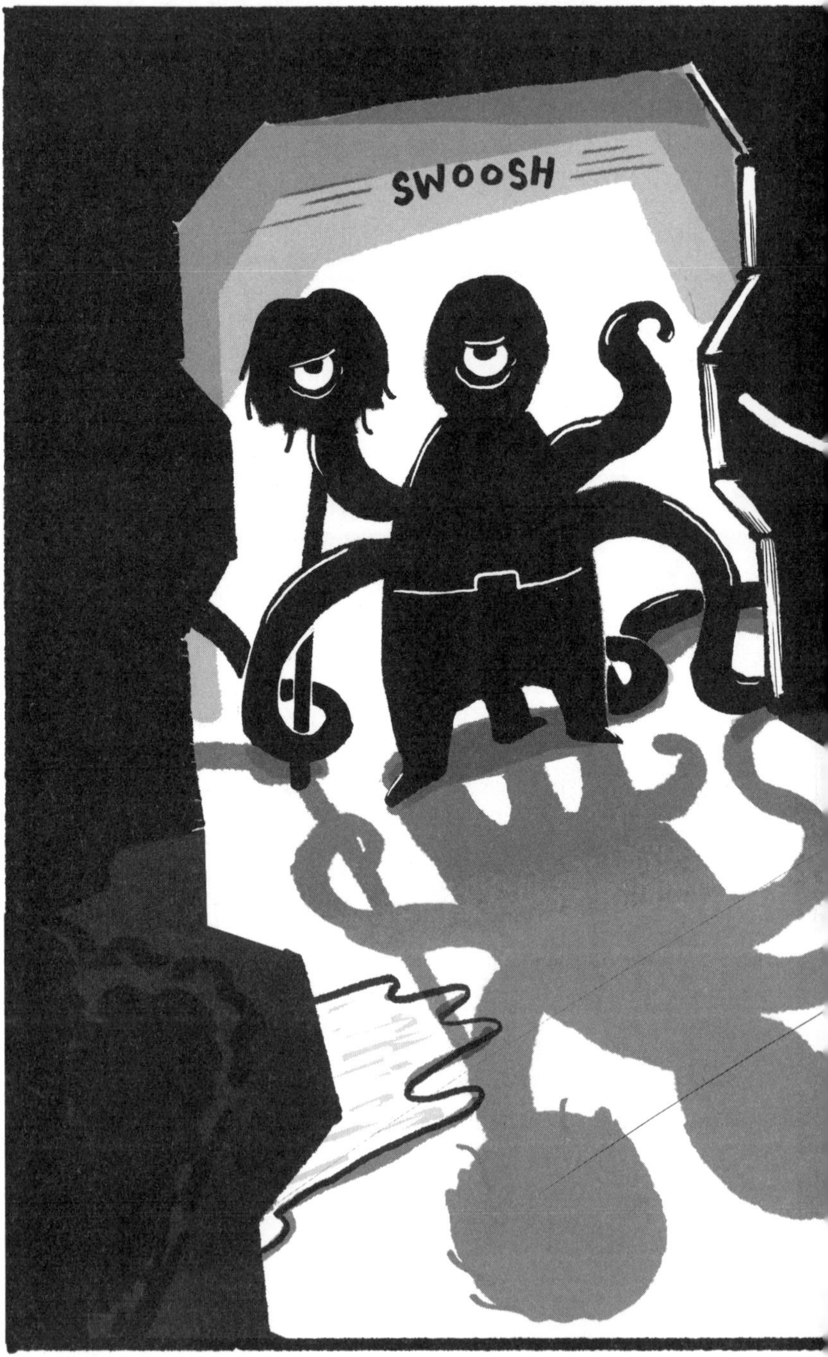
SWOOSH

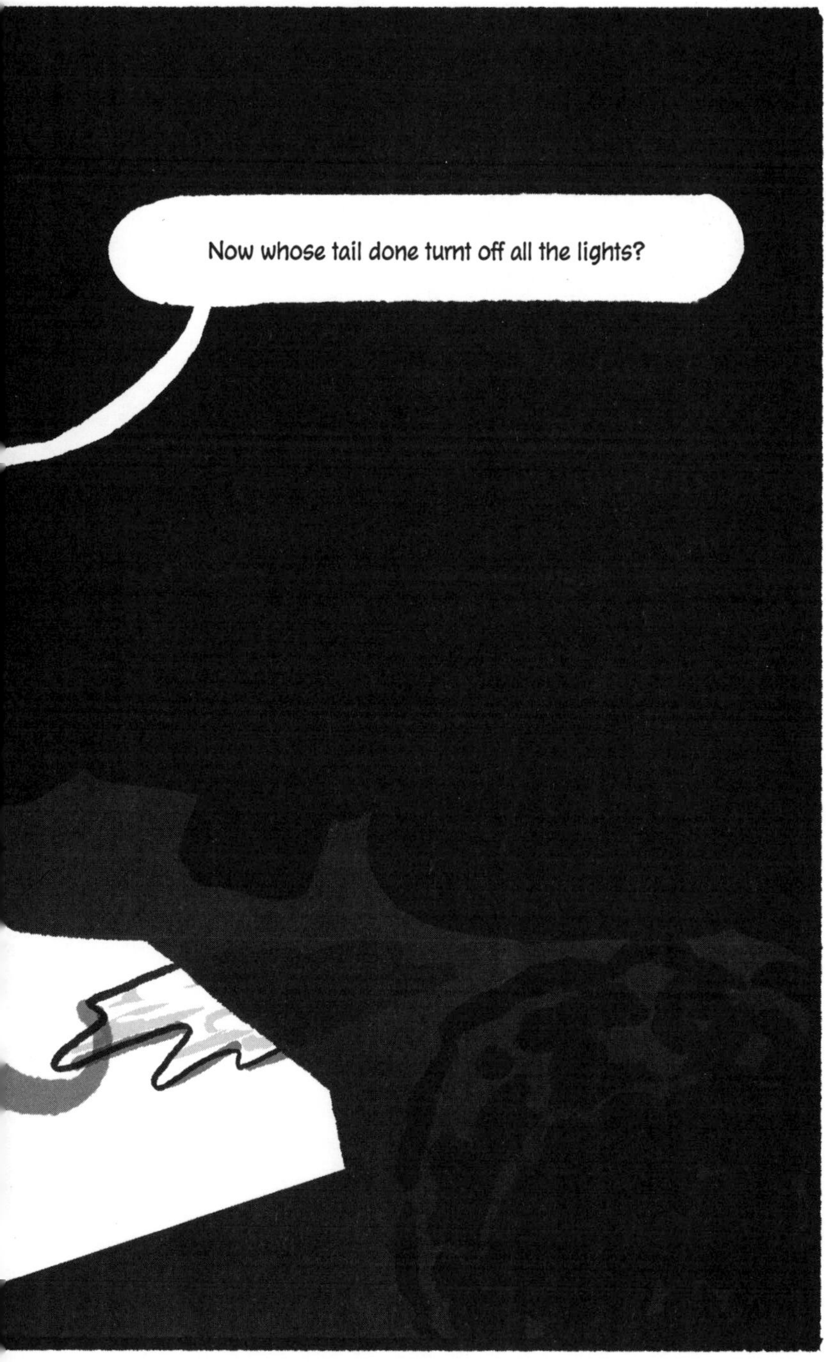
Now whose tail done turnt off all the lights?

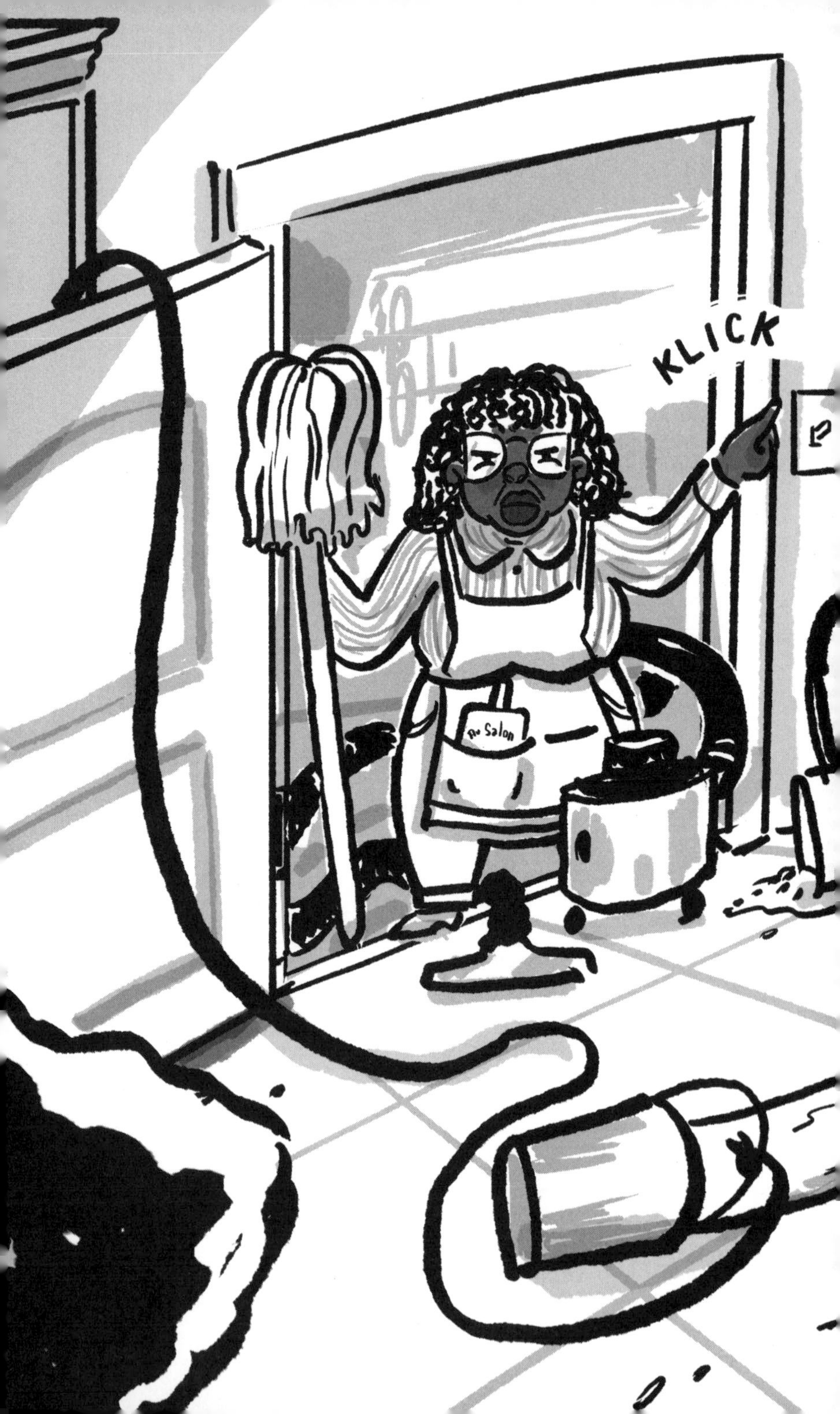
KLICK
Salon

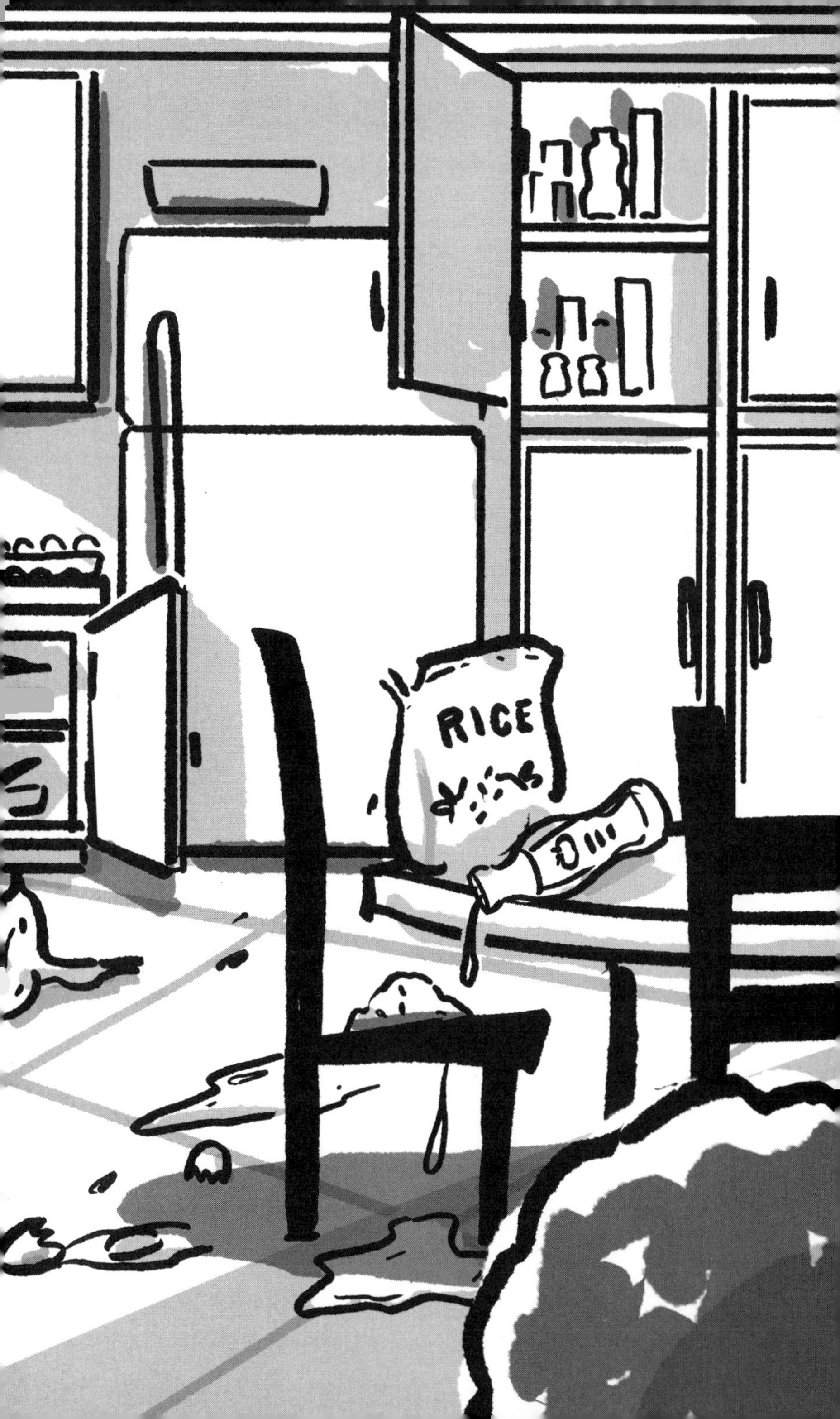
RICE

CHAPTER ELEVEN

WHAT'S A HERO'S WORST NIGHTMARE?

Worse than being raided by no-good space pirates on a distant alien planet?

Worse than being captured by the space pirates and forced to walk the plank into the vacuum of space?

A ten-minute timeout in the bathroom.

No toys.
No games.
Just a seat and a simmer.

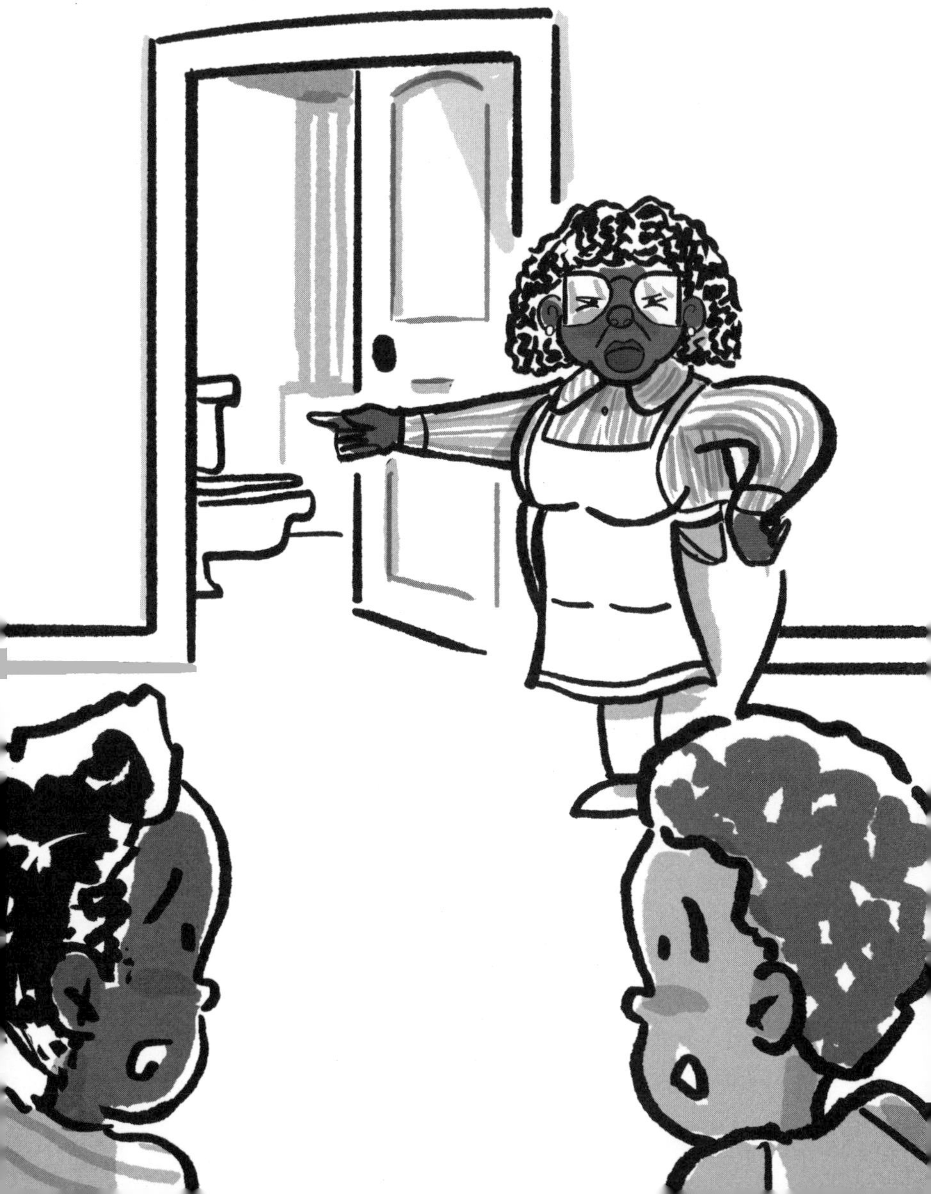

CHAPTER TWELVE

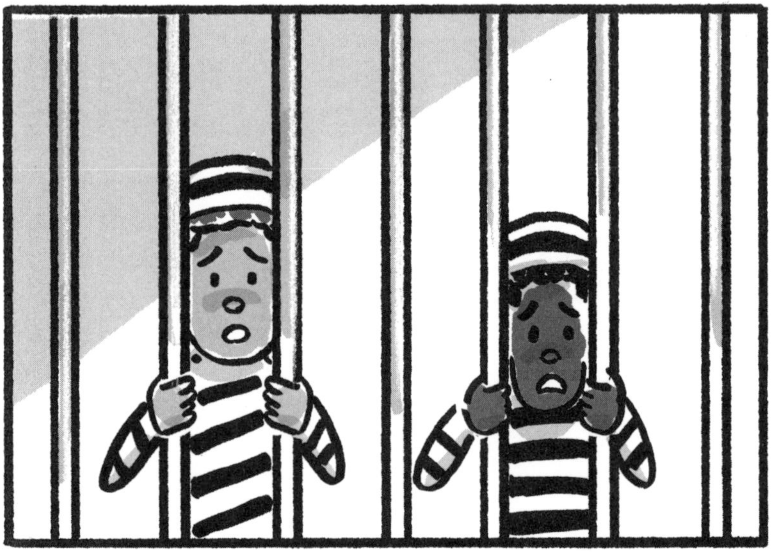

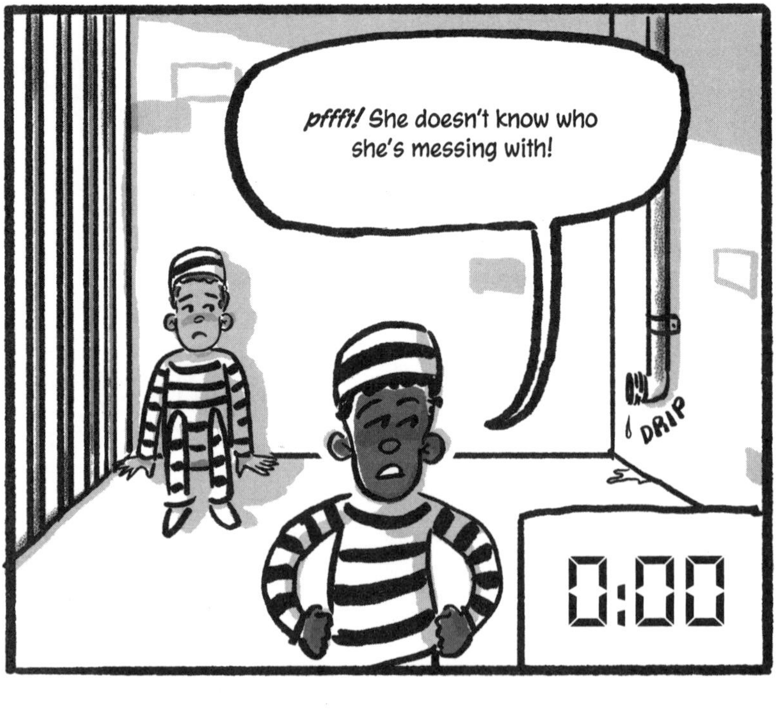
pffft! She doesn't know who she's messing with!
DRIP
0:00

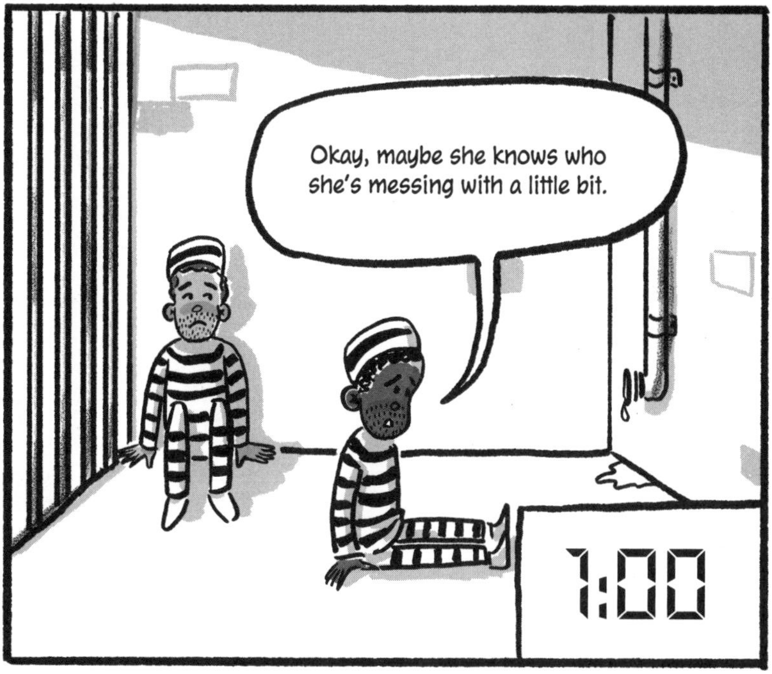
Okay, maybe she knows who she's messing with a little bit.
1:00

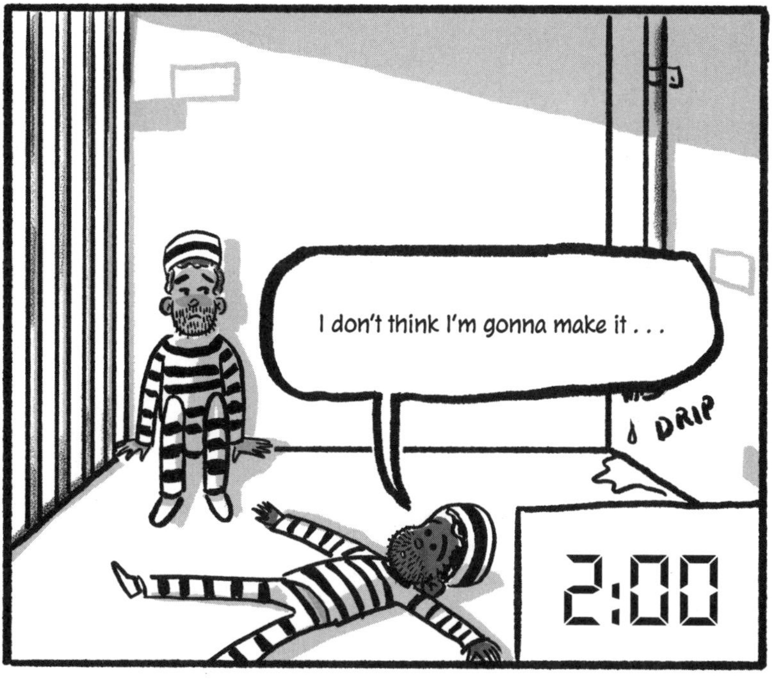
I don't think I'm gonna make it . . .
DRIP
2:00

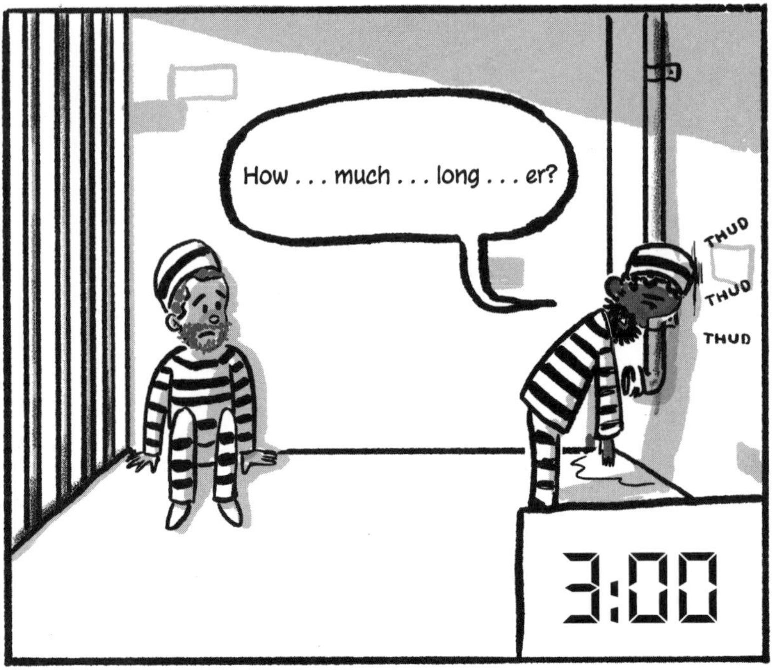
How . . . much . . . long . . . er?
THUD
THUD
THUD
3:00

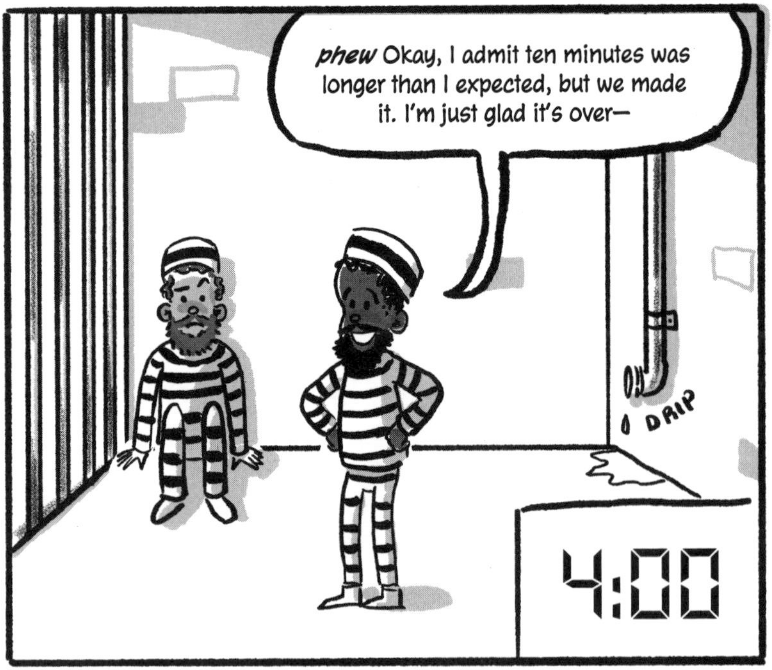
phew Okay, I admit ten minutes was longer than I expected, but we made it. I'm just glad it's over—
DRIP
4:00

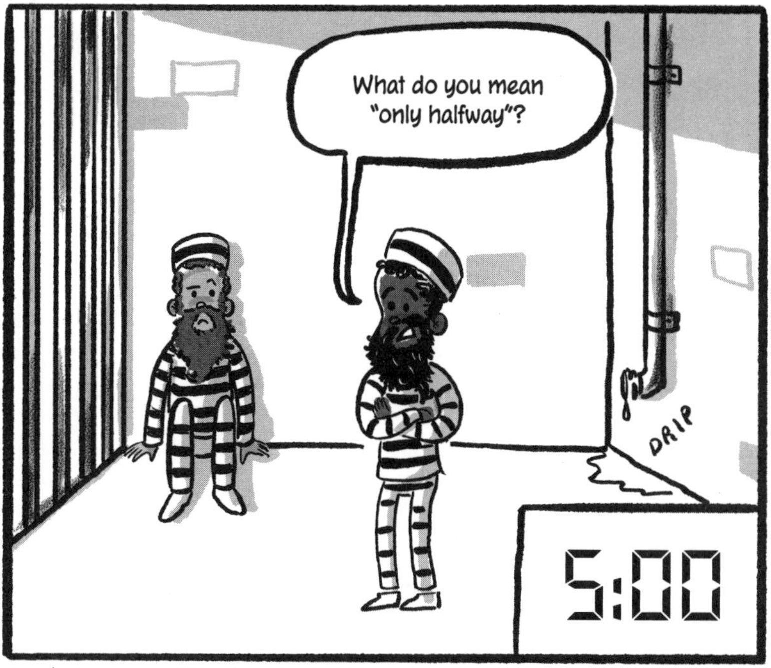
What do you mean "only halfway"?
DRIP
5:00

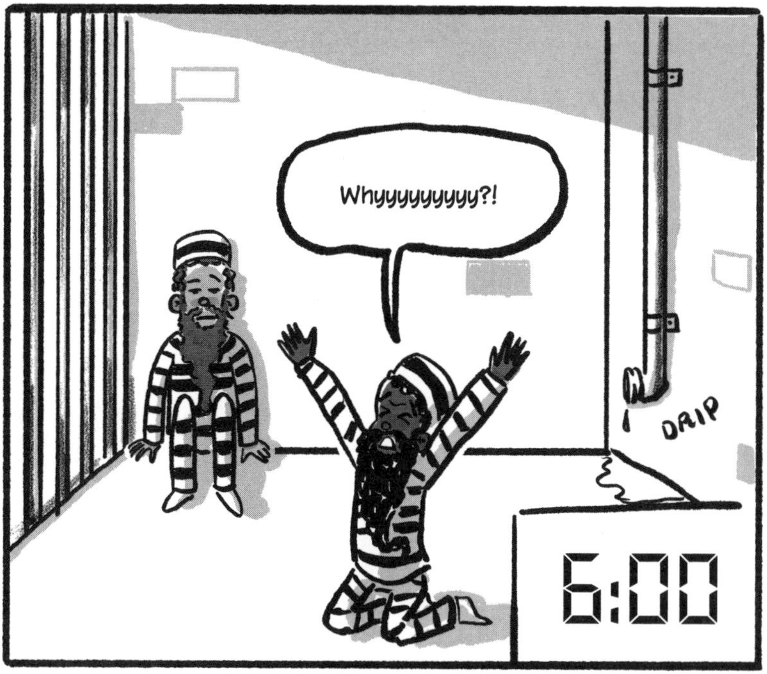
Whyyyyyyyyy?!
DRIP
6:00

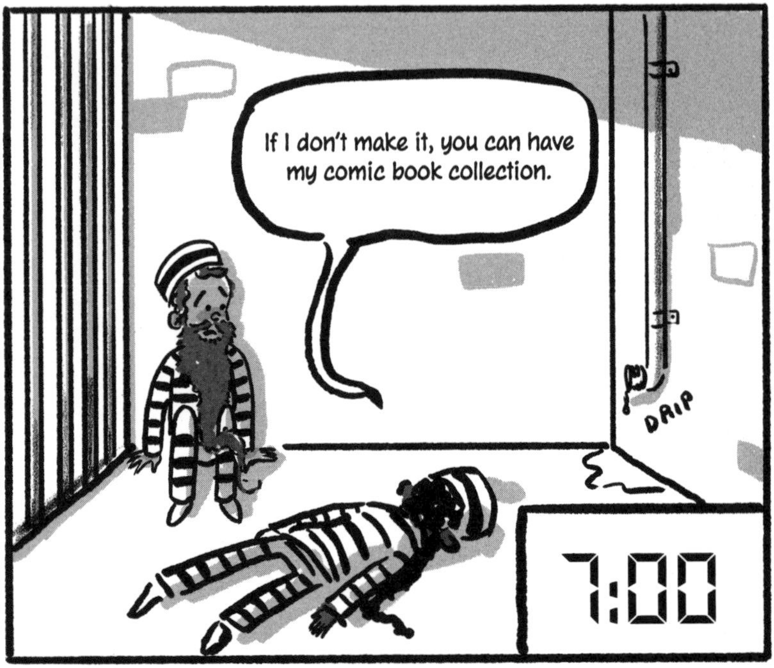
If I don't make it, you can have my comic book collection.
DRIP
7:00

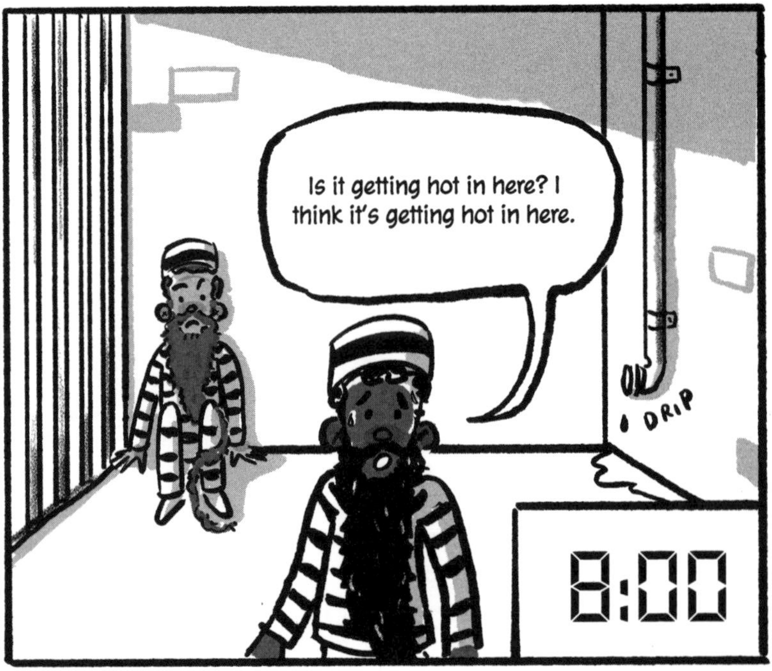
Is it getting hot in here? I think it's getting hot in here.
DRIP
8:00

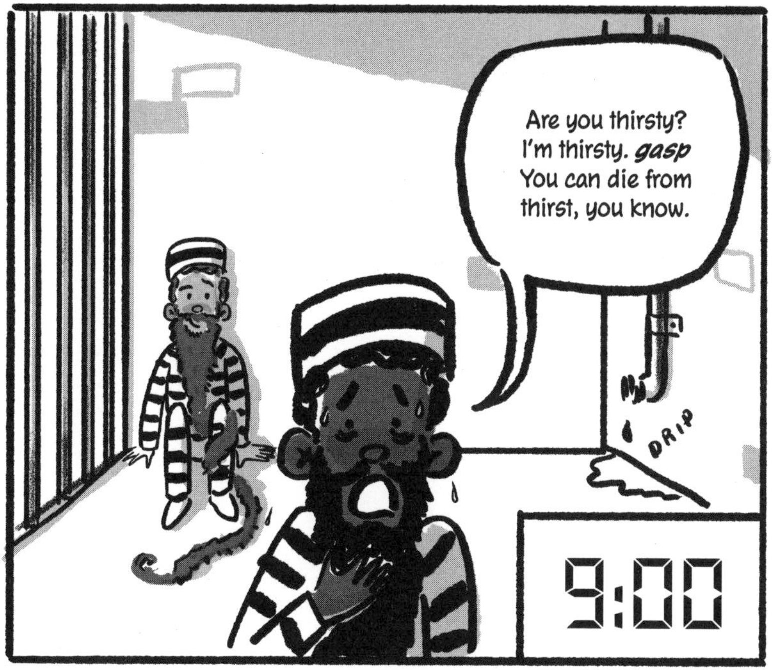
Are you thirsty? I'm thirsty. *gasp* You can die from thirst, you know.
DRIP
9:00

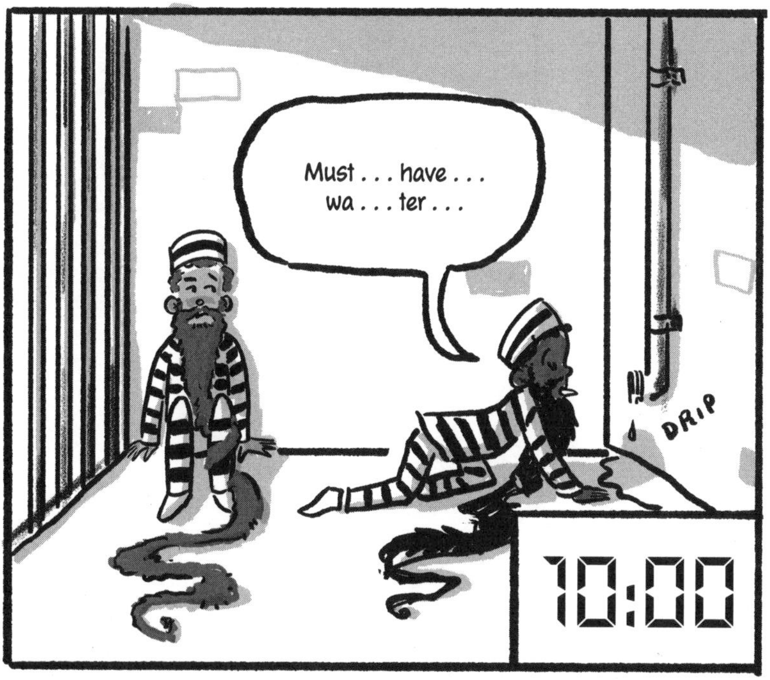
Must . . . have . . . wa . . . ter . . .
DRIP
10:00

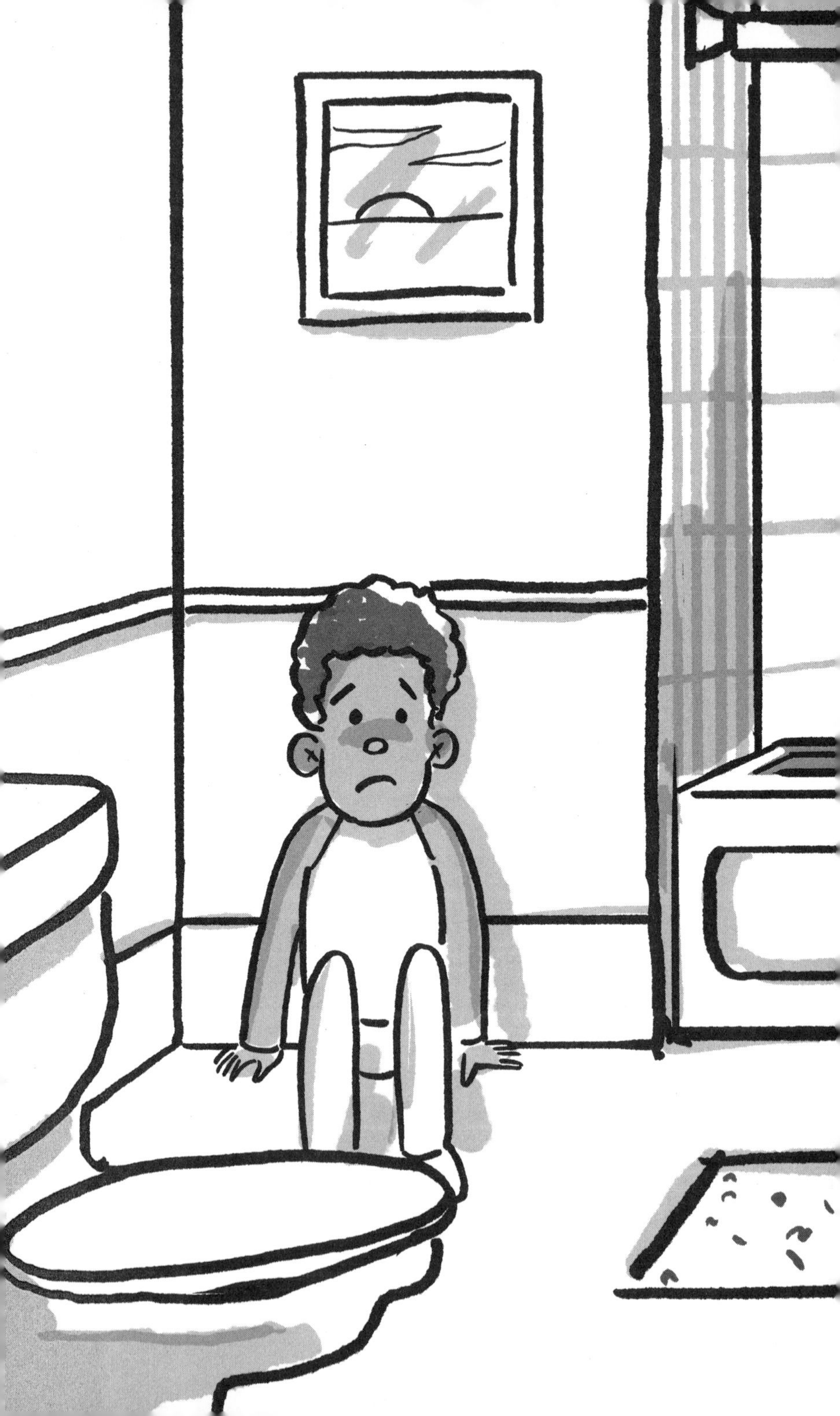

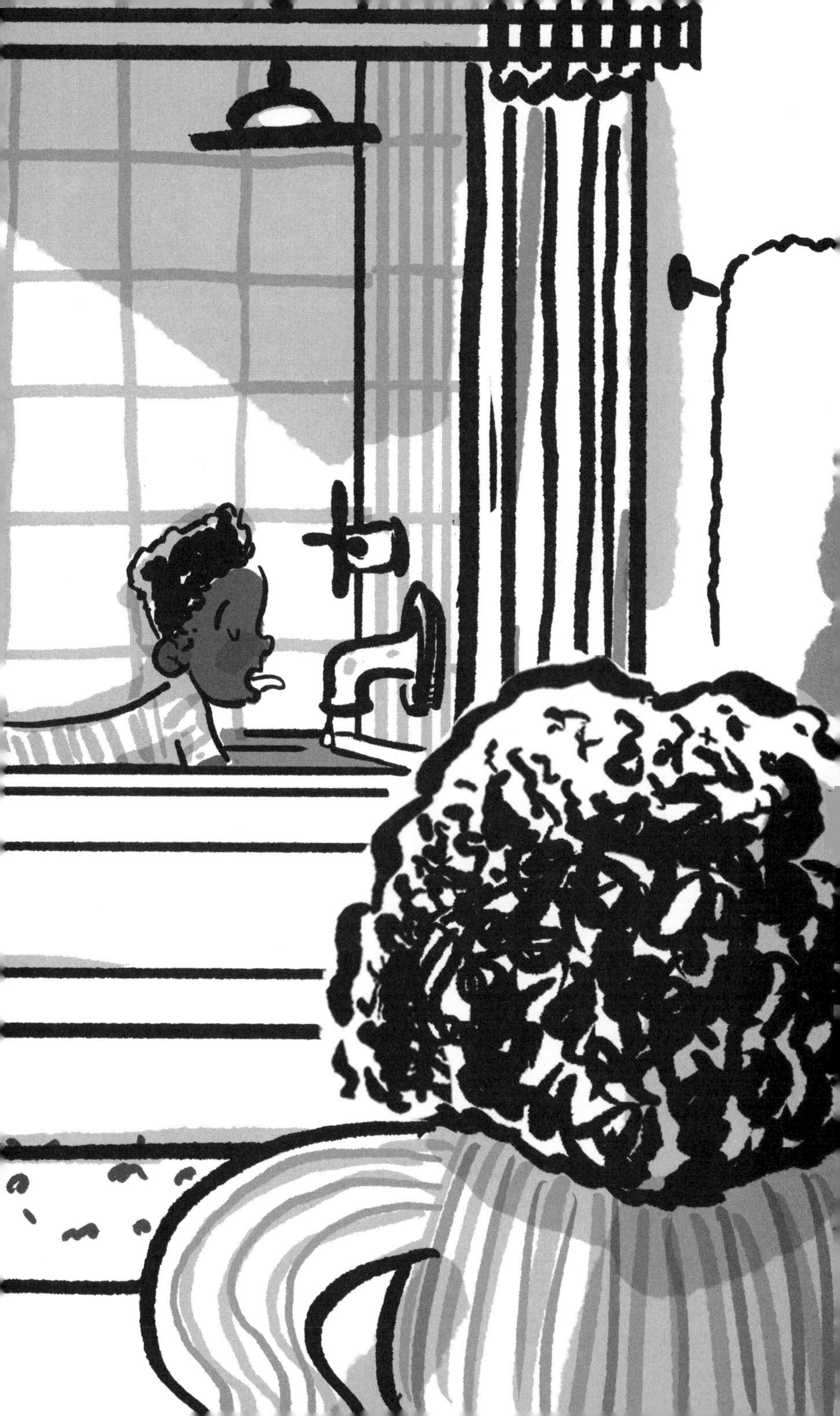

CHAPTER THIRTEEN

AS IT TURNED OUT, TEN MINUTES OF TOYLESS, gameless, sit-and-think-about-your-actions time in the bathroom wasn't the worst of it.

Ms. Joyce stood in the doorway, holding a basket of laundry. Link and Hud looked up from the floor.

"Now, let's get this straight from the start. Your mama and daddy put me in charge. What's that mean?" She didn't wait for an answer. "That means I'm the boss. When they not here, this my house. You do what I say."

Link and Hud started to protest but Ms. Joyce kept right on going.

"You both twice-lucky I was gon' clean that kitchen and hadn't already. Your poor parents work all day, and I don't mean to let them come home to unruly kids in a messy house. Next time, we gon' do better. Ain't that right?"

Link and Hud stared up at Ms. Joyce. Neither spoke. Ms. Joyce stared back and sucked her gold tooth.

“Listen, I done raised fifteen brothers and sisters, six of my own kids, thirteen grandbabies, a great-grandbaby, and sixty-two nieces and nephews. You ain’t gotta say a word for me to know what you thinkin’—you want me gone.”

Hud gasped. She *did* know what he was thinking. Link looked at Hud in a way that said *I can’t believe you fell for that.*

Ms. Joyce smiled, her gold tooth gleaming. “We’ll all get along just fine long as y’all remember you ain’t done nothin’ I ain’t seen before.”

Link thought, *We’ll see about that.*

Hud thought, *Just in case you’re reading my mind right now, I’m gonna think happy thoughts about my favorite things, like my favorite food, Fruity Rings; my favorite video game,* Boomer Bros.; *and my favorite comic-book hero, Wonder Willis. I’m definitely NOT gonna think about anything embarrassing like my favorite—*

Ms. Joyce held up a pair of underwear from the laundry basket. They were yellow and purple and covered in little lightning bolts. “I swear there ain’t nothin’ they won’t put on drawers these days.”

Hud gasped again. Then he blushed.

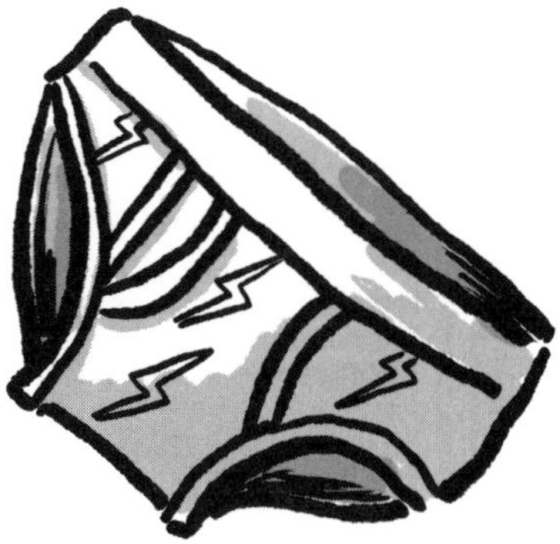

“Now,” Ms. Joyce continued, “go on and take a seat over on the couch. Y’all can help me fold all this laundry while I watch my stories.”

Link and Hud stood up and shuffled out of the bathroom. Just before they entered the den, Link's jaw dropped. The kitchen, which had been a complete disaster only ten minutes ago, was sparkling clean, cleaner than he'd ever seen it before. He elbowed Hud.

Hud was looking down and muttering to himself, "*Nothing . . . nothing.* Just think *nothing.*" He stopped and looked up, annoyed. "What?"

"Look." Link pointed to the kitchen.

Hud shrugged and started muttering to himself again.

Link threw his hands up. Now *he* was annoyed.

The boys entered the den and went to sit down on the couch. Ms. Joyce's large purse was in the way.

"Watch it now—don't sit on my pocketbook. Move it over yonder." Ms. Joyce waved her hand toward the coffee table.

Link and Hud looked at each other like they were both waiting on the other to do it. Neither volunteered. Instead, Link made a fist with one hand and held it out. Hud did the same. "Rock. Paper. Scissors. Shoot." Link turned his fist into bunny ears and laid it out. Scissors. At the same time, Hud left his fist as a fist and laid it out. Rock.

Hud smiled. Link rolled his eyes.

"C'mon, now," said Ms. Joyce. "It ain't gon' bite you."

As Link moved the purse to the coffee table, he scrunched his nose at the strong smell of vinegar and peppermint.

The boys took a seat and Ms. Joyce placed the laundry basket between them. Then she turned on the TV. "Now get to foldin' and keep quiet. *The Lost and the Lonely* is fixin' to start."

If you've never heard of *The Lost and the Lonely*, don't feel bad. Link and Hud had never heard of it, either.

"What's *The Lost and the Lonely*?" asked Hud.

"Shhh!" said Ms. Joyce, as she snapped a towel and started folding it, her eyes glued to the TV.

Link didn't care what *The Lost and the Lonely* was. He was too busy thinking about what he'd just seen in the kitchen. *They'd destroyed that place. How'd Ms. Joyce clean it so fast? Why hadn't she left it for them to clean? Weren't grown-ups supposed to make you clean up your own messes? What would she tell their parents? He knew one thing for sure, he did want her gone. But how were they going to get rid of her and why . . . why was that guy making those gross kissy faces at that lady?*

"Scarlett, my darling."
"Oh, Denzel!"
smooch

If you have a TV in your house, you probably recognize what just happened. You've probably been in the middle of doing something yourself when, just for a moment, you look at the TV and get distracted. You stop doing whatever it was you were doing, and instead you say, *Oh, that's interesting.* And before you know it, you've forgotten all about what you were doing before you ever looked at the TV. That's what just happened to Link. All of a sudden, getting answers to what happened in the kitchen, even getting rid of Ms. Joyce, didn't seem so urgent.

Link and Hud spent the rest of the afternoon absentmindedly folding laundry on the couch. Link mismatched several pairs of socks. Hud folded the same pair of his favorite underwear five times and never realized it. All the while, they watched Denzel make more kissy faces at Scarlett—*ewww!*—whom he thought he'd lost forever—*awww!*—but was only lost in the hospital—*yay!*—in a coma—*no!*—that she was faking—*whoa!*—because she really had amnesia—*what!*—and feared she'd always be a snow cone—*huh?*

CHAPTER FOURTEEN

"FEARED SHE'D ALWAYS BE A WHAT?" SAID MRS. Dupré over dinner that night.

"A snow cone," said Hud.

"I think you probably heard that wrong, buddy," said Dr. Dupré.

"Told you," said Link.

"Anyway, as interesting as *The Lost and the Lonely* is, there's something more important we need to discuss," said Mrs. Dupré.

Uh-oh. Link knew this was coming. He set his fork down and prepared himself for a talking-to. Hud picked up a long green bean with his fingers and started wiggling it.

"Now, we know you didn't want Ms. Joyce to watch you after school," said Mrs. Dupré, "but with the practice and Au Salon—"

"And running out of neighbors," interjected Dr. Dupré.

"Yes, that too," said Mrs. Dupré. "Well, we really had no choice."

Link looked down to avoid eye contact. Hud studied the green bean closely and nibbled nervously on the end.

"All we asked," continued Mrs. Dupré, "was that you two behave—"

"And stay out of the garage," interjected Dr. Dupré.

"Right. That too," said Mrs. Dupré. "But instead,"—here it came—"you went above and beyond."

Link looked up, surprised at what he'd just heard. Hud stopped mid-slurp, half the green bean hanging out of his mouth.

"Don't look so surprised," said Mrs. Dupré with a big smile on her face. "I've always known my boys were perfect little gentlemen, but it never hurts to hear someone else say it."

Link and Hud looked at each other, confused.

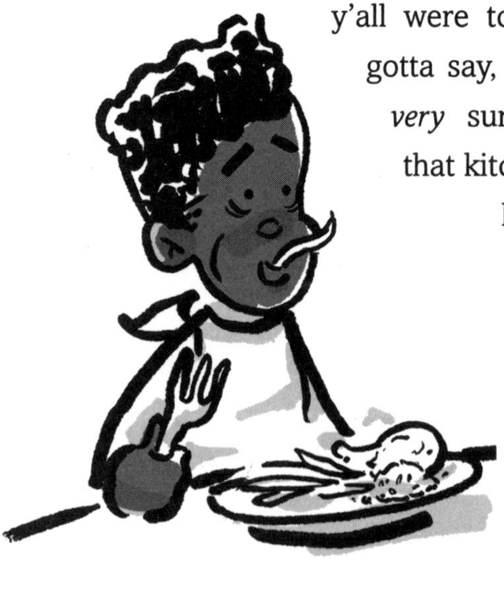

"Ms. Joyce told us all about how helpful y'all were today," said Dr. Dupré. "I gotta say, unlike your mama, I was *very* surprised. I've never seen that kitchen so clean! And all that laundry too—ooh wee!" Dr. Dupré shook his head like he couldn't believe what he was saying. "Call me impressed. If y'all aren't careful, I might just have to put y'all to work for Au

Salon." He chuckled and looked at Mrs. Dupré. "Lord knows it could use the help."

"Anyhoo," said Mrs. Dupré, "we just wanted to say thank you for giving Ms. Joyce a chance—"

"And that we're having pecan pie for dessert!" interjected Dr. Dupré.

"And that too," said Mrs. Dupré. "Pecan pie for my sweetie pies." She beamed at Link and Hud.

"I'll go get the ice cream!" said Dr. Dupré.

"Can you believe that?" said Hud. "I don't even remember cleaning the kitchen."

Link and Hud were in their bunks for the night: Link up top, Hud down below. Their bedroom was dark except for the flashlight Hud was using to flip through his comic book.

"We didn't clean the kitchen," said Link with an eye roll to the ceiling. "Ms. Joyce didn't tell them what really happened."

"Oh, right. I knew that," said Hud without looking up from his comic book. He turned the page. "Isn't that a good thing?"

Link hung over the edge of his bed and looked down at Hud. "Don't you get it? She made herself look like the best babysitter ever. Mom and Dad will never get rid of her now, and that is definitely not good for us."

Hud pointed his flashlight up at Link. "Well, we got pecan pie tonight, didn't we? I think that's pretty good for us—"

Link snatched the flashlight from Hud's hand and pointed it back in his face. "Do you want to do more hard time in the bathroom? Huh? Do you?"

Hud shut his eyes at the bright light and shuddered at the thought. "No. Way."

Link tossed the flashlight down to Hud's feet and then rolled back over to look up at the ceiling. "Me neither. I'd never eat pecan pie again if it meant no more Ms. Joyce."

Hud reached down, picked up the flashlight, and went back to flipping through his comic book. After a few minutes of silent page-turning, he said, "You know, Ms. Joyce kinda reminds me of Dr. Nebulo."

"That evil scientist from *Wonder Willis?*" said Link.

"Yeah," said Hud. "Dr. Nebulo had everyone on planet Woopton fooled. They all thought he was a good guy until issue #23, *Wonder Warriors of Planet Woopton*, when Wonder Willis discovered his secret."

Link waited in the dark, expecting Hud to share Dr. Nebulo's secret.

"Well? What was it?" said Link when Hud didn't.

"What was what?" said Hud.

"His secret!"

"Oh. That he was a bad guy—duh."

"Right. Okay. I'm going to sleep," said Link. He rolled over onto his side, punched his pillow to fluff it, and closed his eyes, annoyed.

"I'm just sayin'," said Hud with a yawn, "if Mom and Dad found out Ms. Joyce was secretly a bad guy, they'd probably get rid of her. I dunno. It worked for Wonder Willis." He turned off his flashlight, put his comic book under his pillow, closed his eyes, and was snoring within seconds.

Link opened his eyes. And then he smiled. Sometimes—and he'd never admit it out loud—little brothers were pretty smart.

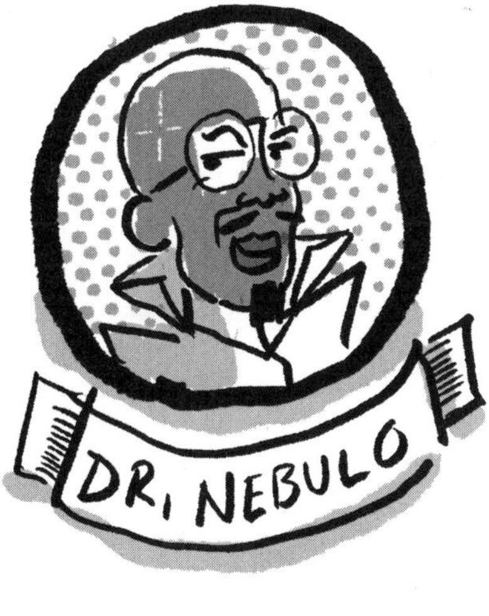
DR. NEBULO

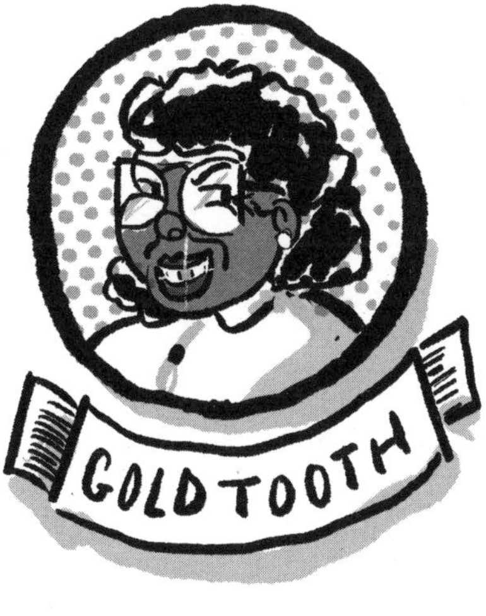
GOLDTOOTH

CHAPTER FIFTEEN

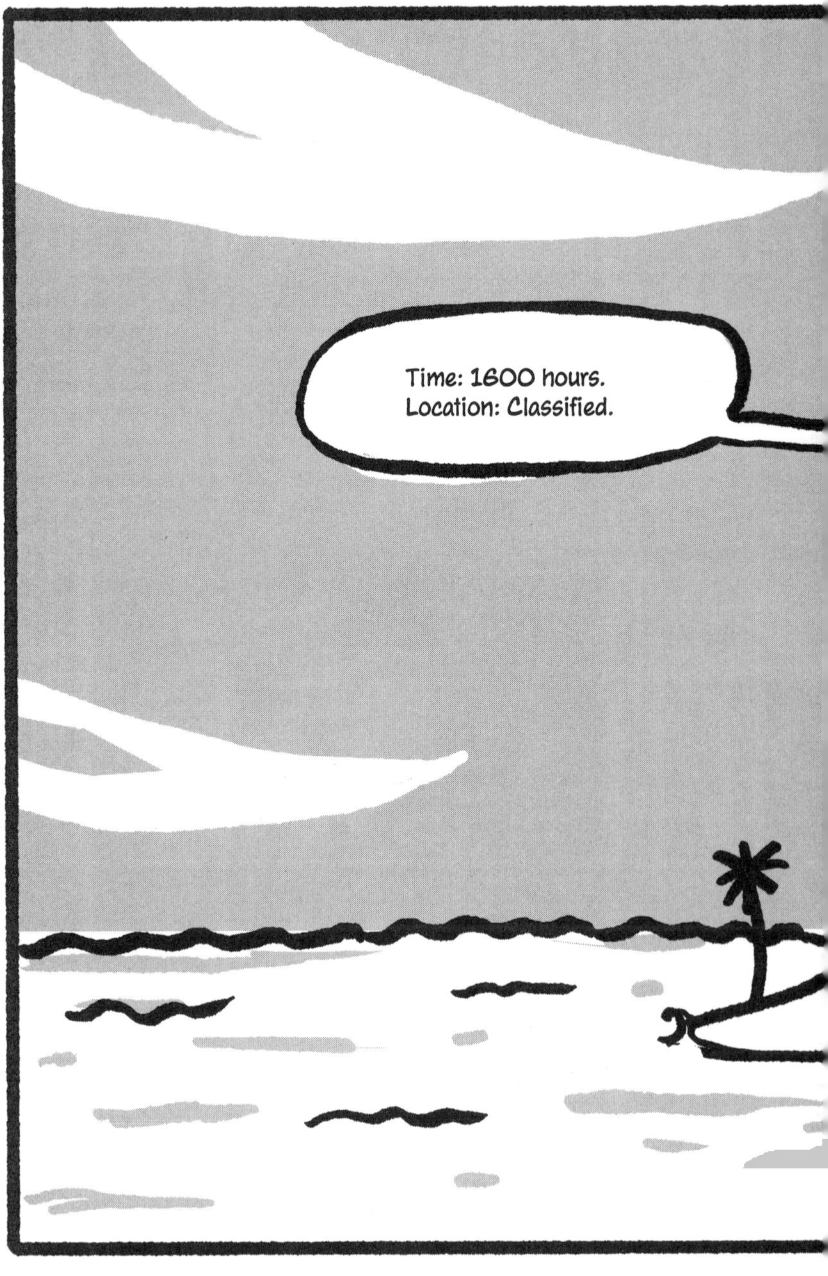
Time: 1600 hours.
Location: Classified.

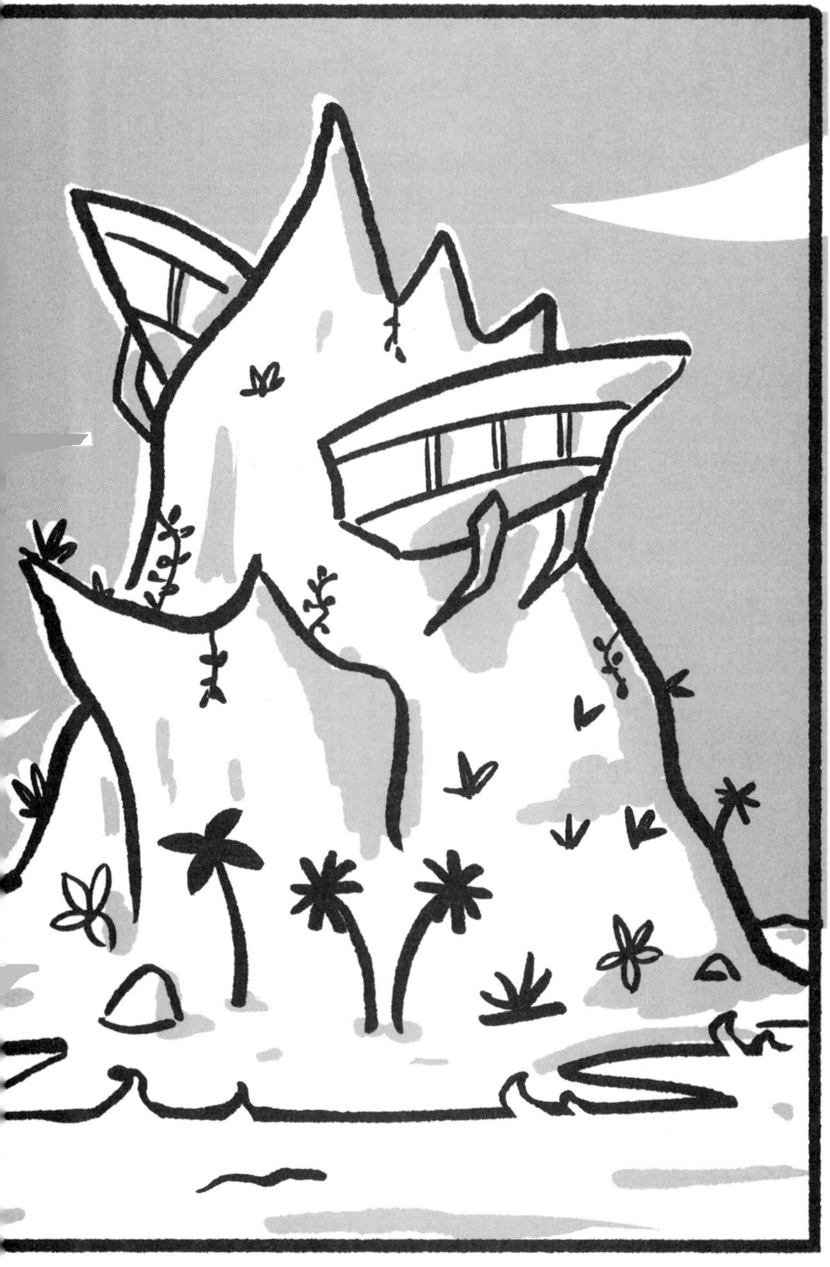

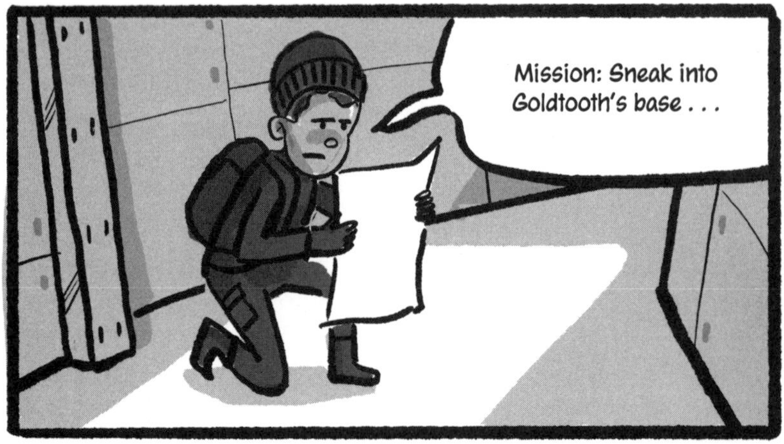
Mission: Sneak into Goldtooth's base . . .

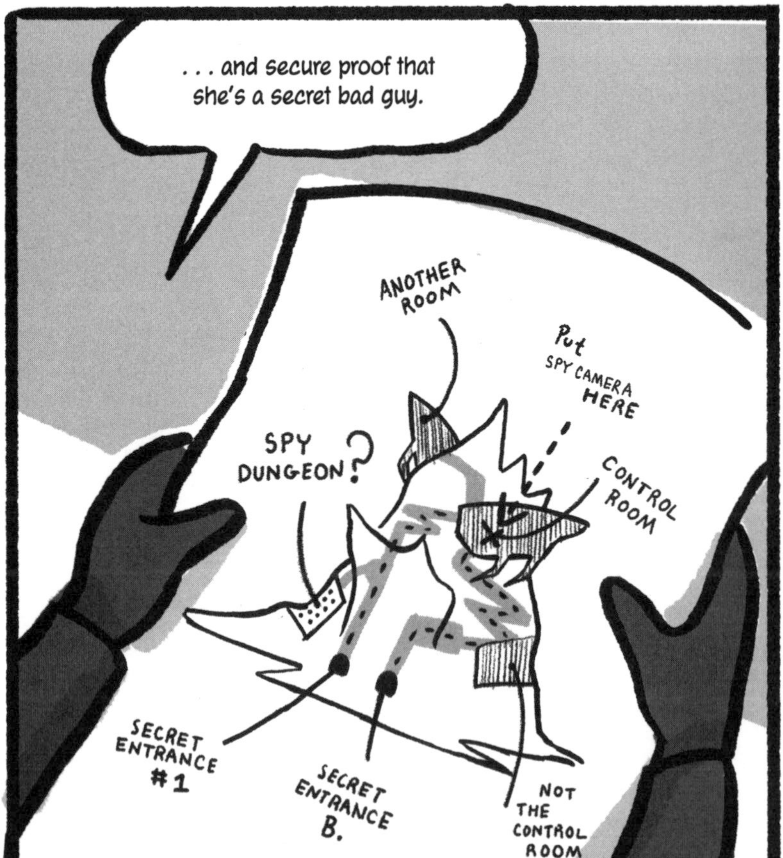
. . . and secure proof that she's a secret bad guy.
ANOTHER ROOM
Put SPY CAMERA HERE
SPY DUNGEON?
CONTROL ROOM
SECRET ENTRANCE #1
SECRET ENTRANCE B.
NOT THE CONTROL ROOM

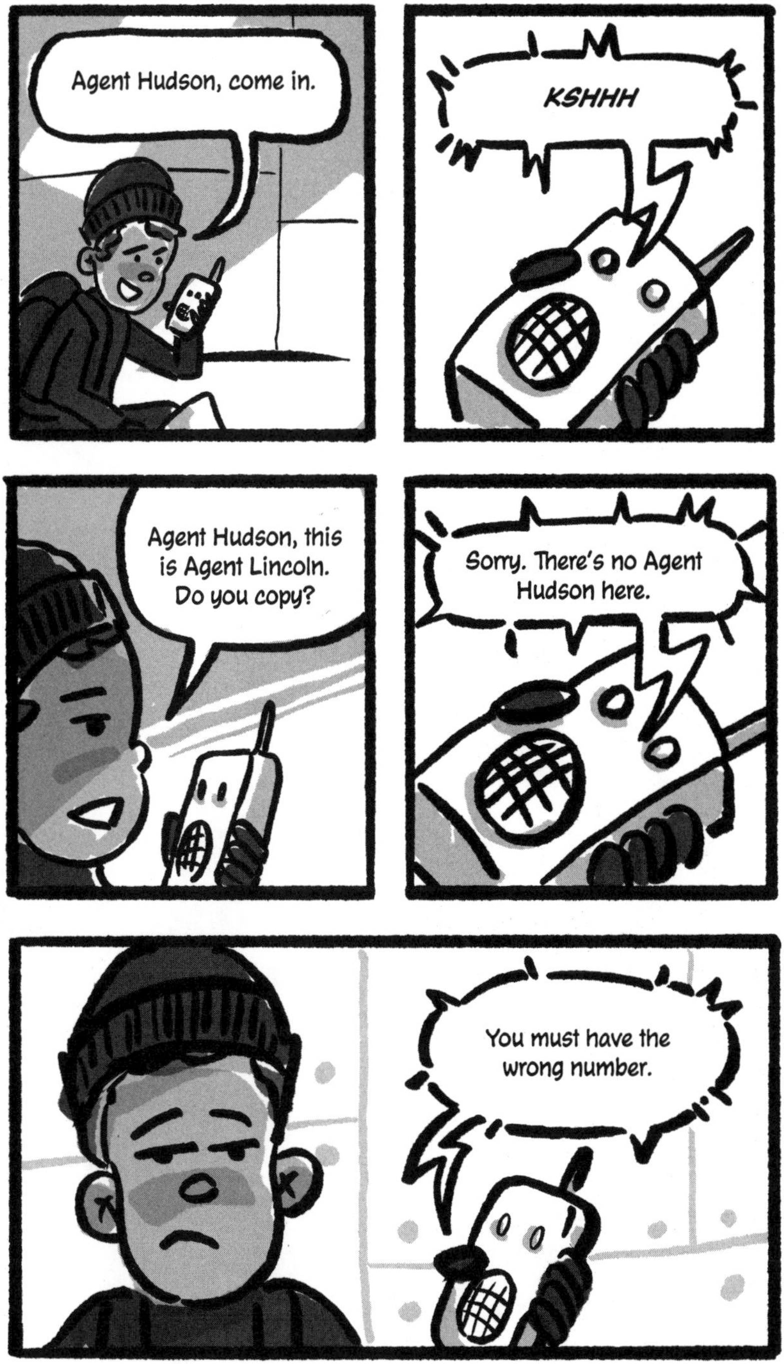
Agent Hudson, come in.
KSHHH
Agent Hudson, this is Agent Lincoln. Do you copy?
Sorry. There's no Agent Hudson here.
You must have the wrong number.

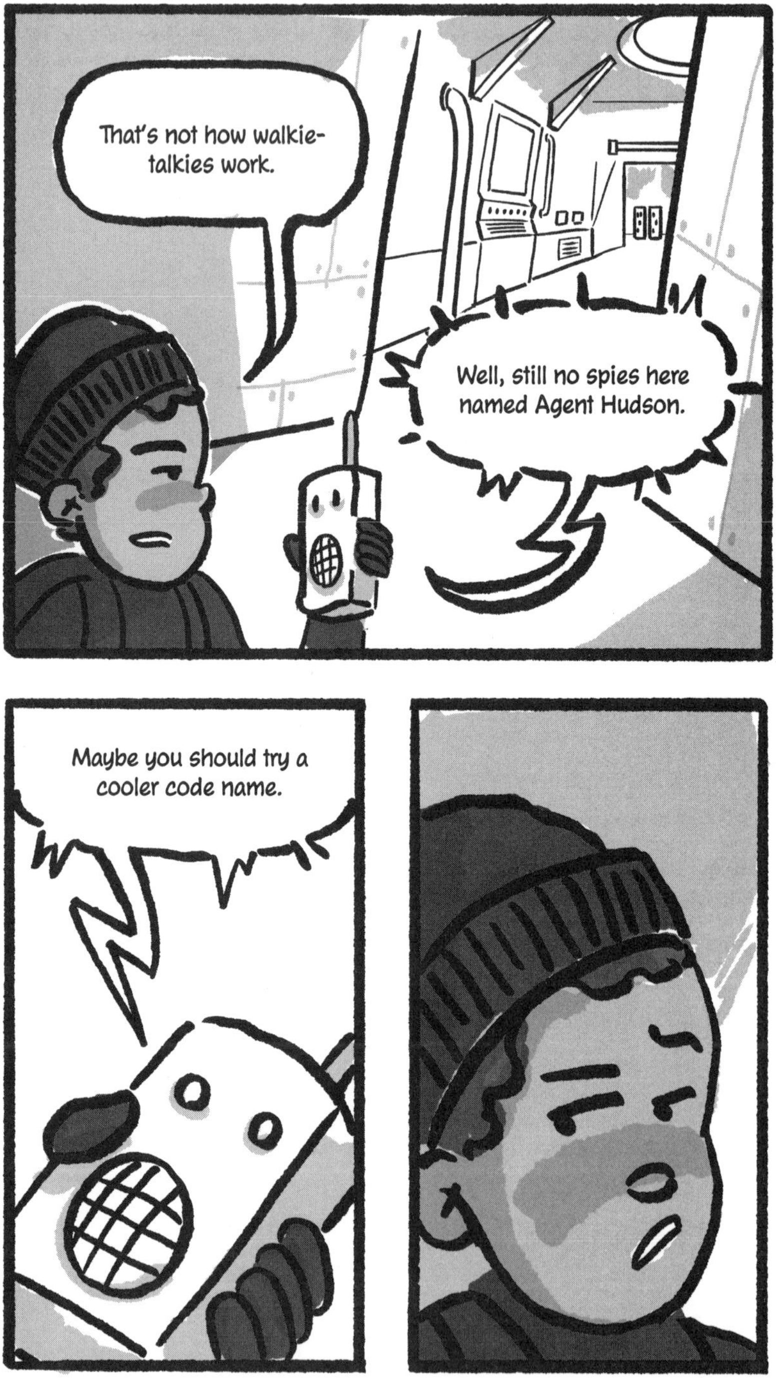
That's not how walkie-talkies work.
Well, still no spies here named Agent Hudson.
Maybe you should try a cooler code name.

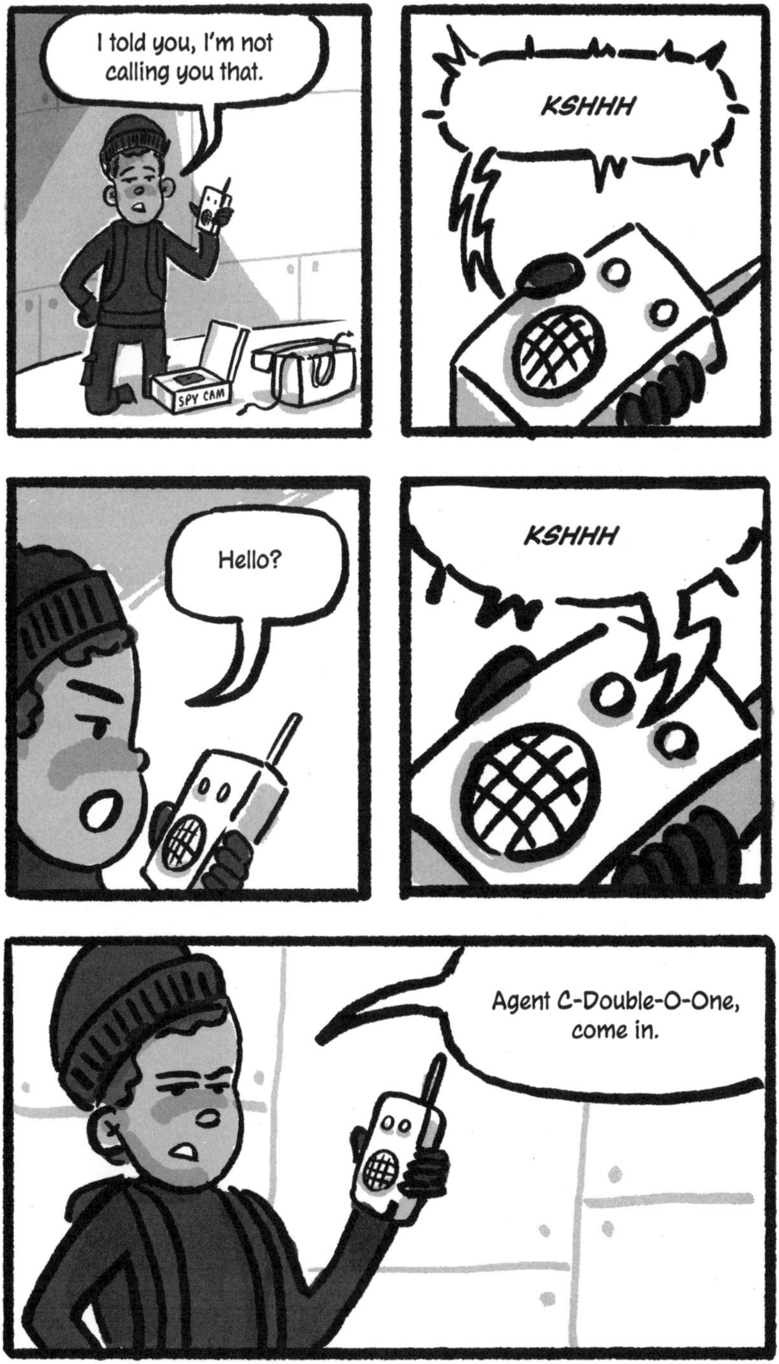
I told you, I'm not calling you that.
KSHHH
Hello?
KSHHH
Agent C-Double-O-One, come in.
SPY CAM

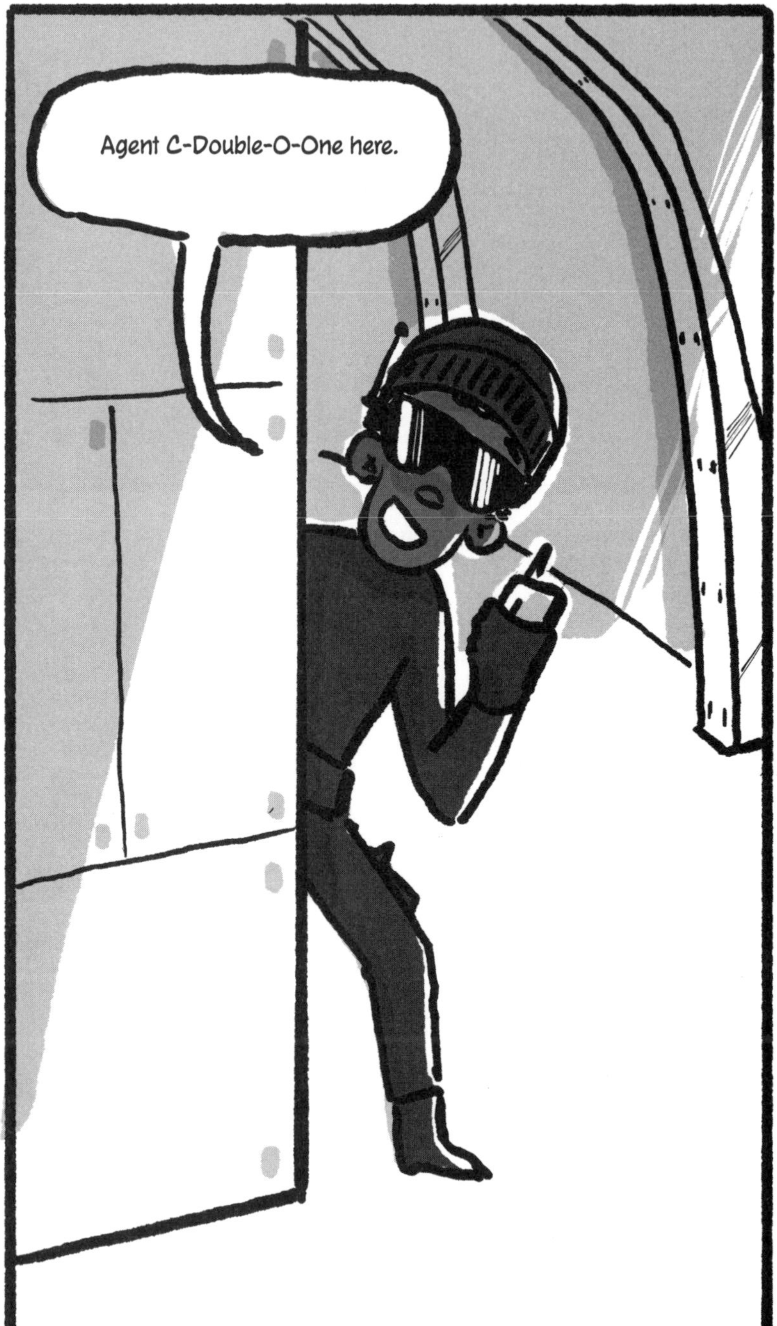
Agent C-Double-O-One here.

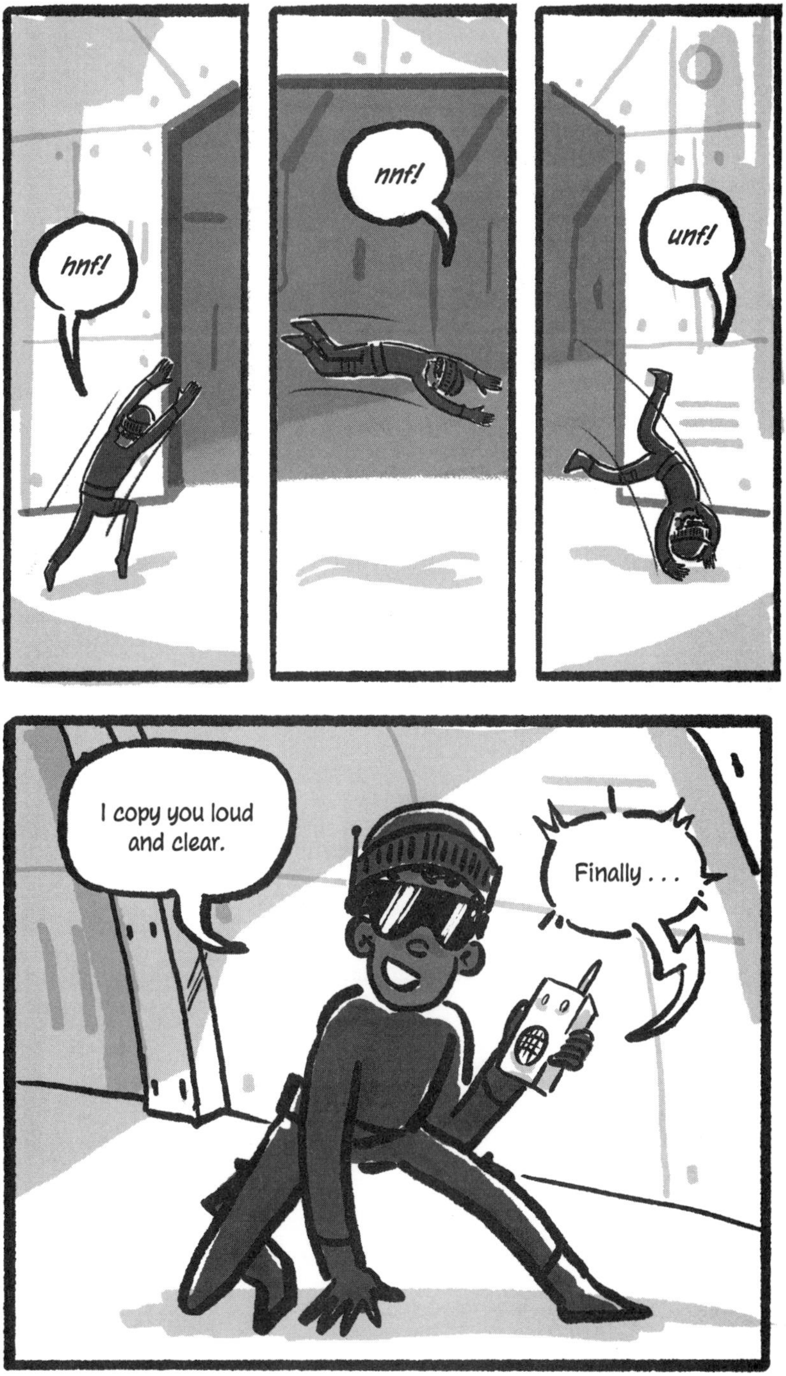
hnf!
nnf!
unf!
I copy you loud and clear.
Finally . . .

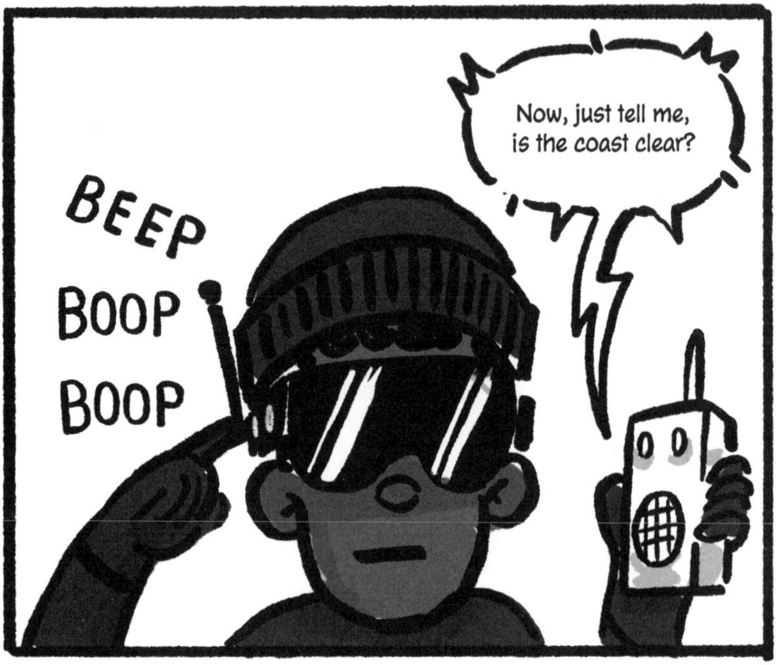
BEEP
BOOP
BOOP
Now, just tell me, is the coast clear?

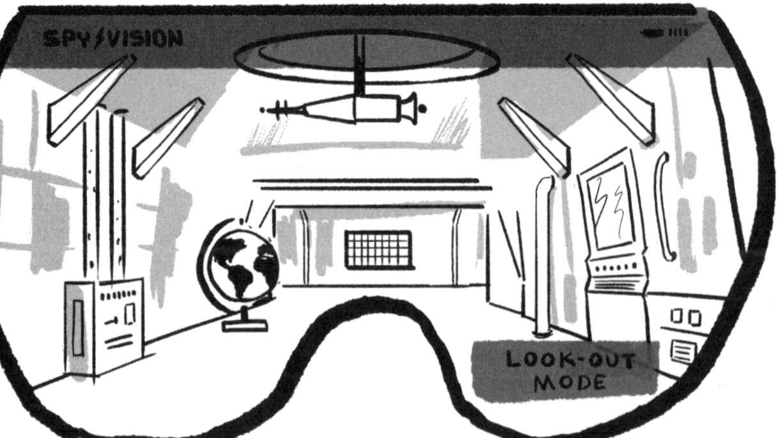
SPY/VISION
LOOK-OUT MODE

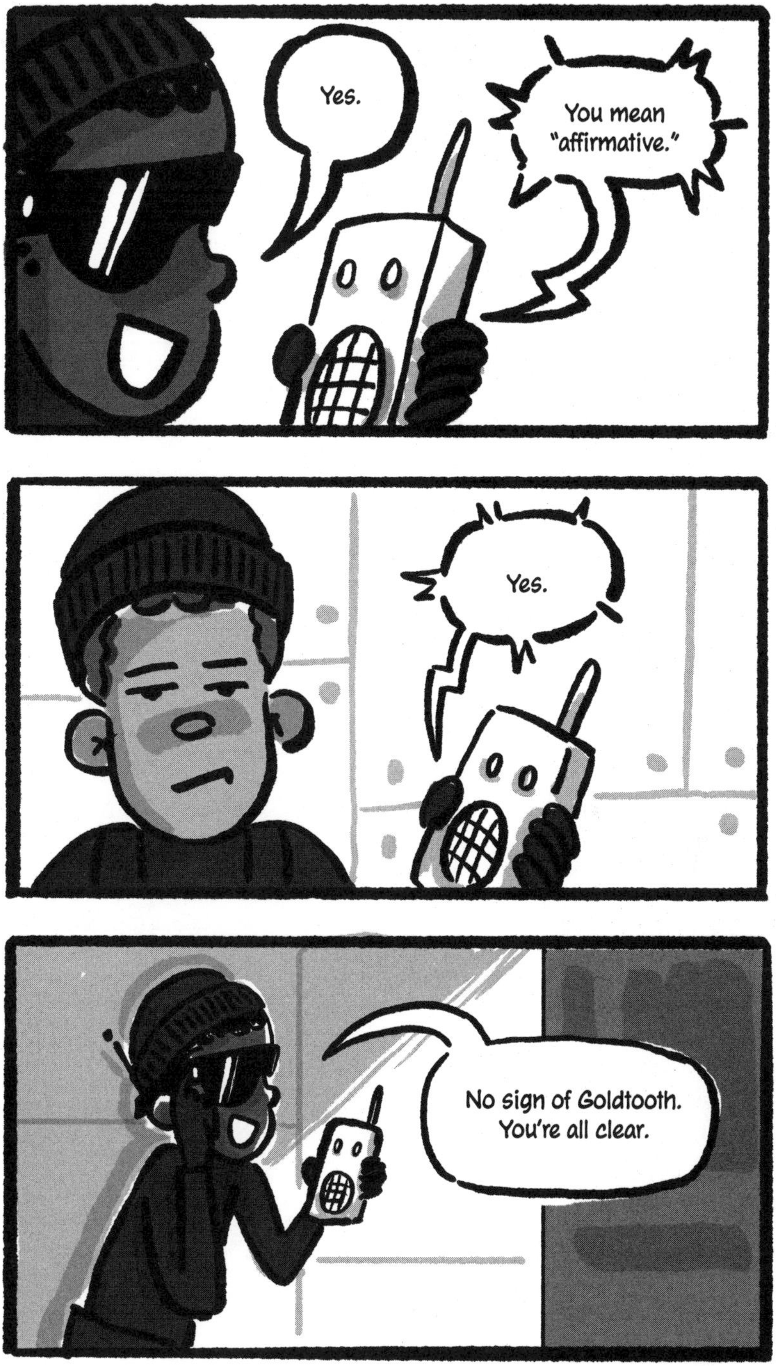
Yes.
You mean "affirmative."
Yes.
No sign of Goldtooth. You're all clear.

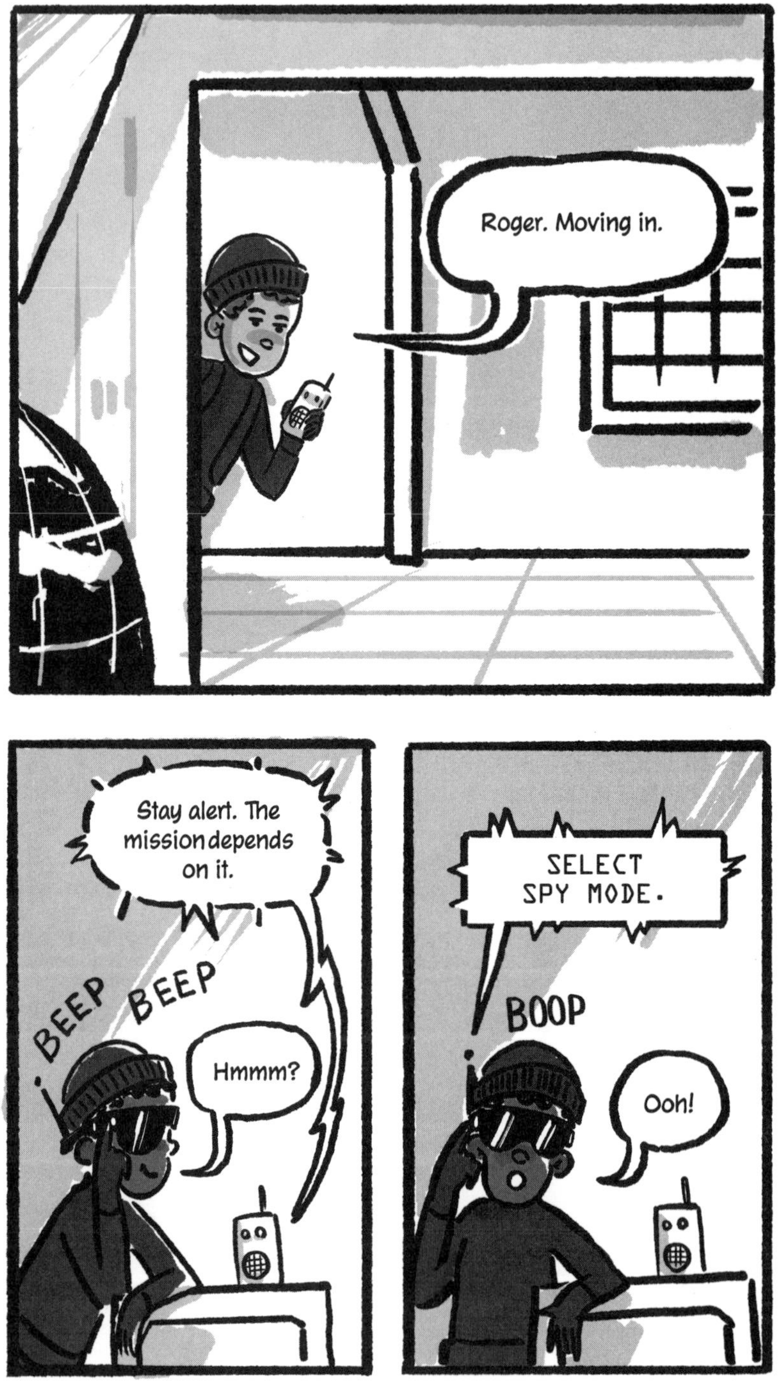
Roger. Moving in.
Stay alert. The mission depends on it.
BEEP BEEP
Hmmm?
SELECT SPY MODE.
BOOP
Ooh!

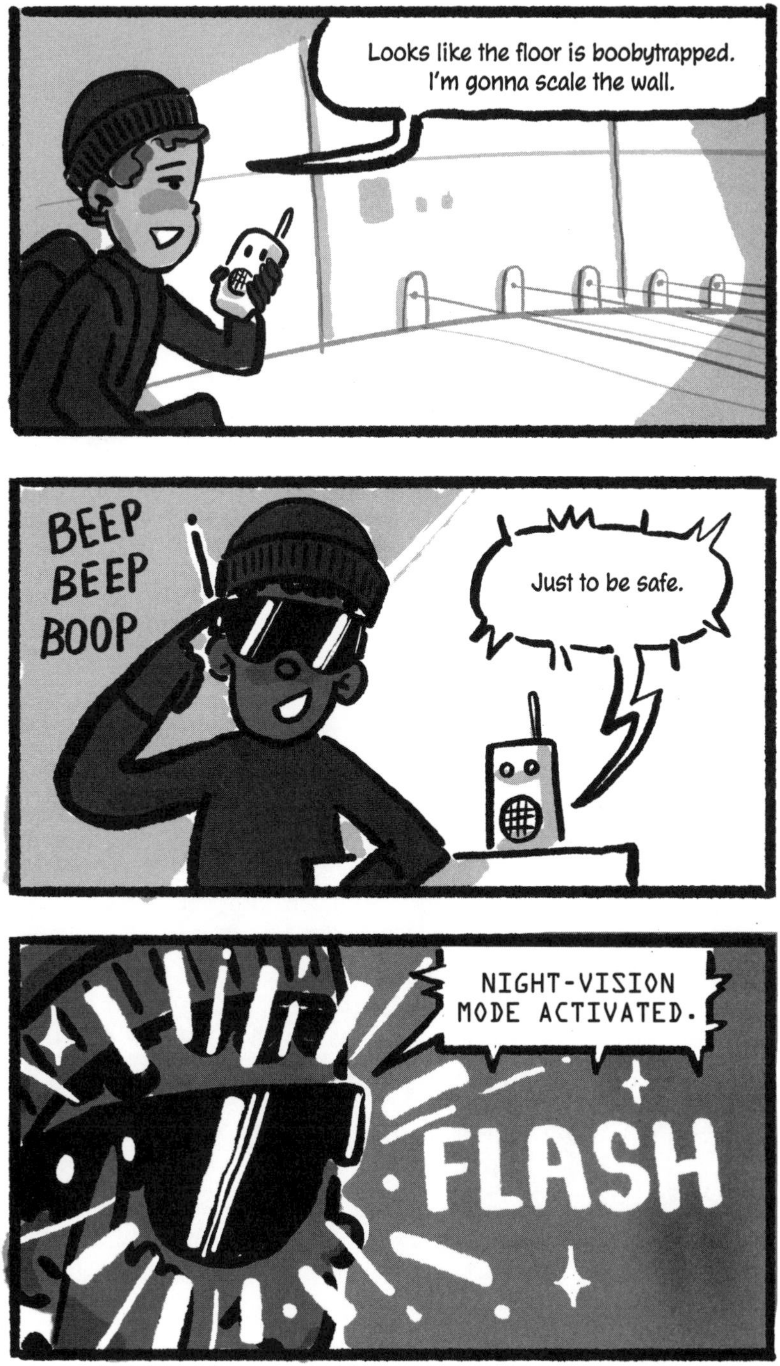
Looks like the floor is boobytrapped. I'm gonna scale the wall.
BEEP BEEP BOOP
Just to be safe.
NIGHT-VISION MODE ACTIVATED.
FLASH

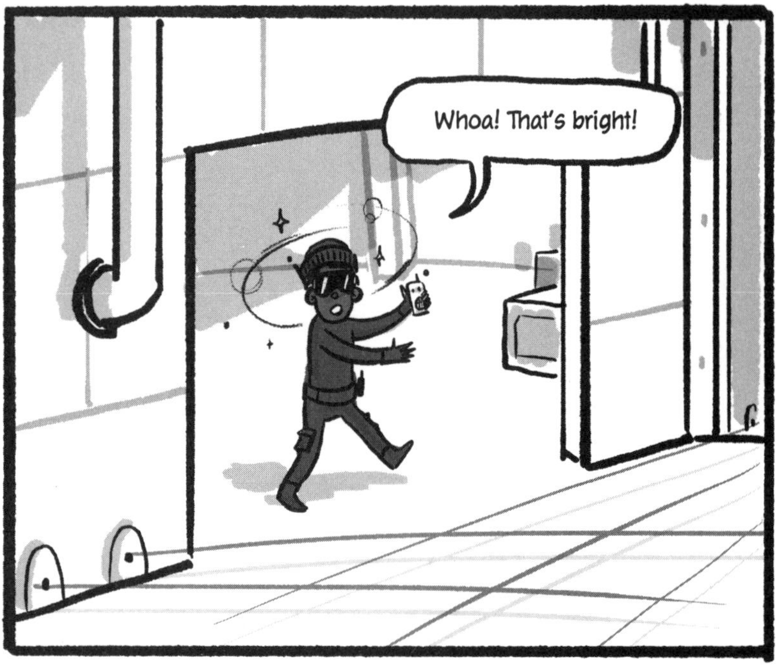
Whoa! That's bright!

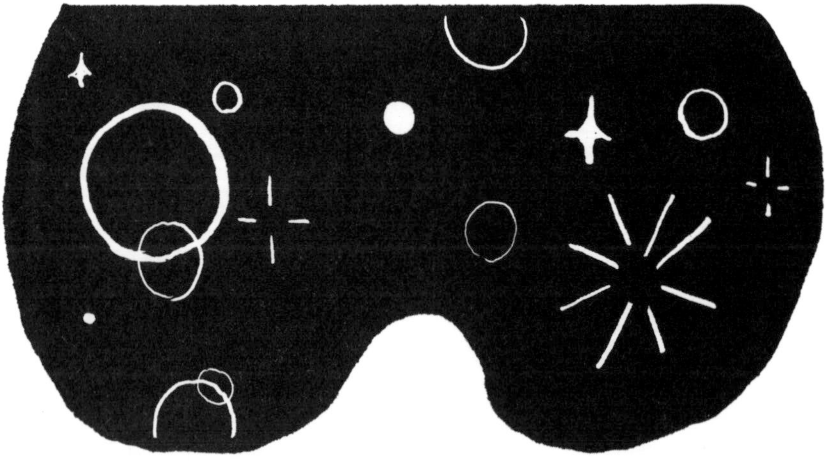

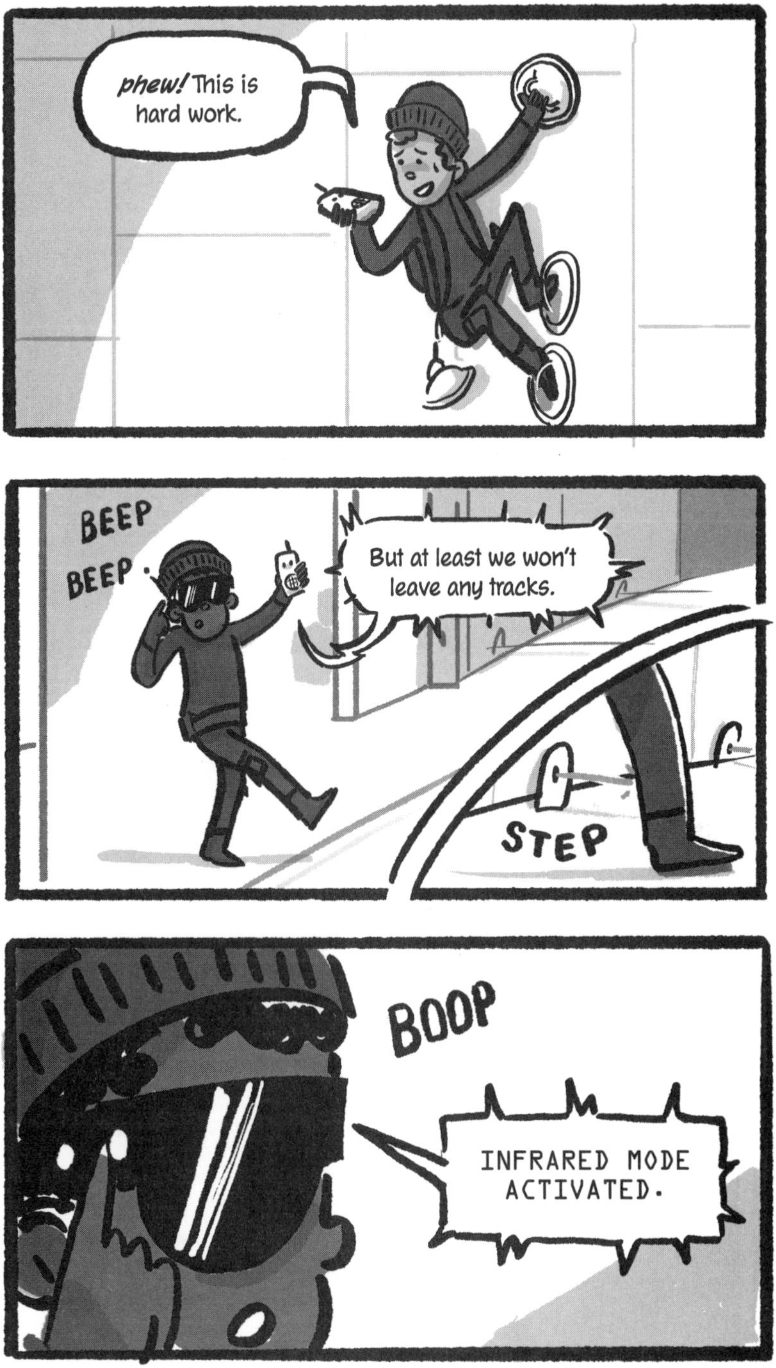
phew! This is hard work.
BEEP
BEEP.
But at least we won't leave any tracks.
STEP
BOOP
INFRARED MODE ACTIVATED.

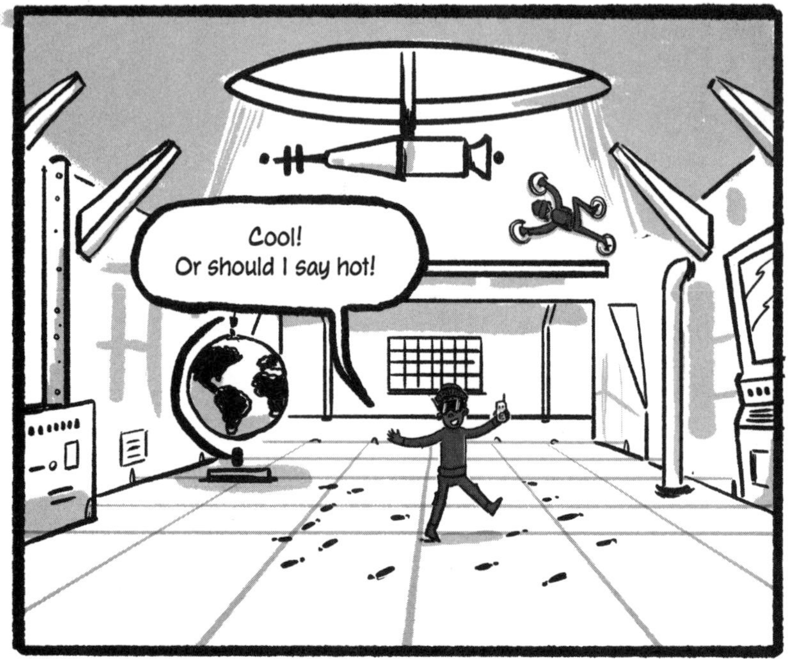
Cool!
Or should I say hot!

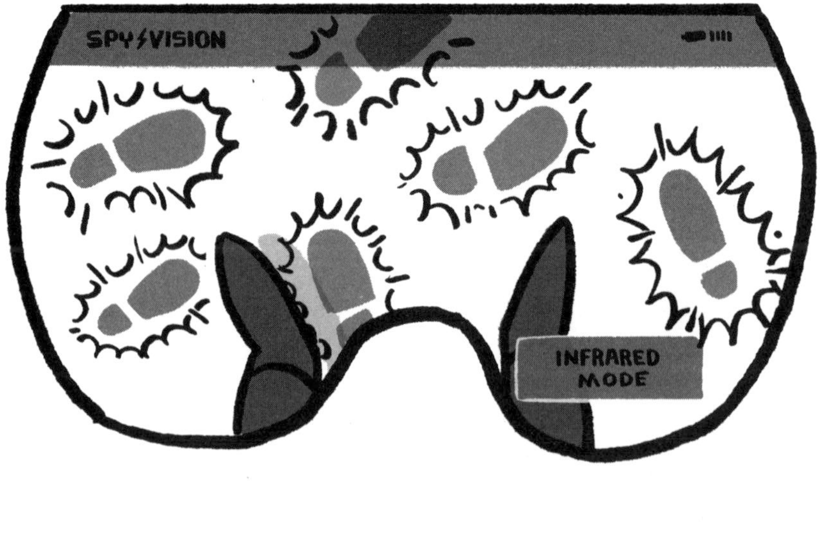
SPY⚡VISION
INFRARED MODE

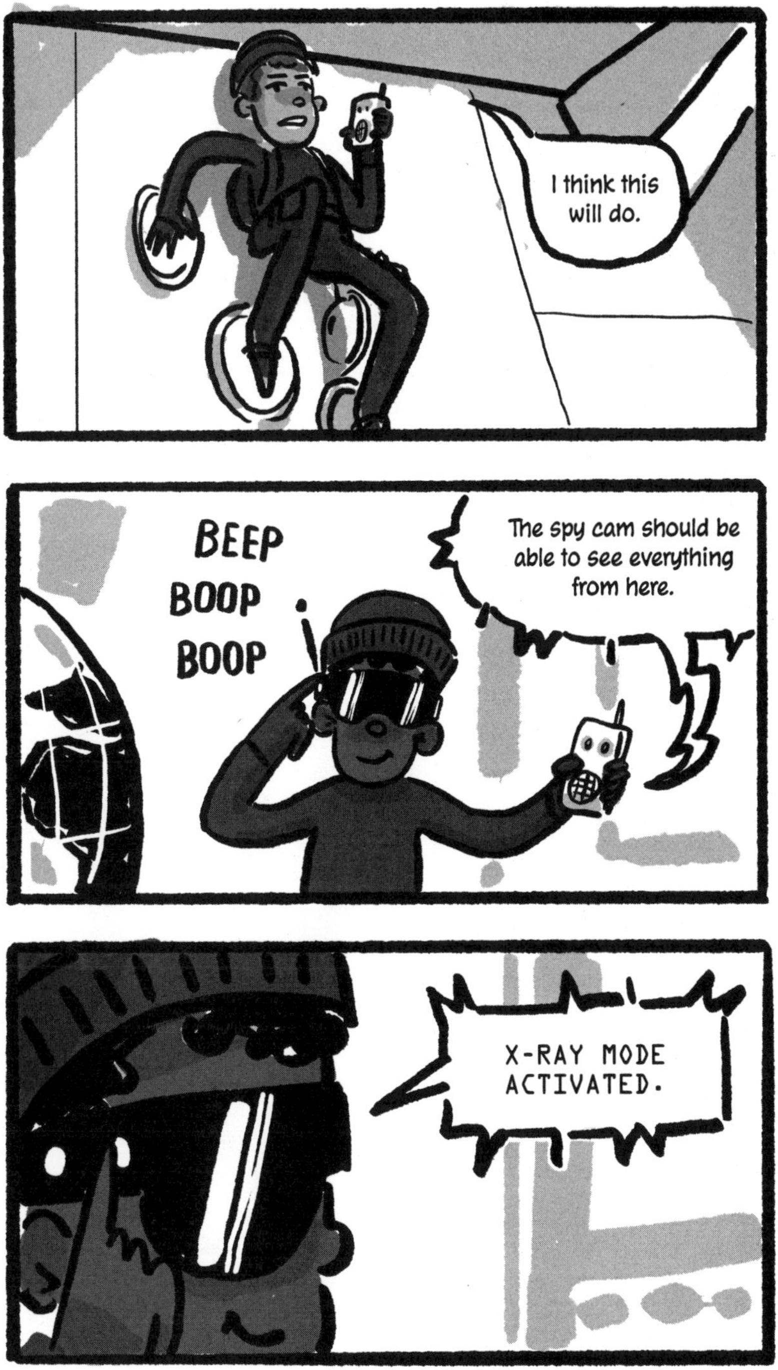
I think this will do.
BEEP BOOP BOOP
The spy cam should be able to see everything from here.
X-RAY MODE ACTIVATED.

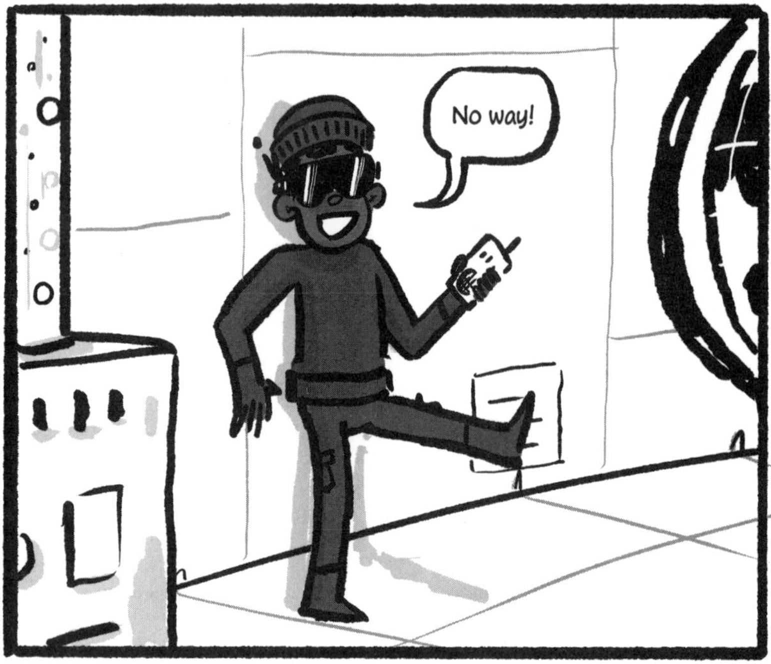
No way!

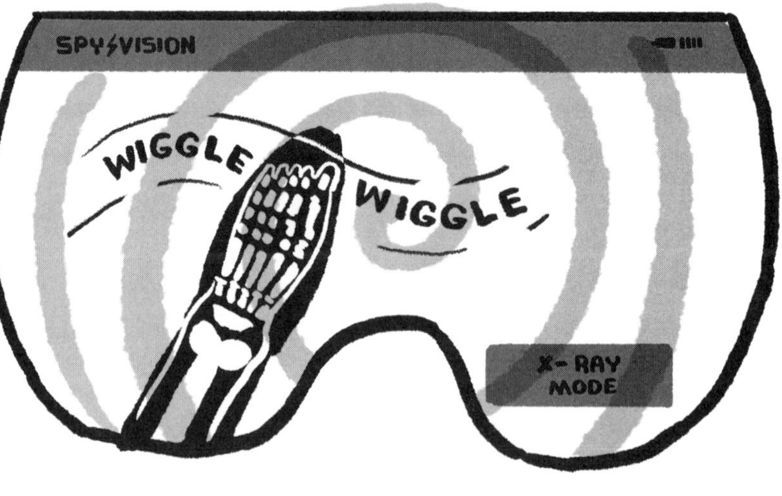
SPY⚡VISION
WIGGLE
WIGGLE
X-RAY MODE

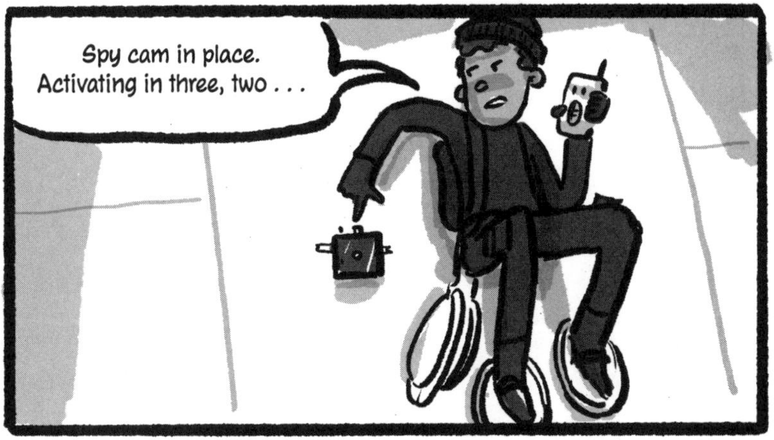
Spy cam in place.
Activating in three, two . . .

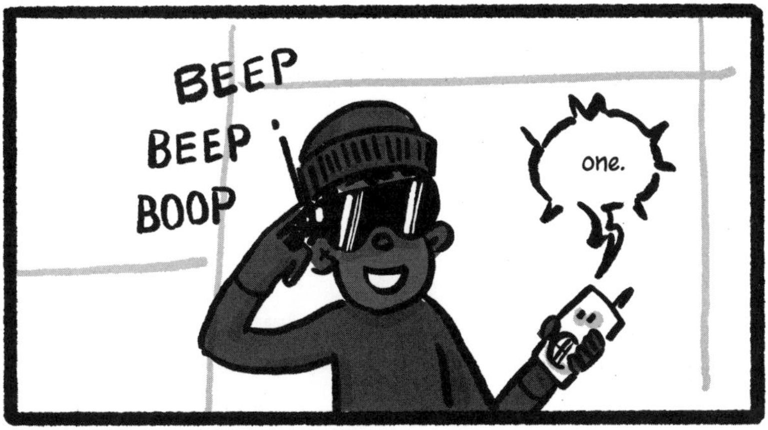
BEEP
BEEP
BOOP
one.

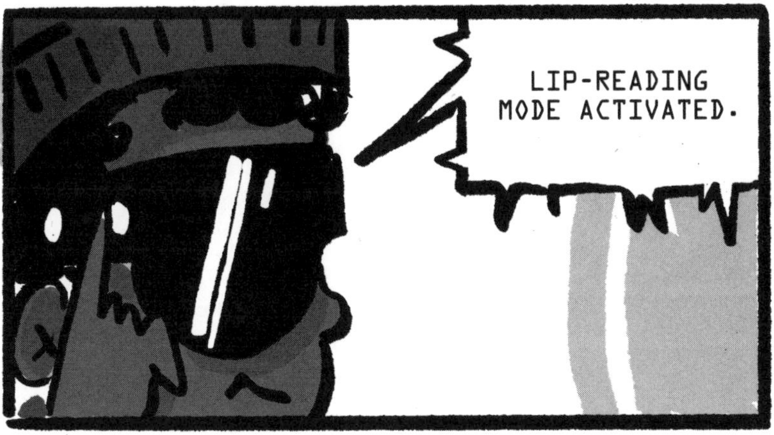
LIP-READING
MODE ACTIVATED.

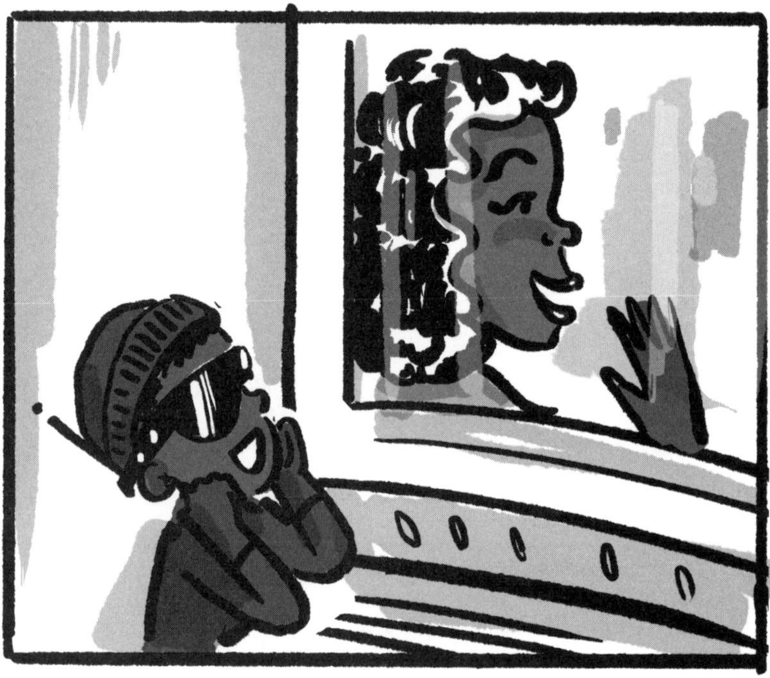

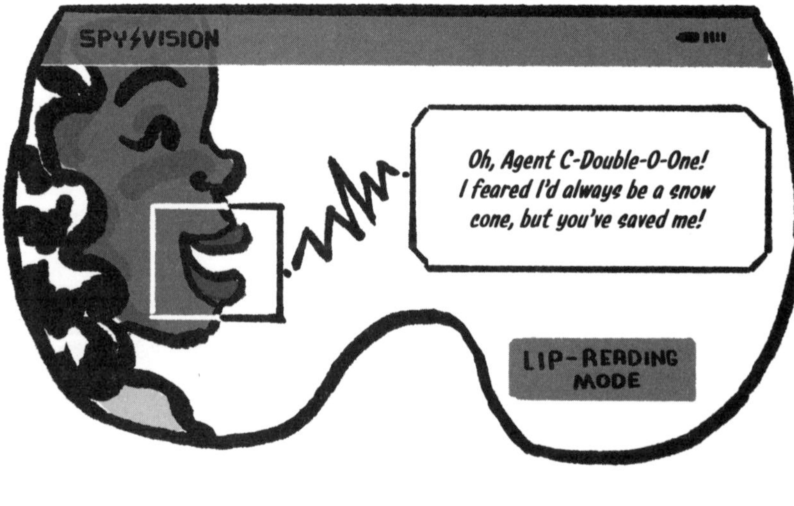
SPYϟVISION
Oh, Agent C-Double-O-One!
I feared I'd always be a snow
cone, but you've saved me!
LIP-READING
MODE

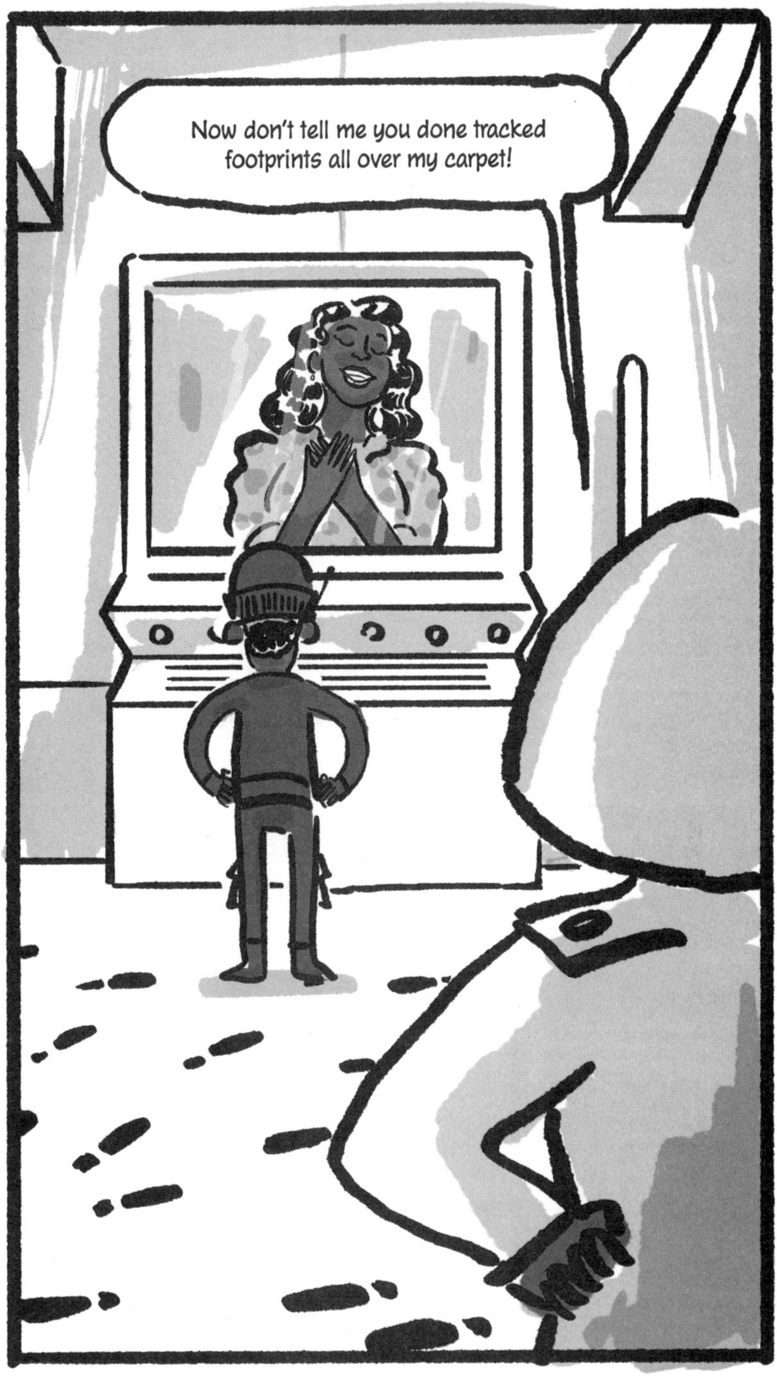
Now don't tell me you done tracked footprints all over my carpet!

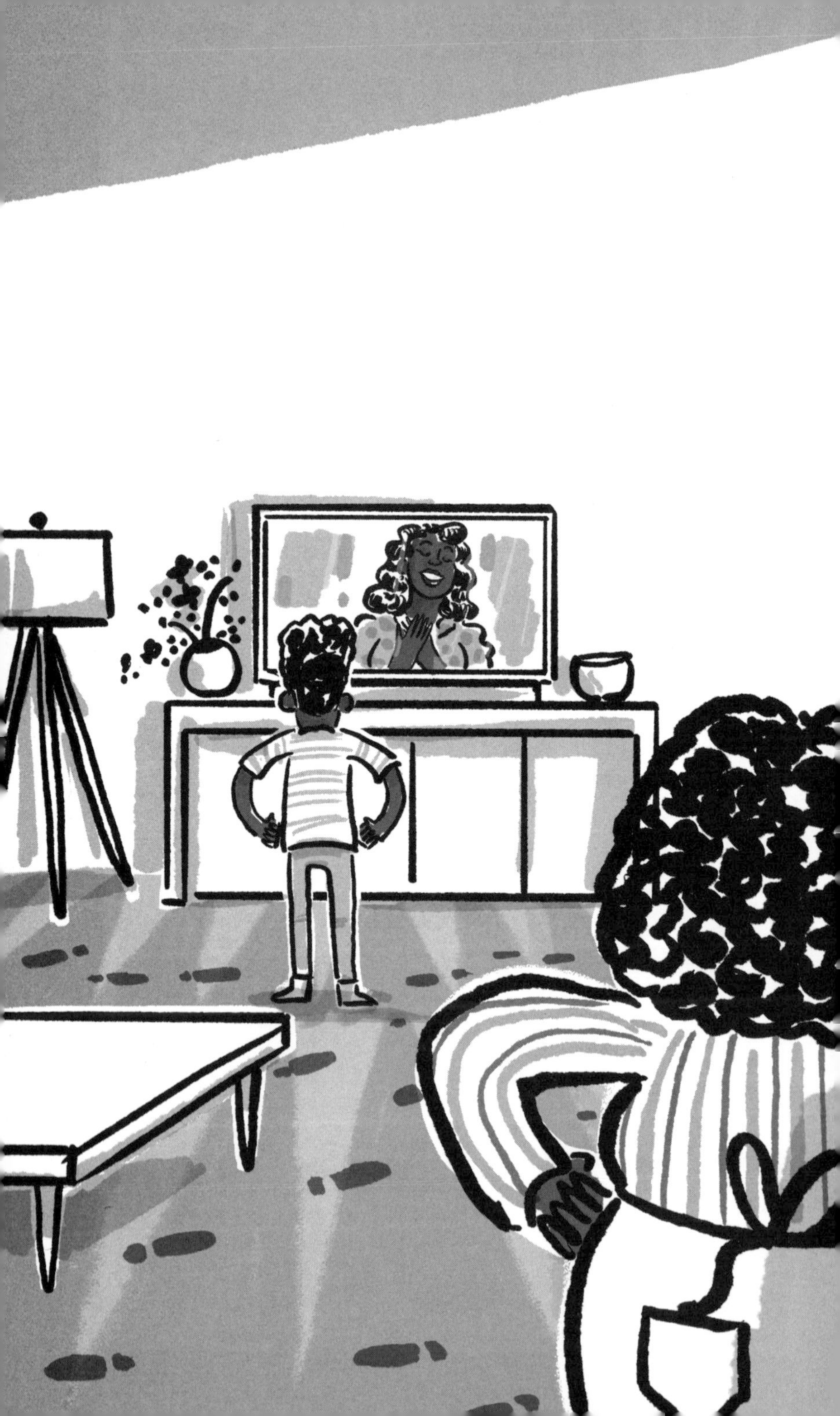

CHAPTER SIXTEEN

VAHROOOOOOM.

"GON' WALK ALL OVER MY CARPET LIKE I DIDN'T JUST VACUUM."

VAHROOOOOOM.

"AND GOT ME MISSIN' MY STORIES TOO."

VAHROOOOOOM.

"LORD, GIVE ME PATIENCE."

VAHROOOOOOM.

Ms. Joyce was talking to herself loudly enough for Link and Hud to hear over the whir of the vacuum. They watched from over the back of the couch as she dragged the vacuum across the den, to and fro, leaving perfectly spaced triangles of light and dark shag in the carpet. Hud's footprints disappeared with each pass.

"WHAT Y'ALL LOOKIN' AT?" Ms. Joyce shouted, looking up at the boys as she continued pulling the vacuum.

VAHROOOOOOM.

"TURN YOUR TAILS AROUND AND GET TO FOLDIN' THAT LAUNDRY LIKE I TOLD YOU."

VAHROOOOOOM.

The boys did as they were told.

VAHROOOOOOM.

Link reached into the laundry basket and picked up a pair of underwear. They were red and blue and covered in little shooting stars. Though they were clean, he held them out and acted like they weren't. He looked at Hud. "This is all your fault, you know—"

VAHROOOOOOM.

"HUH?" shouted Hud. He cupped his hand near his ear. "WHAT'D YOU SAY?"

VAHROOOOOOM.

Link flung the underwear at Hud's face. "I SAID, THIS IS ALL YOUR FAULT!"

VAHROOOOOOM.

Hud flinched as the underwear hit him. "SORRY. GEEEEZ—"

VAHROOOOOOM.

Hud pulled his second-favorite pair of underwear from his face and folded them. Then he set them down on the coffee table next to Ms. Joyce's purse, which was taking up most of the space. "I DIDN'T SEE HER."

VAHROOOOOOM.

"DUH." Link rolled his eyes. "YOU'RE JUST LUCKY I

GOT DAD'S CAMCORDER SET UP."

VAHROOOOOOM.

"Oh, yay. Lucky me," Hud said to himself, as he picked up a pair of plain white underwear from the laundry basket and started fake gagging. "SO, NOW WHAT?" He flung the tighty-whities at Link.

VAHROOOOOOM.

Link snatched his underwear out of the air midflight and looked at Hud. "NOW WE—"

"AHEM." Ms. Joyce was done vacuuming behind the couch and was ready to vacuum in front of the couch. Link and Hud's feet were in the way. "UP. UP. LIFT 'EM UP."

The boys both lifted their feet.

VAHROOOOOOM.

VAHROOOOOOM.

"NOW BACK TO IT," Ms. Joyce shouted over the vacuum, "THAT LAUNDRY AIN'T GON' FOLD ITSELF."

Link and Hud put their feet back down, and then Hud reached into the basket for more laundry as Link folded his underwear and set them on the coffee table. Ms. Joyce pushed the vacuum away, working her way toward the TV.

VAHROOOOOOM.

VAHROOOOOOM.

As Link sorted through the laundry basket with his left hand, looking for the match to the sock in his right, he looked at Hud again. "NOW WE—"

"OH, DENZEL!" the TV blared. Link and Hud looked over, startled. Ms. Joyce had just cranked the TV's volume all the way up as she went past with the vacuum.

VAHROOOOOOM.

"I THOUGHT—"

VAHROOOOOOM.

"LOST YOU—"

VAHROOOOOOM.

"FOREVER! smooch"

VAHROOOOOOM.

Ms. Joyce stopped pulling the vacuum and turned it off.

ROOOOOOOMMmmmmmmmmmmmmmmm.

The vacuum wound down. Ms. Joyce didn't. "SCARLETT, YOU'S SOMETHIN' ELSE. YOU KNOW THAT AIN'T DENZEL!" she shouted at the TV. Then she unplugged the vacuum, coiled up the cord, and pushed it out of the room.

Link eyed Ms. Joyce as she left and then leaned in toward Hud over the laundry basket. "Now we just—"

"WAIT!" blared the TV. (Ms. Joyce hadn't turned the volume back down.) *"HE'S NOT DENZEL—I'M DENZEL!"*

Link and Hud both stared at the too-loud TV, forgot about everything else, and didn't even notice . . .

They didn't notice Ms. Joyce come back into the den.

They didn't notice her leave again with the clothes they'd finished folding.

They *did* notice her block the TV as she turned the

volume down and shouted, "YES, YOU WOULD, GIRL! DON'T BELIEVE HER, DENZEL!"

But they didn't notice their parents arriving home or Ms. Joyce leaving for the day.

Link and Hud just sat on the couch watching TV. And besides kind of noticing their mom walk through the den with a stack of something (because she walked in front of the TV) and sort of noticing their dad say something about the carpet and cocoa butter (because he talked louder than the TV), they didn't notice much of anything else.

What's worse, they didn't notice they didn't notice.

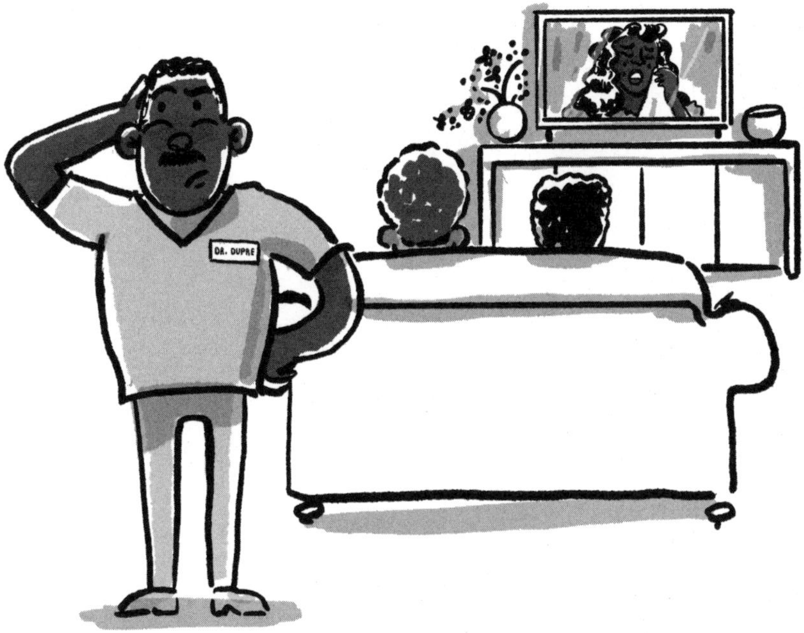
DR. DUPRE

CHAPTER SEVENTEEN

IF YOU EVER WANT TO DO ANYTHING IMPORTANT, like, say, placing a spy cam in a secret bad guy's base or recording that secret bad guy doing secret-bad-guy things, don't turn on the TV. Or at the very least, if you don't control the TV, don't watch it if you can help it. Because if you do, before you notice, that spy cam will be gone and that recording long lost.

Just ask Link and Hud.

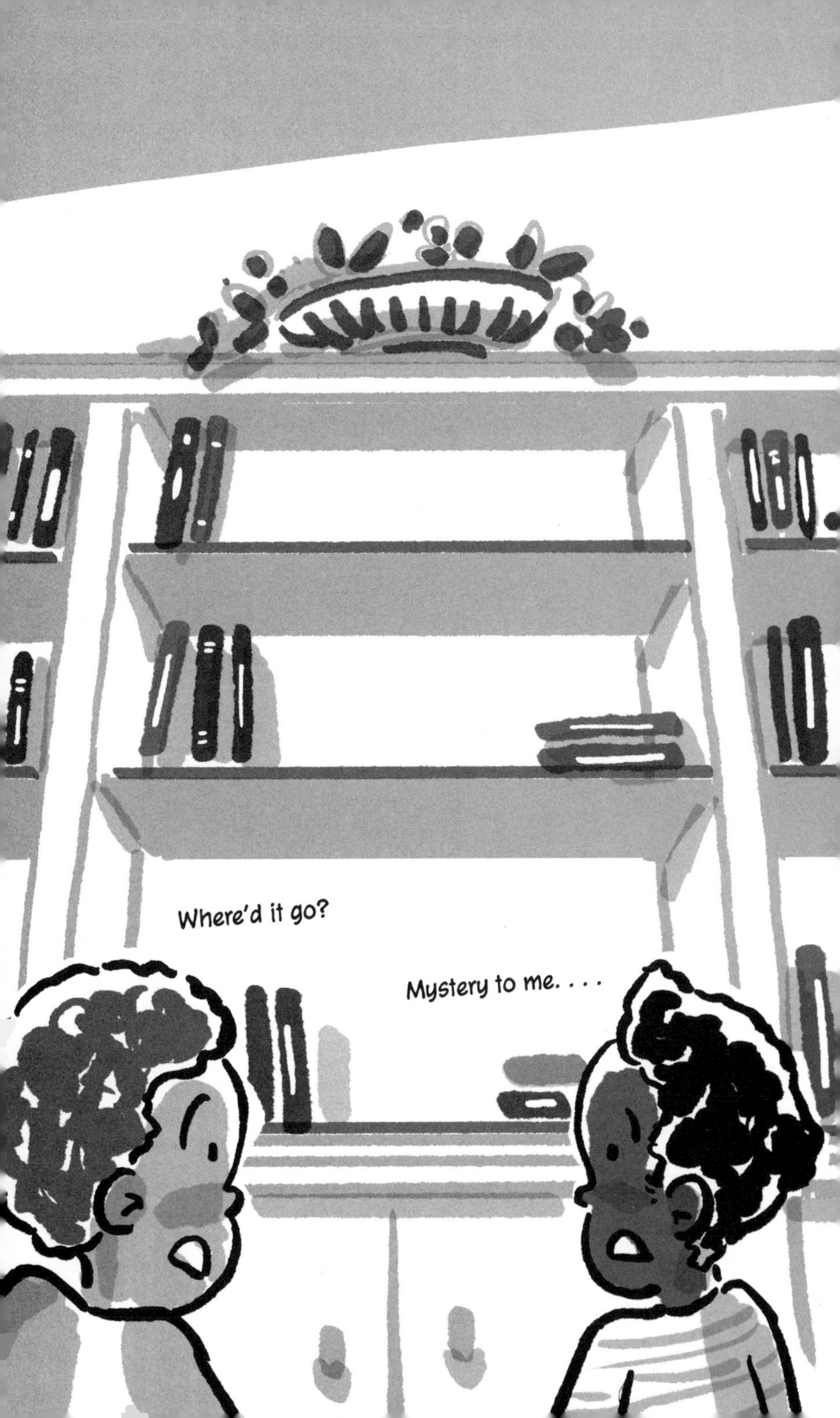
Where'd it go?
Mystery to me. . . .

CHAPTER EIGHTEEN

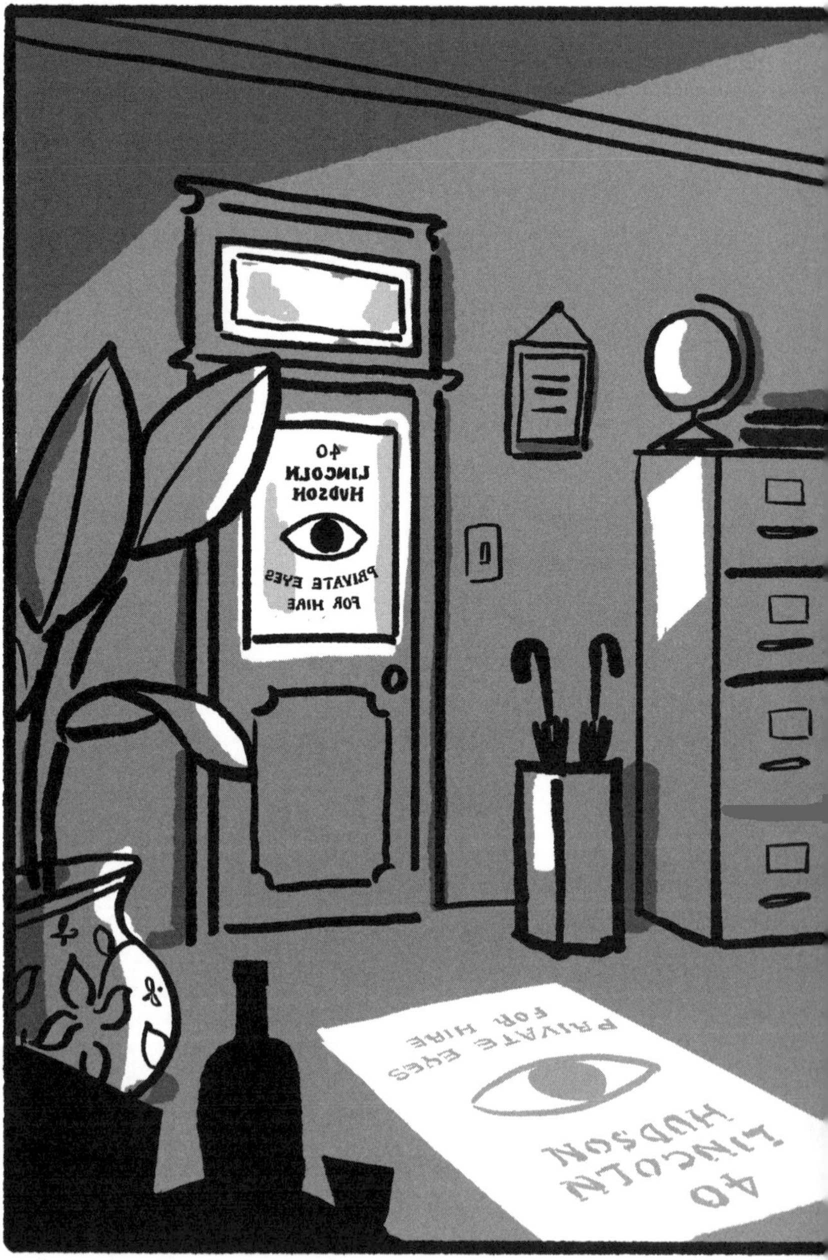
40
LINCOLN
HUDSON
PRIVATE EYES
FOR HIRE
40
LINCOLN
HUDSON
PRIVATE EYES
FOR HIRE

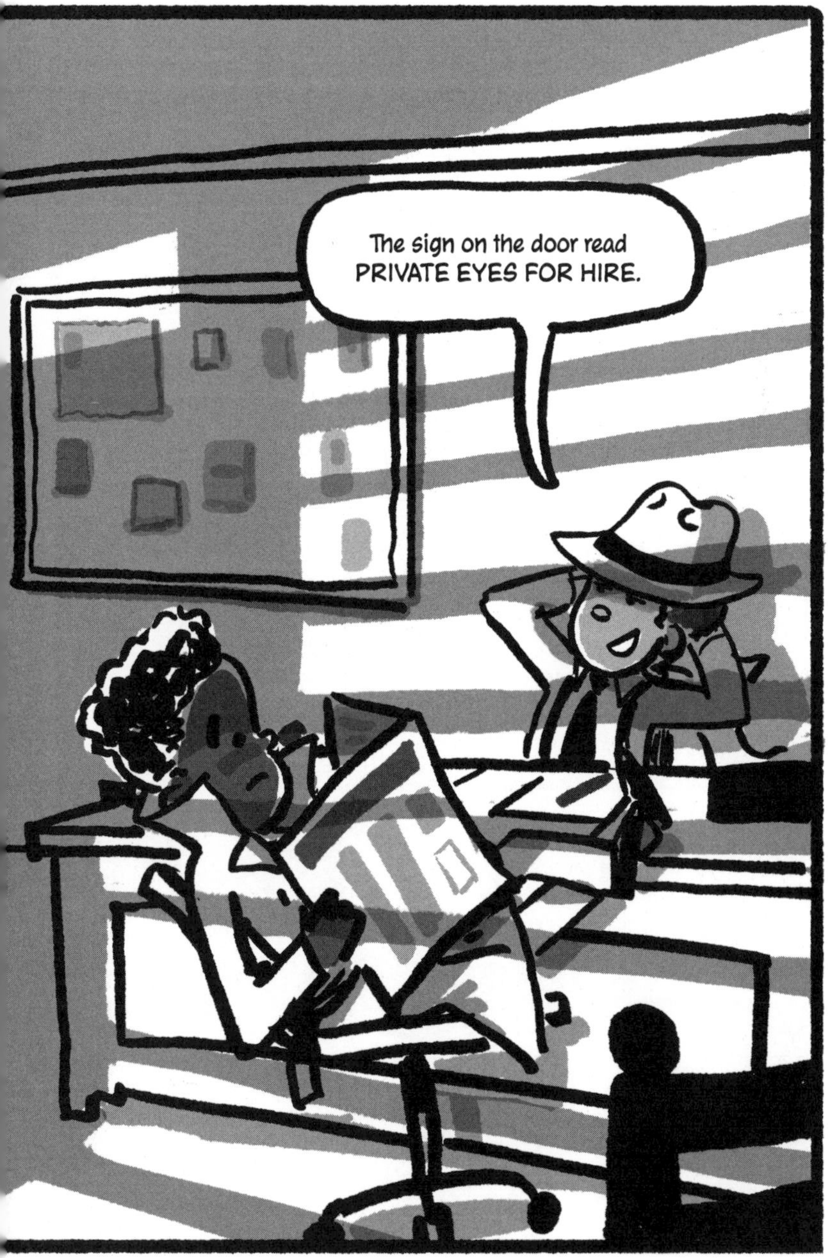
The sign on the door read
PRIVATE EYES FOR HIRE.

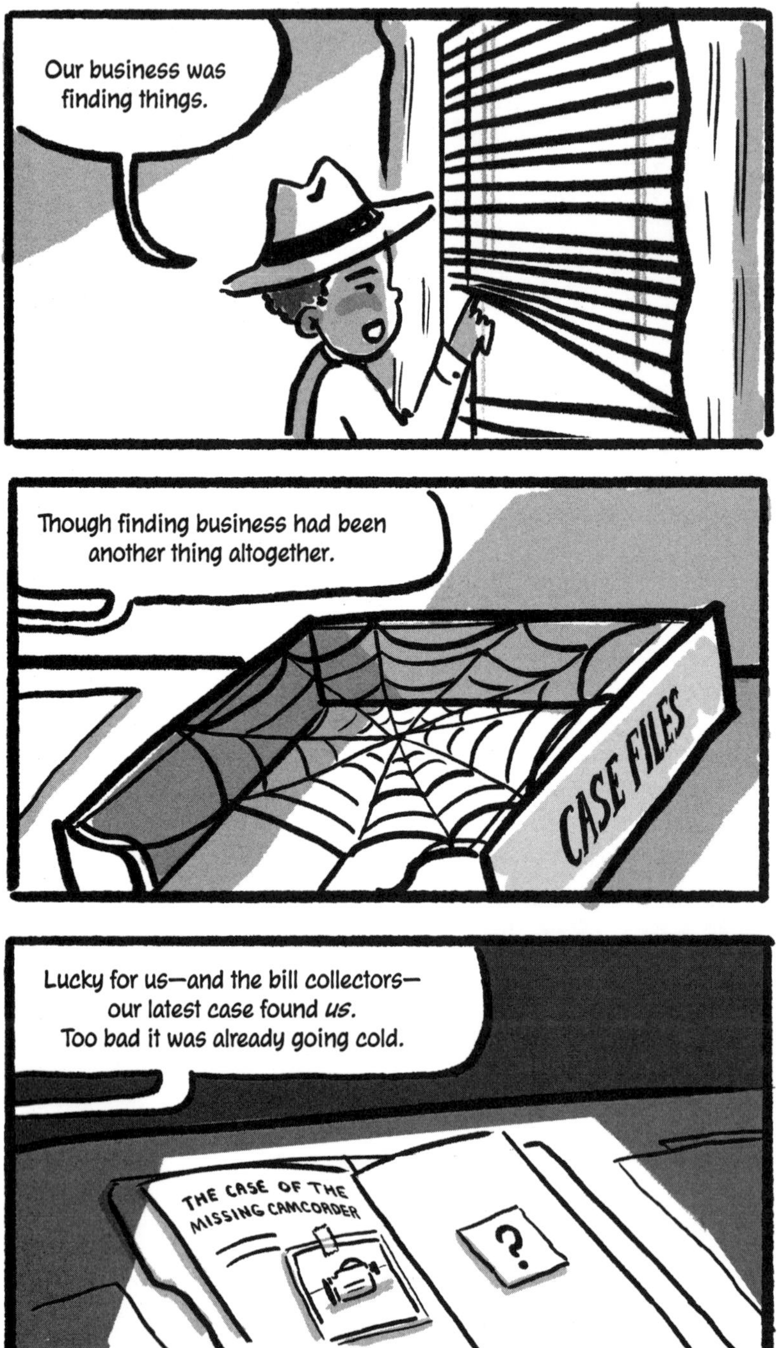
Our business was finding things.
Though finding business had been another thing altogether.
CASE FILES
Lucky for us—and the bill collectors—our latest case found *us*. Too bad it was already going cold.
THE CASE OF THE MISSING CAMCORDER
?

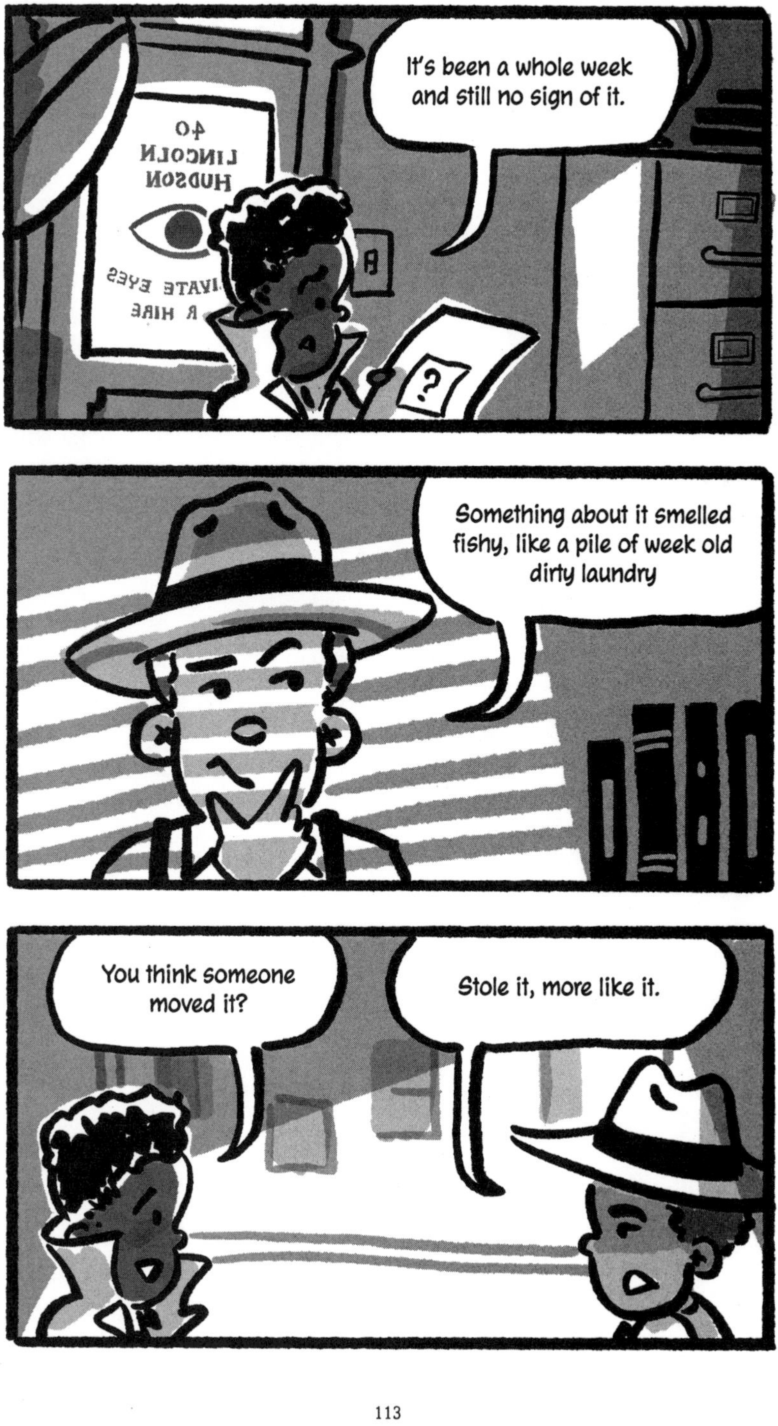
It's been a whole week and still no sign of it.
Something about it smelled fishy, like a pile of week old dirty laundry
You think someone moved it?
Stole it, more like it.

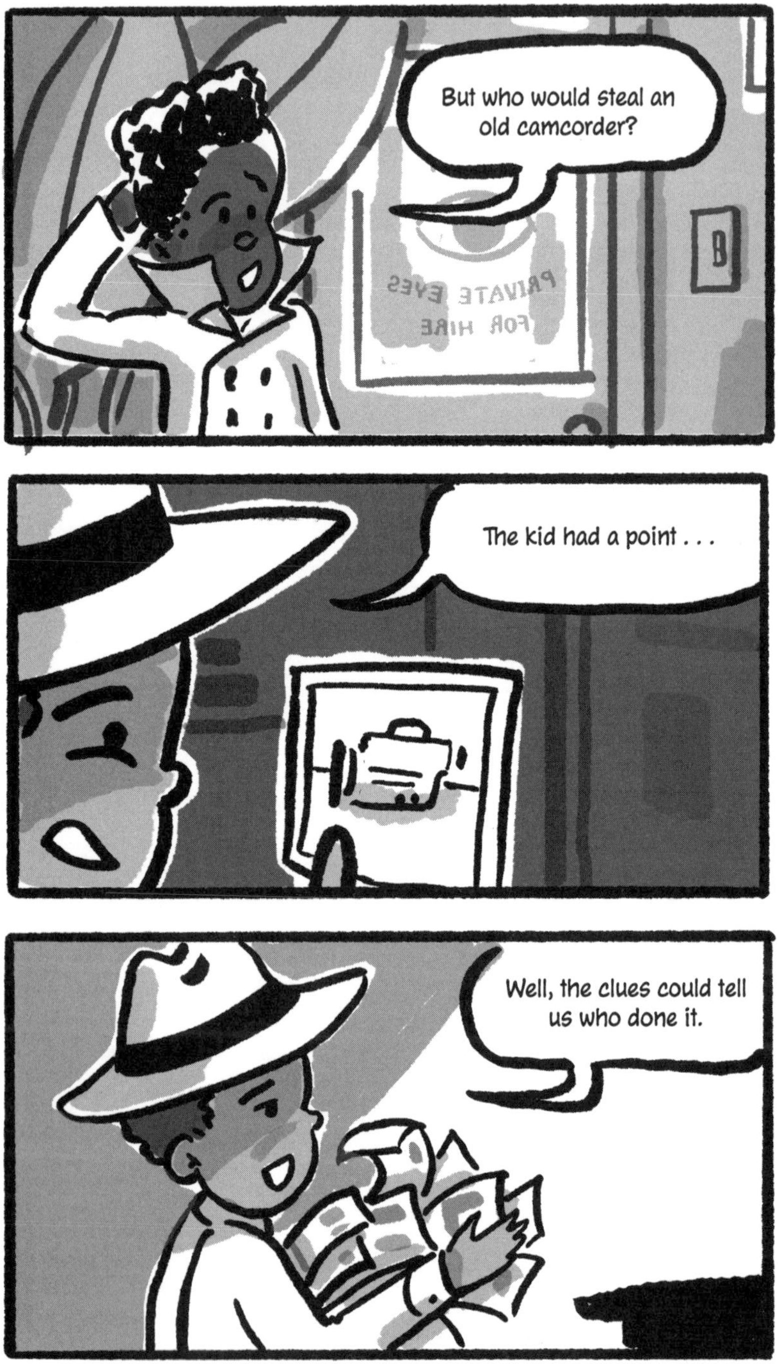
But who would steal an old camcorder?
PRIVATE EYES FOR HIRE
The kid had a point . . .
Well, the clues could tell us who done it.

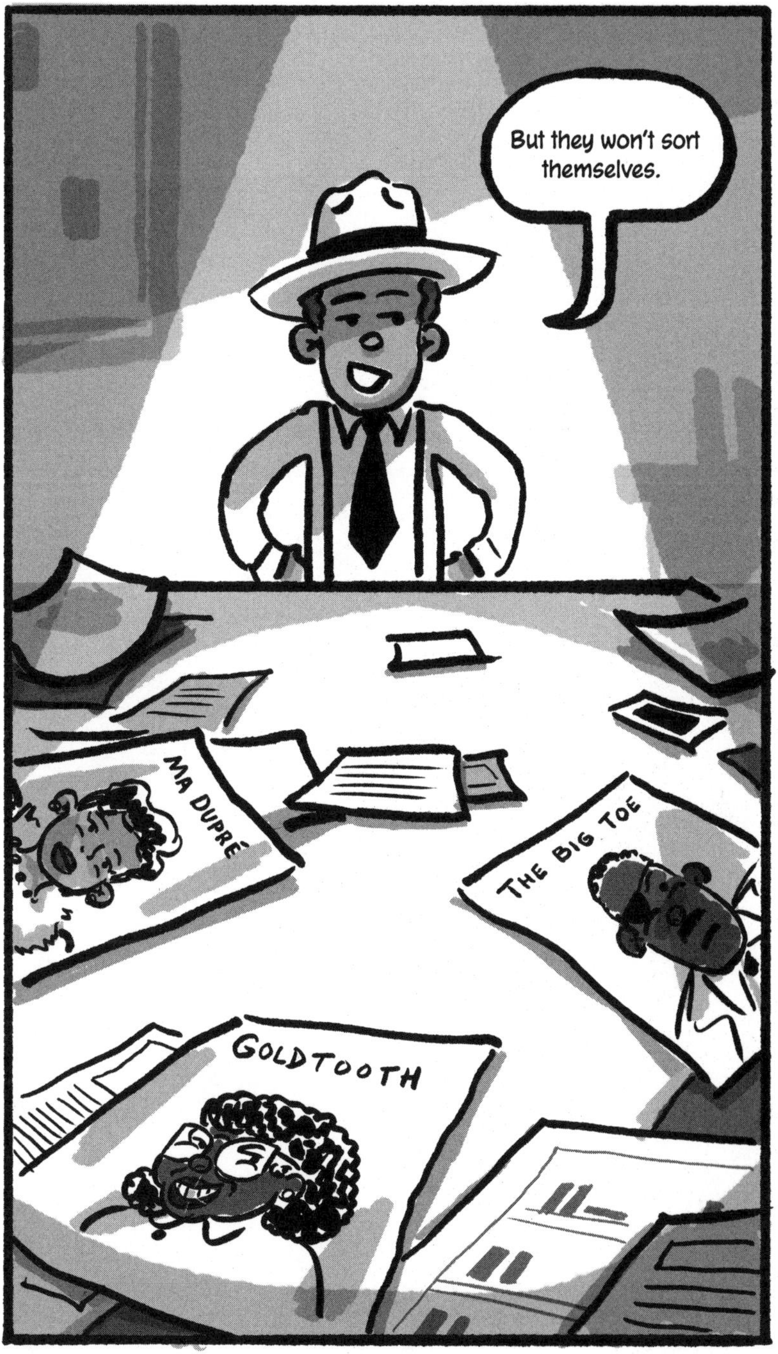
But they won't sort themselves.
MA DUPRÉ
THE BIG TOE
GOLDTOOTH

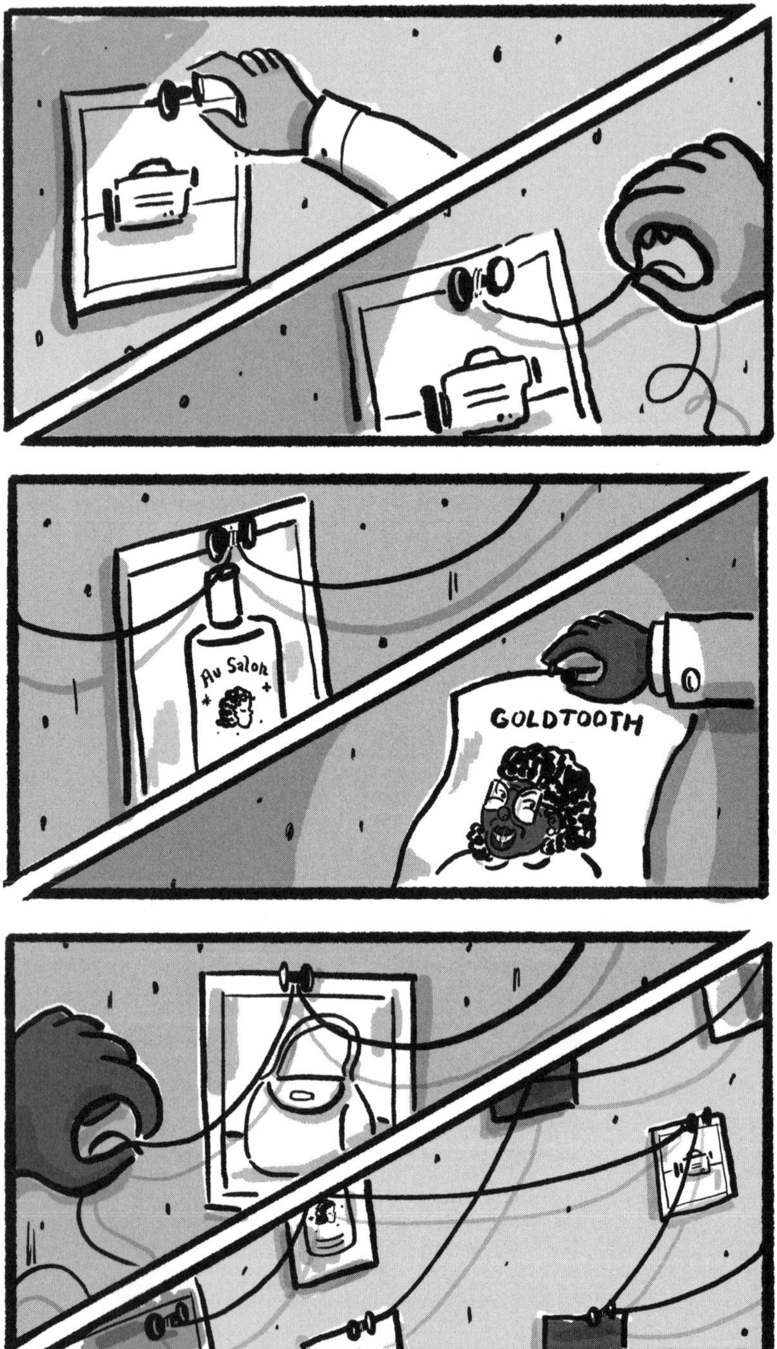
Au Salon
GOLDTOOTH

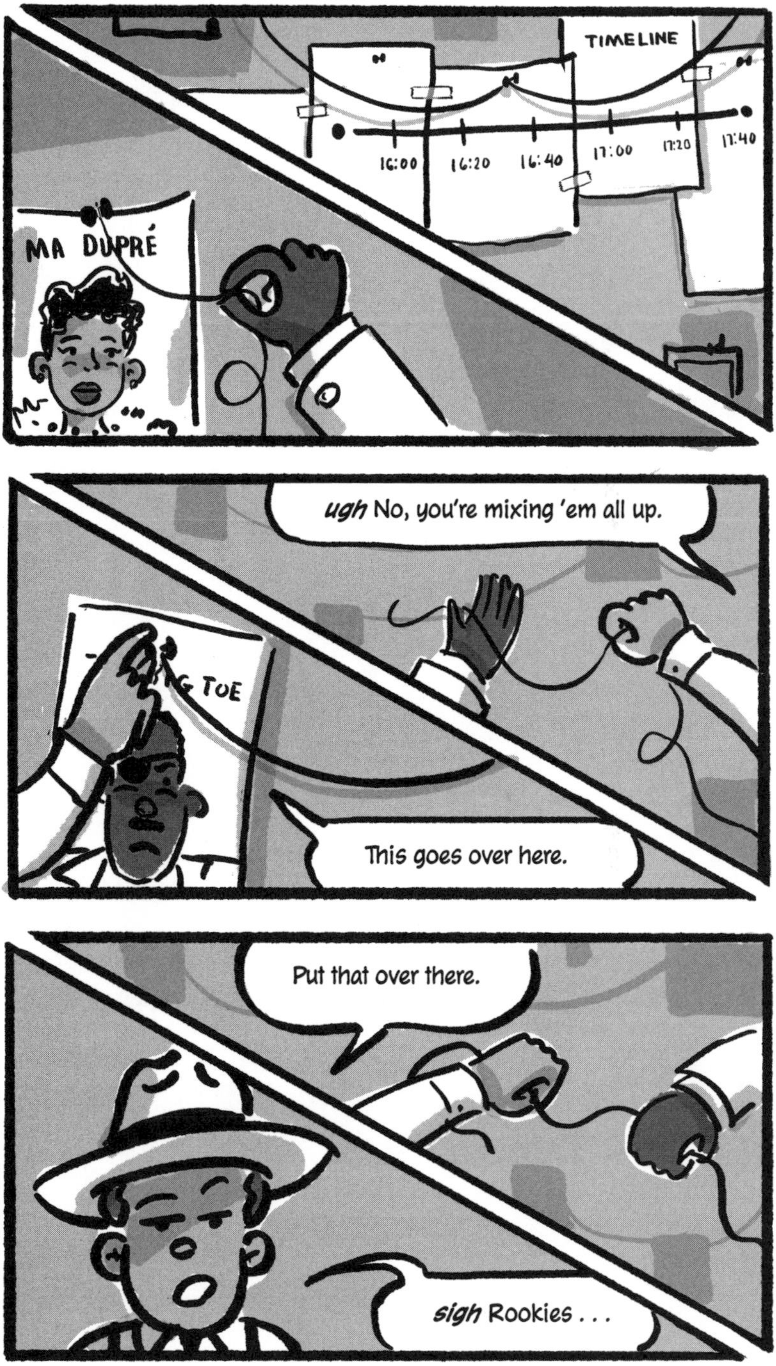
TIMELINE
16:00
16:20
16:40
17:00
17:20
17:40
MA DUPRÉ
ugh No, you're mixing 'em all up.
This goes over here.
Put that over there.
sigh Rookies . . .

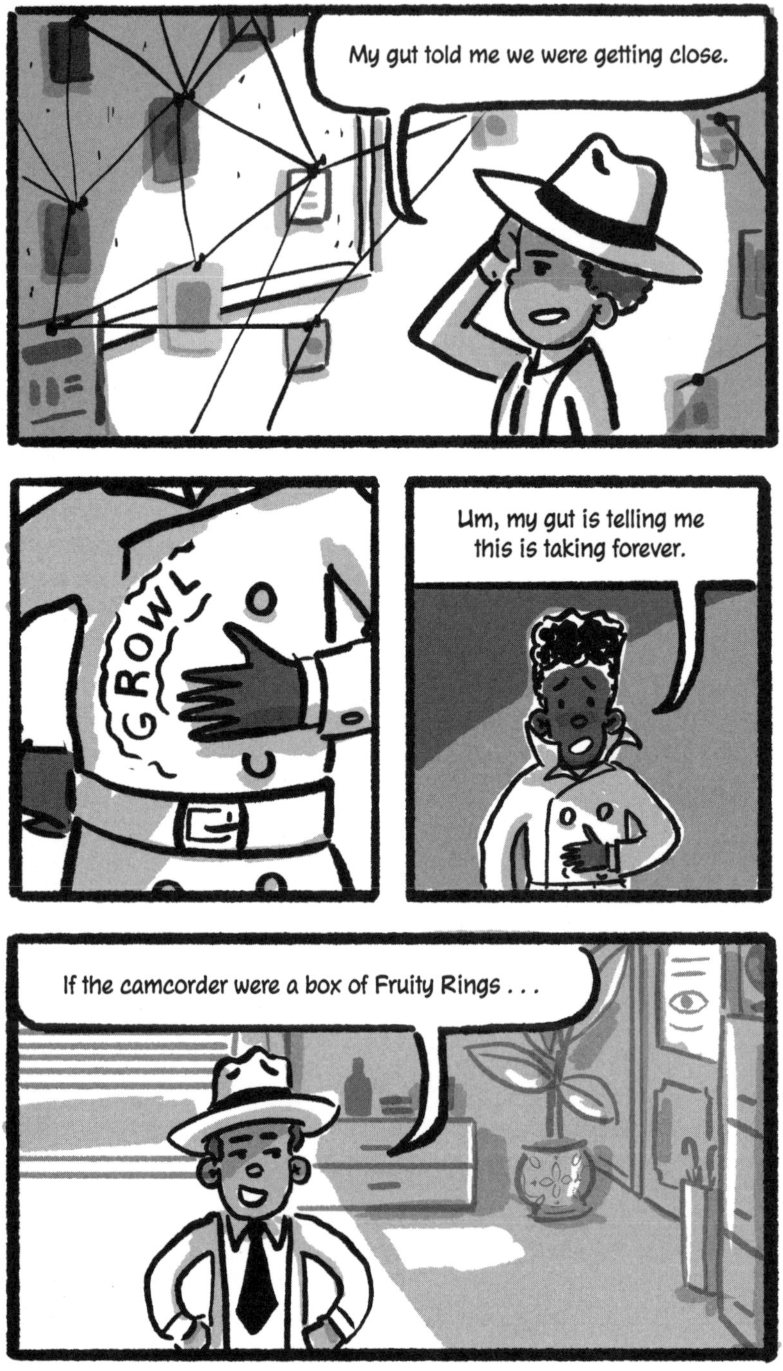
My gut told me we were getting close.
GROWL
Um, my gut is telling me this is taking forever.
If the camcorder were a box of Fruity Rings . . .

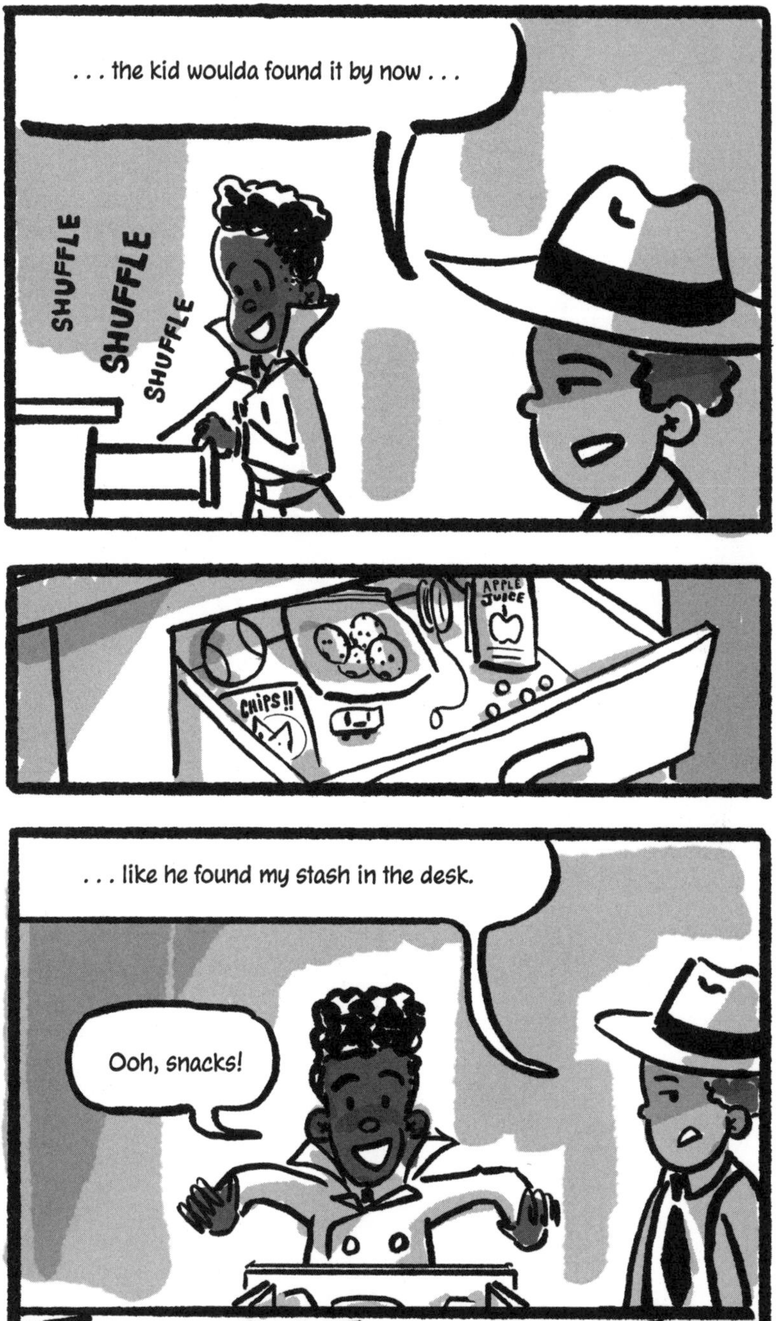
. . . the kid woulda found it by now . . .
SHUFFLE
SHUFFLE
SHUFFLE
APPLE JUICE
CHIPS!!
. . . like he found my stash in the desk.
Ooh, snacks!

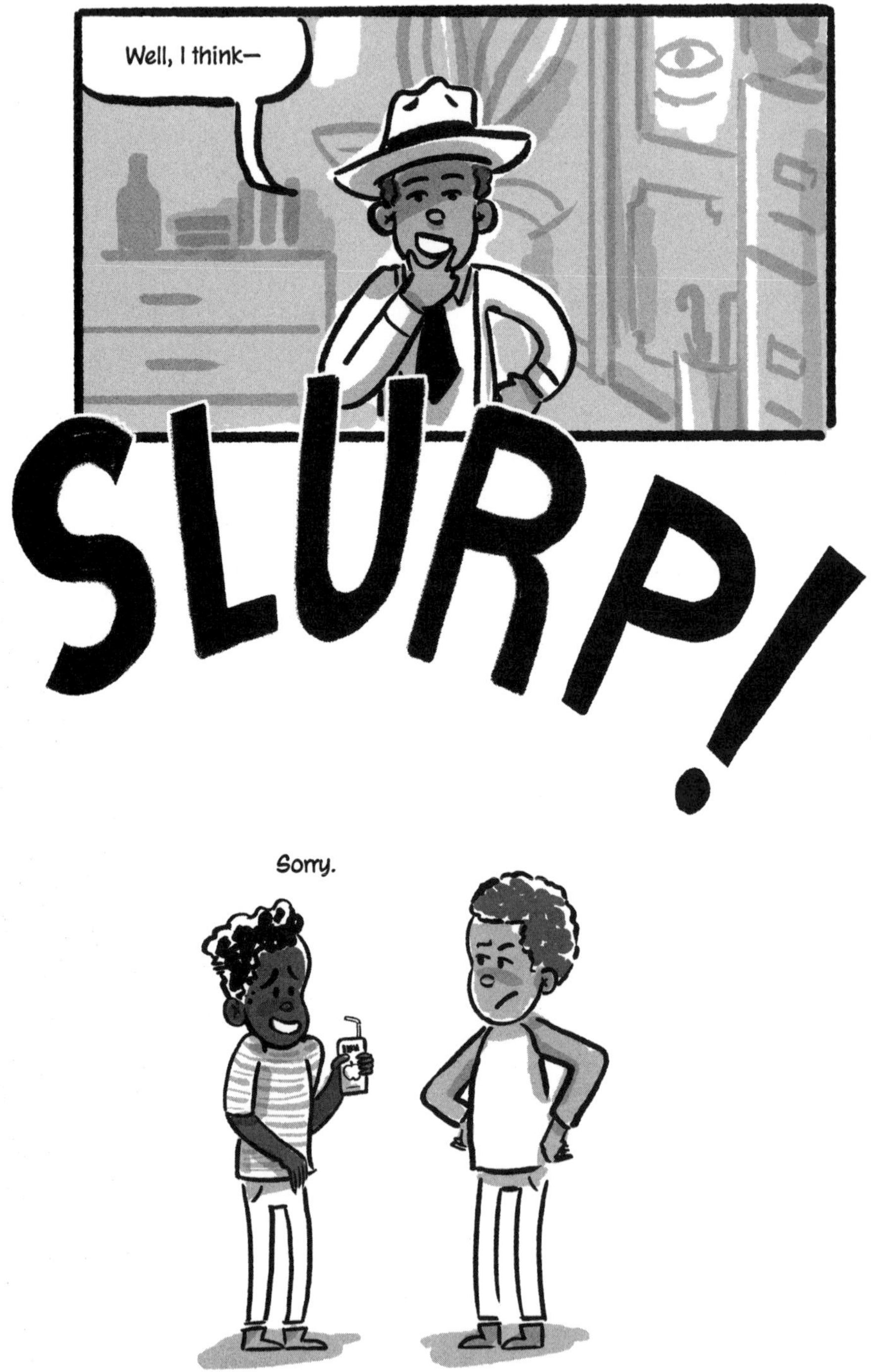
Well, I think—
SLURP!
Sorry.

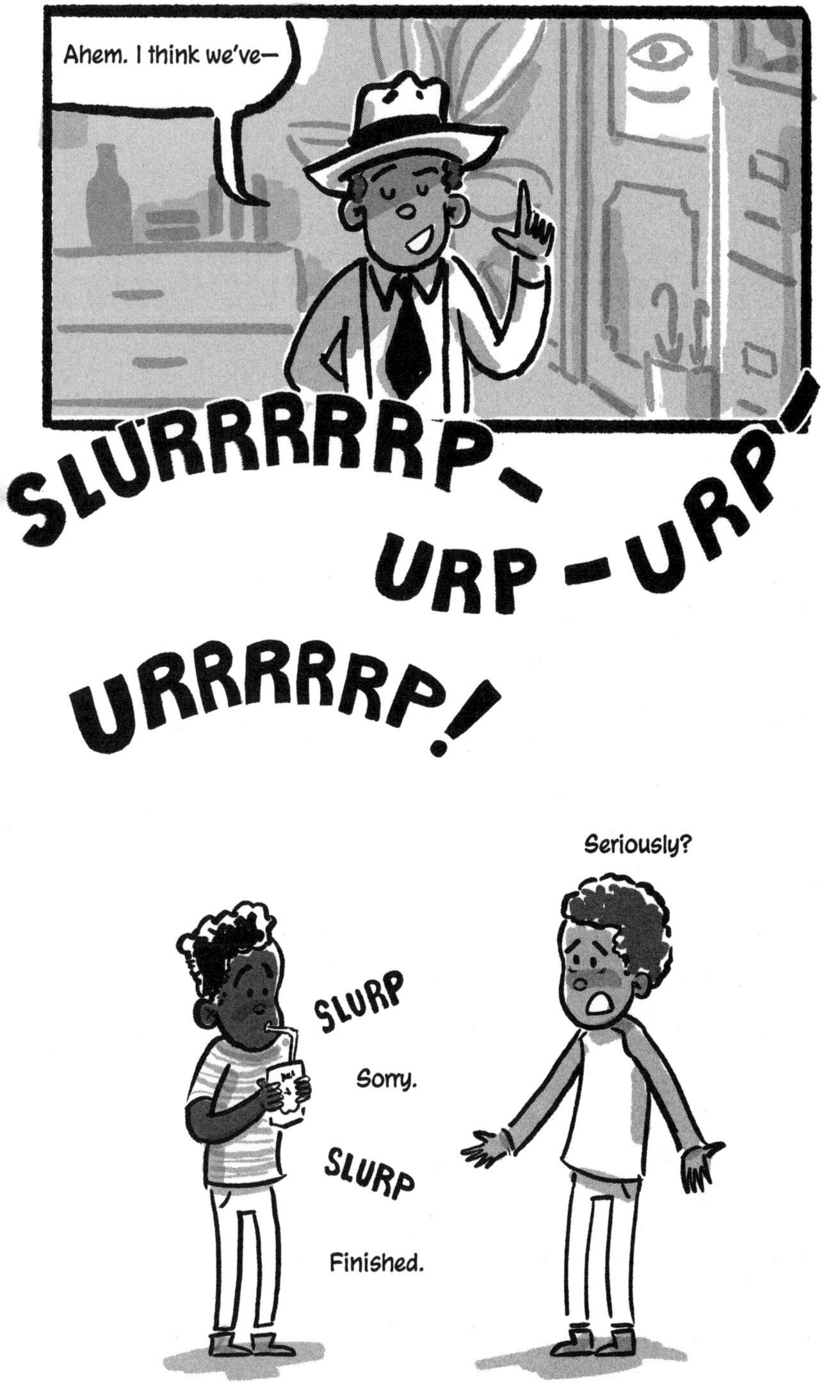
Ahem. I think we've—
SLURRRRRP-URP-URP-URRRRRP!
Seriously?
SLURP
Sorry.
SLURP
Finished.

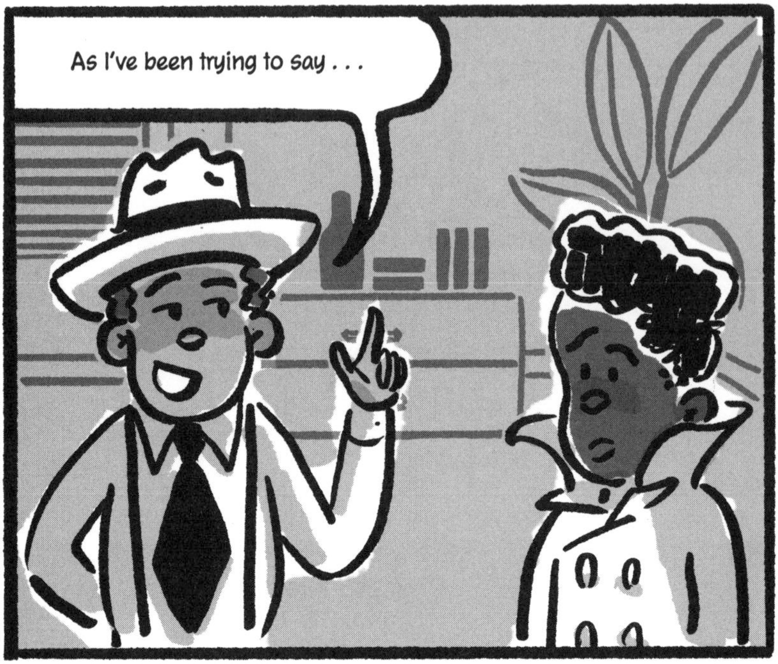
As I've been trying to say . . .

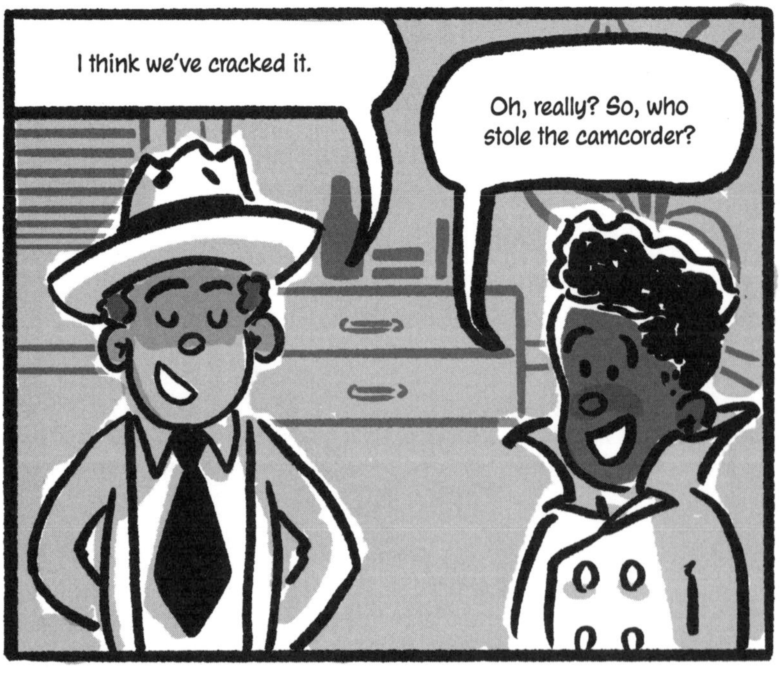
I think we've cracked it.
Oh, really? So, who stole the camcorder?

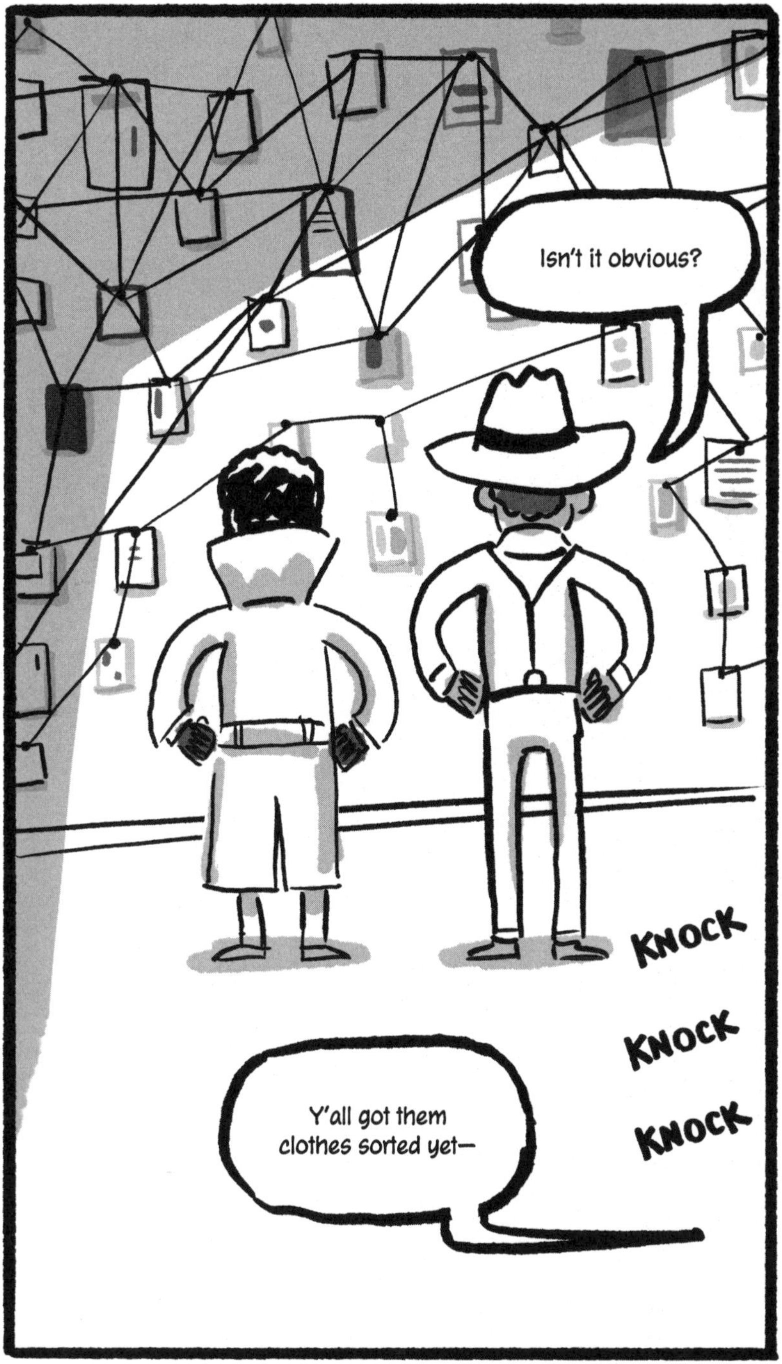
Isn't it obvious?
KNOCK
KNOCK
KNOCK
Y'all got them clothes sorted yet—

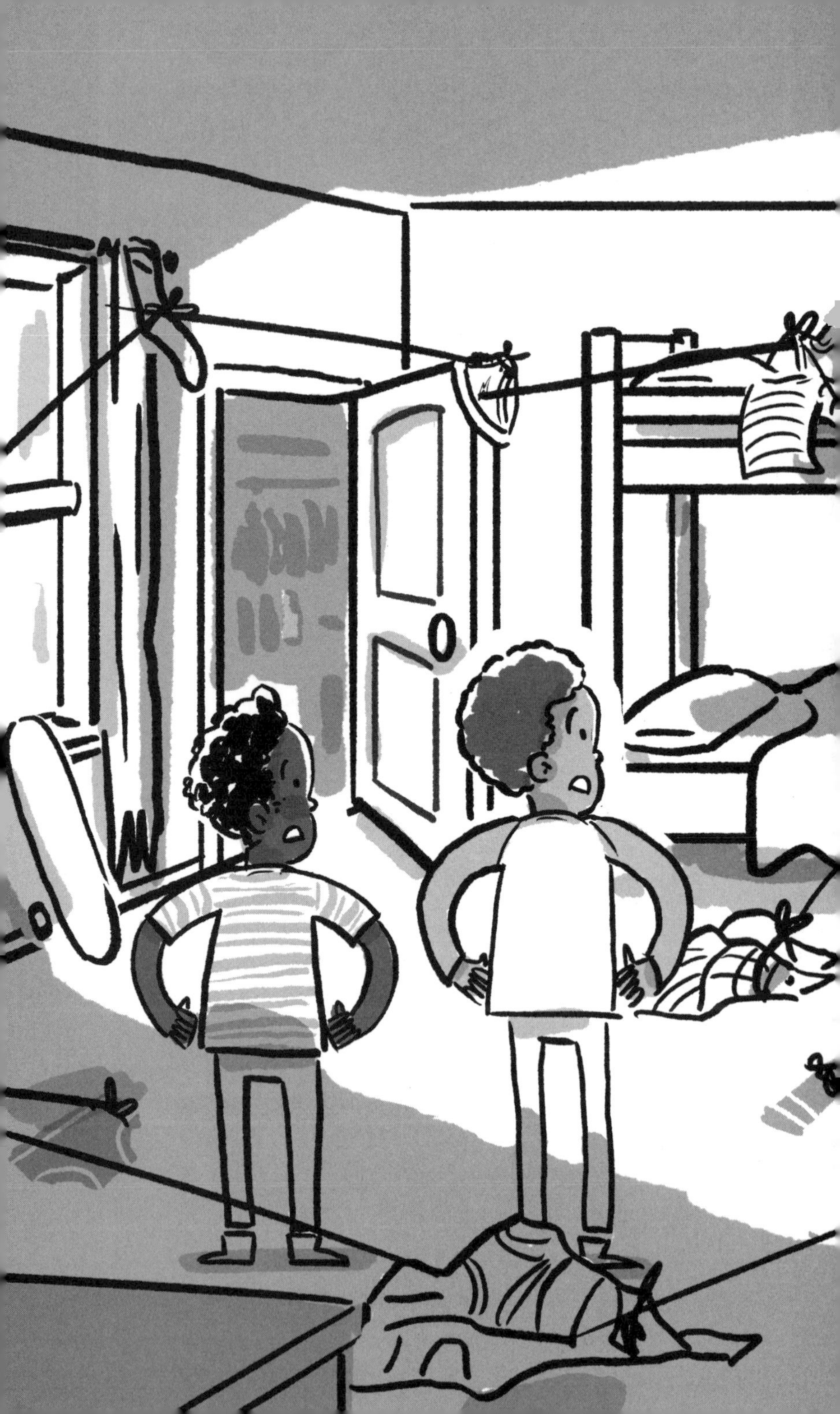

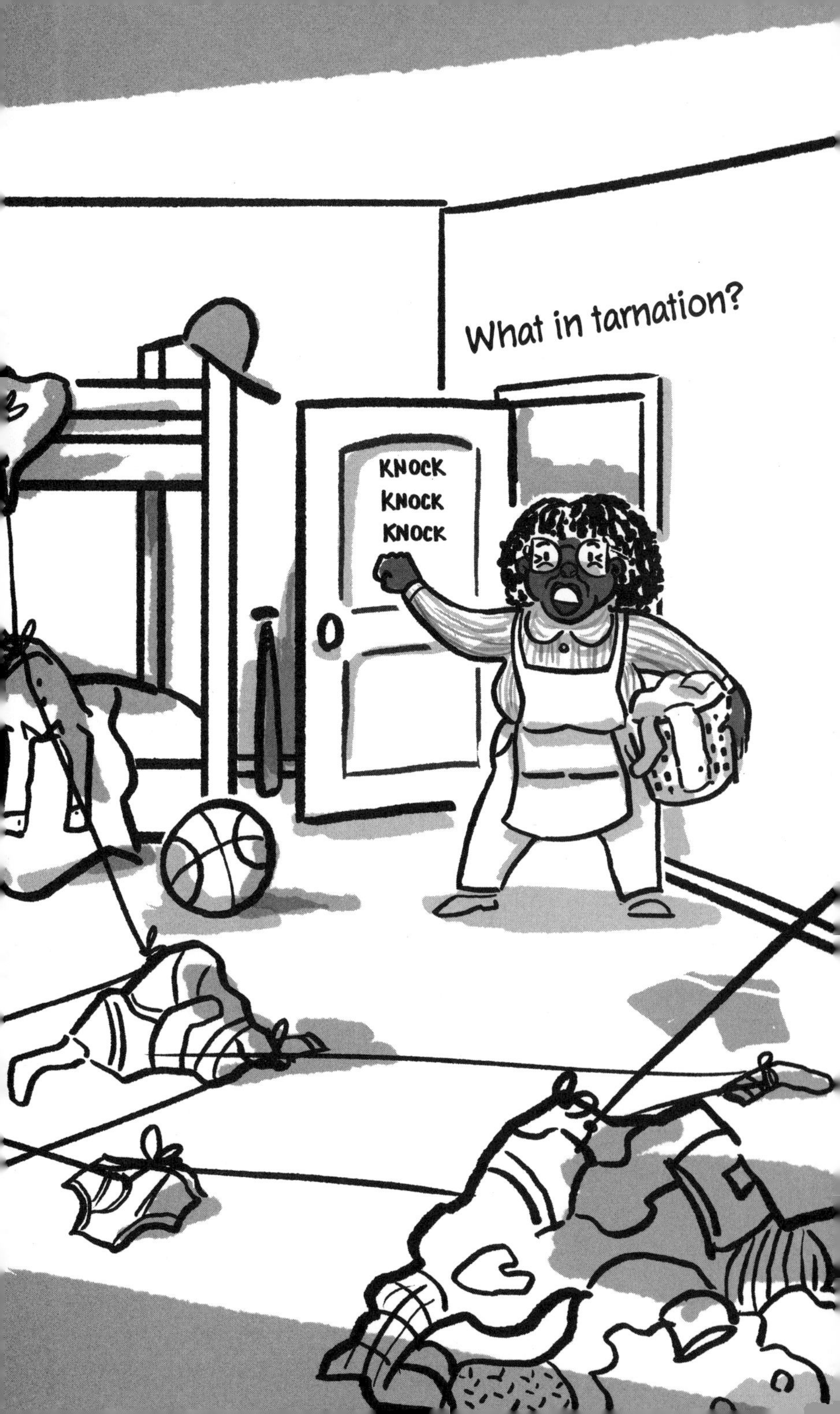
What in tarnation?
KNOCK
KNOCK
KNOCK

CHAPTER NINETEEN

LINK AND HUD FOLLOWED MS. JOYCE DOWN THE hallway toward the kitchen. She hadn't stopped talking to herself since they left the bedroom. "'Bout as helpful as a steerin' wheel on a mule. Got me tired, Lord. Tie. Red." She shook her head and then looked back at the boys. "C'mon, keep up. Got me runnin' behind now."

The boys were each struggling with a large pile of re-sorted laundry. *Why re-sorted?* you ask. Ms. Joyce had plenty to say on that farther down the hallway.

"Gon' make umpteen piles of laundry. All of 'em teeny-tiny. Lord, what I'm supposed to do with umpteen teeny-tiny piles of laundry? I said three piles. Towels. Colors. Whites. Did they listen? 'Course not."

Ms. Joyce shifted the laundry basket she was carrying from one hip to the other. It held the towels.

Link carried the colors. He hugged them in his arms, piled so high, he could barely see where he was going.

Hud carried the whites. His pile was smaller, but so was he, so he wasn't much better off.

Both boys left a trail of socks and underwear behind them as they staggered toward the kitchen, dropping laundry as they went.

"Don't worry 'bout those," Ms. Joyce called over her shoulder. "Y'all can come back for those." She led them through the kitchen and out into the garage. As she approached the washer and dryer, she pointed to the floor in front of the machines. "Drop 'em here."

Hud dropped his pile and exhaled in relief. *phew!*

Link didn't. "We're not supposed to be out here," he said. "Au Salon business only." His arms tightened around his pile.

Ms. Joyce sighed, set the laundry basket on top of the dryer, then leaned against the washer, and crossed her arms. "Well, go 'head then. You can stand there holdin' y'all's dirty drawers in your face if you want."

Link dropped the laundry and jumped back. "Ew!"

"That's what I thought." She chuckled and then smiled, her gold tooth flashing. "See, listenin' to Ms. Joyce don't smell so bad now, do it?"

Link winced like he could still smell the dirty laundry on his face. Hud stifled a giggle.

Ms. Joyce turned a knob on the washer and then pulled it. She opened the lid, and the boys could hear the machine filling with water. Then she bent over and started picking through the whites. Link and Hud watched as she reached down, picked up a few pieces, turned them right side out if they needed it, and then dropped them into the washer. She did it over and over again, without complaint.

Hud stared at Ms. Joyce in disbelief. *How could anyone like doing laundry?*

Link thought they'd better not stare or she'd make them do it, so he scanned the garage instead. There was plenty of other stuff to look at. He saw the fridge and the freezer (next to the washer and dryer); the lawn mower (the pushing kind, not the riding kind); four bikes (their bikes, which were covered in mud, and their parents' bikes, which looked brand-new); the folding basketball hoop (that their dad could roll out into the driveway and unfold); two basketballs (one that was flat and one that wasn't); the bicycle pump (for inflating their bike tires, but mostly for inflating the flat basketball); the big tall thing in the corner (a water heater or something; he couldn't remember—he just knew they weren't supposed to touch it); the ladder hanging on the wall (that they weren't supposed to touch); some old paint cans on the shelf (that they weren't supposed to touch); the big bags of packing peanuts and the Au Salon boxes (that they touched but weren't supposed to); and—the camcorder!

Link gasped—

"They just drawers," said Ms. Joyce.

"Huh?" said Link, confused. He looked at her. She was eyeing him as she turned a pair of underwear right side out.

His underwear. *Oh, no.*

"We all wear 'em," she said, shaking her head. "At least they ain't covered with none of those snazzy colors or pictures." She looked at him over her glasses, which had slid down her nose from all the bending over. "Plain white. You ask me, best way to see if they covered with anything *else*." She winked at him, smirked, and then dropped his underwear into the washer.

Link blushed and palmed his face, embarrassed. Hud laughed.

"Oh, don't you worry, Mr. Chuckles." Ms. Joyce shifted her gaze to Hud. "I can see what your snazzy drawers are covered in just fine."

Hud stopped laughing and Link started.

"Whyn't y'all go on back inside now. I can take it from here." Ms. Joyce reached down for more whites and then turned to face the washer.

Link and Hud happily turned to leave. As they walked toward the door, Link nudged Hud and pointed out what he'd spotted in his survey of the garage.

Hud's eyes got big. His voice got loud. "That's the camcorder!"

shhh! Link put a finger to his lips and looked over his shoulder, waiting for Ms. Joyce to react. She didn't. "I know it's the camcorder," he whispered with an eyeroll. "Duh. I pointed it out."

"Oh, right," Hud whispered back.

"Imma go get it. Stay here and watch my back."

"Um, don't you think I should watch Ms. Joyce's back? I can signal you if she turns around."

Link rolled his eyes again. "Right. Do that."

Hud smiled and gave a silent thumbs up.

As quietly as he could, Link snuck behind the Au Salon boxes, between the big bags of packing peanuts, and across the garage to their dad's workbench. He picked up the camcorder, checked he hadn't missed a signal from Hud, and then made his way back. Wow. That was easier than he expected.

Not believing their luck, the boys headed to the door. As they reached it, Hud grabbed the doorknob. Before he could turn it, something made their stomachs drop.

"Hold up!" It was Ms. Joyce.

They froze without turning around. Link did his best to conceal the camcorder with his body. Hud didn't let go of the doorknob.

"Don't forget to grab that laundry y'all dropped. And hurry it up, already. Ain't got all day."

They exhaled and relaxed. ***phew!*** Then Hud opened the door, and they went inside.

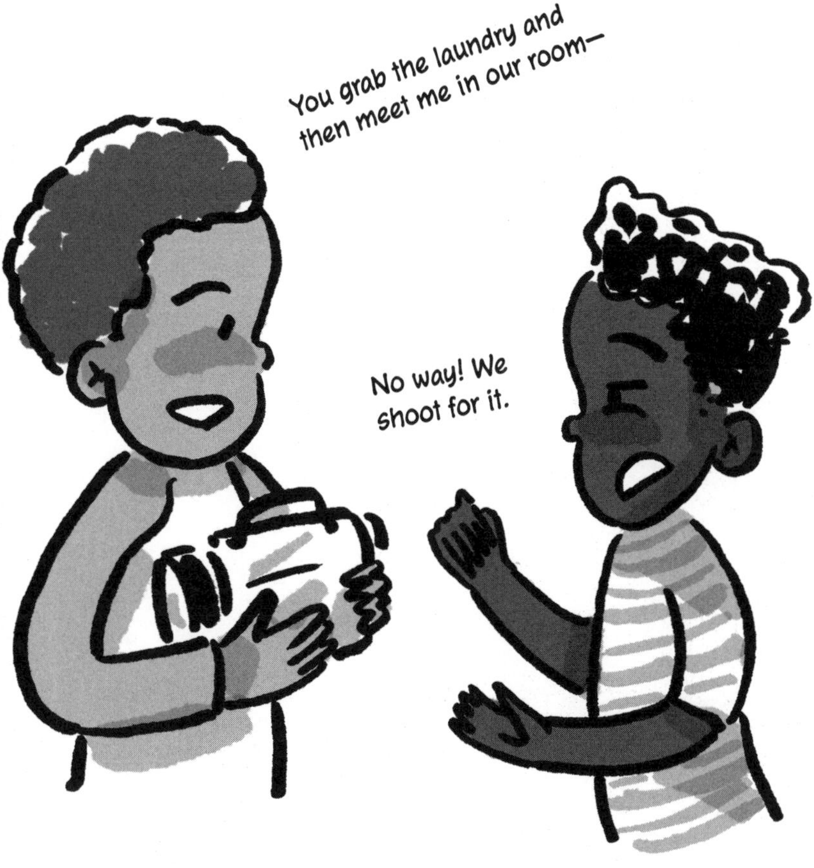
You grab the laundry and then meet me in our room—
No way! We shoot for it.

CHAPTER TWENTY

HAVE YOU EVER HAD TO DO SOMETHING YOU really didn't want to do when there was something way more exciting waiting for you instead?

Hud has.

He started in the kitchen.

Ugh. I shoulda picked scissors.

He picked up a sock. *This isn't even my sock!*

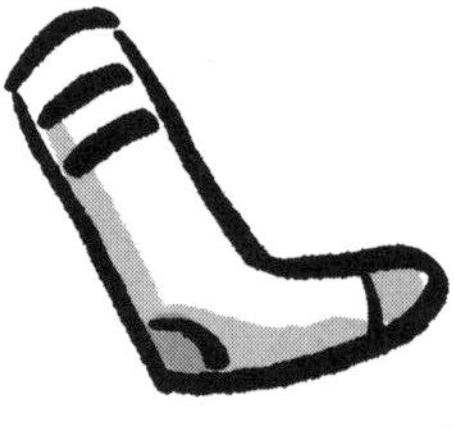

He crossed the kitchen toward the hallway.

Dumb paper. Everyone knows a real rock would win. Rock should always win.

He picked up another sock. *Not mine again!*

He entered the hallway.

Dumb brother, more like it. Who thinks paper is stronger than a rock?

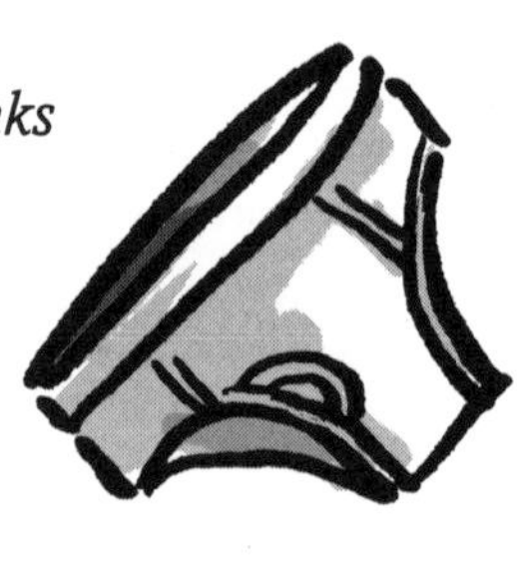

He picked up a pair of underwear. *Hmph. Dumb plain white underwear.*

He passed the den. The TV was off.

Hmmm. I wonder if Scarlett's made it out of the hospital yet.

He picked up another pair of underwear. *Now, this is cool underwear. I don't care what she says. And that's, um, definitely just another, uh, little lightning bolt, yeah.*

He passed the bathroom.

"*No toys. No games.*" No way, *more like it. Ha!*

He picked up a sock. *Ugh. How much more is there—*

He stopped and looked over his shoulder.

What was that noise?

He didn't see anything.

Huh, maybe I'm hearing things.

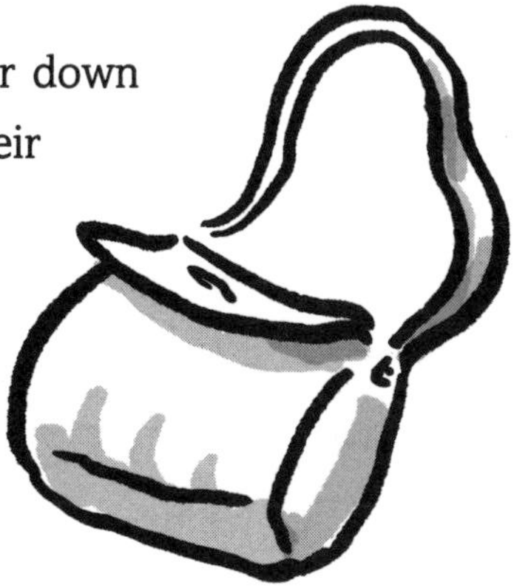

He ignored it and walked farther down the hallway. He stopped outside their bedroom door.

Link better not watch it until I get back.

He picked up the last piece of clothing. It was another sock. *Finally.*

He turned around, walked back down the hallway, back past the bathroom, back past the den, back to—

"Ahh!" he shouted as he threw all the socks and underwear into the air.

"Ahh!" Ms. Joyce shouted as she threw her purse into the air.

The two looked at each other, both startled.

"Lord, child," said Ms. Joyce, covering her heart. "You tryin' to give me a heart attack?"

Hud's heart thumped in his chest. He was breathing hard. "I . . . uh . . . didn't . . . uh . . . see you . . . there."

Ms. Joyce stood in the doorway to the den. Hud had walked right past her and not seen her.

"I came in for my pocketbook," she said, reaching down to pick up her purse, "not heart palpitations—Lord!" She inhaled and let out a deep breath as she patted her chest. "What you sneakin' 'round in here for?"

"Uh, I was getting the clothes we dropped, like you, uh, said." He looked around at the clothes on the floor.

"Well, go on then. Pick 'em up," she said. She sucked her gold tooth.

Hud reached down and picked up the socks and underwear.

Ms. Joyce put her purse over her shoulder and clutched it under her arm. "Give 'em here." She reached out to take the dirty laundry.

Hud passed it over.

"Now go on and stop all that sneakin' 'round. I gots laundry to finish." She walked past Hud into the kitchen and out into the garage.

Hud watched her close the door and then turned around to head to their room.

He passed the den.

Sneaking? I wasn't sneaking. She *was sneaking!*

He passed the bathroom.

Why'd she need her big ol' purse to do laundry, anyway?

He stopped outside their bedroom door and looked back down the hallway.

What's she up to?

He opened the door and walked in.

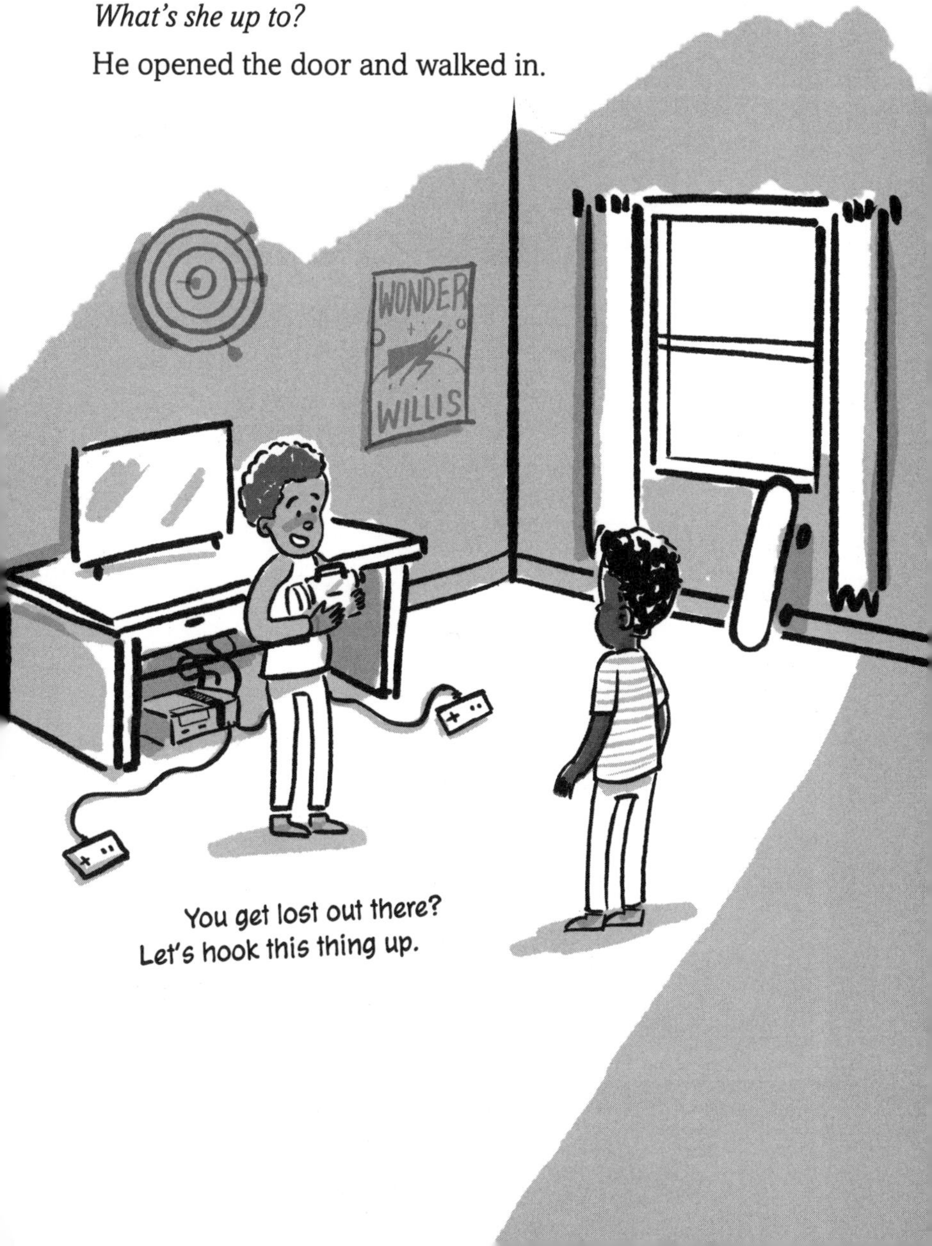
WONDER
WILLIS
You get lost out there?
Let's hook this thing up.

CHAPTER TWENTY-ONE

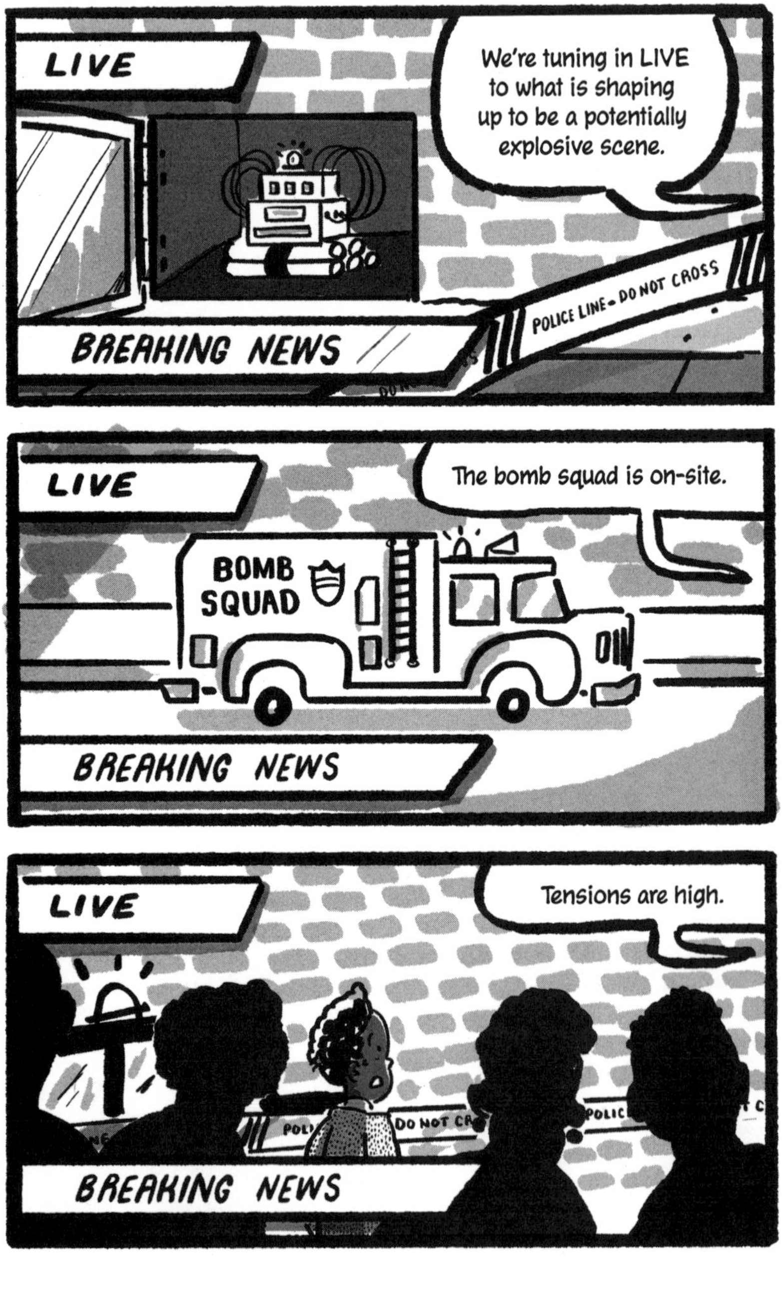
LIVE
We're tuning in LIVE to what is shaping up to be a potentially explosive scene.
POLICE LINE - DO NOT CROSS
BREAKING NEWS
LIVE
The bomb squad is on-site.
BOMB SQUAD
BREAKING NEWS
LIVE
Tensions are high.
BREAKING NEWS

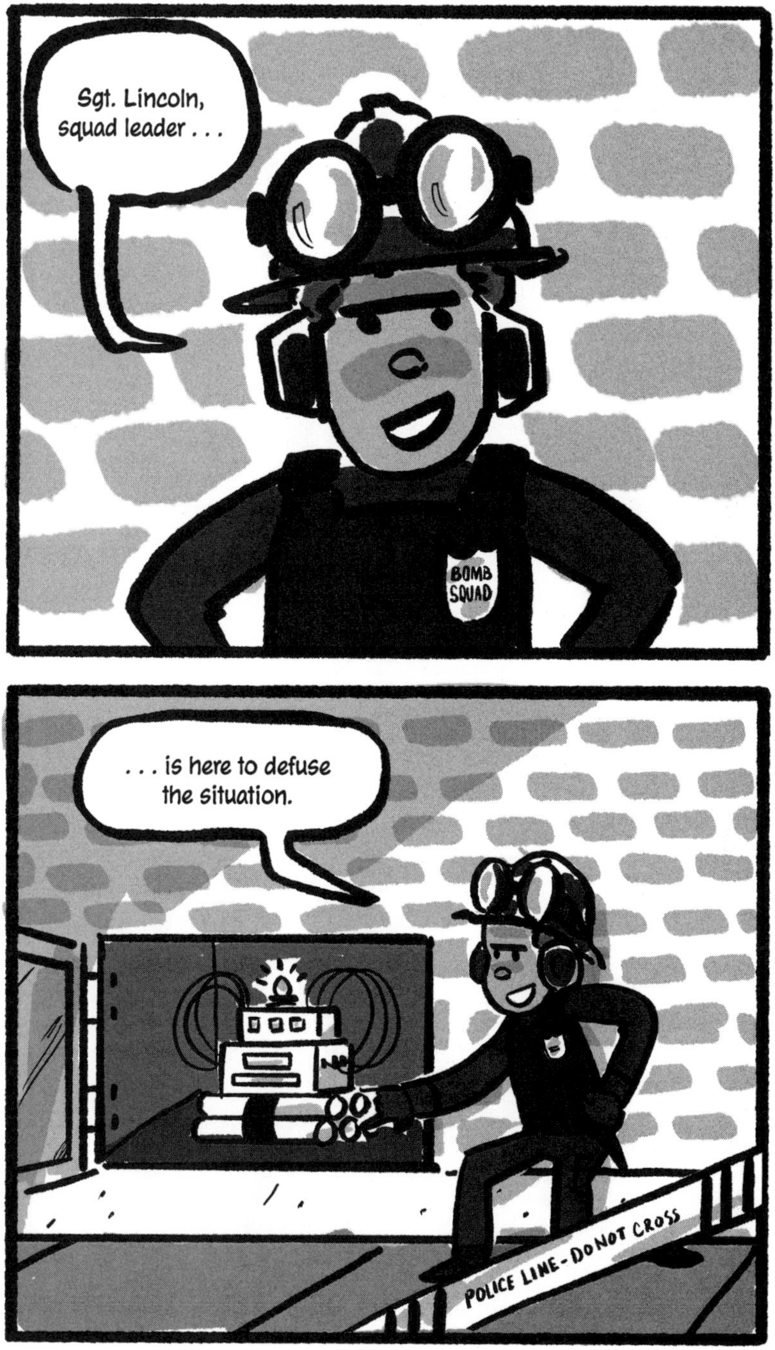
Sgt. Lincoln, squad leader . . .
BOMB SQUAD
. . . is here to defuse the situation.
POLICE LINE - DO NOT CROSS

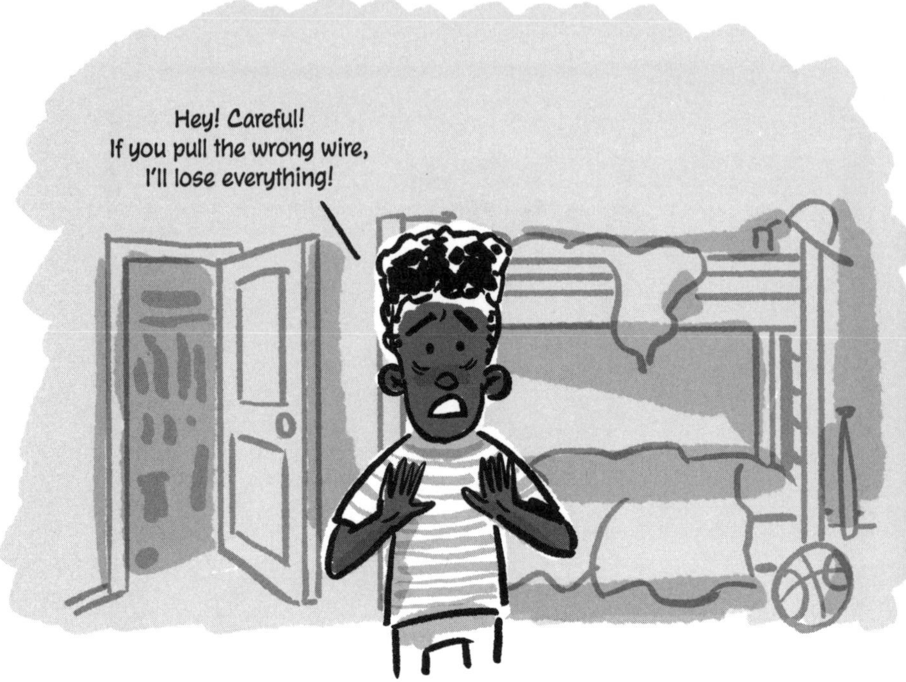
Hey! Careful!
If you pull the wrong wire,
I'll lose everything!

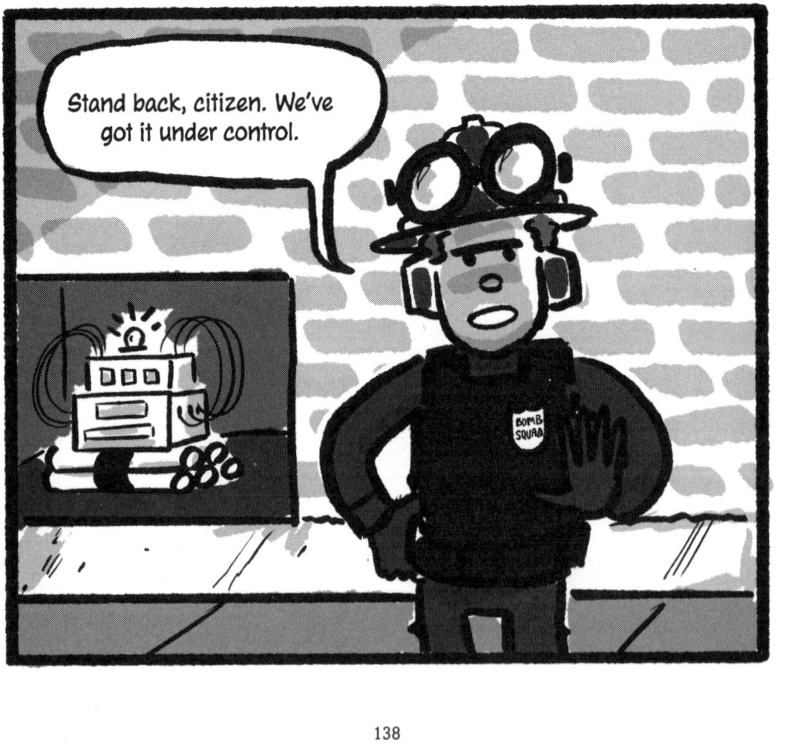
Stand back, citizen. We've
got it under control.
BOMB
SQUAD

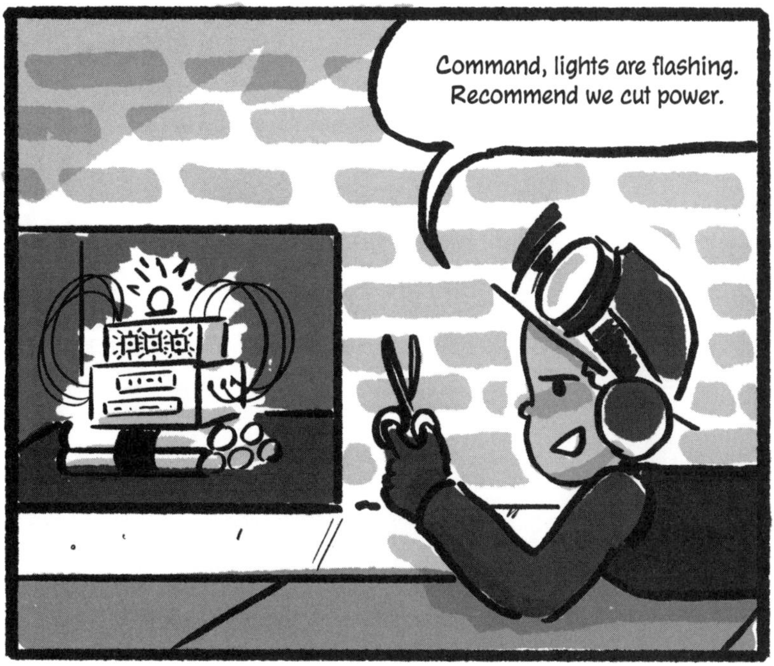
Command, lights are flashing.
Recommend we cut power.

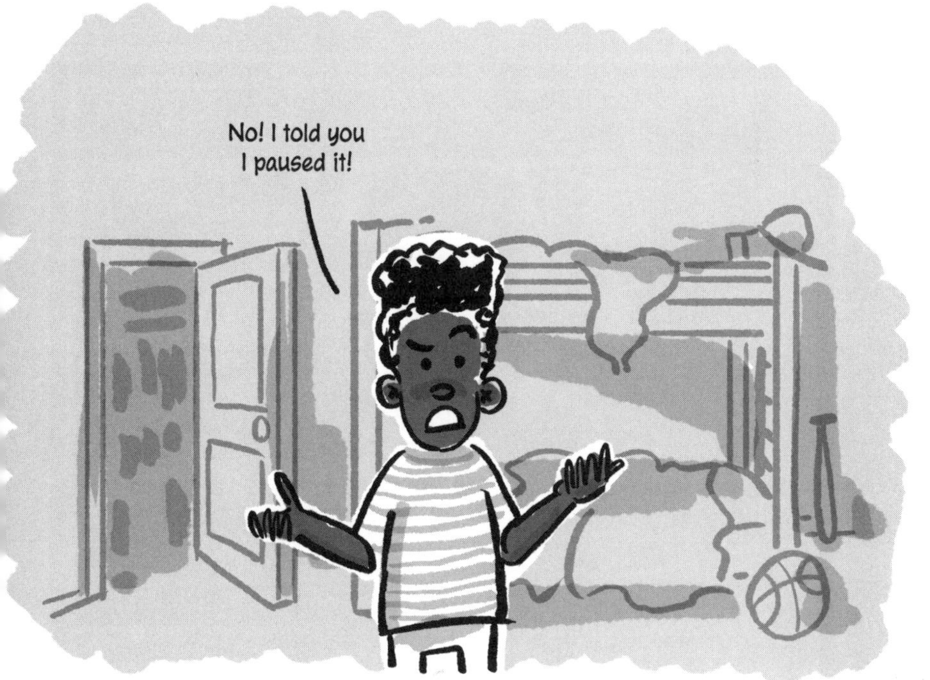
No! I told you
I paused it!

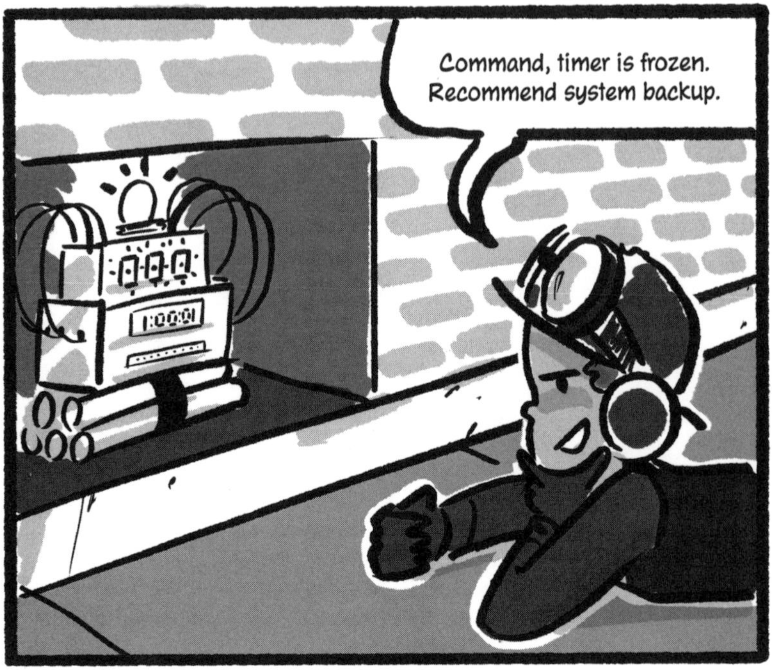
Command, timer is frozen. Recommend system backup.

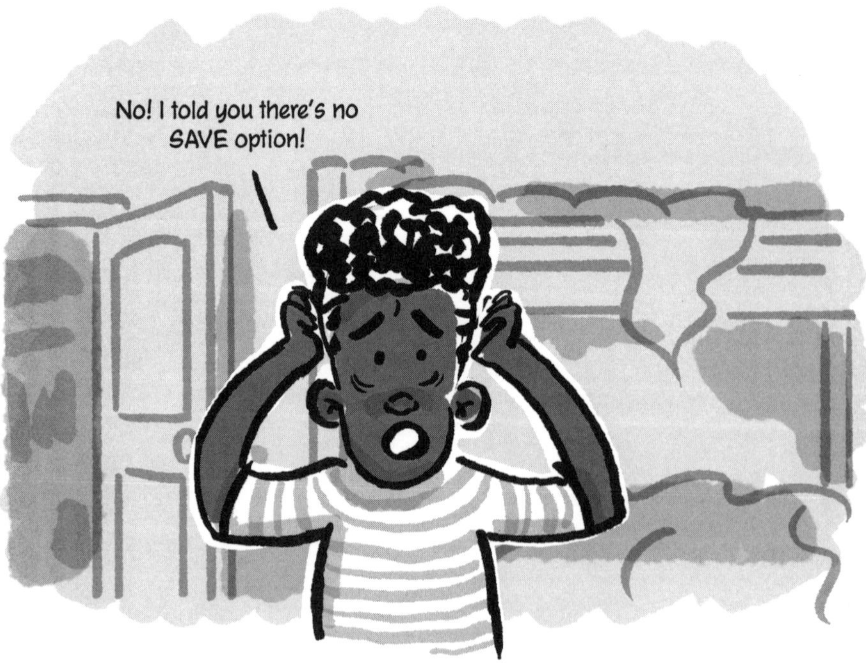
No! I told you there's no SAVE option!

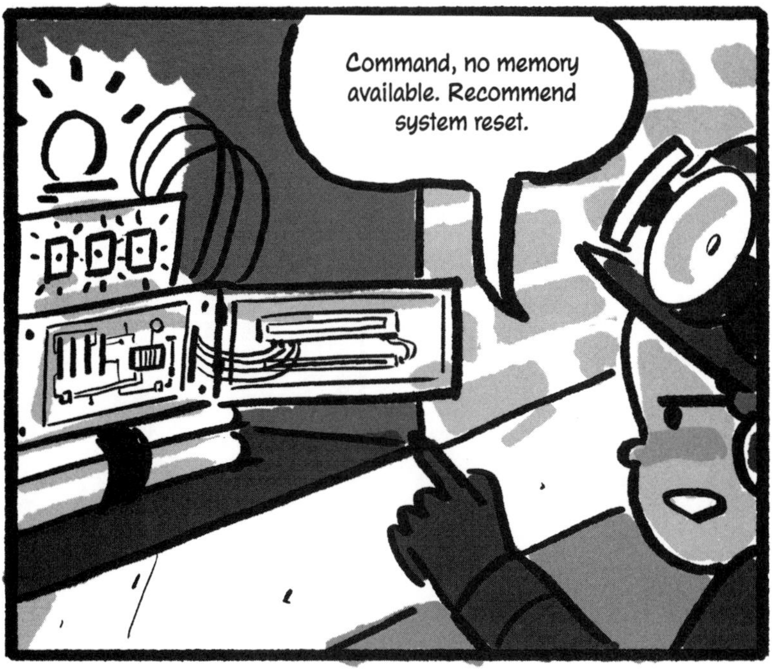
Command, no memory available. Recommend system reset.

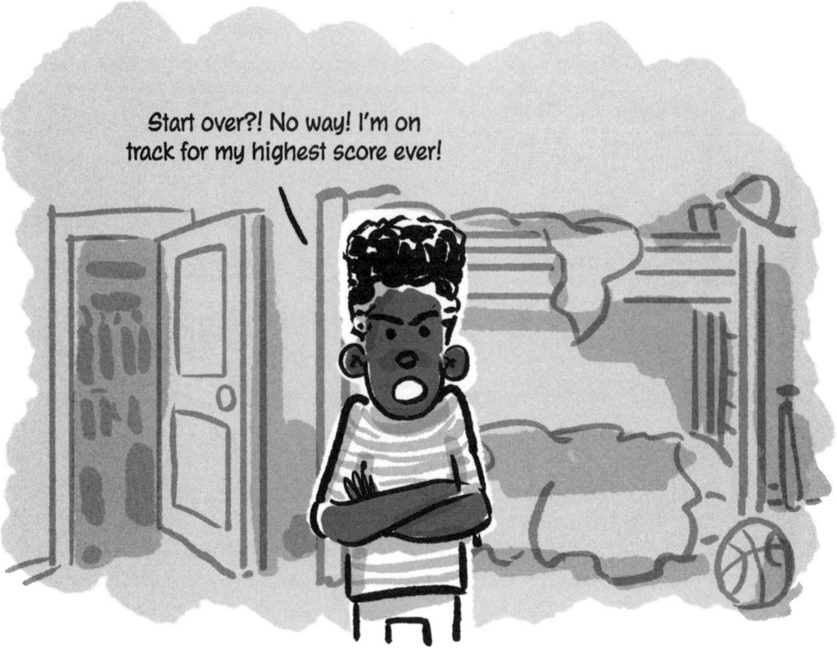
Start over?! No way! I'm on track for my highest score ever!

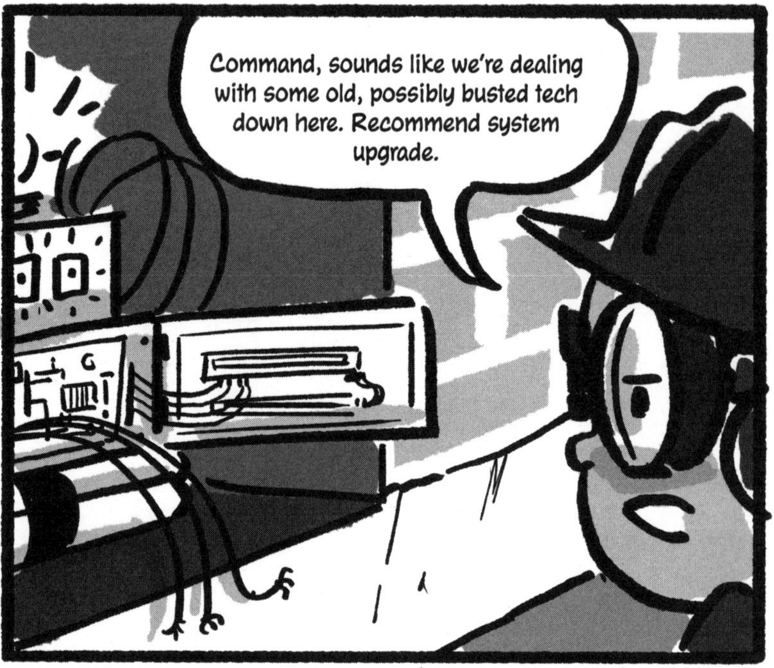
Command, sounds like we're dealing with some old, possibly busted tech down here. Recommend system upgrade.

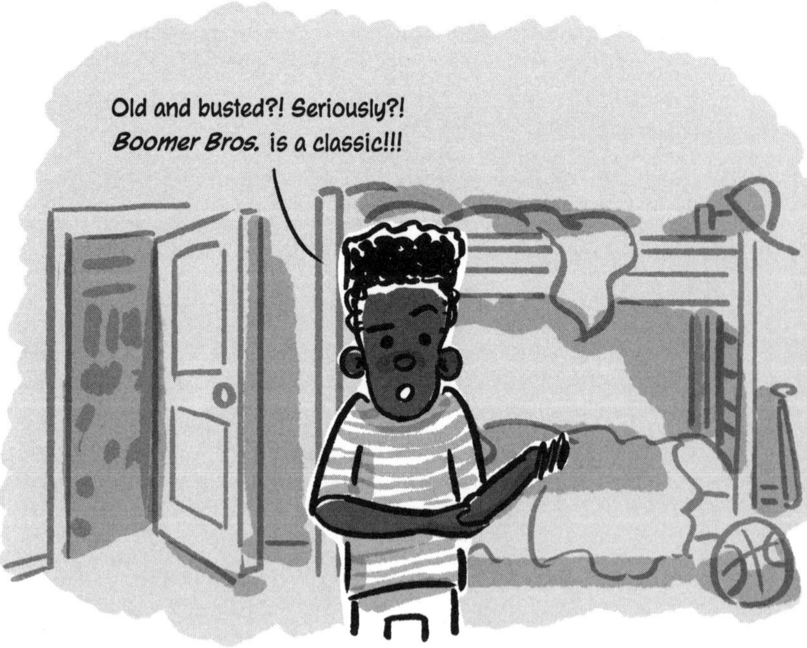
Old and busted?! Seriously?! *Boomer Bros.* is a classic!!!

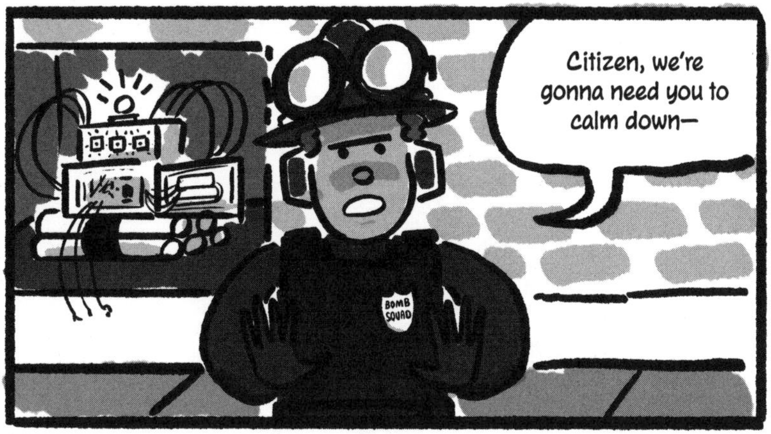
BOMB SQUAD
Citizen, we're gonna need you to calm down—

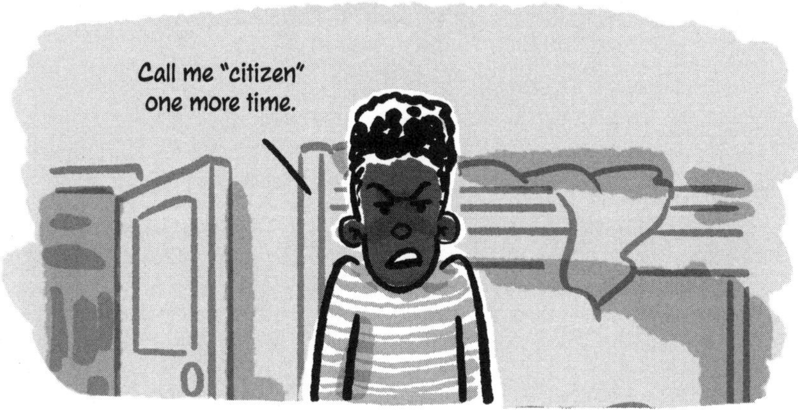
Call me "citizen" one more time.

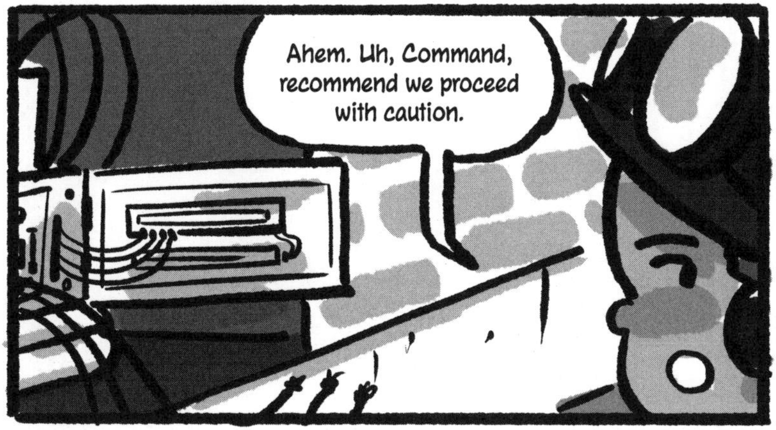
Ahem. Uh, Command, recommend we proceed with caution.

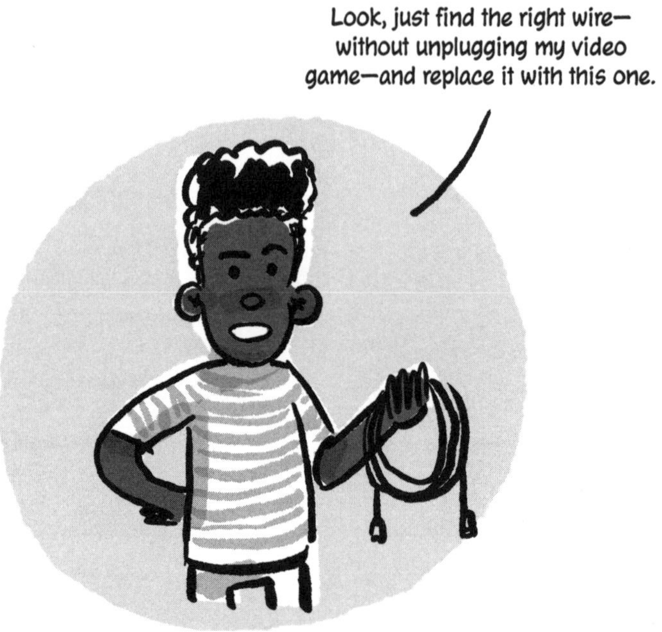
Look, just find the right wire—without unplugging my video game—and replace it with this one.

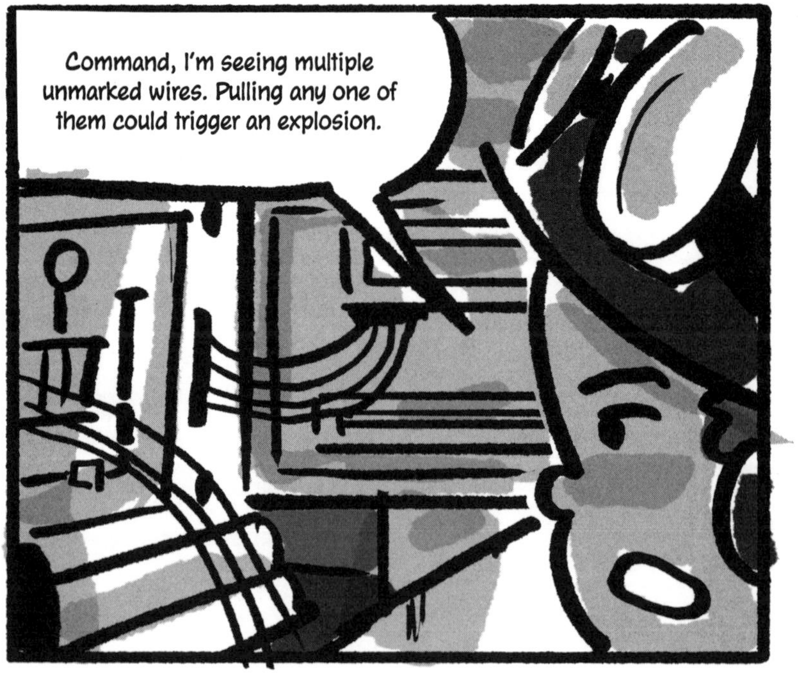
Command, I'm seeing multiple unmarked wires. Pulling any one of them could trigger an explosion.

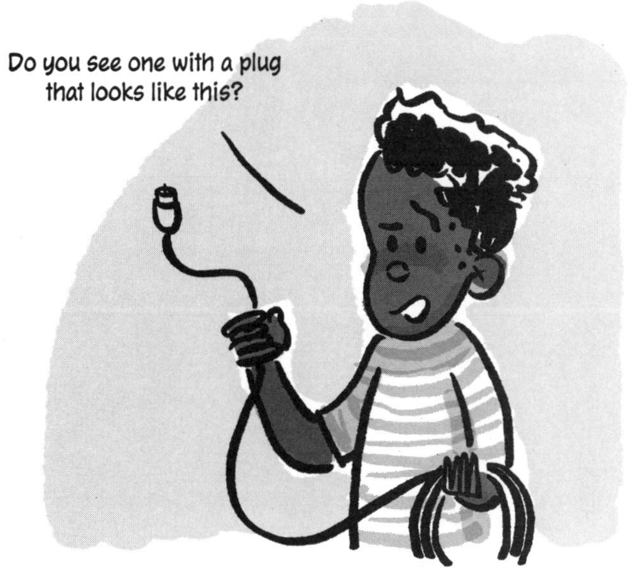
Do you see one with a plug that looks like this?

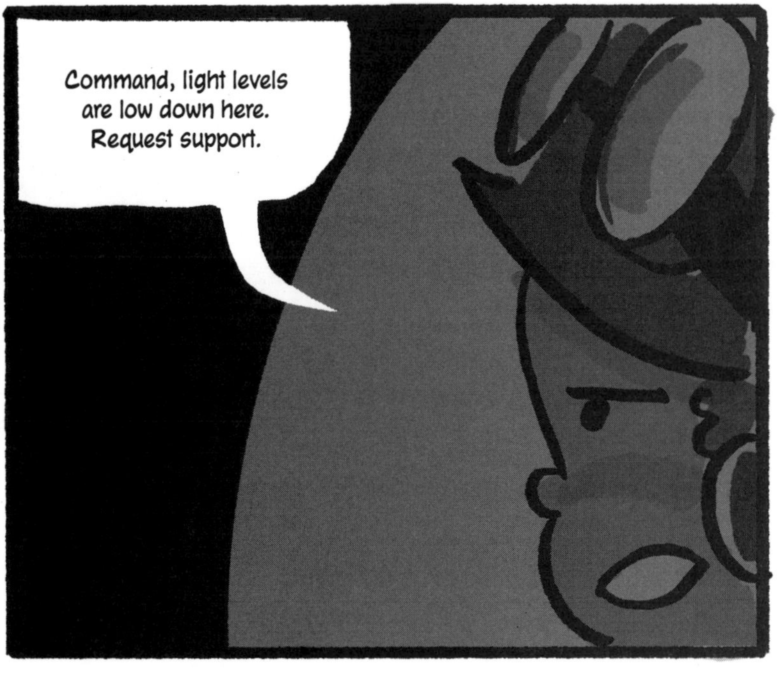
Command, light levels are low down here. Request support.

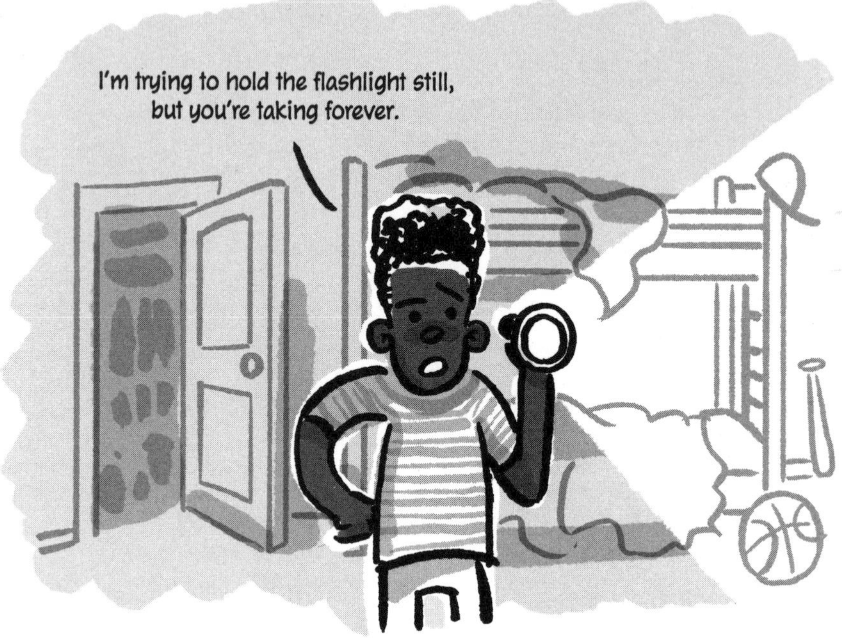
I'm trying to hold the flashlight still, but you're taking forever.

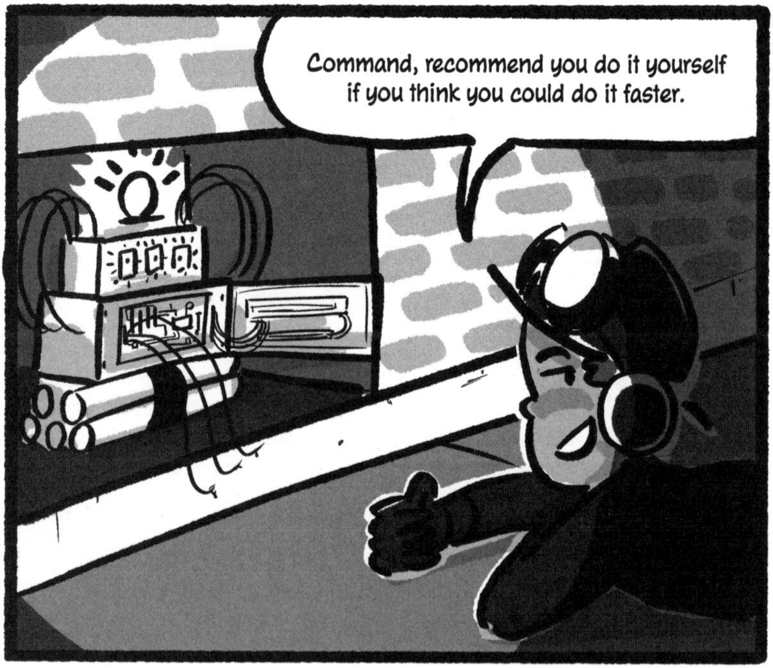
Command, recommend you do it yourself if you think you could do it faster.

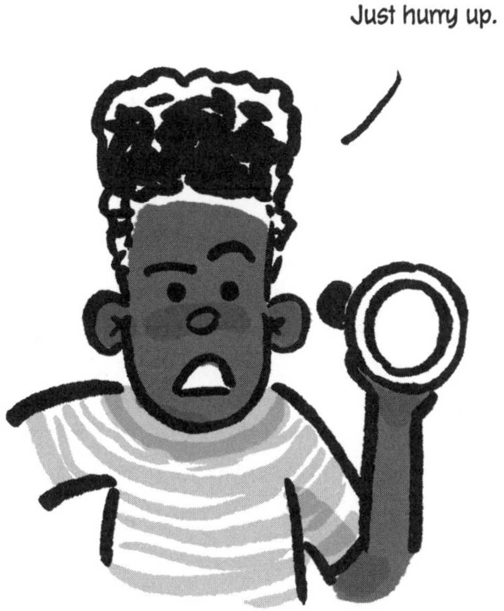
Just hurry up.

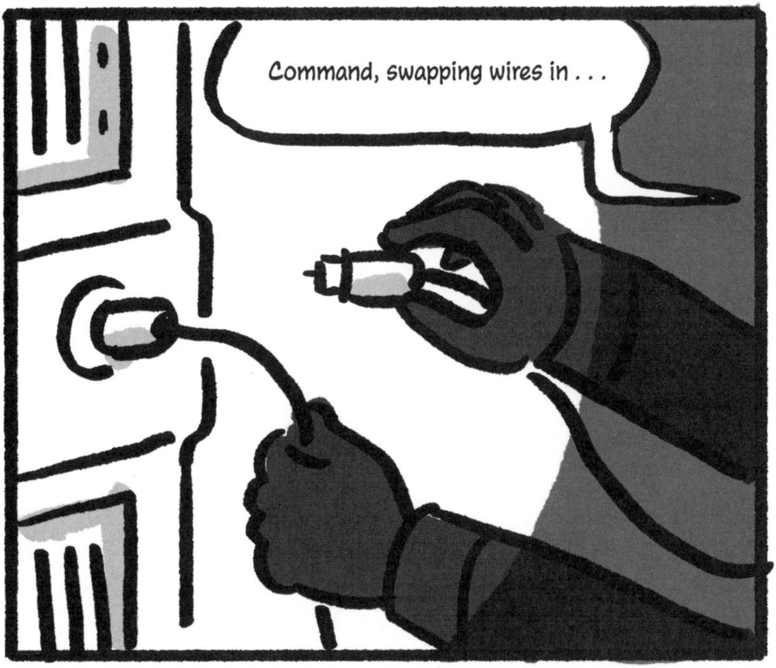
Command, swapping wires in . . .

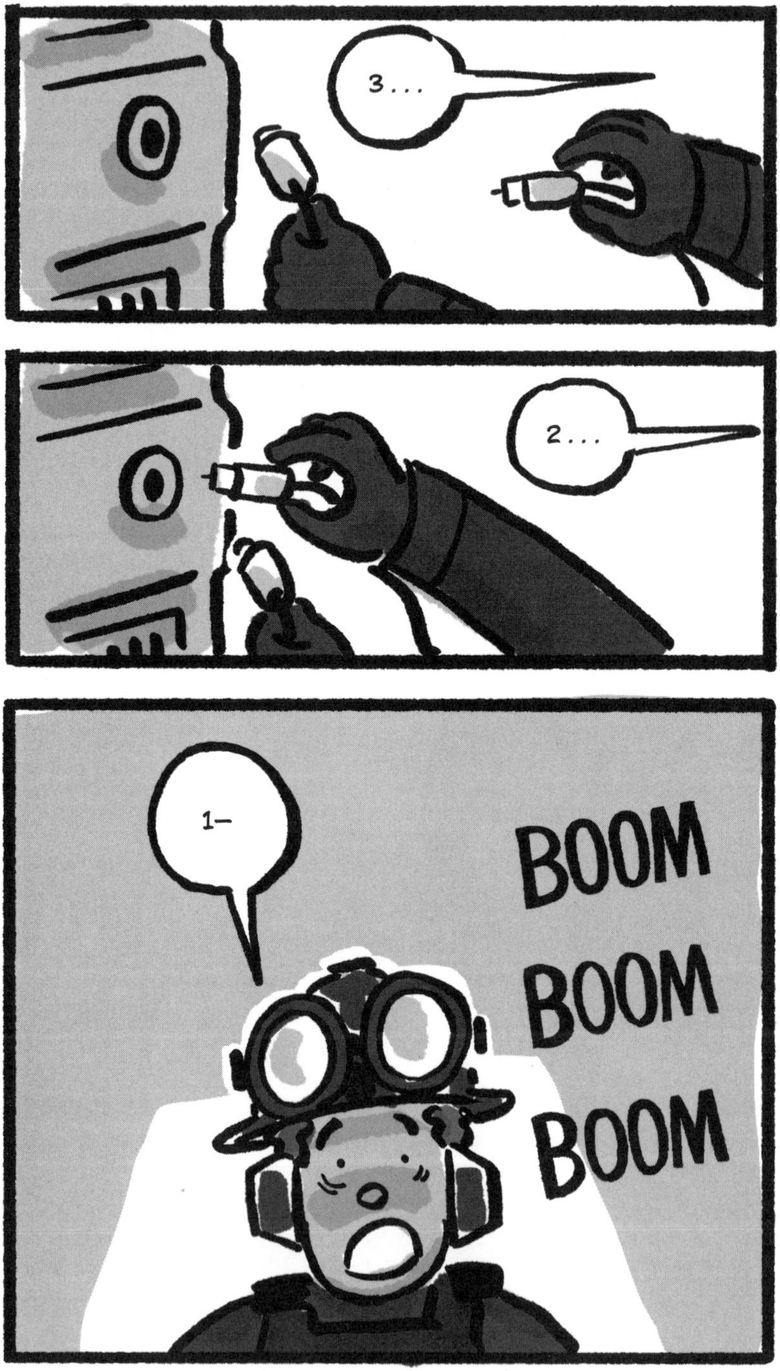
3...
2...
1—
BOOM
BOOM
BOOM

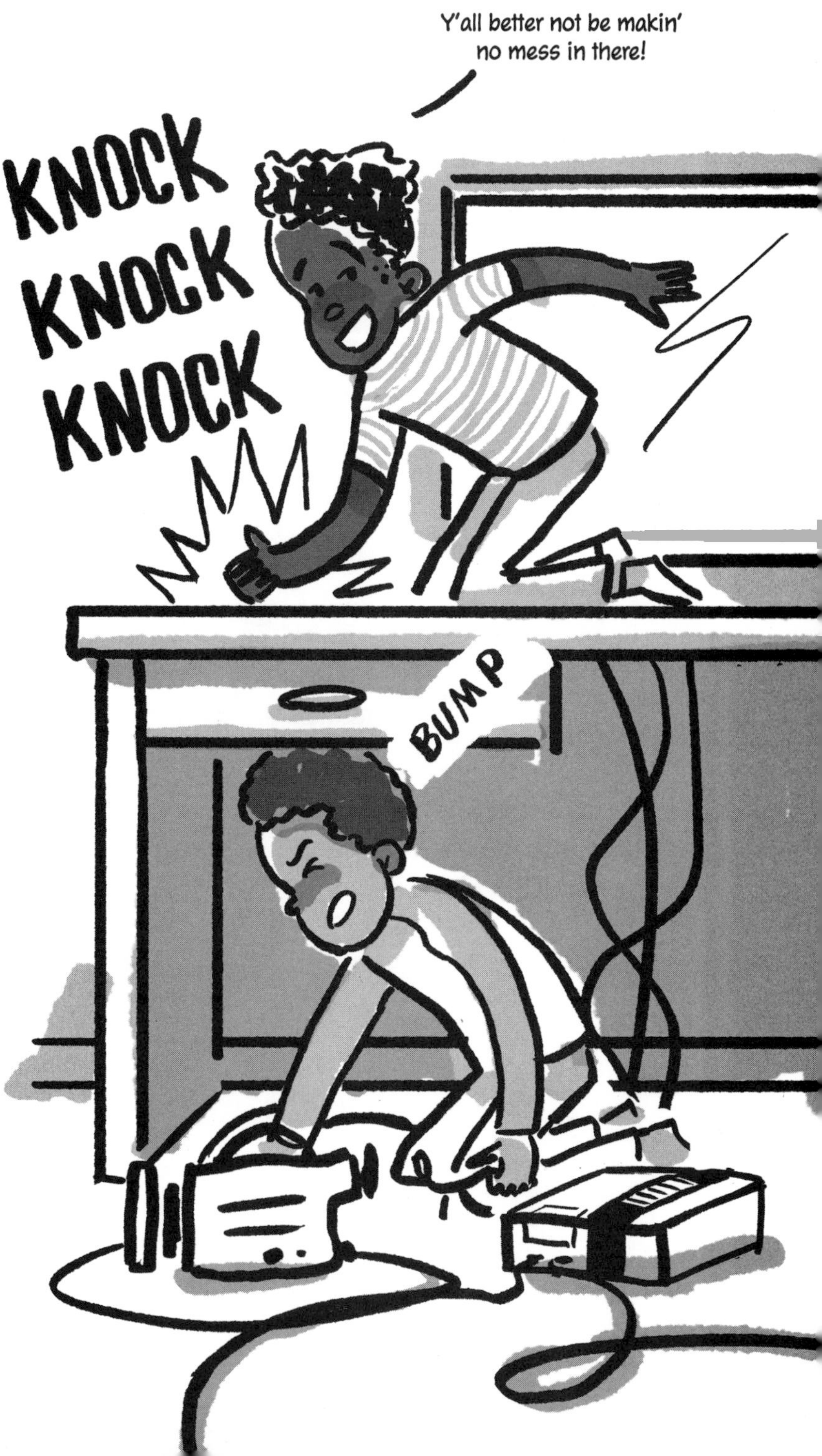
Y'all better not be makin' no mess in there!
KNOCK KNOCK KNOCK
BUMP

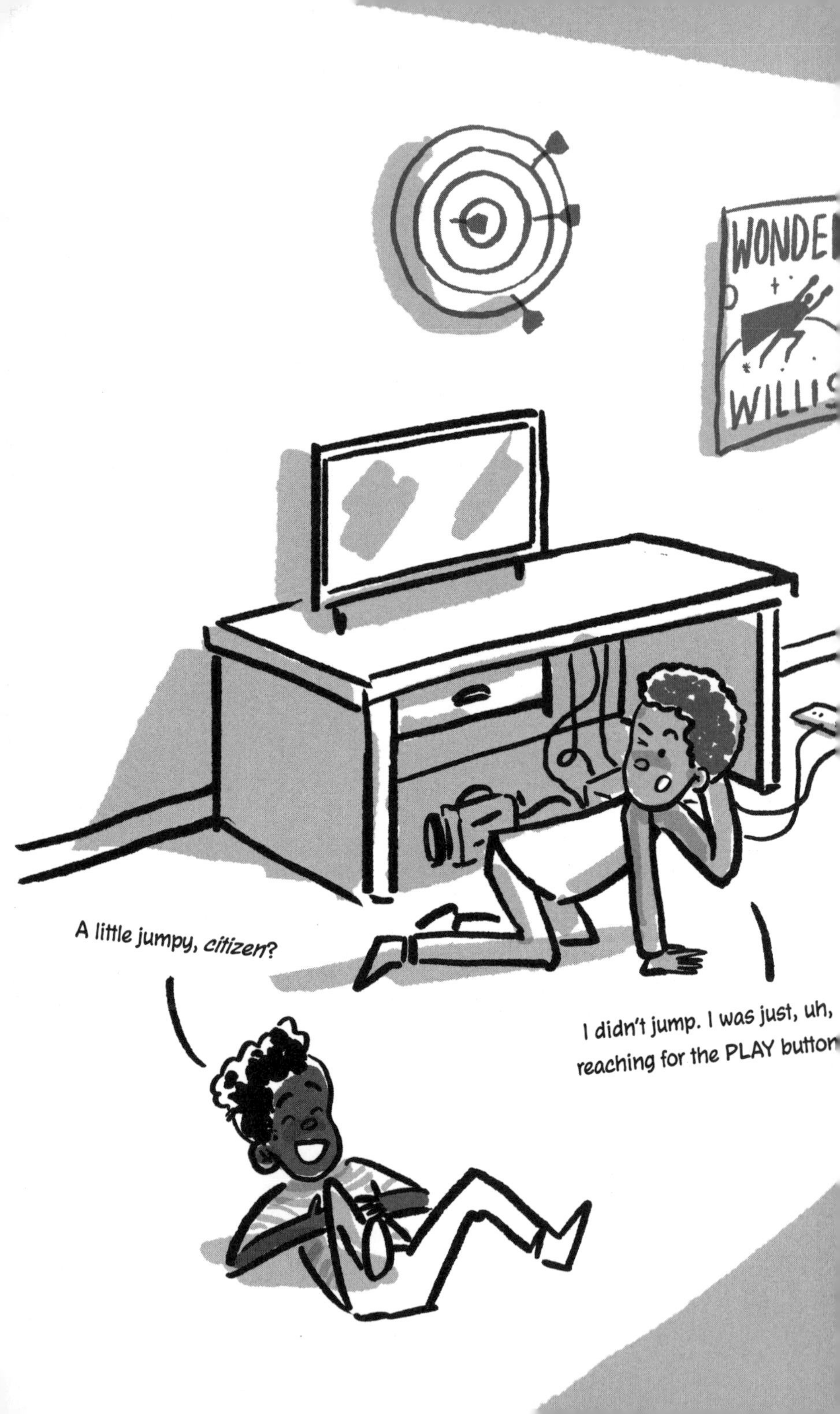
WONDE
WILLIS
A little jumpy, *citizen*?
I didn't jump. I was just, uh, reaching for the PLAY button

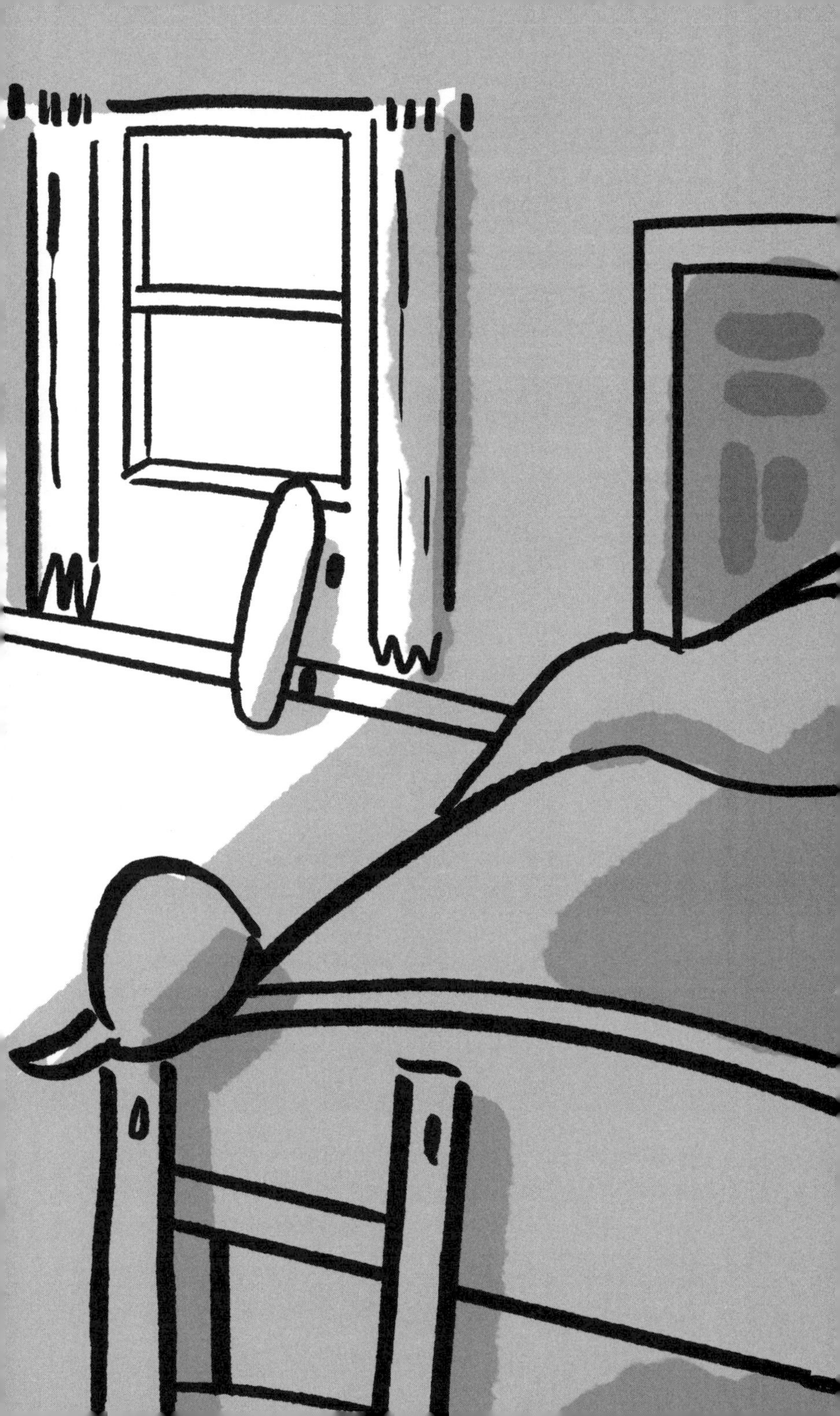

CHAPTER TWENTY-TWO

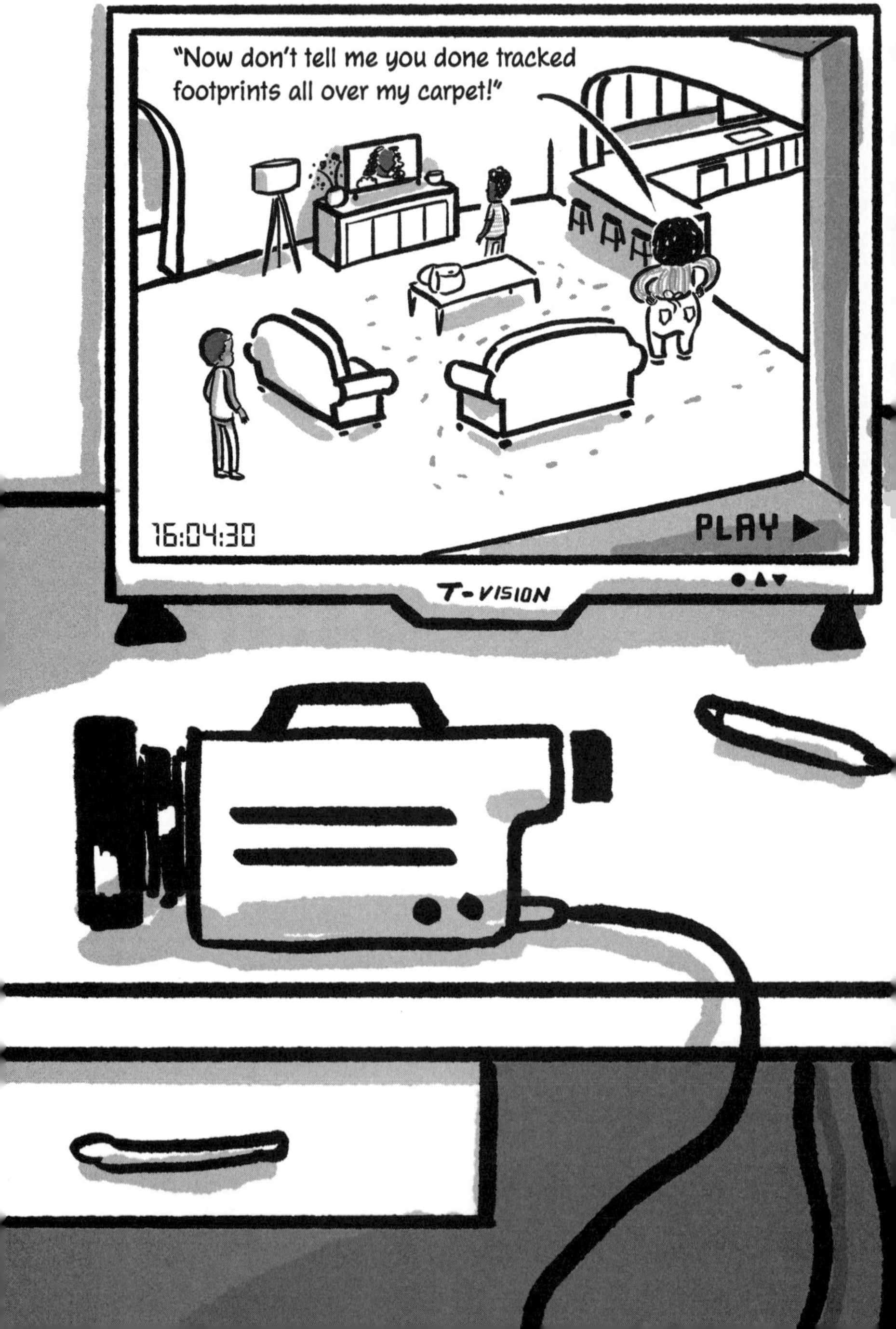
"Now don't tell me you done tracked footprints all over my carpet!"
16:04:30
PLAY ▶
T-VISION

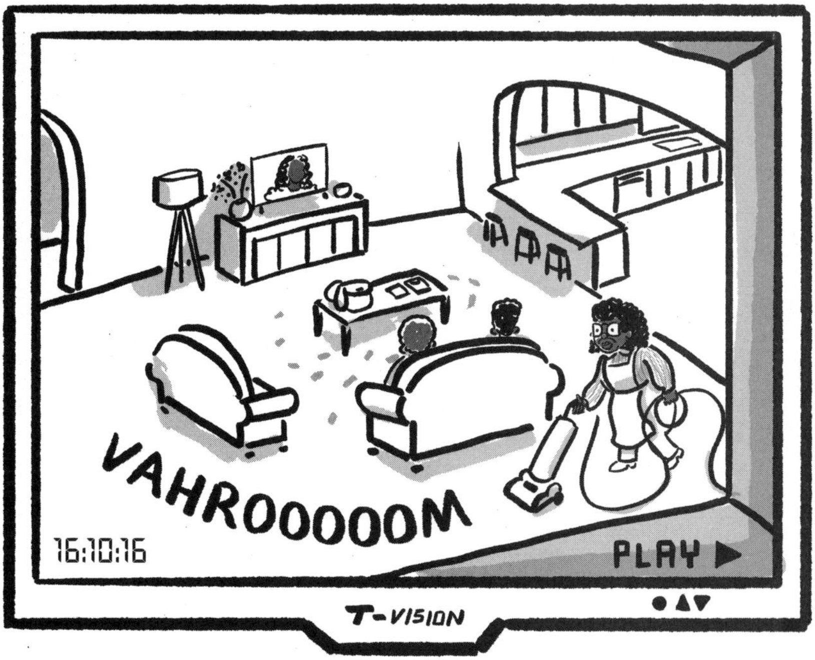
VAHROOOOOM
16:10:16
PLAY ▶
T-VISION

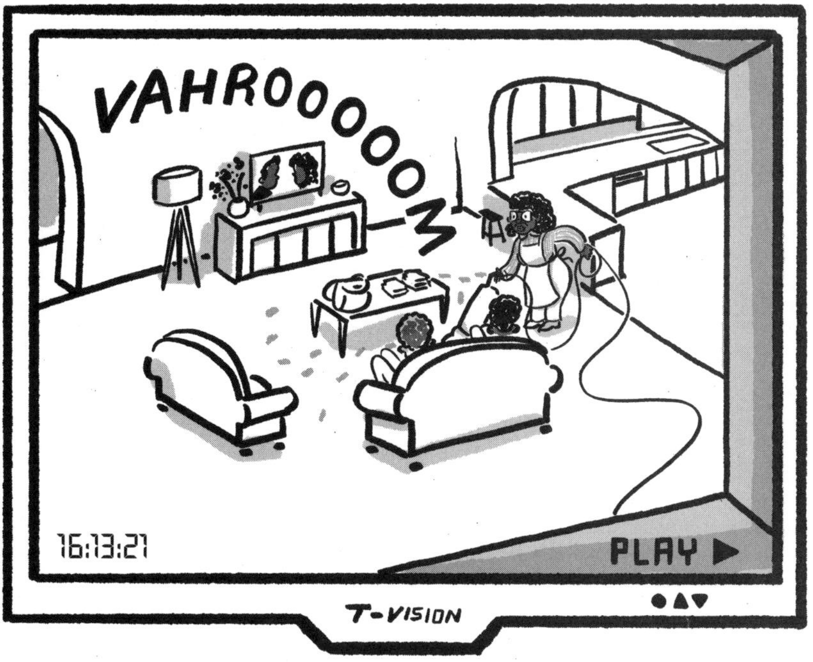
VAHROOOOOOM
16:13:21
PLAY ▶
T-VISION

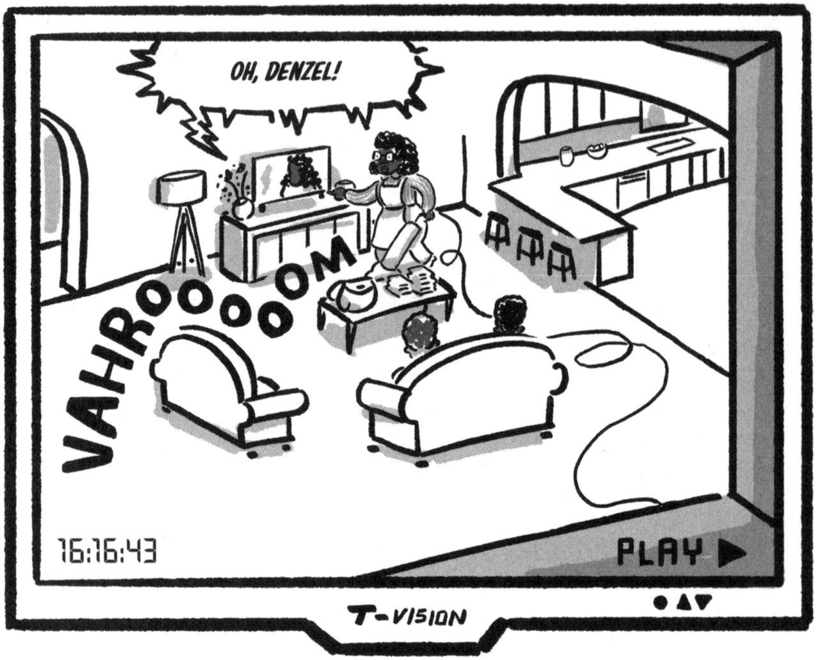
OH, DENZEL!
VAHROOOOOOM
16:16:43
PLAY
T-VISION

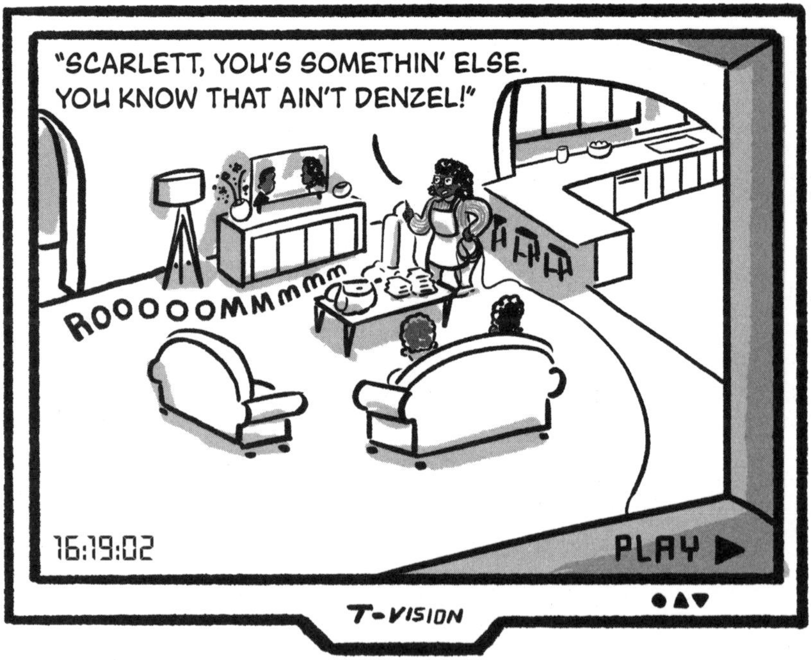
"SCARLETT, YOU'S SOMETHIN' ELSE. YOU KNOW THAT AIN'T DENZEL!"
ROOOOOOMMmmm
16:19:02
PLAY
T-VISION

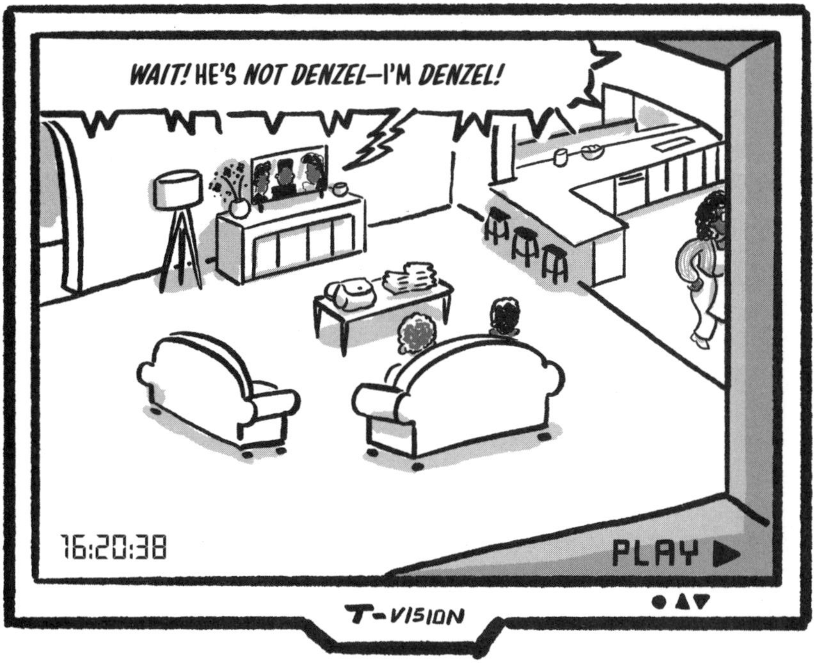
WAIT! HE'S NOT DENZEL—I'M DENZEL!
16:20:38
PLAY
T-VISION

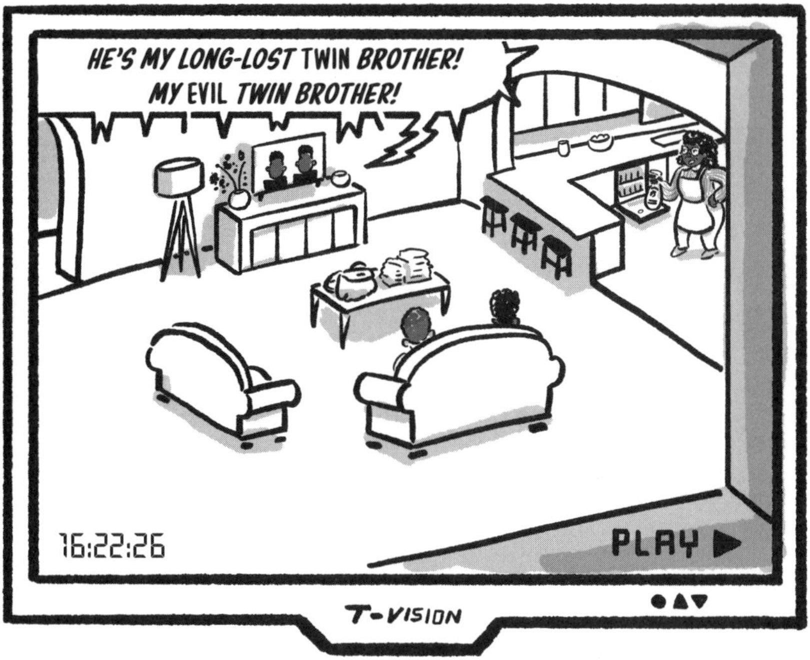
HE'S MY LONG-LOST TWIN BROTHER! MY EVIL TWIN BROTHER!
16:22:26
PLAY
T-VISION

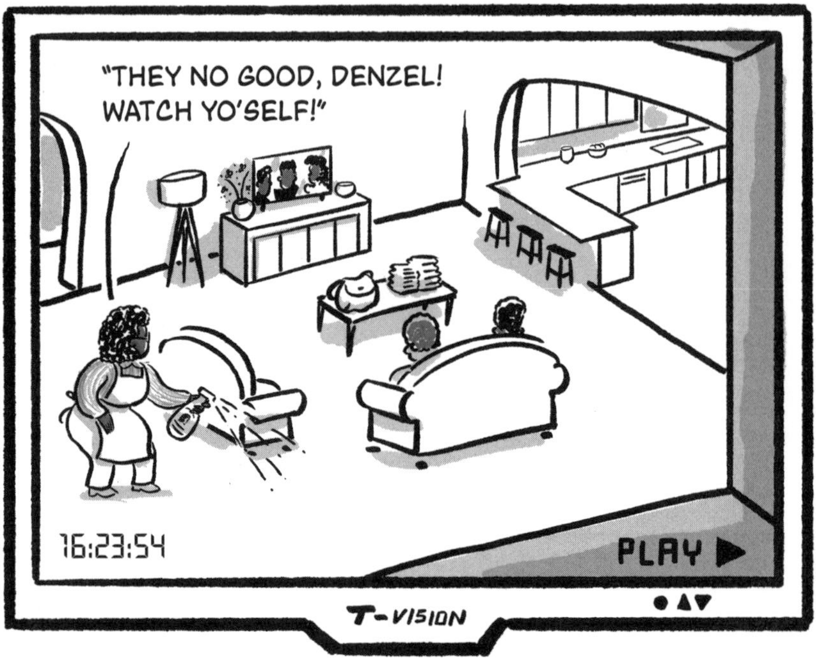
"THEY NO GOOD, DENZEL! WATCH YO'SELF!"
16:23:54
PLAY
T-VISION

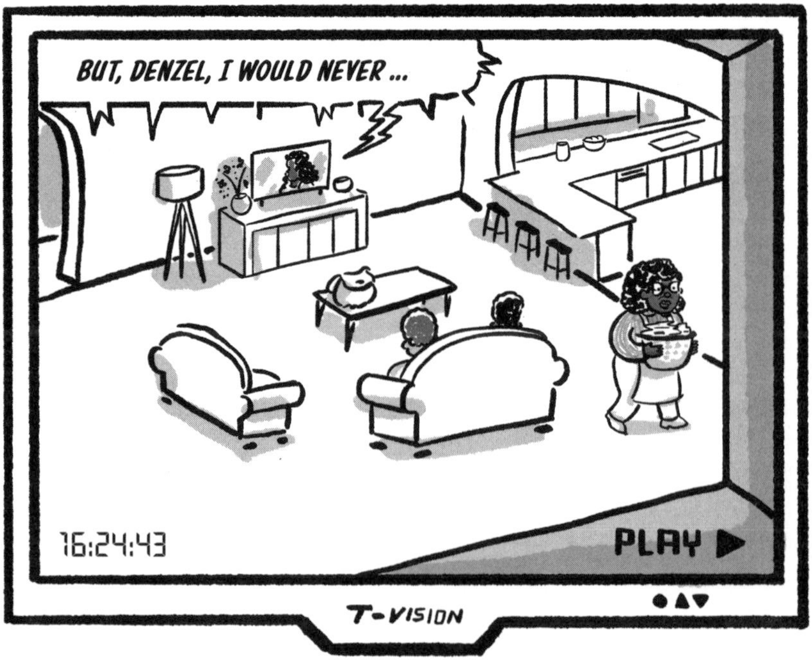
BUT, DENZEL, I WOULD NEVER ...
16:24:43
PLAY
T-VISION

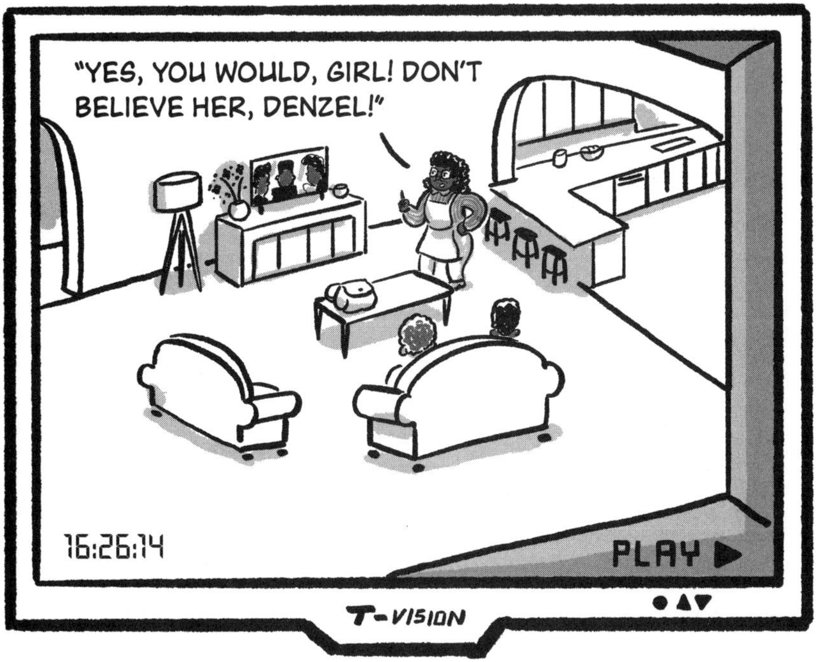
"YES, YOU WOULD, GIRL! DON'T BELIEVE HER, DENZEL!"
16:26:14
PLAY
T-VISION

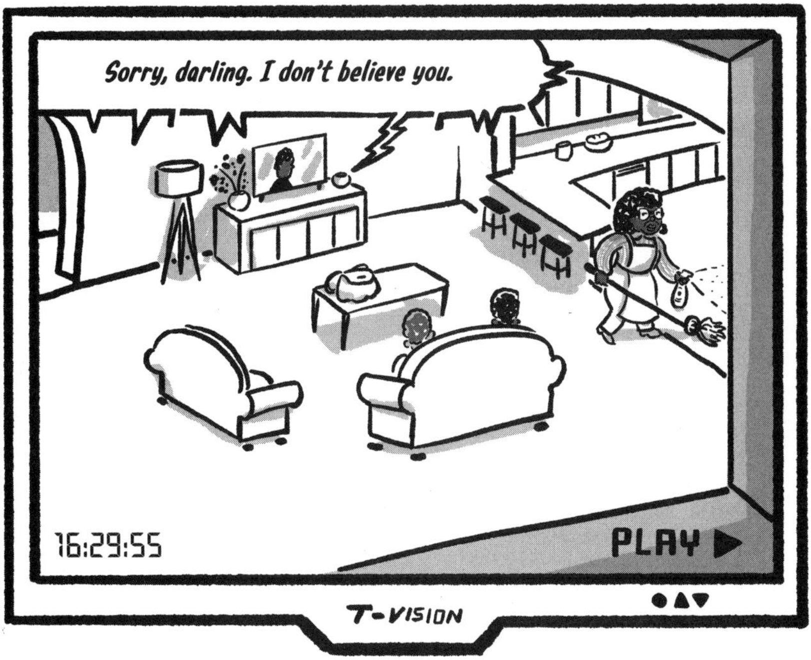
Sorry, darling. I don't believe you.
16:29:55
PLAY
T-VISION

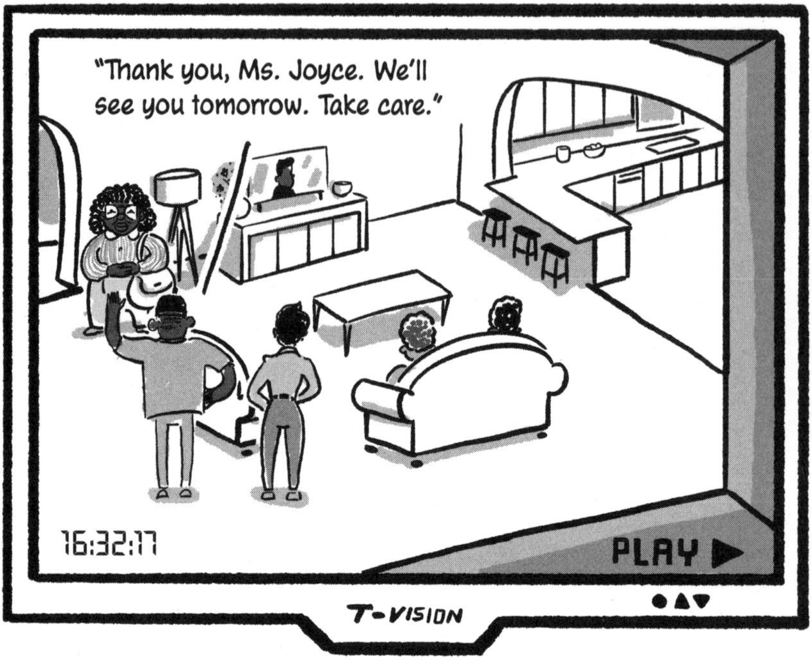
"Thank you, Ms. Joyce. We'll see you tomorrow. Take care."
16:32:17
PLAY
T-VISION

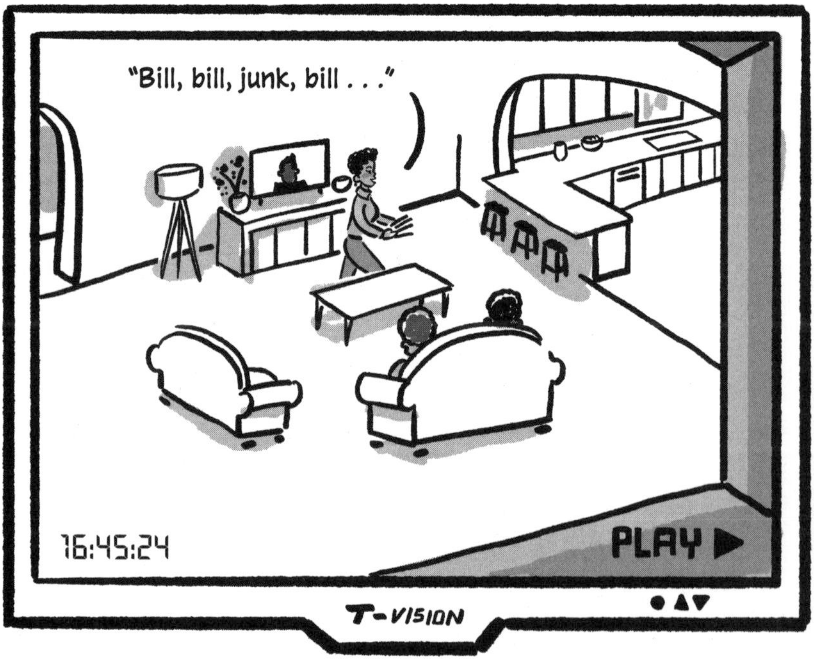
"Bill, bill, junk, bill . . ."
16:45:24
PLAY
T-VISION

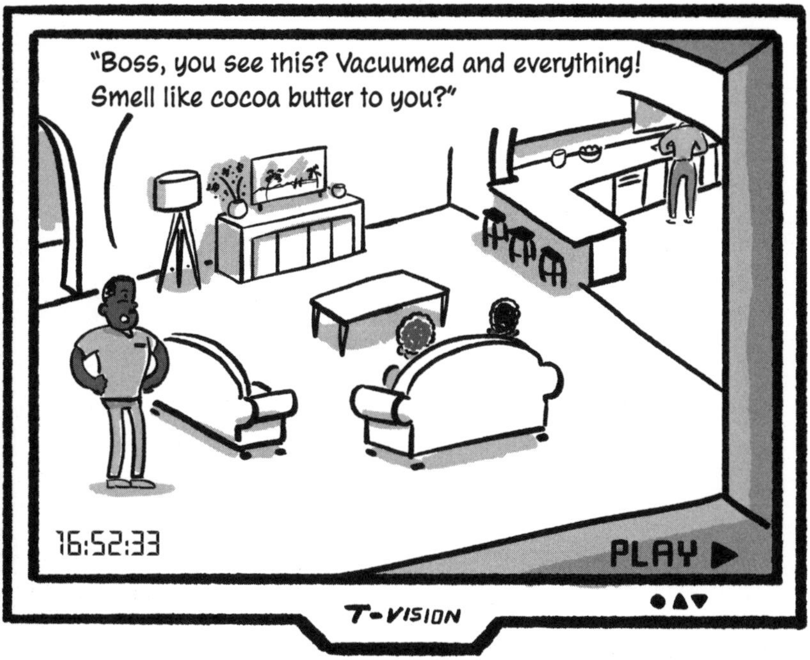
"Boss, you see this? Vacuumed and everything! Smell like cocoa butter to you?"
16:52:33
PLAY
T-VISION

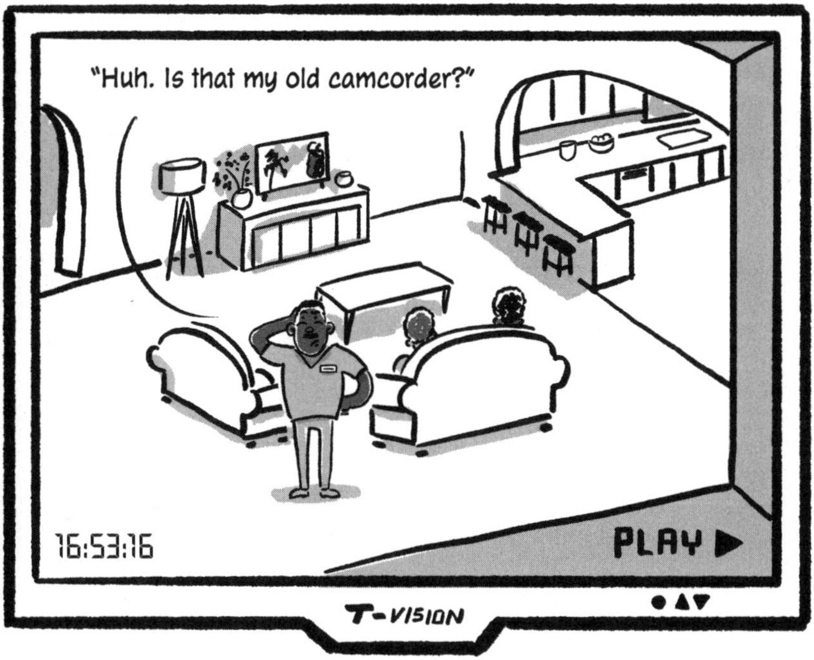
"Huh. Is that my old camcorder?"
16:53:16
PLAY
T-VISION

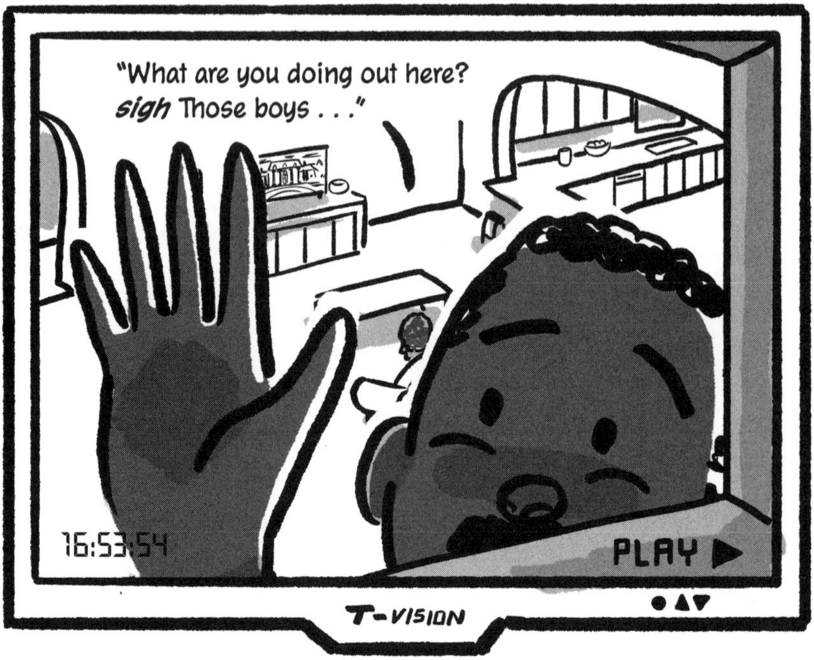
"What are you doing out here? *sigh* Those boys . . ."
16:53:54
PLAY
T-VISION

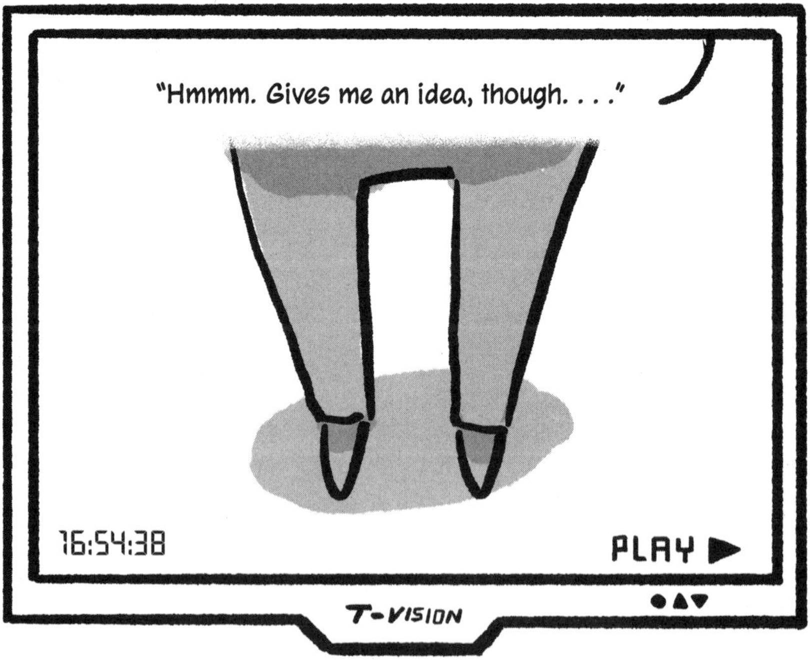
"Hmmm. Gives me an idea, though. . . ."
16:54:38
PLAY
T-VISION

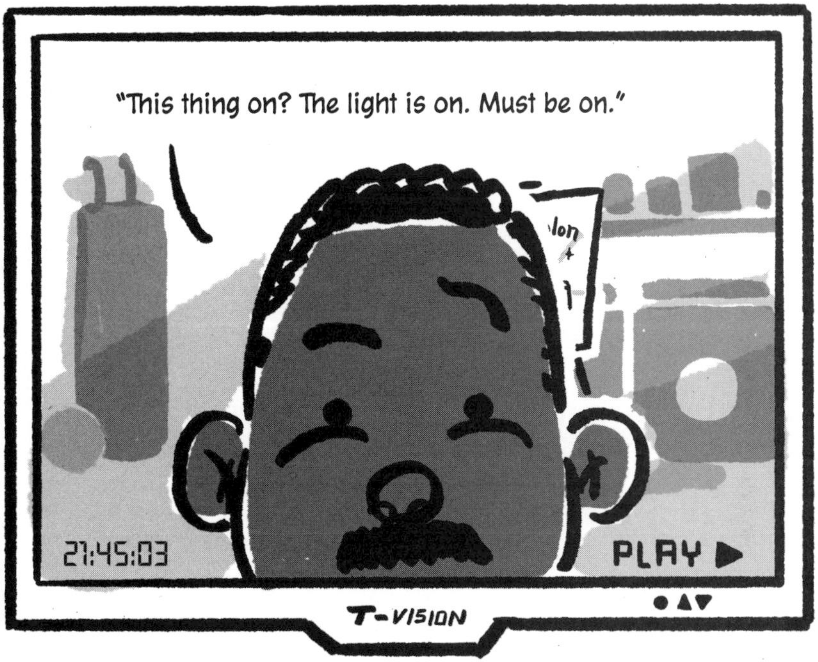
"This thing on? The light is on. Must be on."
lon
21:45:03
PLAY
T-VISION

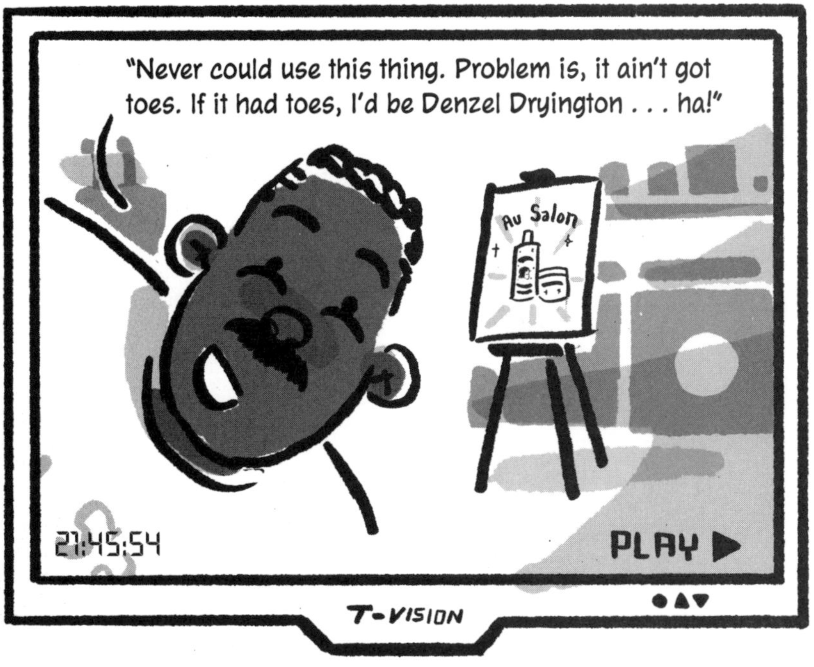
"Never could use this thing. Problem is, it ain't got toes. If it had toes, I'd be Denzel Dryington . . . ha!"
Au Salon
21:45:54
PLAY
T-VISION

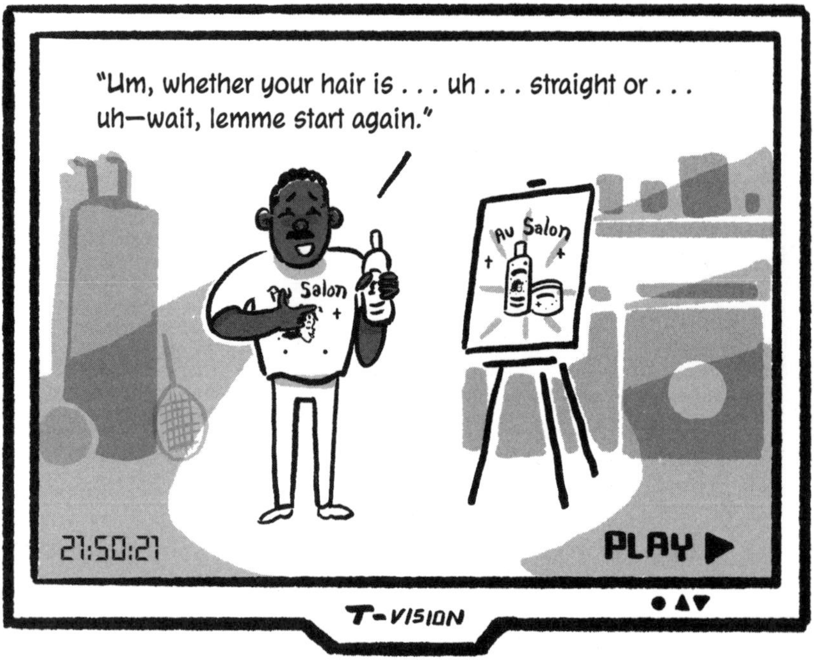
"Um, whether your hair is . . . uh . . . straight or . . . uh—wait, lemme start again."
Au Salon
Au Salon
21:50:21
PLAY
T-VISION

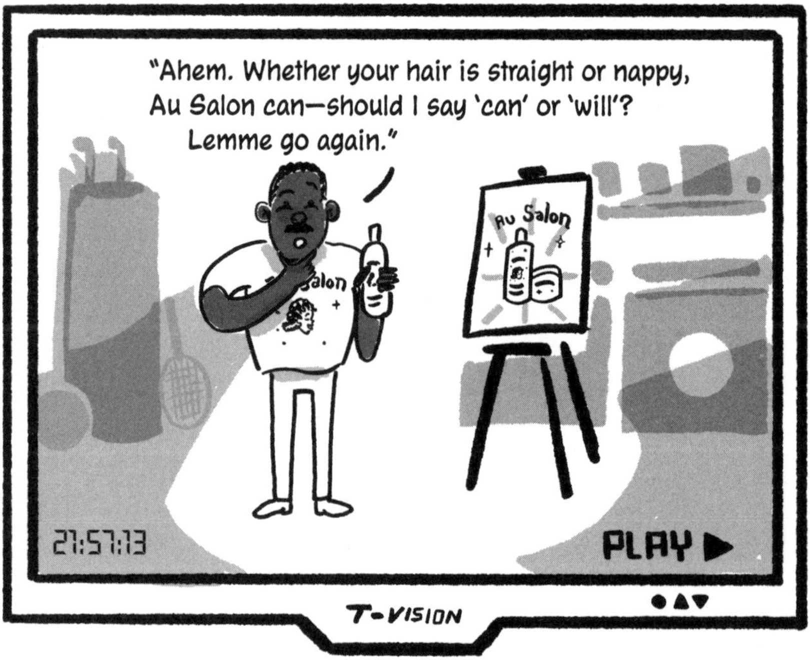
"Ahem. Whether your hair is straight or nappy, Au Salon can—should I say 'can' or 'will'? Lemme go again."
Au Salon
21:57:13
PLAY
T-VISION

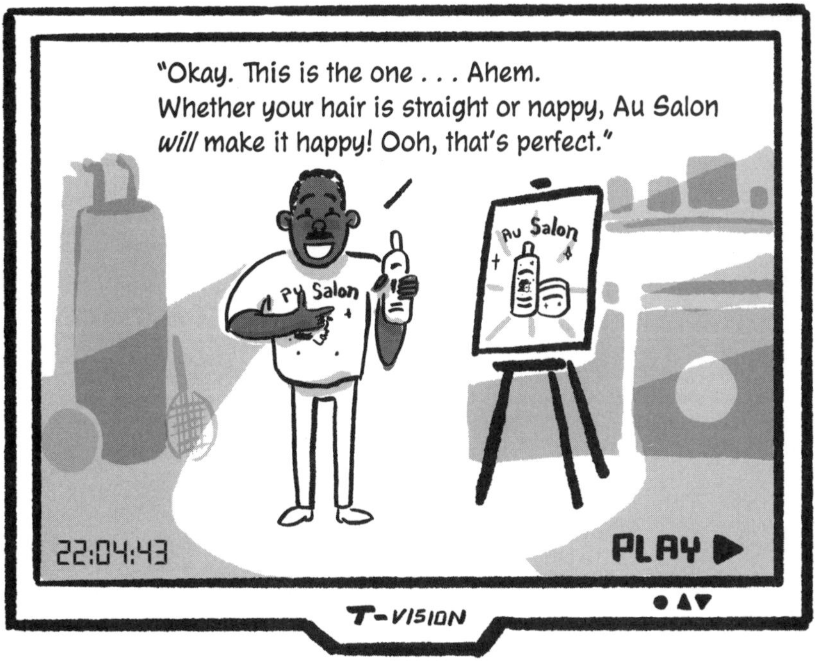
"Okay. This is the one . . . Ahem.
Whether your hair is straight or nappy, Au Salon *will* make it happy! Ooh, that's perfect."
Au Salon
Au Salon
22:04:43
PLAY
T-VISION

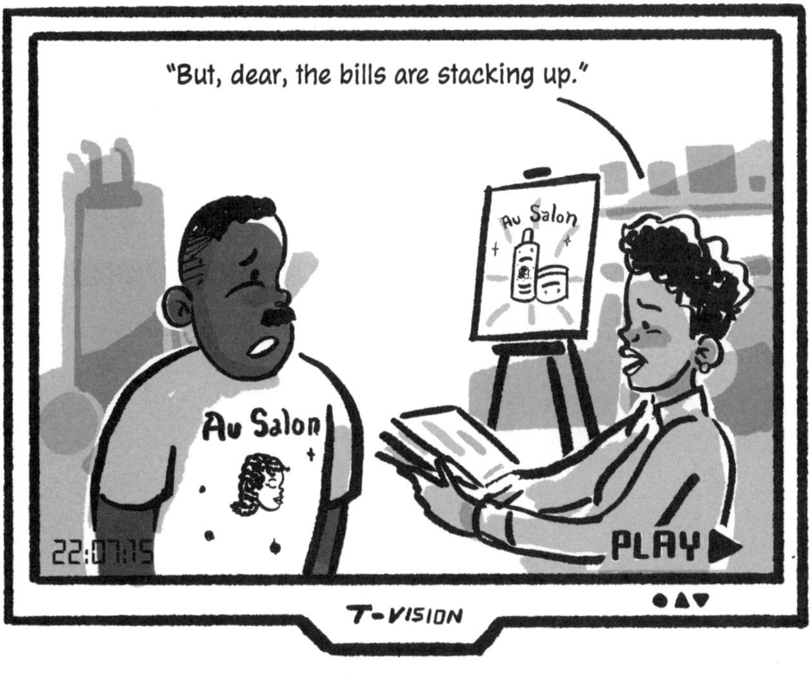
"But, dear, the bills are stacking up."
Au Salon
Au Salon
PLAY
T-VISION

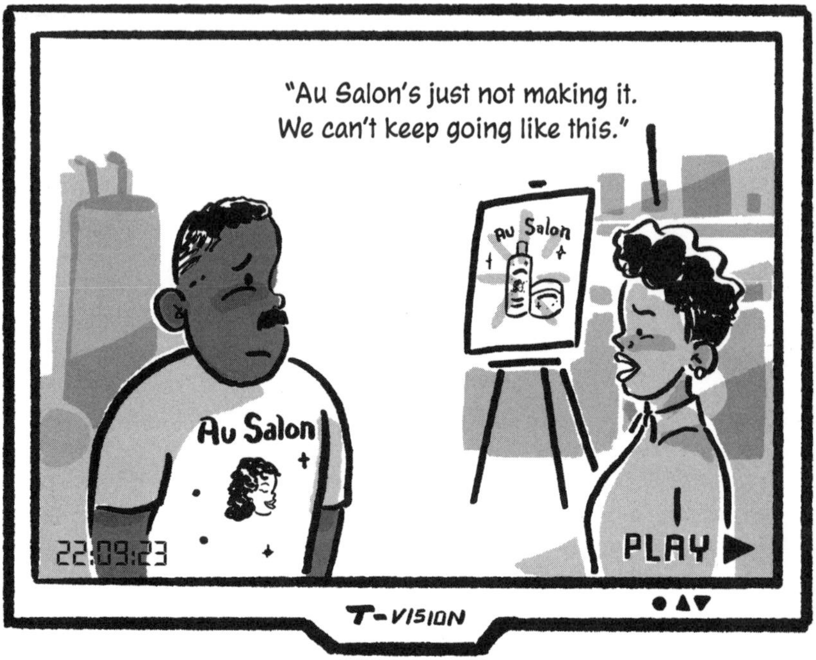
"Au Salon's just not making it.
We can't keep going like this."
Au Salon
Au Salon
22:09:23
PLAY
T-VISION

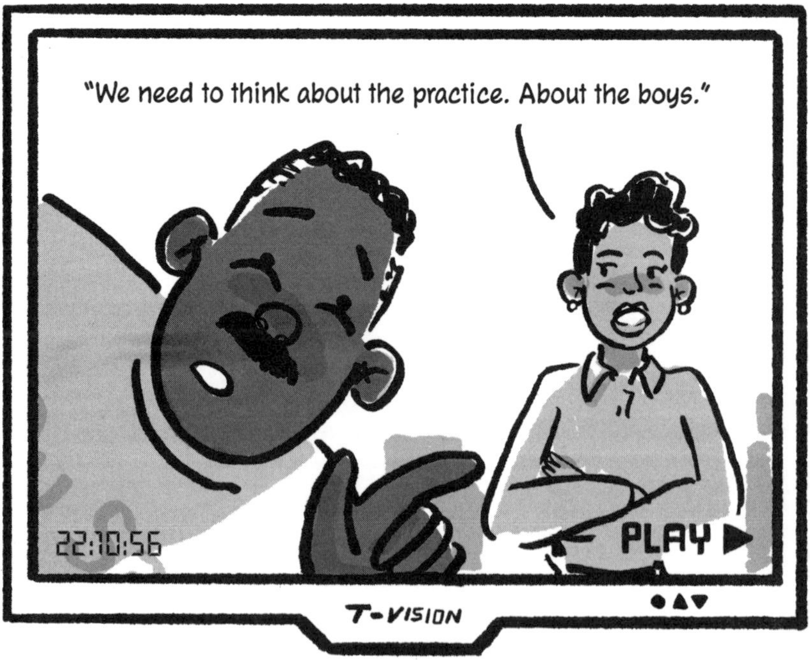
"We need to think about the practice. About the boys."
22:10:56
PLAY
T-VISION

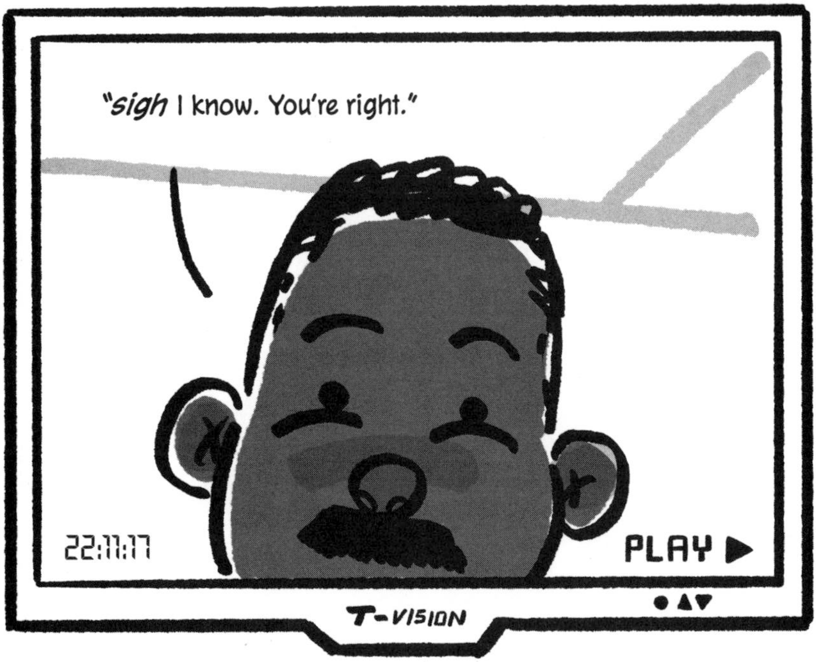
"sigh I know. You're right."
22:11:17
PLAY ▶
T-VISION

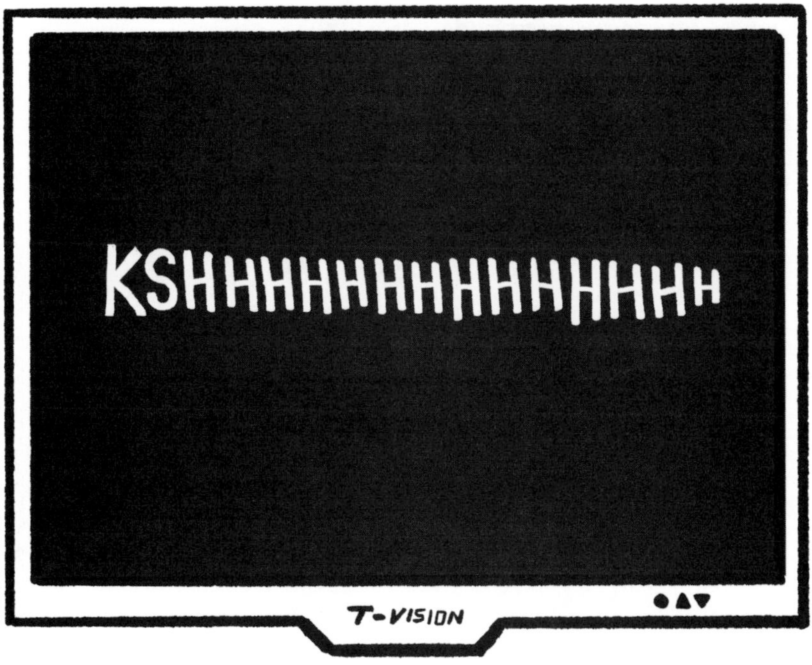
KSHHHHHHHHHHHHHHHH
T-VISION

CHAPTER TWENTY-THREE

LINK HIT THE STOP BUTTON ON THE CAMCORDER and turned off the TV. Then he plopped down into the chair at the desk.

Hud sat on his bed.

Neither spoke. They just sat there, replaying the video over and over in their heads.

After a few minutes, Link said, "I didn't know Au Salon wasn't doing well, did you?"

Hud shook his head. "Unh-unh."

They sat there thinking more.

"Did you see Dad's face?" asked Link.

"Uh-huh," said Hud.

"And Mom," said Link. "She looked so stressed out."

"Yeah," said Hud. "We should have never messed with that dumb old camcorder." He wished he could unsee the looks on their parents' faces, unhear their private conversation.

The boys sat there in silence a few minutes more. Then

Link stood up and started pacing. "So, what are we gonna do about it?" he said. "We gotta do something, right?"

"What do you mean?" said Hud.

"I mean, we're heroes," said Link. "And heroes save the day, right?"

"We're not real heroes," said Hud. "Not in the way that would help Mom and Dad fix Au Salon. We couldn't even get rid of Ms. Joyce."

Link looked at Hud in a way that said *Something about what you just said helped me connect some dots.*

"What?" said Hud at the odd look on Link's face.

Link didn't answer. Instead, he turned the TV back on and hit the PLAY button on the camcorder. The screen was black. He hit the REWIND button and they watched as the video played back in reverse. They watched their parents moving backward in the garage and then again in the den until they saw Ms. Joyce moving backward throughout the house. When they saw her walking backward in the kitchen

away from the dishwasher, Link hit the PLAY button. "Look!" He pointed to the screen. Ms. Joyce was squirting something into the dishwasher. "Look at what she's holding."

Hud got up from the bed and leaned in to have a closer look. It was a bottle of Au Salon. "Hmmm. That's weird."

Link hit the FAST-FORWARD button on the camcorder. The tape squealed forward until he hit the PLAY button again. Now they were watching Ms. Joyce mist something onto the carpet in the den. He pointed at what she was holding again. "Look!"

Hud leaned in again. It was another bottle of Au Salon. "Okaaaay. That's strange."

Again, Link hit the FAST-FORWARD button on the camcorder. And again, the tape squealed forward until he hit the PLAY button. Now they were watching Ms. Joyce back in the kitchen. This time, she was holding a mop and spraying something on the floor. For the third time, Link pointed at what she was holding. "Loo—"

"I see it!" said Hud, realization flashing across his face. "Ms. Joyce has been using Au Salon to clean the house!"

"Not just using it," said Link. "What's another word for 'using something that doesn't belong to you'?"

"Um." Hud thought for a moment. "'Borrowing'?"

"No!" Link rolled his eyes. "'Stealing'!"

Hud gasped as he remembered his encounter with Ms. Joyce and her purse in the hallway. "That's probably why she needed her big ol' purse out in the garage!"

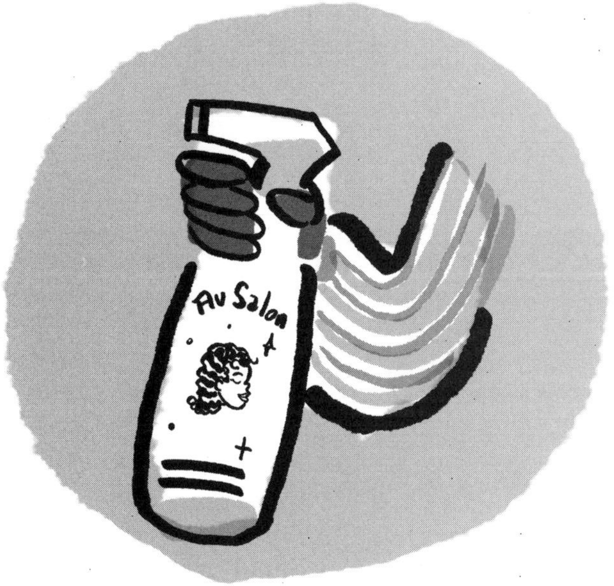
Au Salon

"Exactly," said Link. "She could steal everything out there with that thing! Of course Au Salon isn't doing well. Mom and Dad can't sell it when Ms. Joyce has been stealing it all."

Hud nodded, convinced. It all made sense to him. "So, what now? If we show Mom and Dad this tape, they can get rid of Ms. Joyce and fix Au Salo—"

"No," said Link, shaking his head. "Ms. Joyce has had Mom and Dad fooled from the start. She'd probably just tell them she's been 'helping' them! Can you believe that?"

Hud shook his head. "I knew she was a bad guy."

"Oh, she's so a bad guy," said Link. "I mean, who's been sneaking out into the garage when it's supposed to be Au Salon business only?"

"Ms. Joyce," said Hud, nodding.

"Who's been covering her tracks by cleaning the house a little too good?"

"Ms. Joyce!" said Hud, getting fired up now.

"And who's been lying to Mom and Dad about what perfect little gentlemen we are?"

"Uh, haven't *we* been lying to Mom and Dad about that?" asked Hud.

"No!" said Link. "I mean, sort of, but no! Ms. Joyce is the bad guy here. We're the heroes."

"Oh, right," said Hud.

"No, if Mom and Dad are gonna fix Au Salon, they're gonna need us to get rid of Ms. Joyce for them." Link plopped back down into the chair at the desk and let out a sigh. "I just wish I knew how we were gonna do that."

Hud fell back onto his bed and then slumped to the floor with a sigh of his own. *How do you get rid of a bad guy?*

"Whatever we do, we've gotta go big, right?" said Link, more to himself than to Hud. "Something so big she can't cover it up."

Hud stretched out his legs and accidentally kicked something. *Huh?*

"Or maybe we go sneaky instead of big?" said Link. "We do something she doesn't see coming."

Hud looked down to his feet, curious. *Hmmm.* It was the video game system sitting on the floor in front of the desk.

"Maybe we go big *and* sneaky?" said Link. "Ugh. I dunno . . ."

Hud spotted his *Boomer Bros.* game cartridge sticking out the top. His eyes lit up.

"Can something even be sneaky if it's big?" said Link. "I mean—"

"Uh, Link," said Hud. "I think I have an idea, but you're probably not gonna like it."

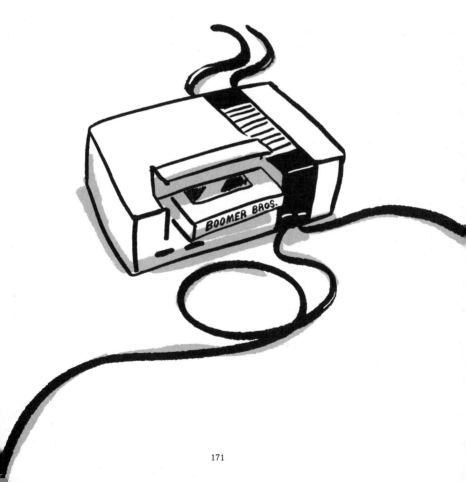

CHAPTER TWENTY-FOUR

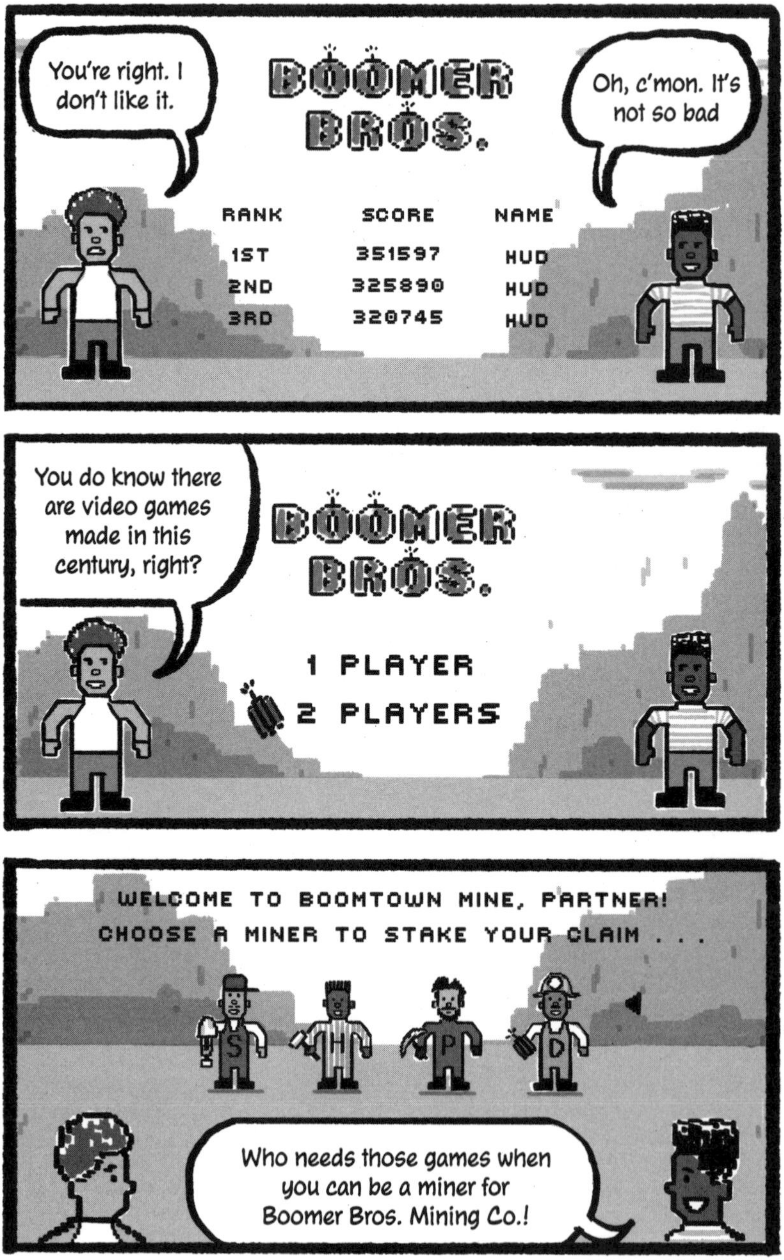
You're right. I don't like it.
BOOMER BROS.
Oh, c'mon. It's not so bad
RANK SCORE NAME
1ST 351597 HUD
2ND 325890 HUD
3RD 320745 HUD
You do know there are video games made in this century, right?
BOOMER BROS.
1 PLAYER
2 PLAYERS
WELCOME TO BOOMTOWN MINE, PARTNER!
CHOOSE A MINER TO STAKE YOUR CLAIM . . .
S
H
P
D
Who needs those games when you can be a miner for Boomer Bros. Mining Co.!

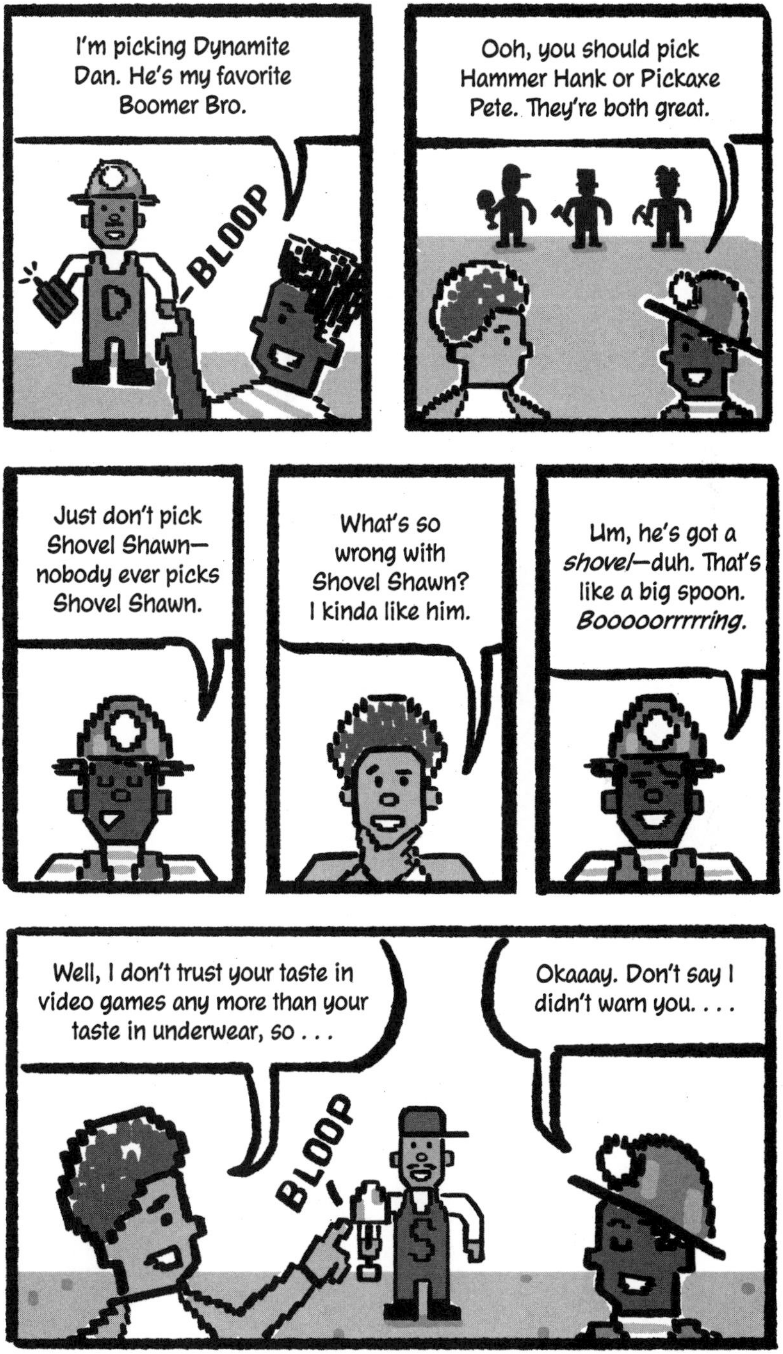
I'm picking Dynamite Dan. He's my favorite Boomer Bro.
BLOOP
Ooh, you should pick Hammer Hank or Pickaxe Pete. They're both great.
Just don't pick Shovel Shawn—nobody ever picks Shovel Shawn.
What's so wrong with Shovel Shawn? I kinda like him.
Um, he's got a *shovel*—duh. That's like a big spoon. *Booooorrrrring.*
Well, I don't trust your taste in video games any more than your taste in underwear, so . . .
BLOOP
Okaaay. Don't say I didn't warn you. . . .

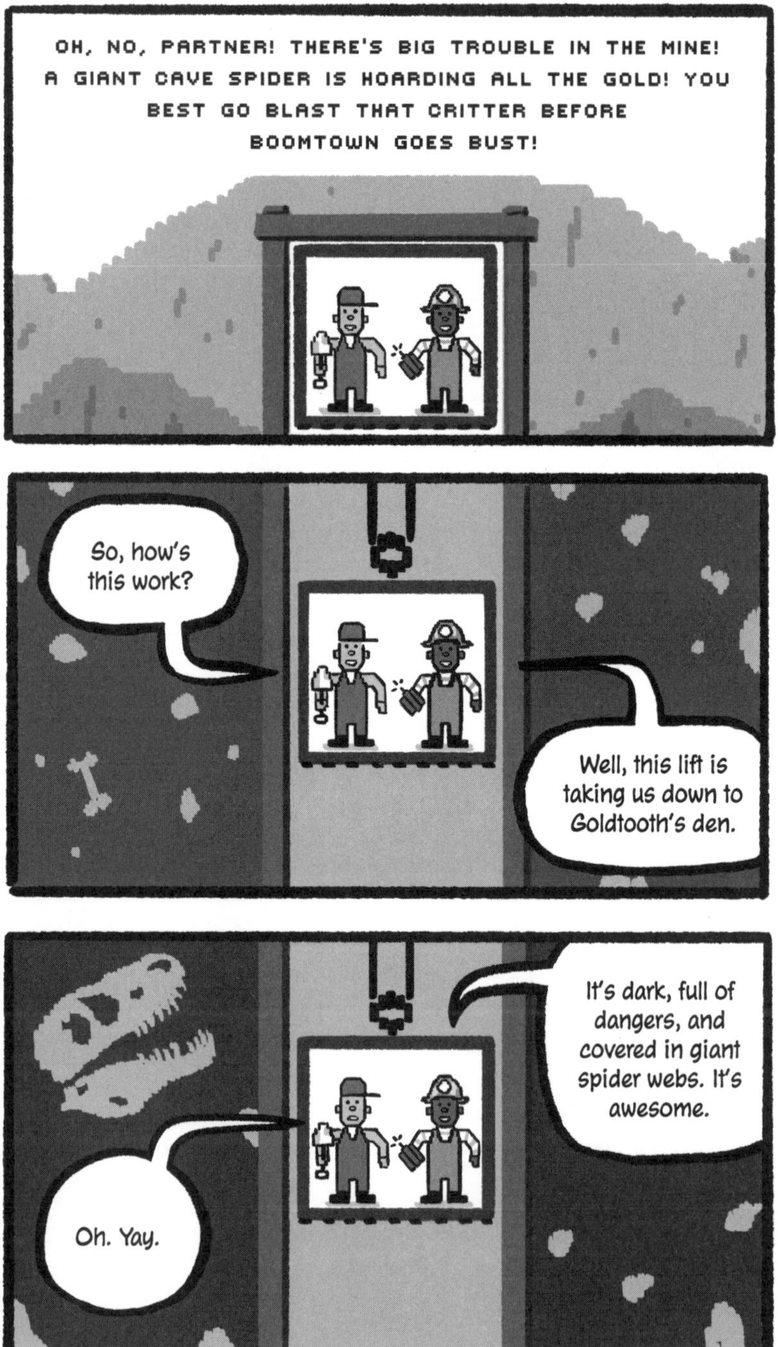
OH, NO, PARTNER! THERE'S BIG TROUBLE IN THE MINE! A GIANT CAVE SPIDER IS HOARDING ALL THE GOLD! YOU BEST GO BLAST THAT CRITTER BEFORE BOOMTOWN GOES BUST!
So, how's this work?
Well, this lift is taking us down to Goldtooth's den.
It's dark, full of dangers, and covered in giant spider webs. It's awesome.
Oh. Yay.

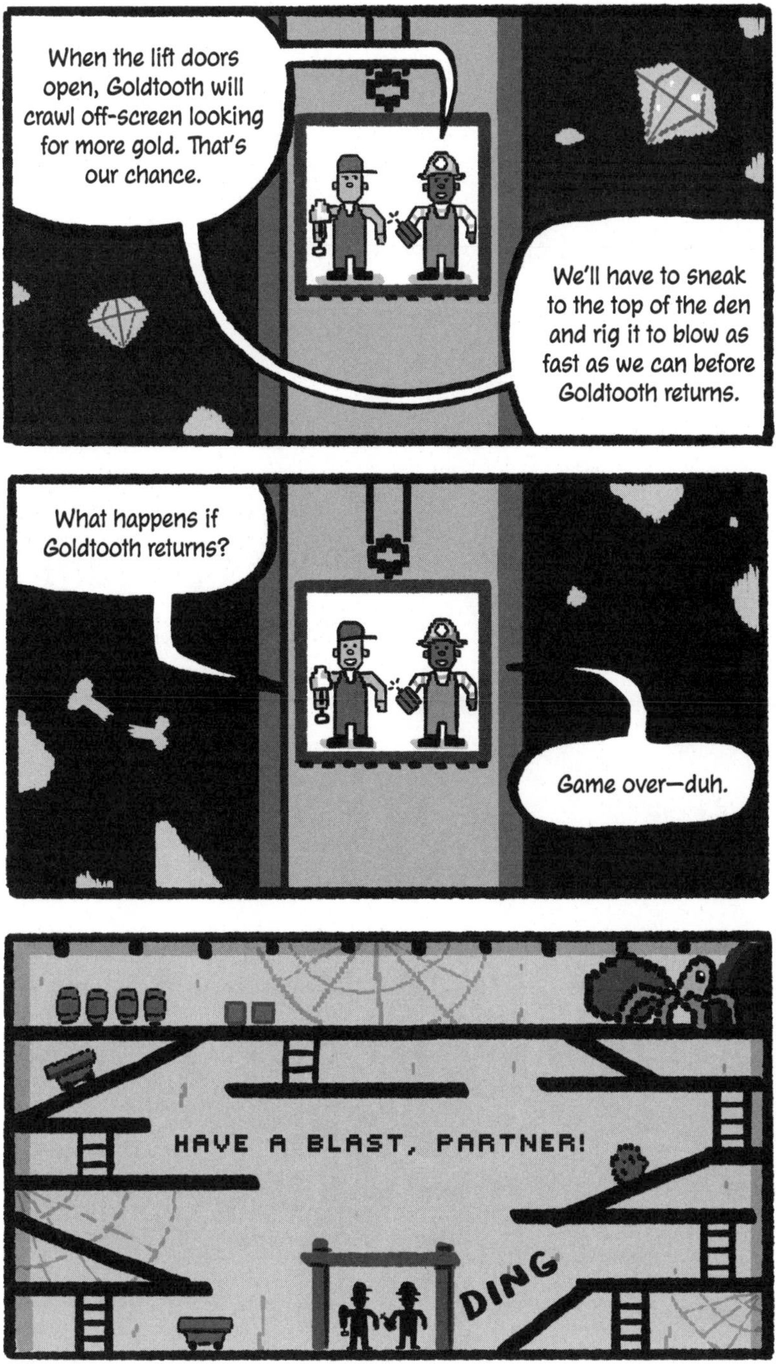
When the lift doors open, Goldtooth will crawl off-screen looking for more gold. That's our chance.
We'll have to sneak to the top of the den and rig it to blow as fast as we can before Goldtooth returns.
What happens if Goldtooth returns?
Game over—duh.
HAVE A BLAST, PARTNER!
DING

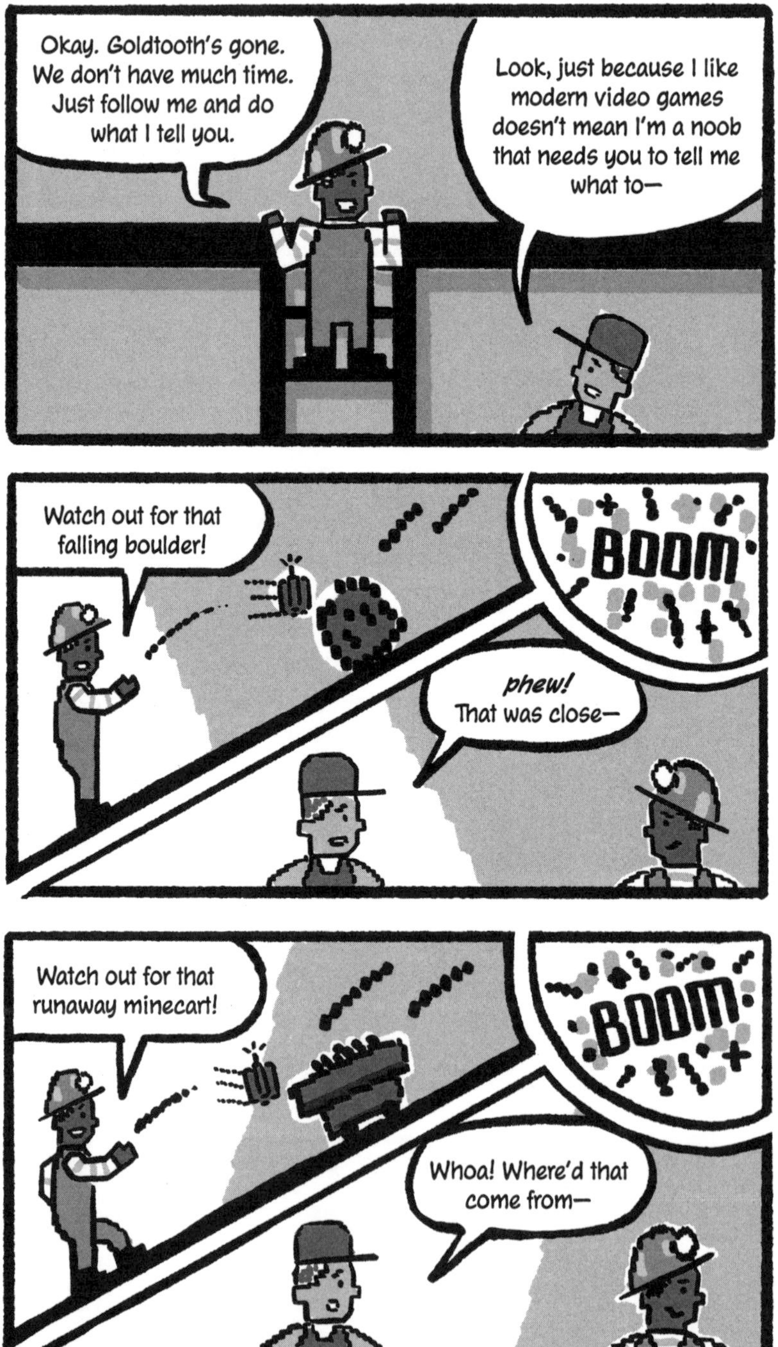
Okay. Goldtooth's gone. We don't have much time. Just follow me and do what I tell you.
Look, just because I like modern video games doesn't mean I'm a noob that needs you to tell me what to—
Watch out for that falling boulder!
BOOM
phew! That was close—
Watch out for that runaway minecart!
BOOM
Whoa! Where'd that come from—

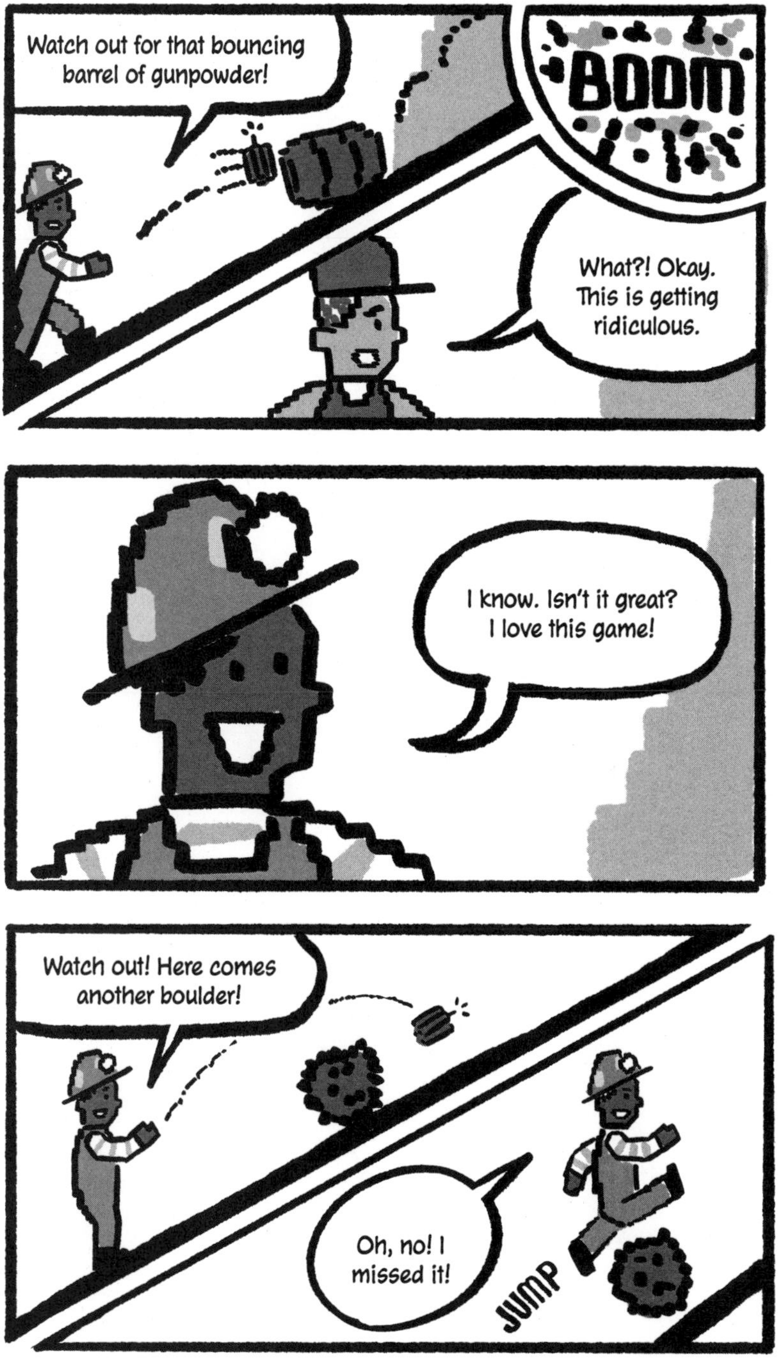
Watch out for that bouncing barrel of gunpowder!
BOOM
What?! Okay. This is getting ridiculous.
I know. Isn't it great? I love this game!
Watch out! Here comes another boulder!
Oh, no! I missed it!
JUMP

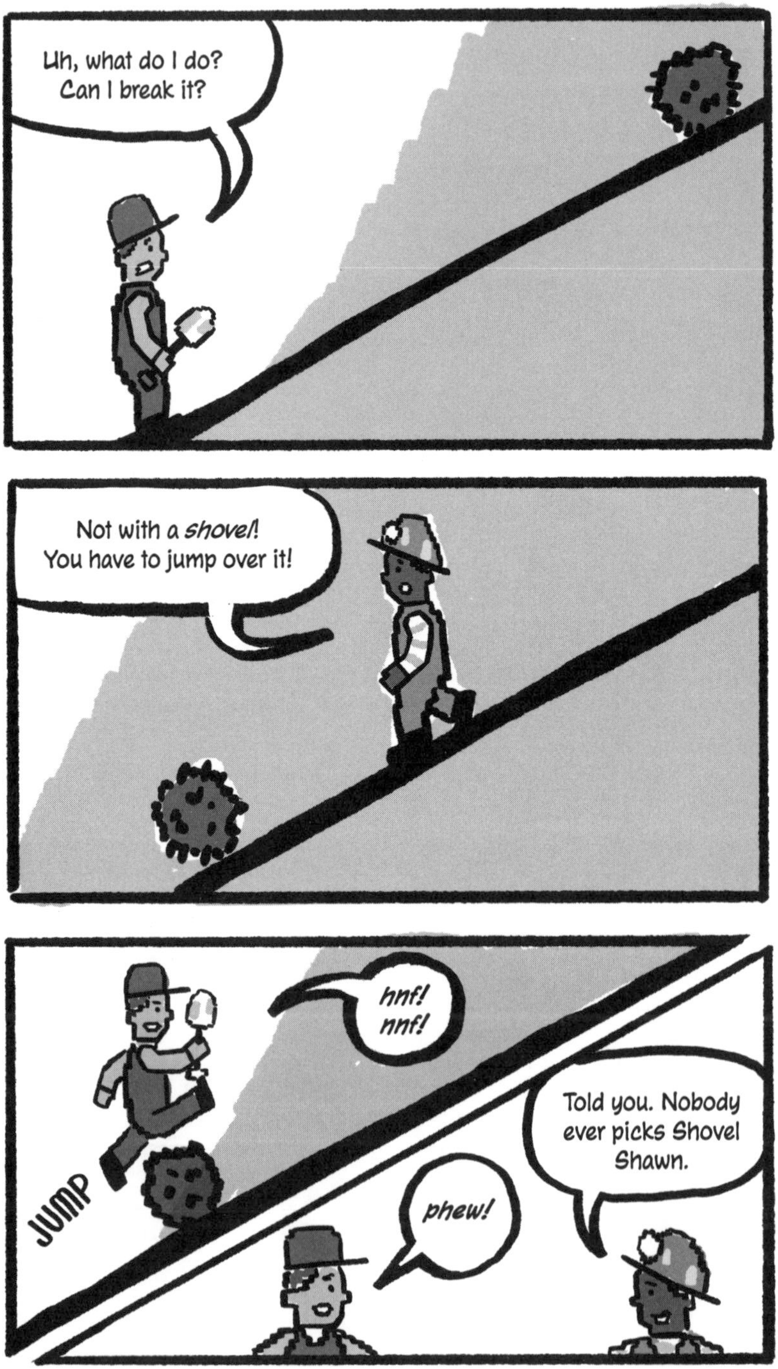
Uh, what do I do? Can I break it?
Not with a *shovel*! You have to jump over it!
hnf! nnf!
JUMP
phew!
Told you. Nobody ever picks Shovel Shawn.

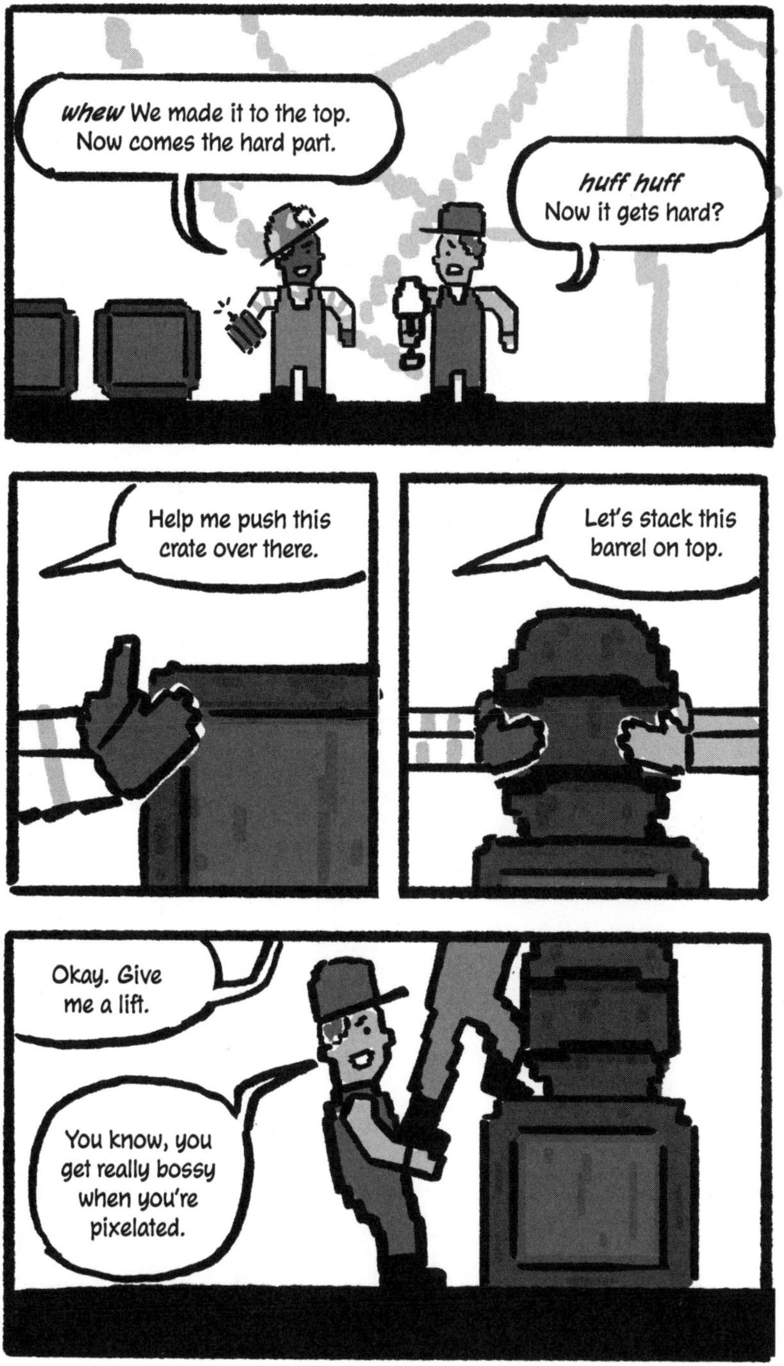
whew We made it to the top. Now comes the hard part.
huff huff Now it gets hard?
Help me push this crate over there.
Let's stack this barrel on top.
Okay. Give me a lift.
You know, you get really bossy when you're pixelated.

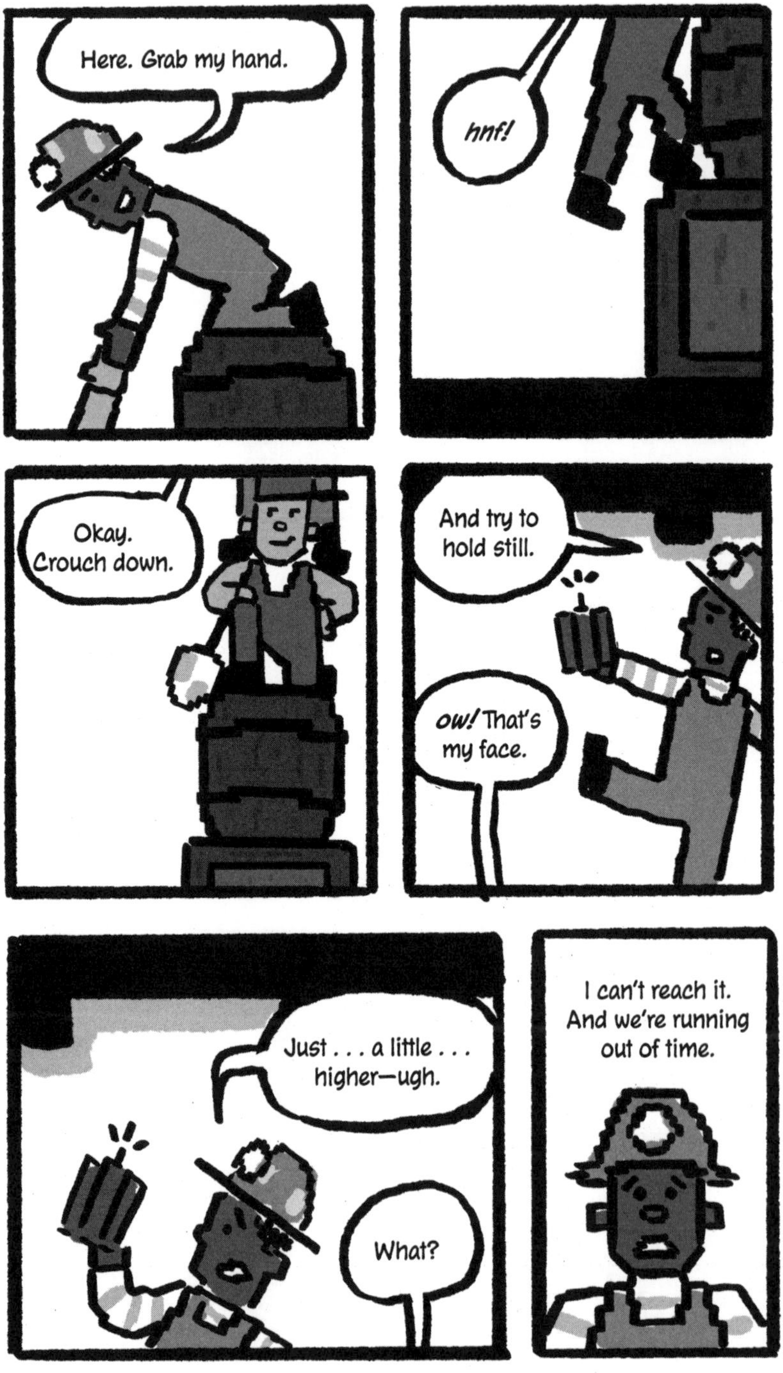
Here. Grab my hand.
hnf!
Okay. Crouch down.
And try to hold still.
OW! That's my face.
Just . . . a little . . . higher—ugh.
What?
I can't reach it. And we're running out of time.

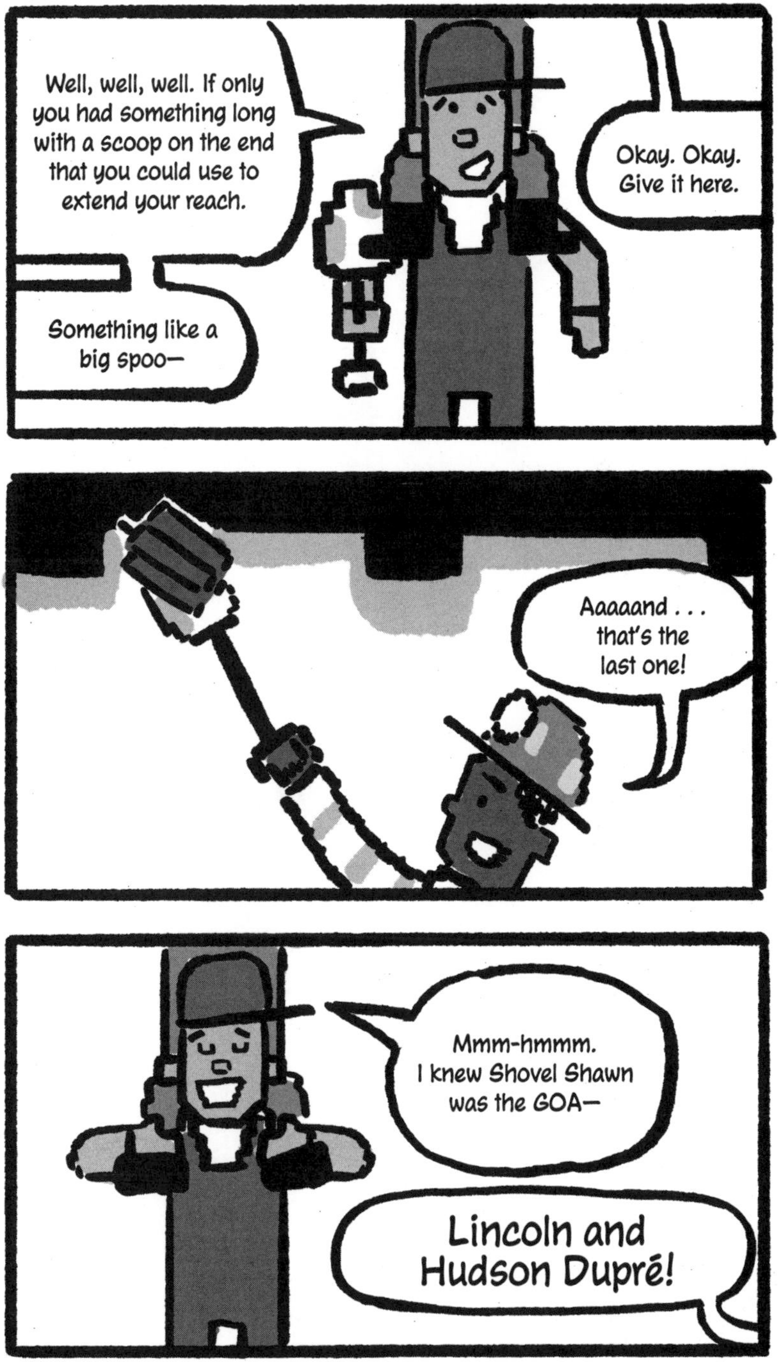
Well, well, well. If only you had something long with a scoop on the end that you could use to extend your reach.
Something like a big spoo—
Okay. Okay. Give it here.
Aaaaand . . . that's the last one!
Mmm-hmmm. I knew Shovel Shawn was the GOA—
Lincoln and Hudson Dupré!

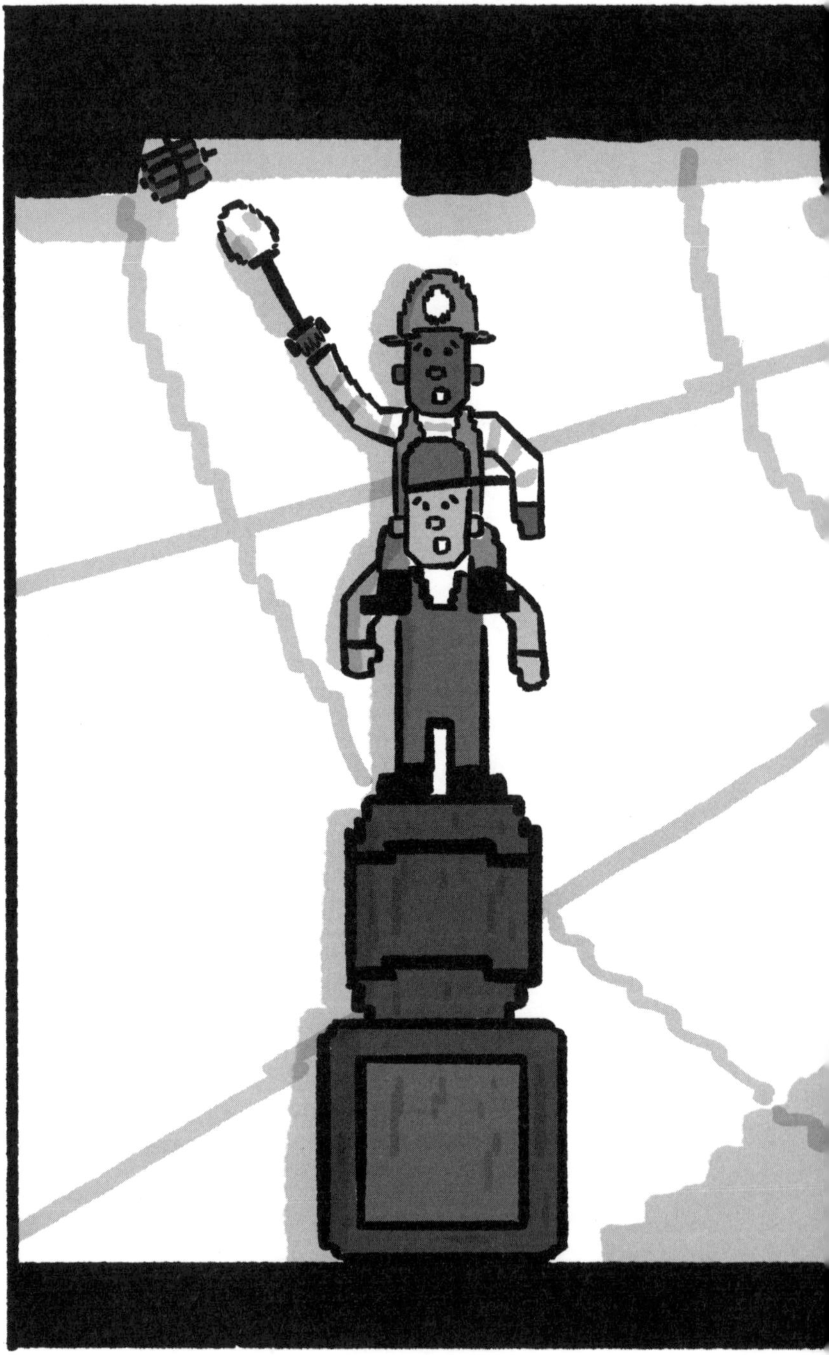

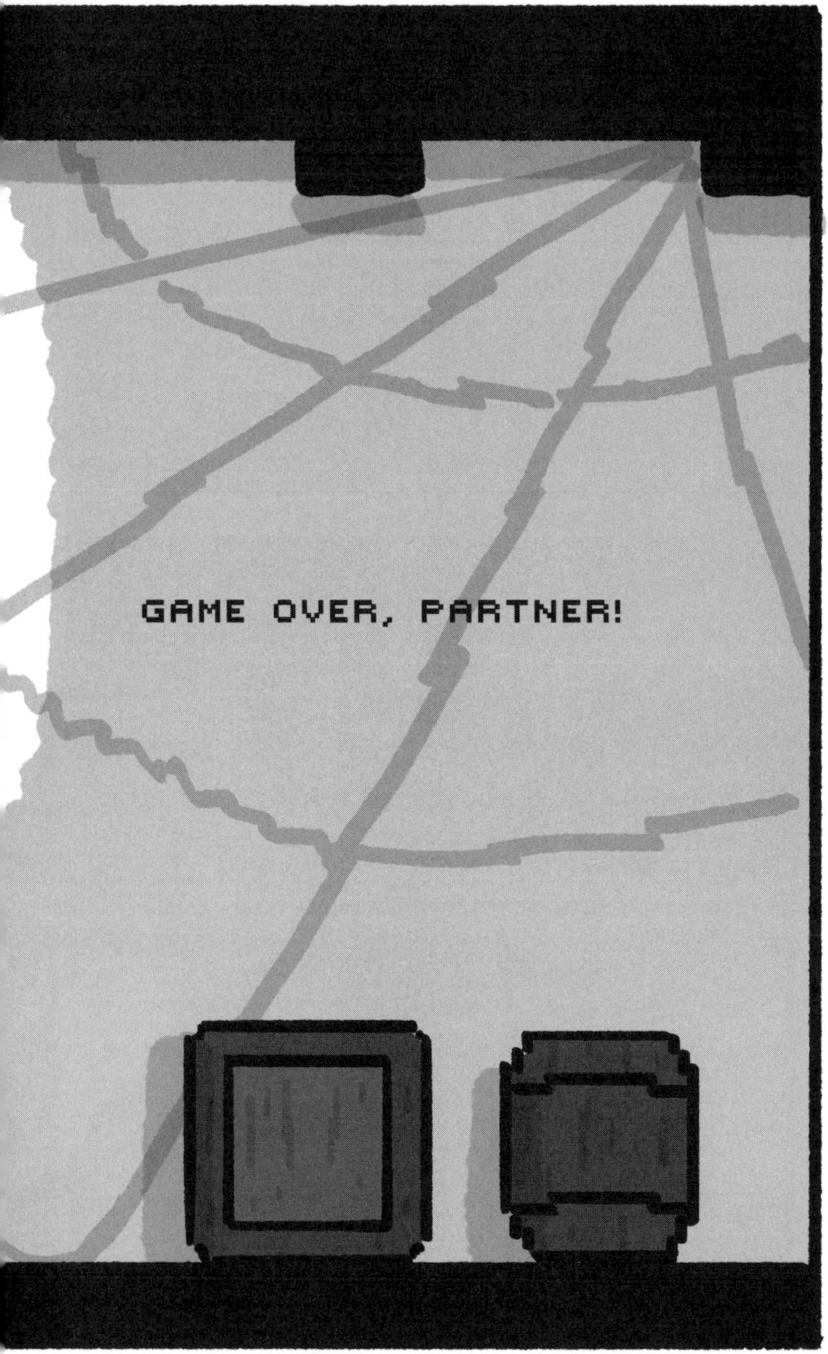
GAME OVER, PARTNER!

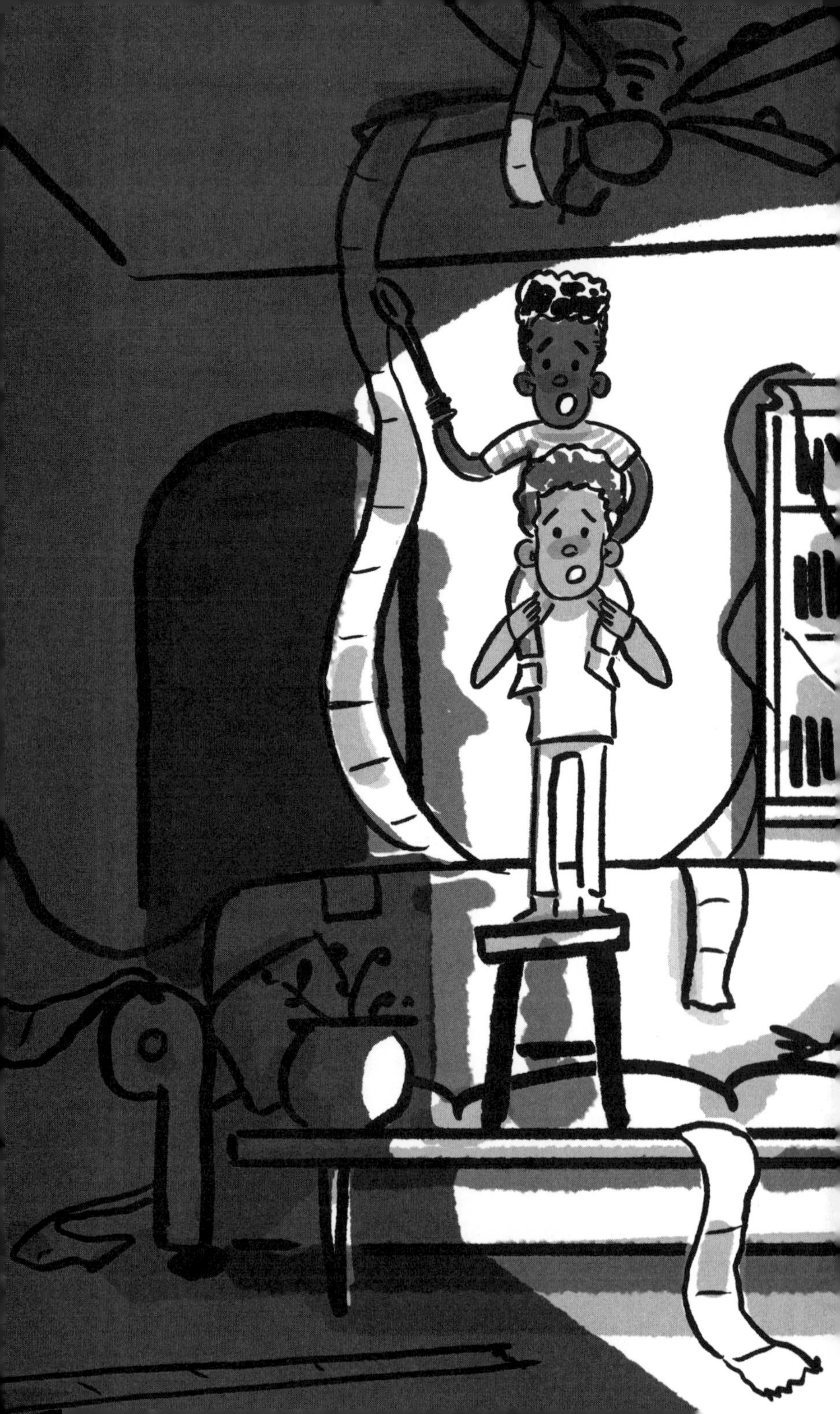

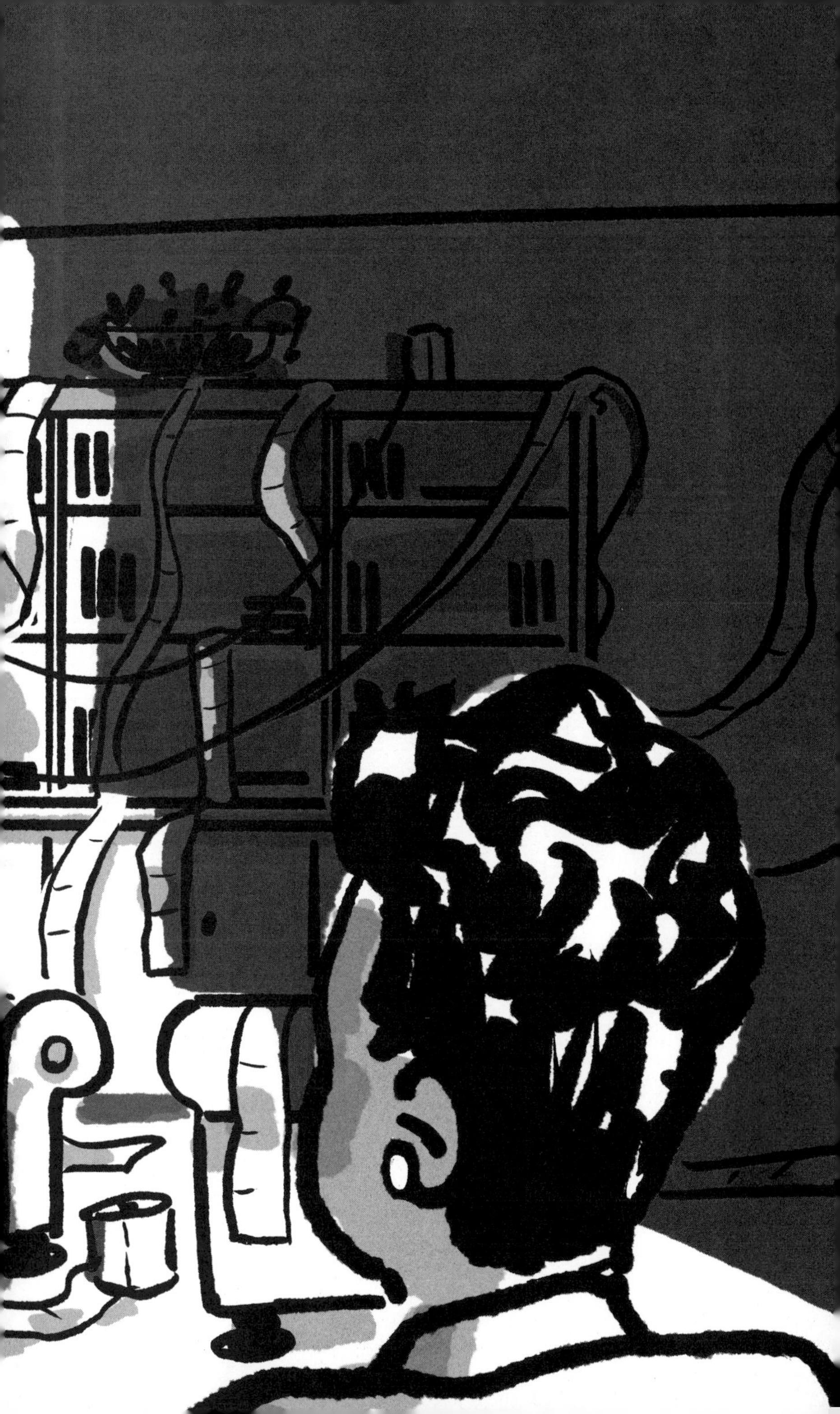

CHAPTER TWENTY-FIVE

"WHAT ON EARTH?"

Hud flinched at the sound of their mom's voice and dropped the spoon. Link flinched at the spoon hitting him in the head and nearly dropped Hud. The boys teetered on the edge of the barstool, which tottered on the edge of the coffee table.

"If you don't get down right this minute!" Mrs. Dupré hurried over to hold the barstool steady as Hud shimmied awkwardly down Link's shoulders. "What were you thinking?! You could have broken something!"

"Well, I told Link we should move the vase off the coffee table," said Hud, as he climbed down the barstool, nearly kicking the vase in the process. "But he said—"

"Not the vase, son!" said Mrs. Dupré. "I don't care about the vase! You could have broken *you* . . . an arm, a leg—your neck!" She pulled Hud in for a hug as he stepped off the coffee table, relieved to have him safe on the ground. "You're so lucky you didn't fall."

Hud could hardly breathe she was holding him so tight.

"And you!" Mrs. Dupré directed her attention at Link, who was just now climbing down the barstool. "You're the older brother. You say you don't need a babysitter, but then you do this?!"

"Sorry, Mom," said Link as he stepped off the coffee table.

As soon as Link had both feet on the ground, Mrs. Dupré pulled him in for a hug also, squishing Hud even more. "You're lucky too," she said, rubbing his back for a moment before patting his behind. "Lucky you didn't drop my baby."

Mrs. Dupré released the boys and looked around the room. "Is that toilet paper?" She shook her head. "I just don't know *what* would make you two do this—"

"Now whose tail done turnt off all the lights this time?" came a voice from the kitchen.

Mrs. Dupré and the boys looked over to see Ms. Joyce standing in the doorway, holding a basket of laundry, her gold tooth flashing in the dark.

"Nothing but junk today, boss," came another voice from the front door.

Mrs. Dupré and the boys turned around to see Dr. Dupré in the entryway, sorting through a stack of mail, the front door still wide open.

"'Bout time," said Dr. Dupré as he turned to close the door. "Another bill woulda broke— Huh? Why's it so dark in here?"

What happened next seemed to happen in slow motion.

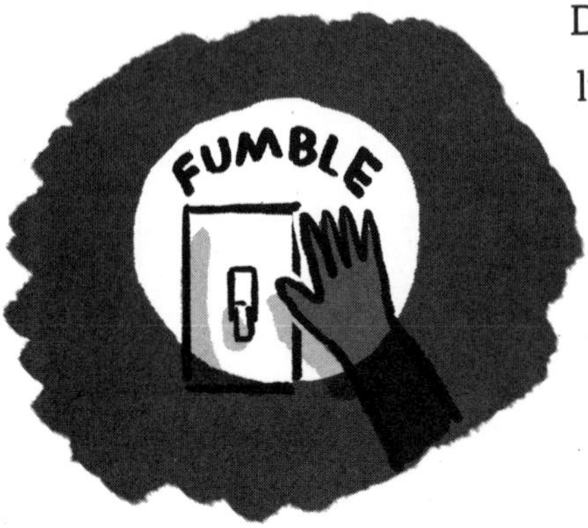
FUMBLE

Dr. Dupré reached for the light switch just inside the den. "I'll get the lights."

Link pulled Hud close enough to hear a panicked whisper. "The water balloons!"

Mrs. Dupré called out to Ms. Joyce. "Don't move, Ms. Joyce. The boys have made a mess in here. Let Dr. D turn on the lights."

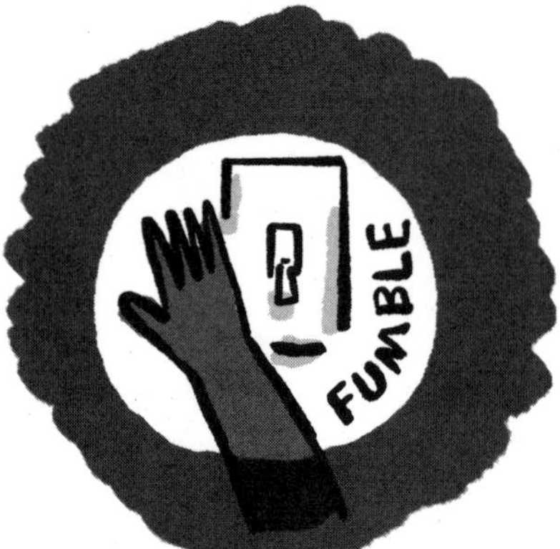
FUMBLE

Ms. Joyce shifted the laundry basket to her hip. "Oh, Lord. What they do now?"

Dr. Dupré fumbled around in the dark, blindly searching the wall for the switch. "It's around here somewhere. One sec."

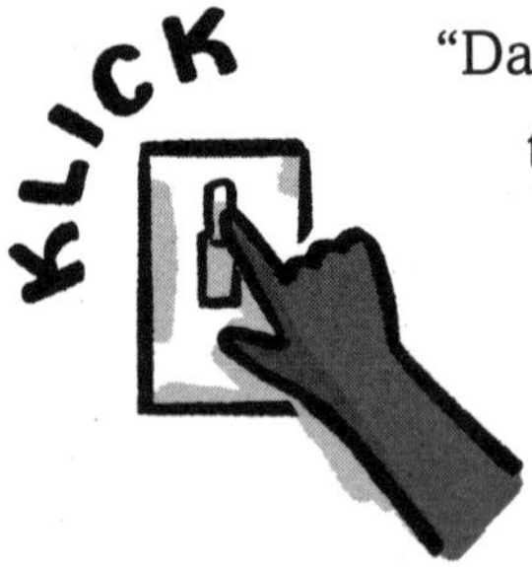
KLICK

Hud lunged toward their dad in the dark. "Dad, wai—" He kicked the edge of the couch and fell to the floor. "Ow!"

Link scrambled onto the coffee table. He reached up for the pull string, the one that controlled the ceiling fan. It was dangling somewhere in the dark above him. "I can't find it!"

Dr. Dupré found the light switch. "Found it."

"NOOOOO!" shouted Link and Hud.

It was too late. Dr. Dupré flipped the switch.

The lights in the den turned on.

So did the ceiling fan.

The water balloons went flying before any of the grown-ups in the room knew what was happening.

The first balloon hit the wall near the bookshelf—*sploosh*!

The second balloon hit the floor near the TV console— *sploosh*!

Link and Hud both winced as the third and final balloon found a more vocal target— *sploosh*!

"LINCOLN AND HUDSON DUPRÉ!"

CHAPTER TWENTY-SIX

DO YOU KNOW WHAT HAPPENS TO TOILET PAPER when it gets wet?

That's right. It gets gloopy.

Mrs. Dupré stood in the middle of the den under the ceiling fan, soaking wet and freezing cold. If that weren't bad enough, the air from the fan started blowing streams of toilet paper across the room.

Can you guess what happened next?

A wet Mrs. Dupré became a wet and gloopy Mrs. Dupré.

Oooooh! Link and Hud were in troublllllllllllle!

Mrs. Dupré stared daggers at the boys. They didn't move. They didn't speak.

Ms. Joyce grabbed a towel from the laundry basket and wrapped it around Mrs. Dupré's shoulders. "Don't need you catchin' no cold."

Dr. Dupré rushed over and pulled the pull string on the ceiling fan to switch it off. He looked at the boys and shook his head. "What were y'all thinking?"

Mrs. Dupré dried her face with the towel and pulled the gloopy toilet paper from her hair. As she pulled a glop of toilet paper from her neck, she looked at the boys and said, "You're both going to clean this den from top to bottom. You're going to clean up every last drop of water and every last shred of toilet paper. You're going to put all the furniture back where it belongs. And when you're done, you're going to go straight to your room and stay there for the night. Am I understood?"

The boys nodded and did as they were told.

While they cleaned up the den, their dad cleaned out their room. He took their TV, their video games, the comic books, and the snack stash.

When they finished in the den and their mom, now showered and gloop-free, had inspected their work, they headed to their room for the night, where there was nothing left to do but lie in their bunks and talk:

Their trap hadn't worked. "Man, Mom and Dad ruined it."

So, Ms. Joyce hadn't been busted. "She shoulda got in trouble. Not us."

But their parents had talked to her after. "What do you think they were saying?"

They had talked in the kitchen. "Couldn't hear from the den."

They had seen them, though. "They were waving their hands around a lot."

So, maybe their parents *had* been mad at her. "Maybe. Hard to tell."

Then their parents had walked her to the front door. "Nothing weird about that."

But their mom had hugged her. "And she never does that."

And their dad had walked her outside. "He never does that, either."

They hadn't had a chance to think about it until now. "But, what if . . ."

knock! knock!

Link and Hud groaned awake, bleary-eyed and groggy. The sun shone through their bedroom window.

"Morning, fellas," said Dr. Dupré as he opened the door. "Let's get moving. Your mama and I need to talk to y'all before y'all head to school."

The boys rolled out of bed, got dressed, and shuffled into the kitchen, still half asleep.

"Good morning, you two," said Mrs. Dupré from the table, as she cut her grapefruit. "Sleep okay?"

"Mmmm," said Link with a nod, as he sat down to join her. He slumped back in his chair and let out a big yawn. *OOOOhhh*!

Hud nodded silently as he shuffled over to the pantry, his eyes half closed.

"Well, I hope you got a chance to think things over," said Mrs. Dupré. "And I hope you'll make better decisions next time." She took a bite of grapefruit, and her lips puckered.

Link nodded, still sleepy. "Mm-hmm."

Hud found the box of Fruity Rings in the pantry and set it on the table, nodding as he shuffled past on his way to the fridge.

Dr. Dupré poured a cup of coffee and then took a seat at the table. "So, I spoke with Layla's folks this morning," he said.

Link perked up. "Hmmm?"

Hud grabbed the milk from the fridge and set it on the table, nodding as he shuffled over to the dishwasher.

“She’ll be here to watch y’all when you get home from school today,” said Dr. Dupré. He took a sip of coffee.

Link sat up, alert now.

Hud pulled a clean bowl from the dishwasher and set it on the table, nodding as he shuffled over to the silverware drawer.

“As much as we care about Ms. Joyce,” said Mrs. Dupré, “after what happened last night,”—she shook her head—“your father and I have decided you might be too much for her to handle.”

Link’s eyes got wide.

Hud picked out a spoon from the drawer and shuffled over to the table. He nodded as he sat down.

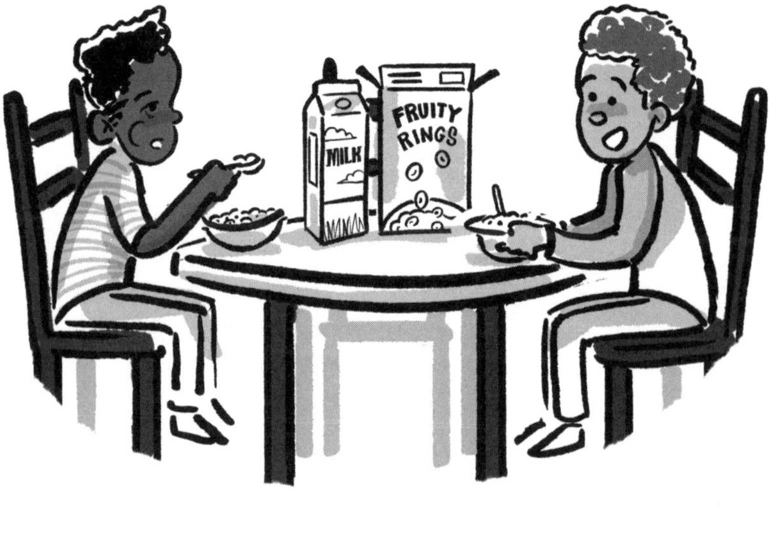
MILK
FRUITY RINGS

"Don't get any ideas," said Mrs. Dupré, seeing the look on Link's face. "You're both still on very thin ice." She took another bite of her grapefruit. Her lips puckered again.

Link tried to look bored about the news. "Mm-hmm."

Hud nodded as he poured Fruity Rings into his bowl.

"This is just until we can figure something else out," said Dr. Dupré. He took another swig of his coffee.

"So, behave yourselves, okay?" added Mrs. Dupré. She took another—and by the look of the wince on her face, the final—bite of her grapefruit. "Ahem. I don't want to hear you've given Layla a hard time. Understood?"

Link nodded and raised his hands as if to say, *I would never.*

Hud nodded as he sloshed milk into his bowl of cereal.

Dr. Dupré finished off his coffee, picked up Mrs. Dupré's plate, and put the dishes in the sink. Mrs. Dupré stood up from the table, and they both turned to leave the kitchen.

"Oh, one more thing," added Dr. Dupré, turning back to look at the boys. "I shouldn't have to say this, but I didn't think I'd have to tell y'all no water balloons in the house, either." He shook his head. "Stay out of the garage. Okay? Au Salon business only." Then he turned and followed Mrs. Dupré.

Link waited for their dad to leave. Then he smiled.

Hud took a big bite of his cereal—*crunch*—and then looked over at Link. "Sho, wush habbenin?"

"We did it!"

CHAPTER TWENTY-SEVEN

"SO, HOW DOES IT FEEL?" SAID LINK.

"What?" said Hud.

"To be a real-life hero—duh!"

The boys were walking home from school, barely able to contain their excitement.

"Oh. It feels awesome," said Hud. "I just wish Mom and Dad felt that way about it."

They turned down their street.

"Real heroes don't do it for the credit," said Link. "I don't even mind Dad taking all our stuff. I can live with no TV, no video games, no comic books, no snacks—"

"Whoa," said Hud. "Don't push it."

They laughed as they reached their driveway.

"I'm just sayin'," Link continued, "Dad can have it all if it means no more laundry, no more hard time in the bathroom—no more Goldtooth!"

They laughed some more as they reached their front door.

“How long do you think we’ll be in trouble?” said Hud.

“I dunno,” said Link. “But I think we’re already past the worst of it.”

They punched in the keycode.

“You do?” said Hud.

“Definitely,” said Link. “Besides, what could possibly be worse than Ms. Joyce?”

They laughed and laughed as they opened the door and went inside.

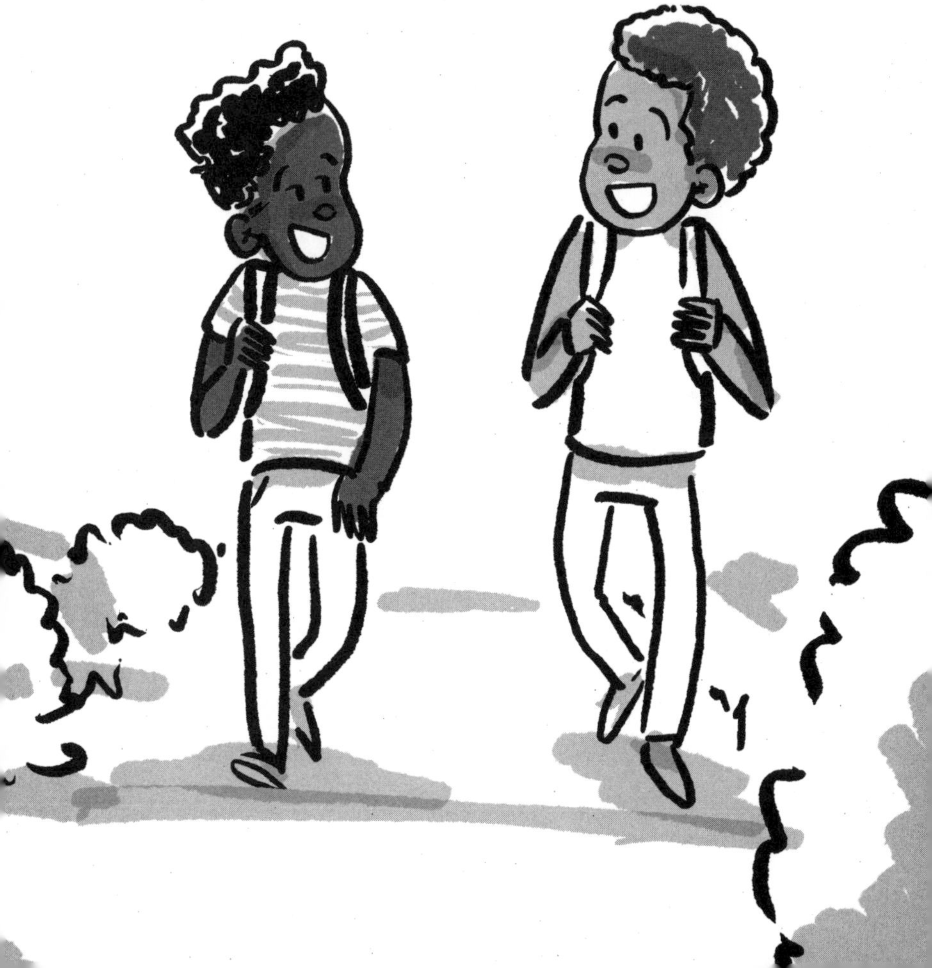

CHAPTER TWENTY-EIGHT

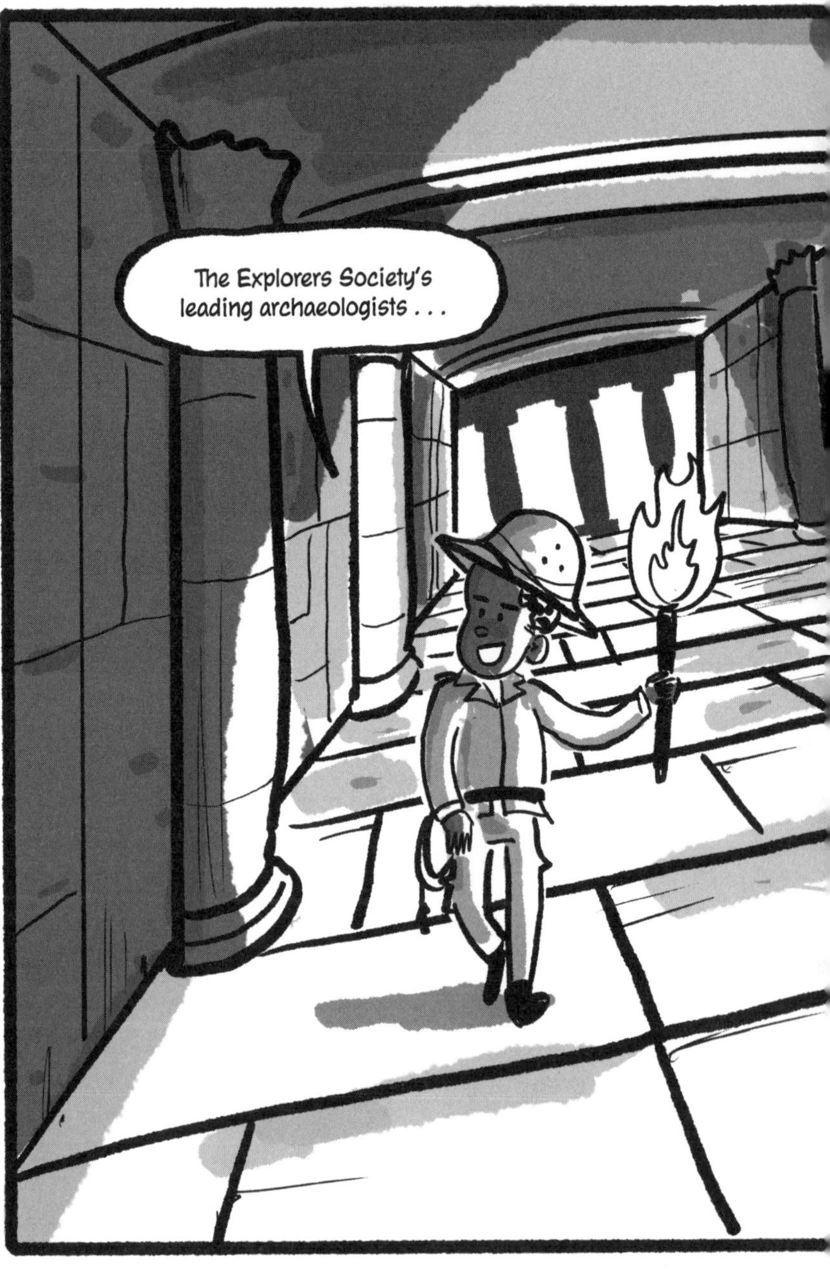
The Explorers Society's leading archaeologists . . .

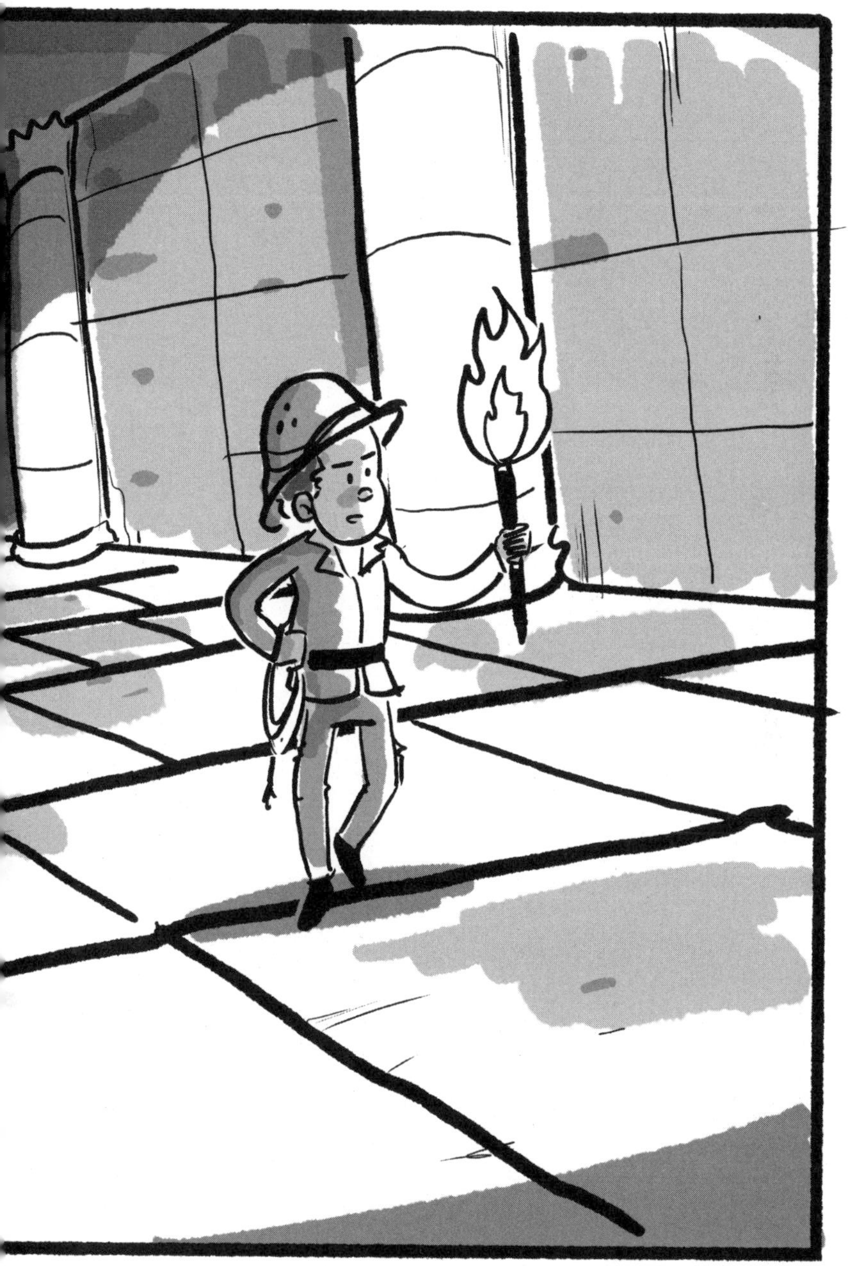

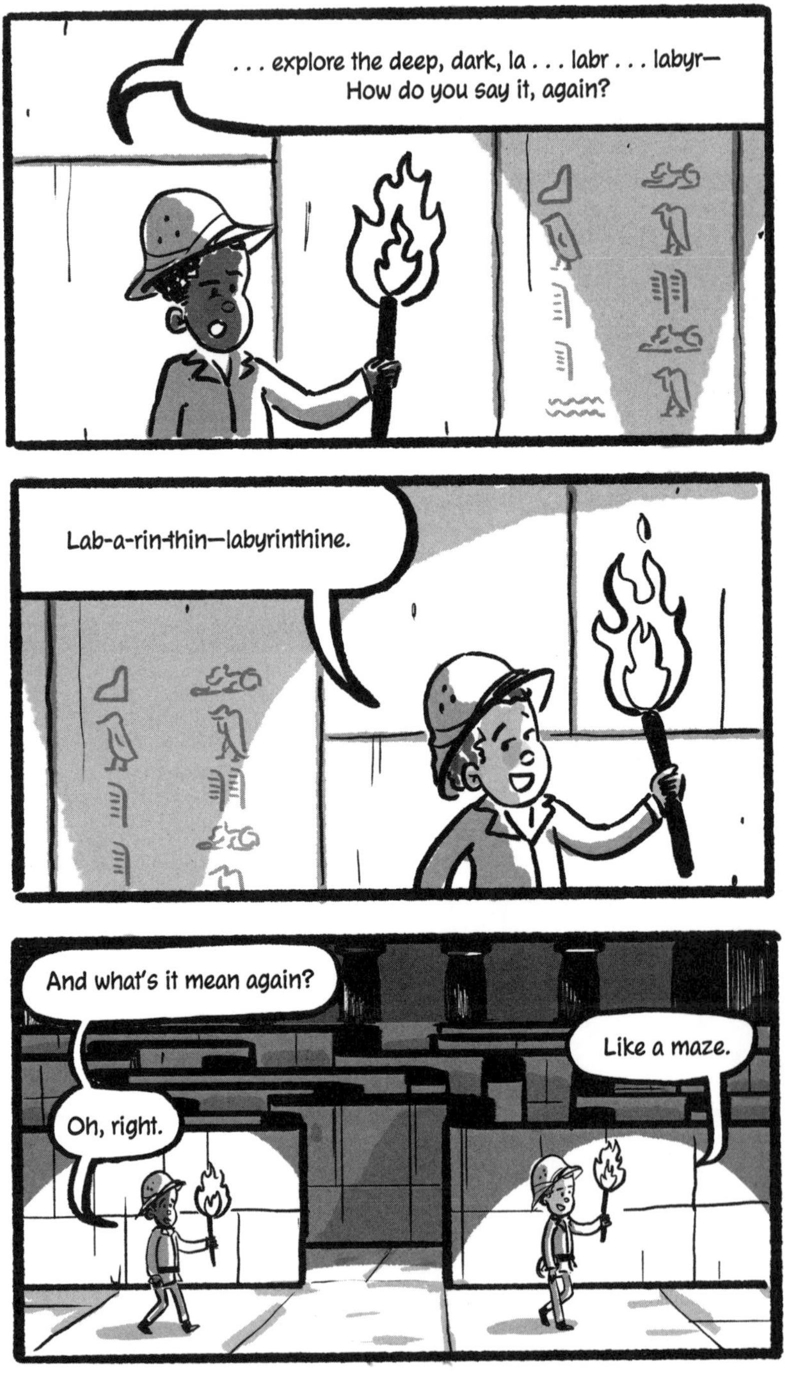
. . . explore the deep, dark, la . . . labr . . . labyr—
How do you say it, again?
Lab-a-rin-thin—labyrinthine.
And what's it mean again?
Like a maze.
Oh, right.

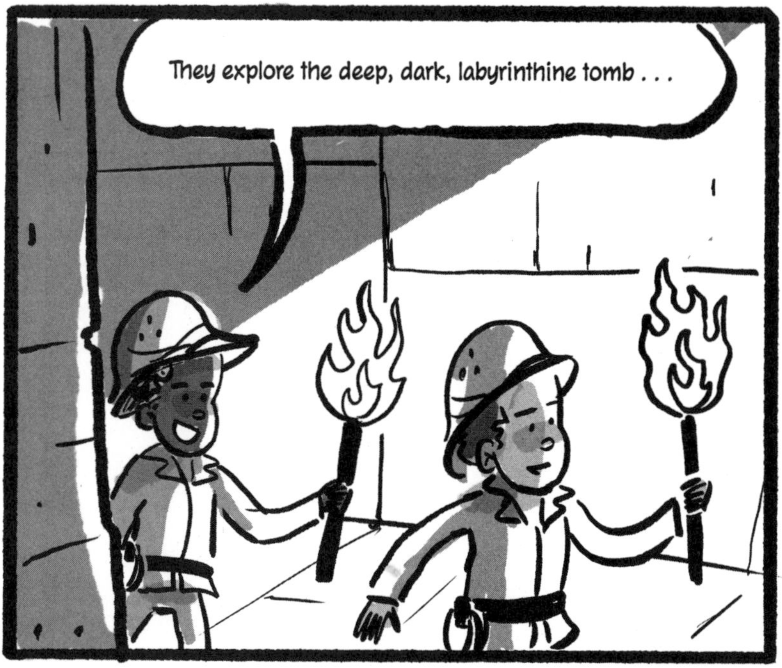
They explore the deep, dark, labyrinthine tomb . . .

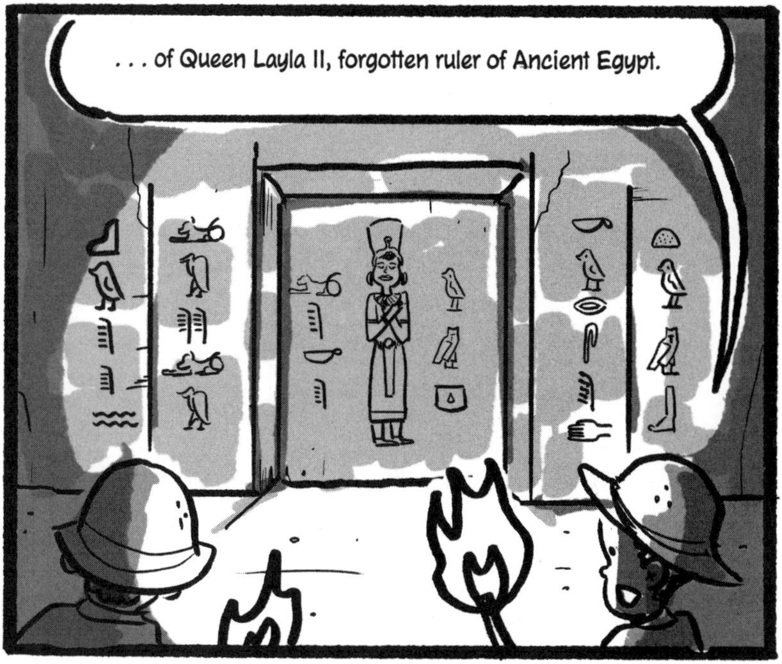
. . . of Queen Layla II, forgotten ruler of Ancient Egypt.

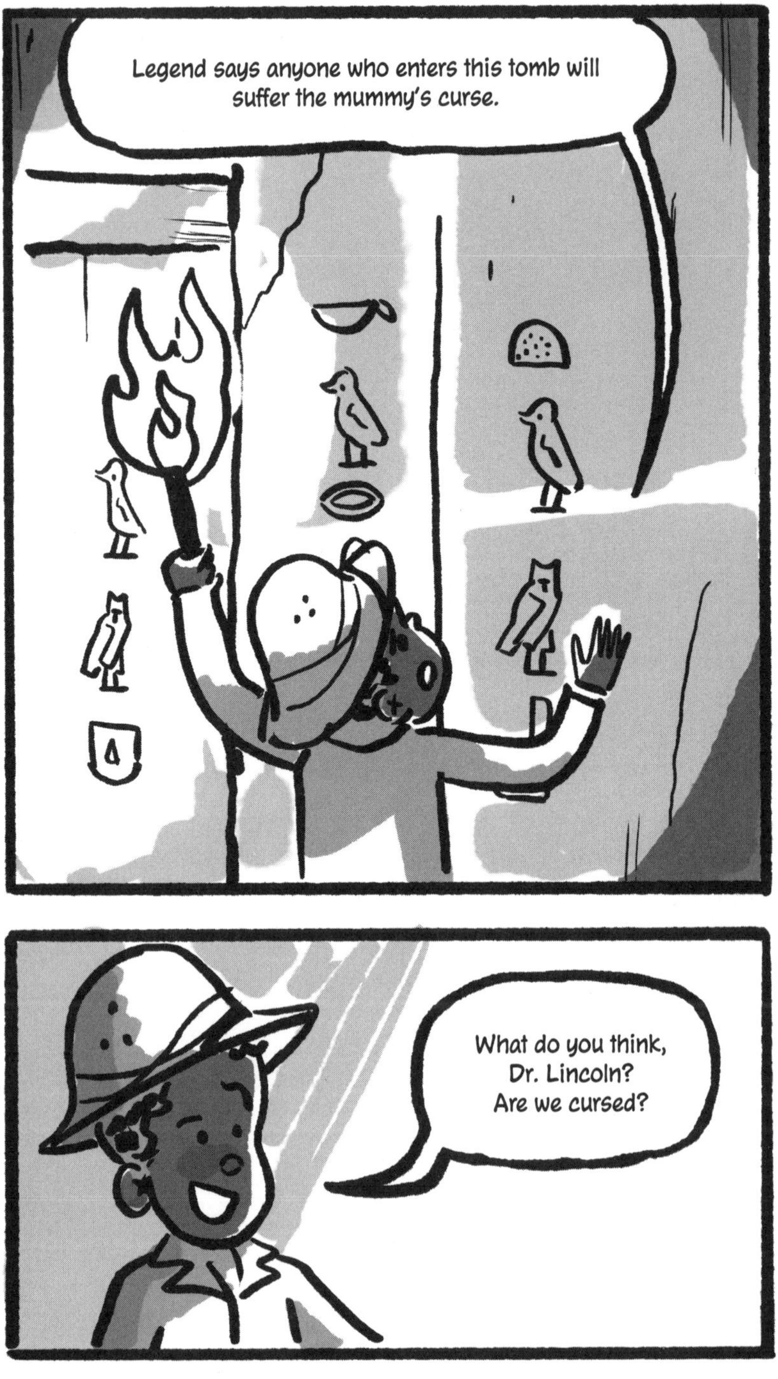
Legend says anyone who enters this tomb will suffer the mummy's curse.
What do you think, Dr. Lincoln? Are we cursed?

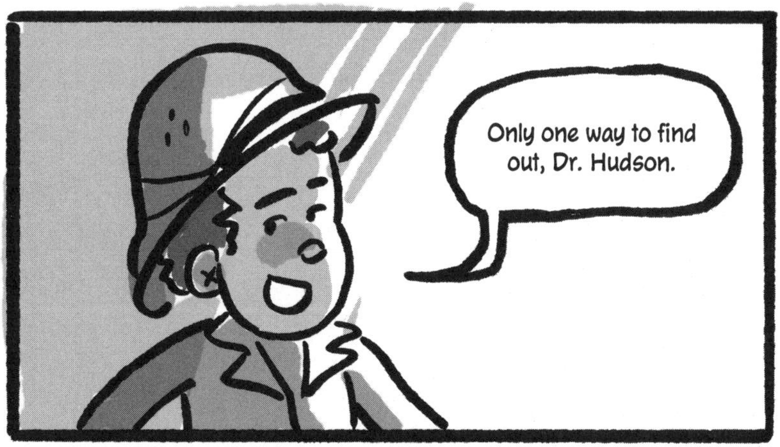
Only one way to find out, Dr. Hudson.

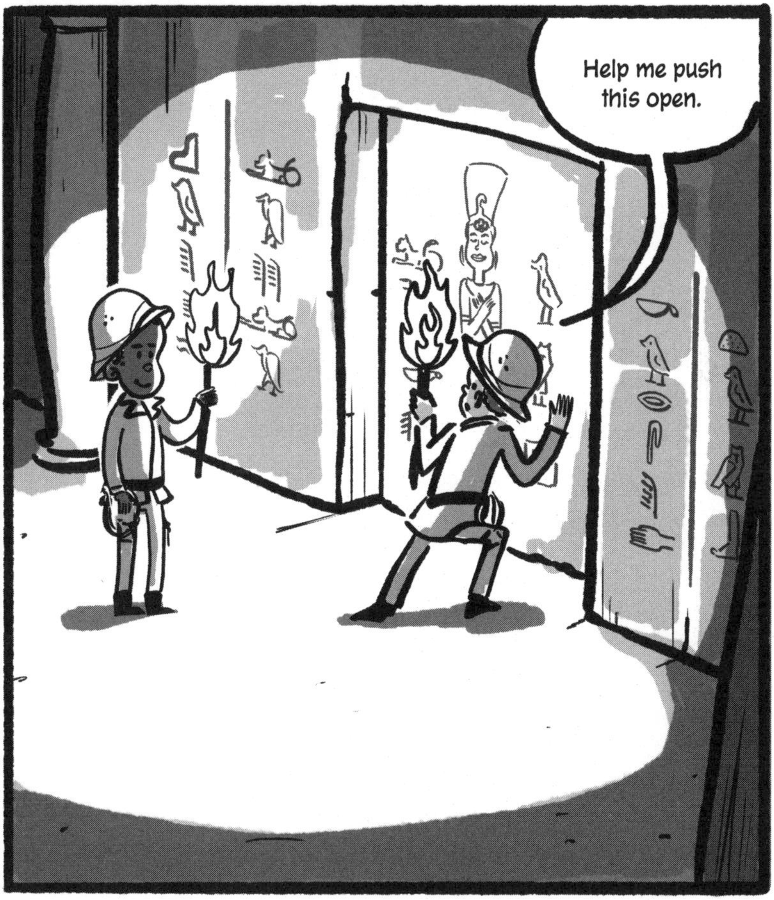
Help me push this open.

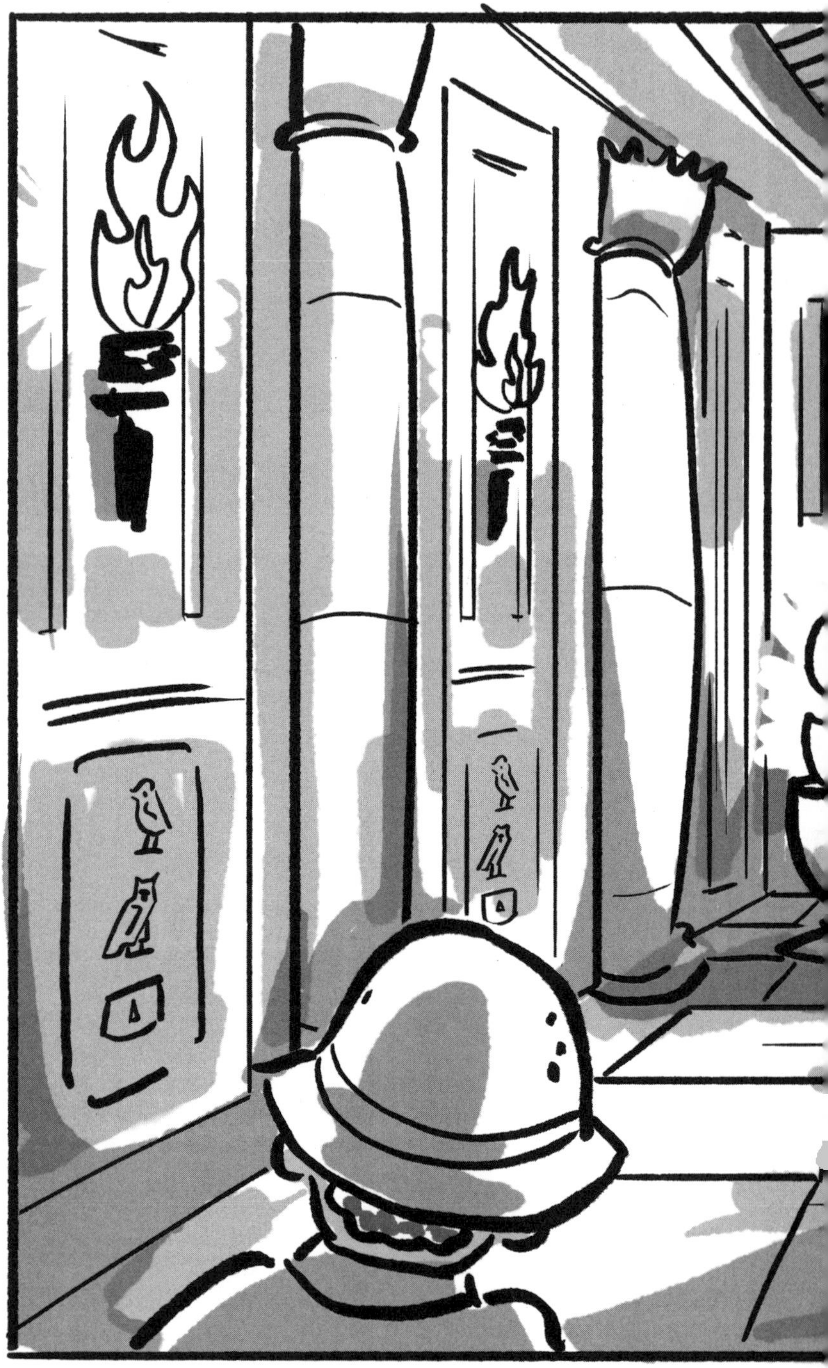

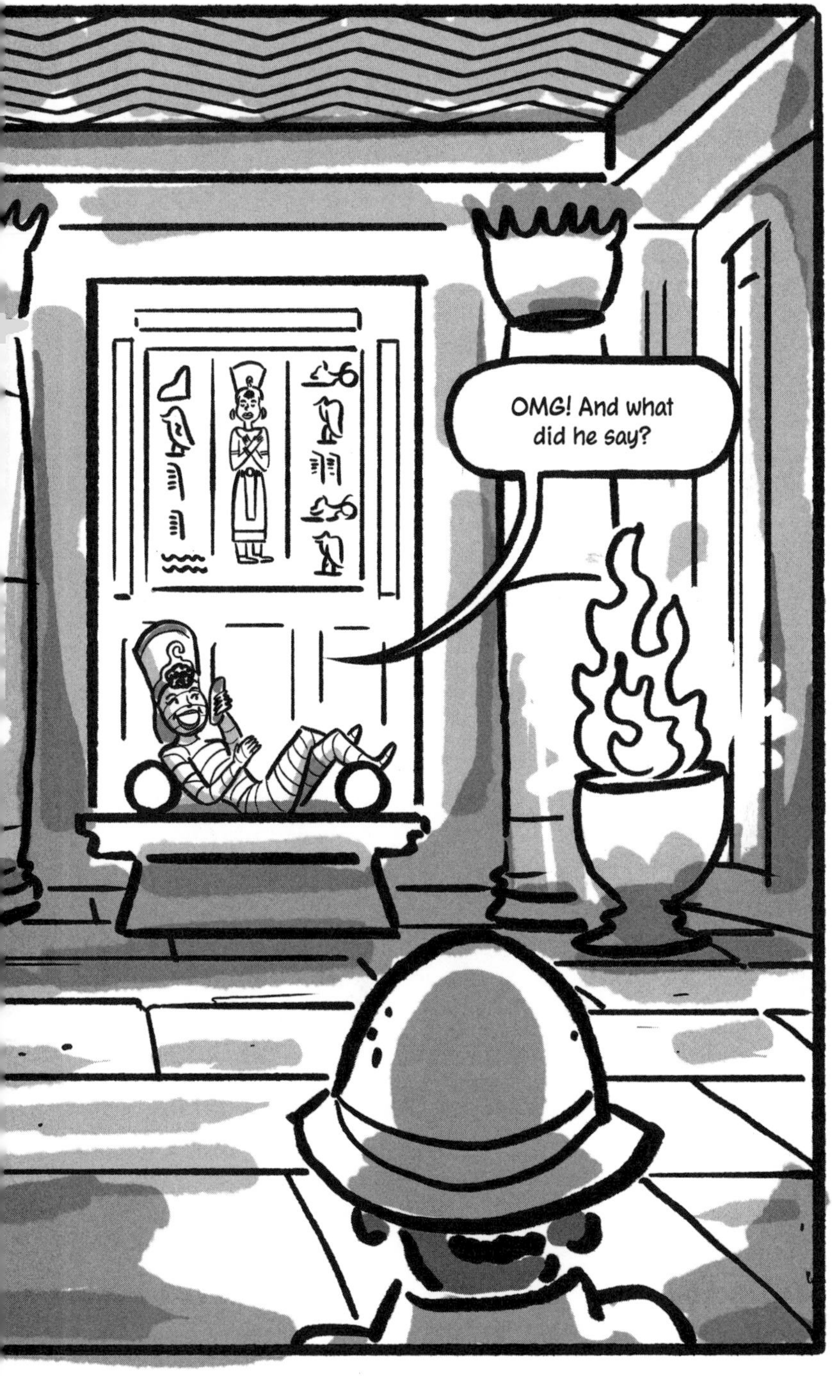
OMG! And what did he say?

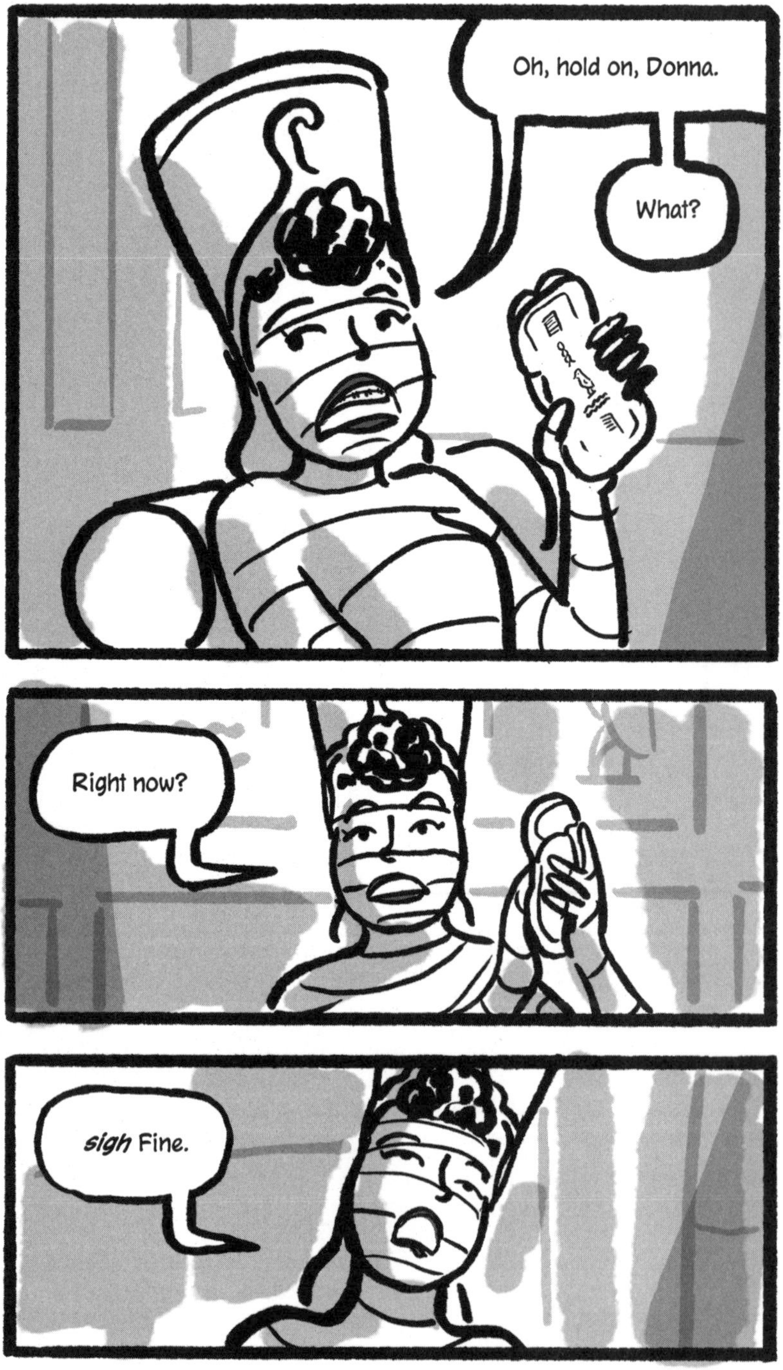
Oh, hold on, Donna.
What?
Right now?
sigh Fine.

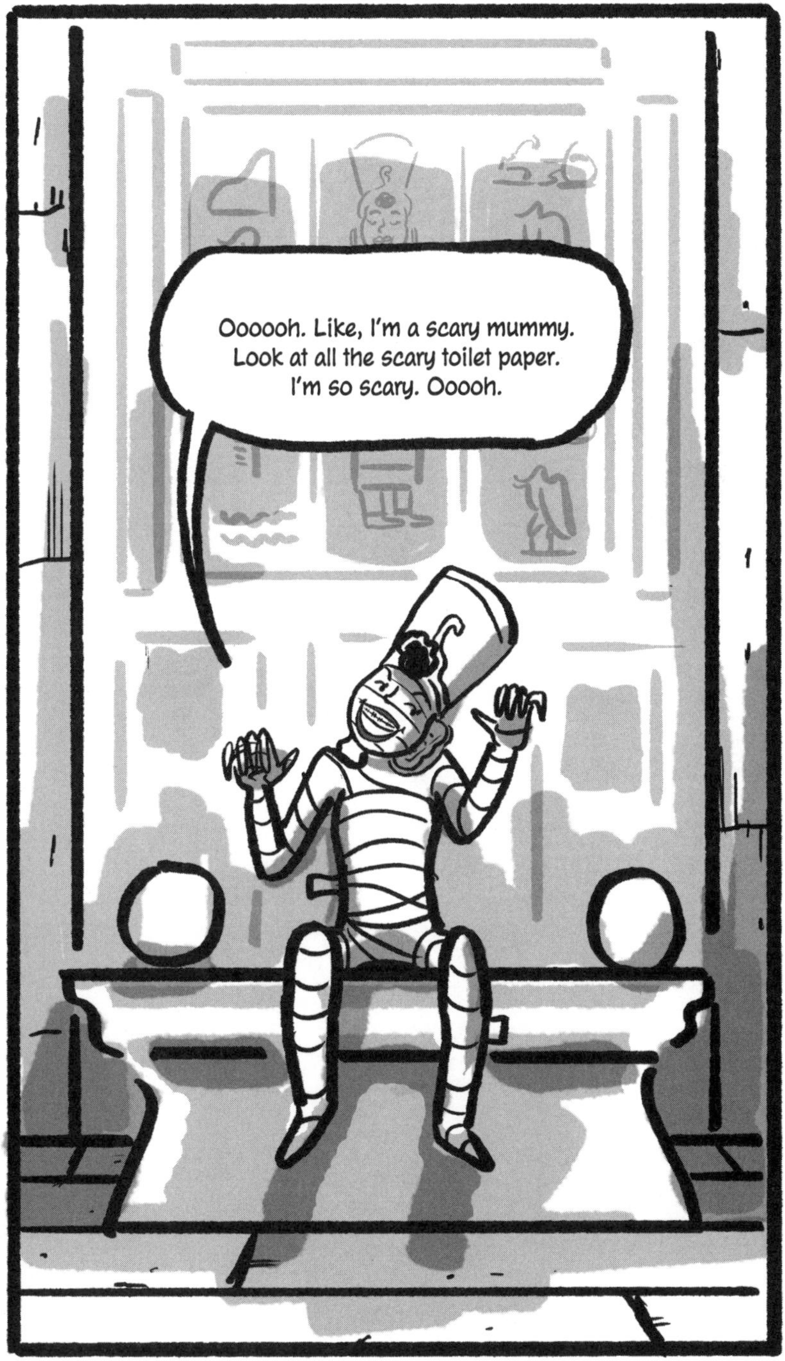
Oooooh. Like, I'm a scary mummy.
Look at all the scary toilet paper.
I'm so scary. Ooooh.

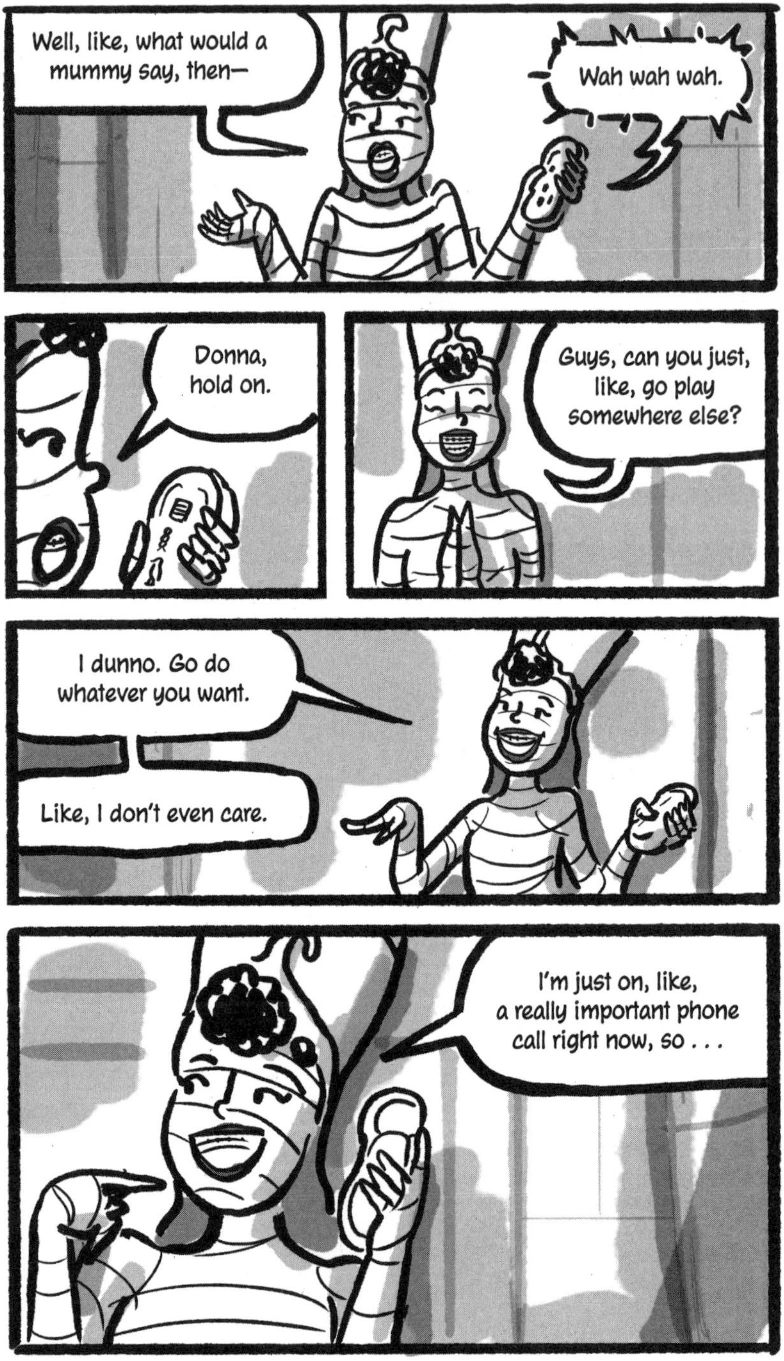
Well, like, what would a mummy say, then—
Wah wah wah.
Donna, hold on.
Guys, can you just, like, go play somewhere else?
I dunno. Go do whatever you want.
Like, I don't even care.
I'm just on, like, a really important phone call right now, so . . .

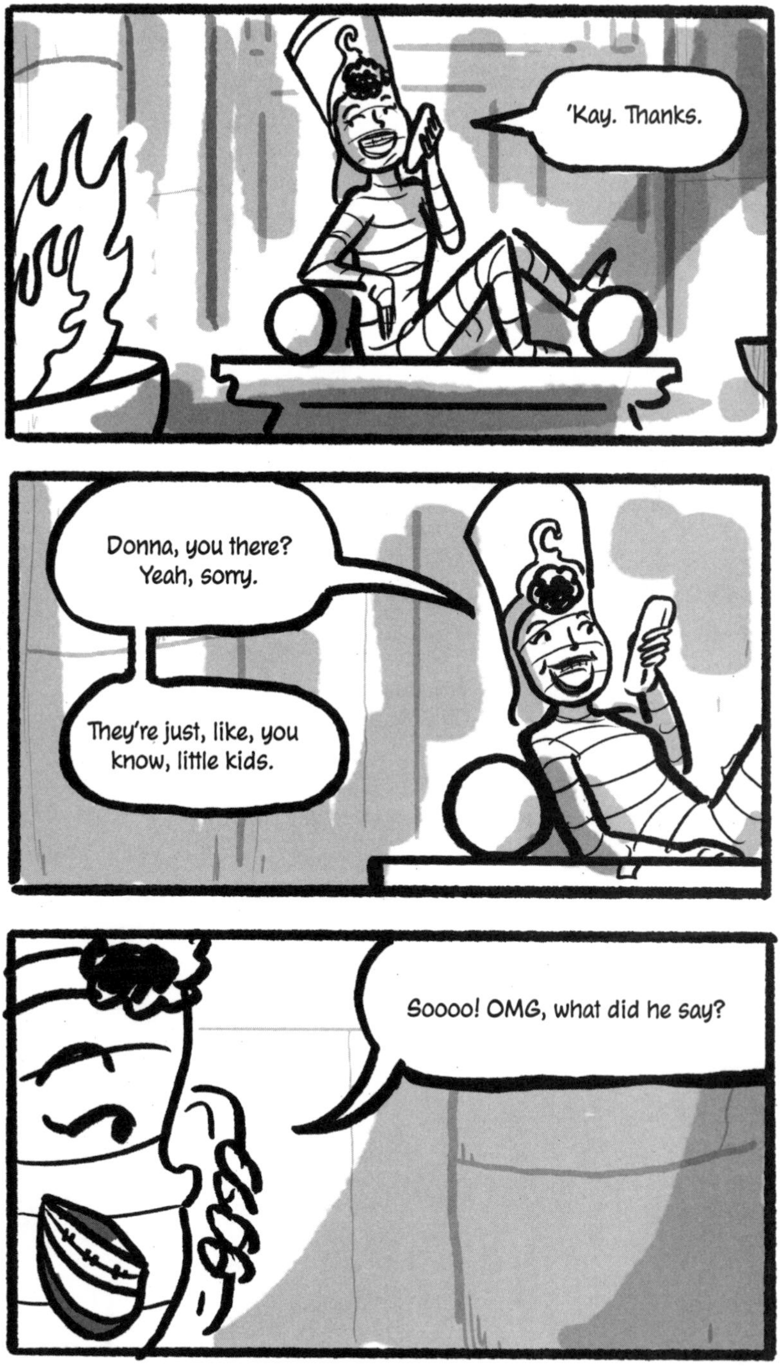
'Kay. Thanks.
Donna, you there? Yeah, sorry.
They're just, like, you know, little kids.
Soooo! OMG, what did he say?

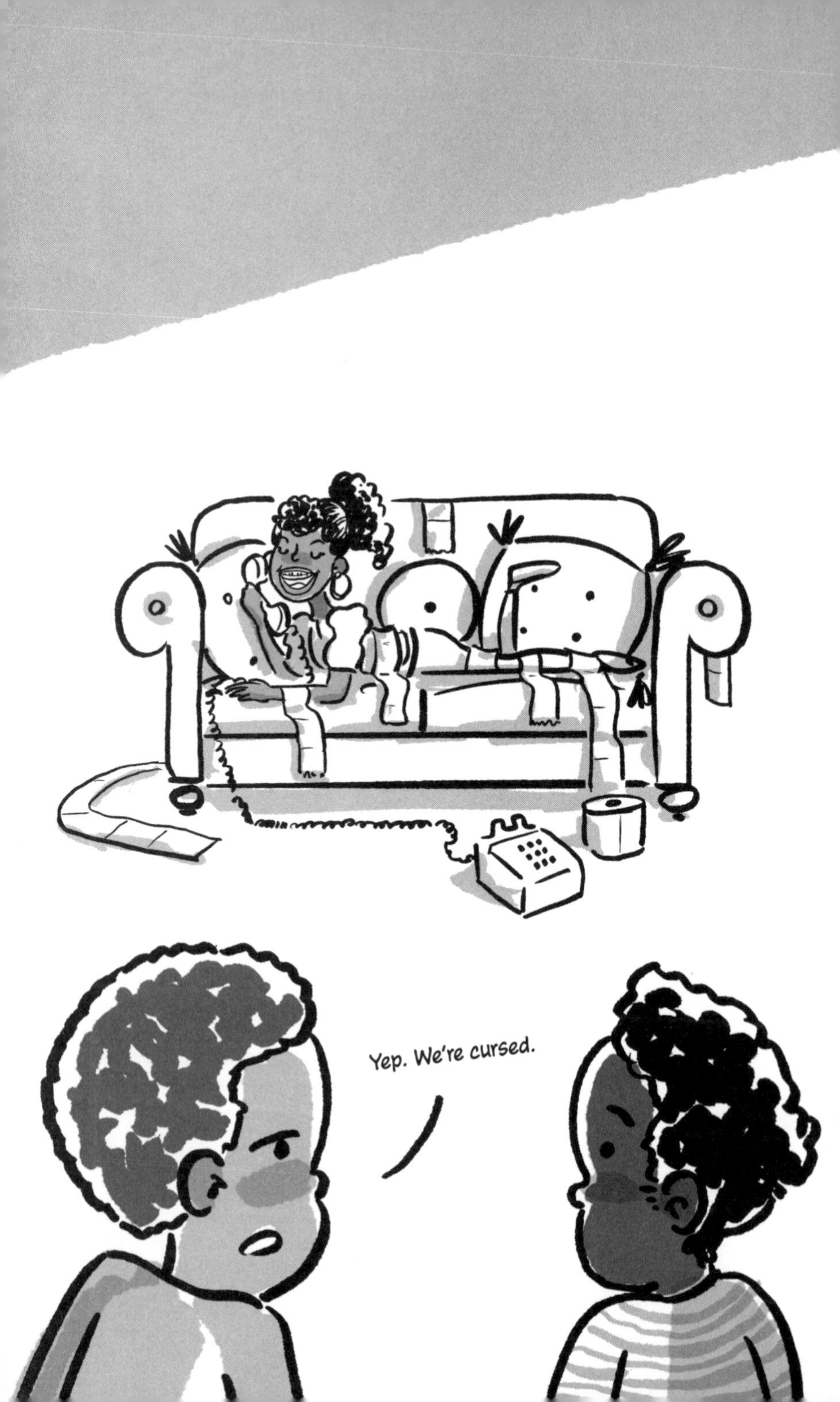
Yep. We're cursed.

CHAPTER TWENTY-NINE

WHAT'S WORSE THAN BEING LOST IN A DEEP, dark, labyrinthine tomb?

Worse than suffering the curse of, like, an ancient Egyptian mummy?

Worse, even, than a ten-minute timeout in the bathroom?

Being a hero without a bad guy.

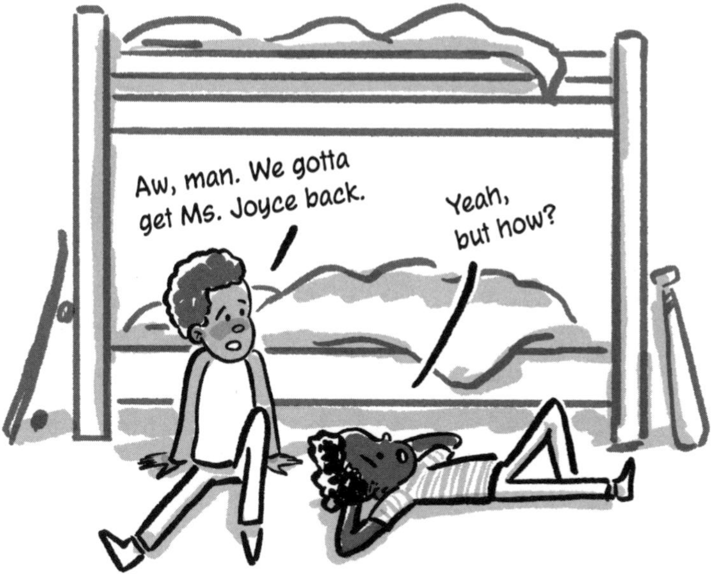
Aw, man. We gotta get Ms. Joyce back.
Yeah, but how?

CHAPTER THIRTY

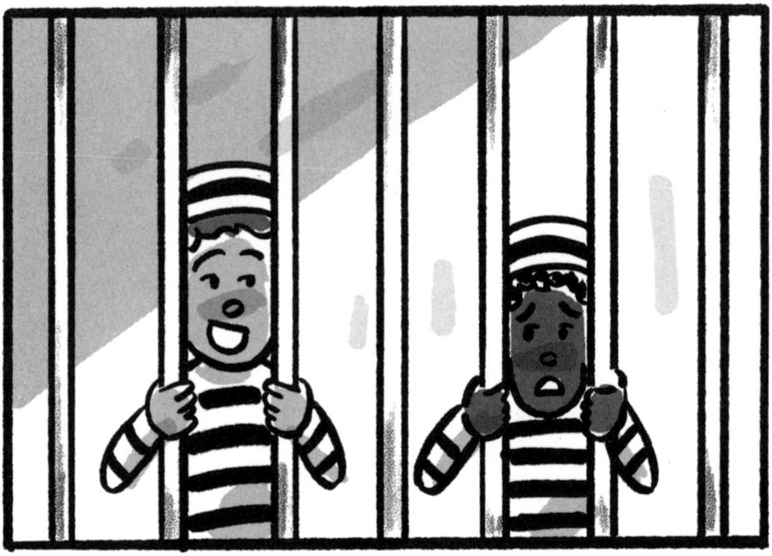

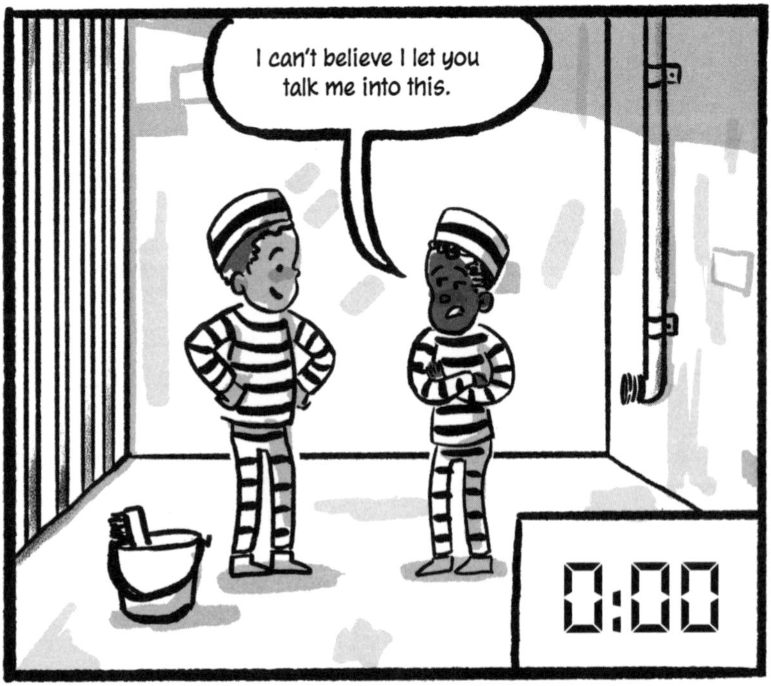
I can't believe I let you talk me into this.
0:00

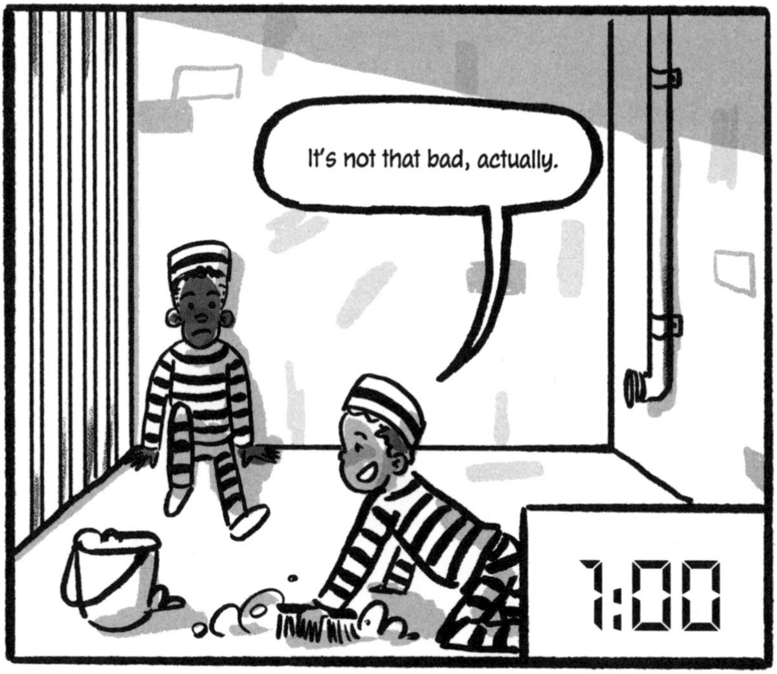
It's not that bad, actually.
7:00

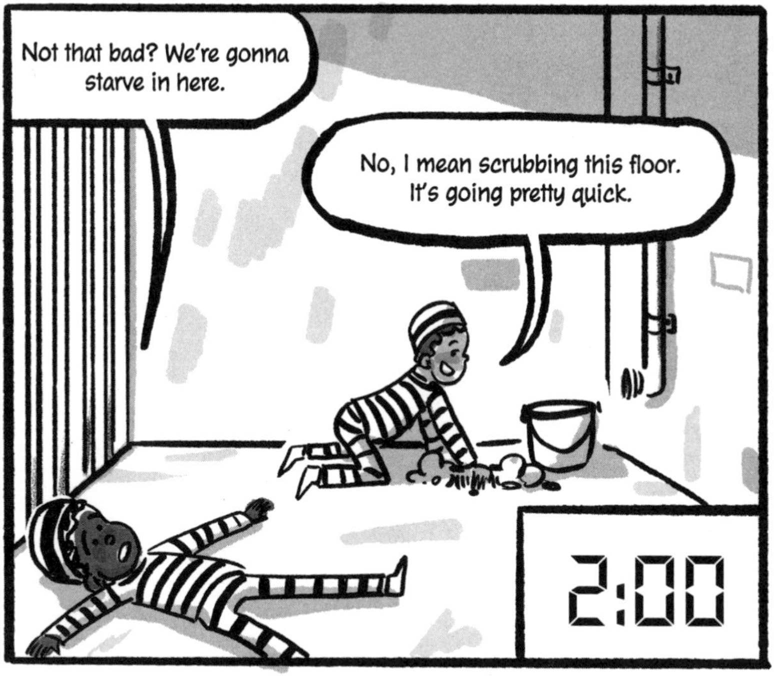
Not that bad? We're gonna starve in here.
No, I mean scrubbing this floor. It's going pretty quick.
2:00

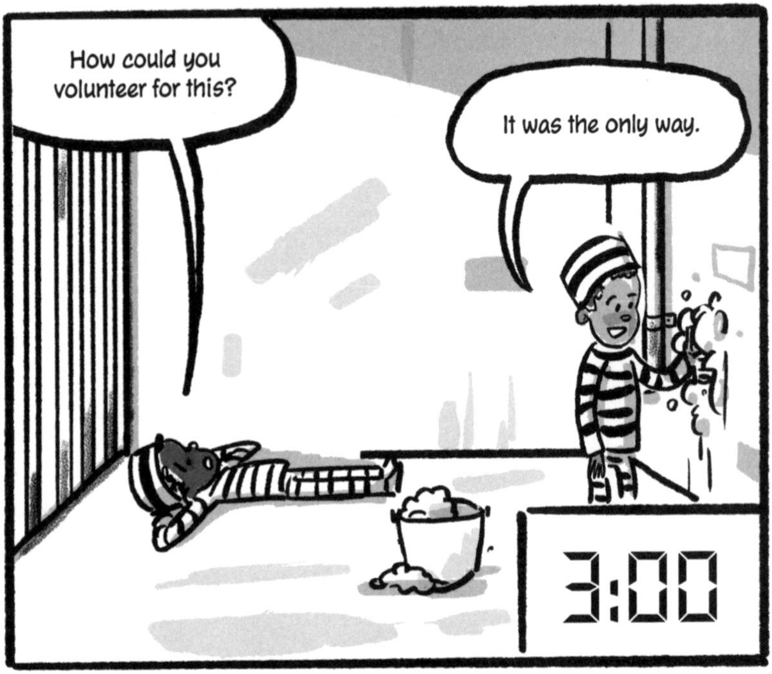
How could you volunteer for this?
It was the only way.
3:00

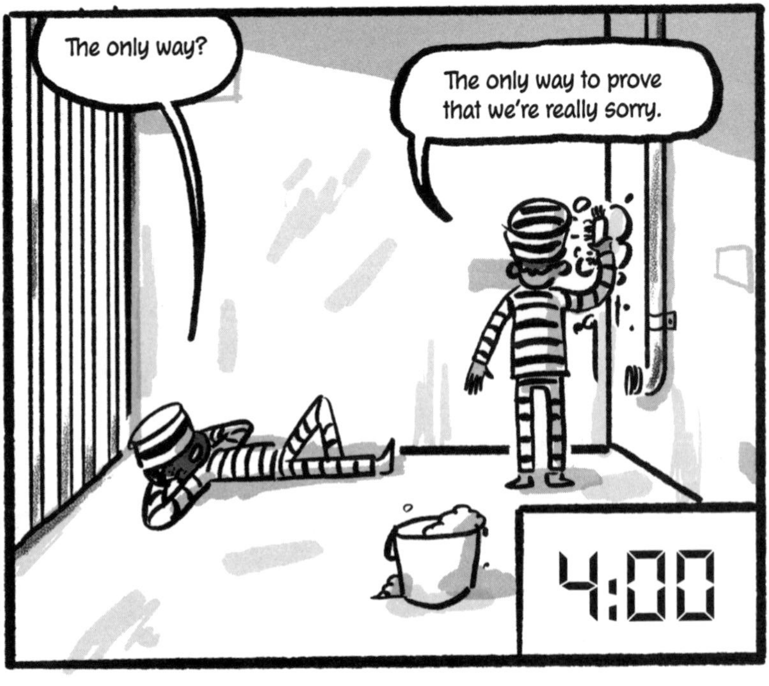
The only way?
The only way to prove that we're really sorry.
4:00

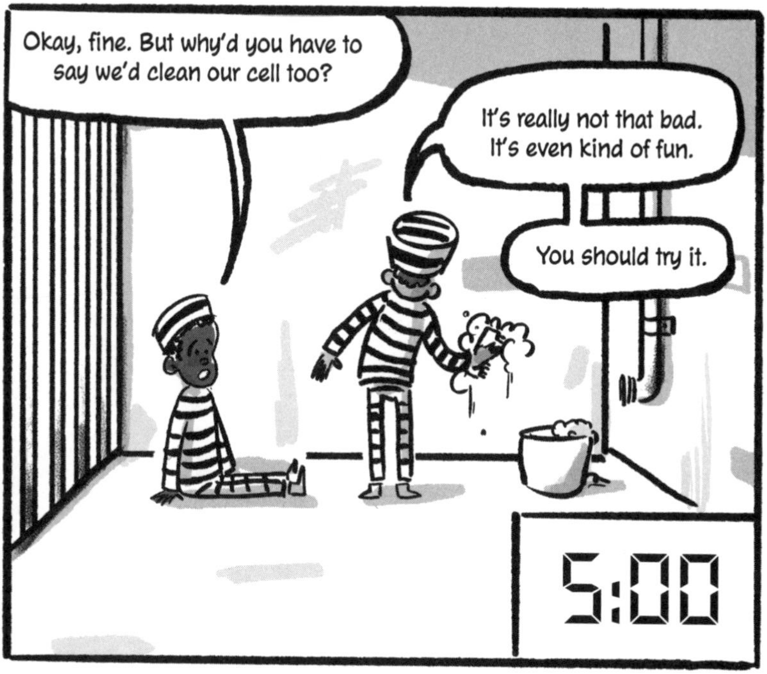
Okay, fine. But why'd you have to say we'd clean our cell too?
It's really not that bad. It's even kind of fun.
You should try it.
5:00

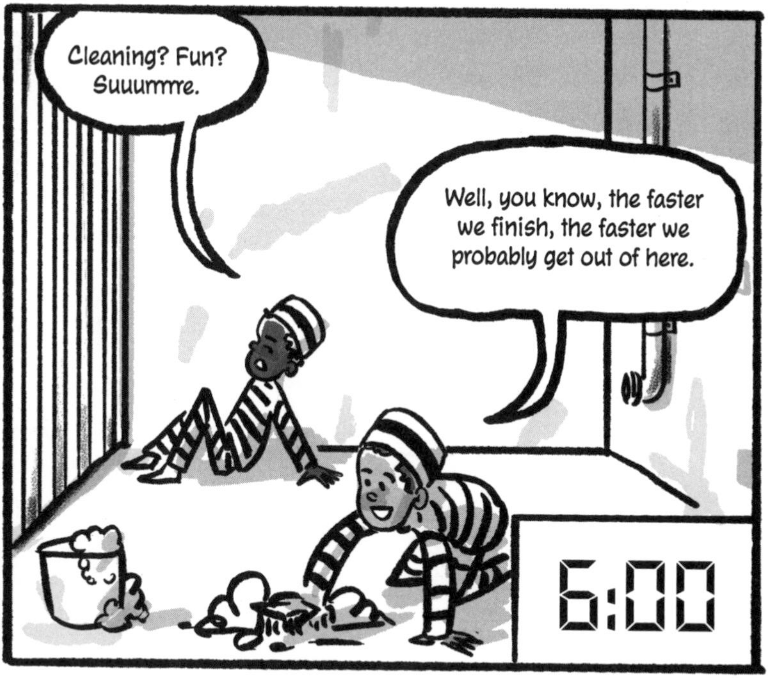
Cleaning? Fun? Suuurrrre.
Well, you know, the faster we finish, the faster we probably get out of here.
6:00

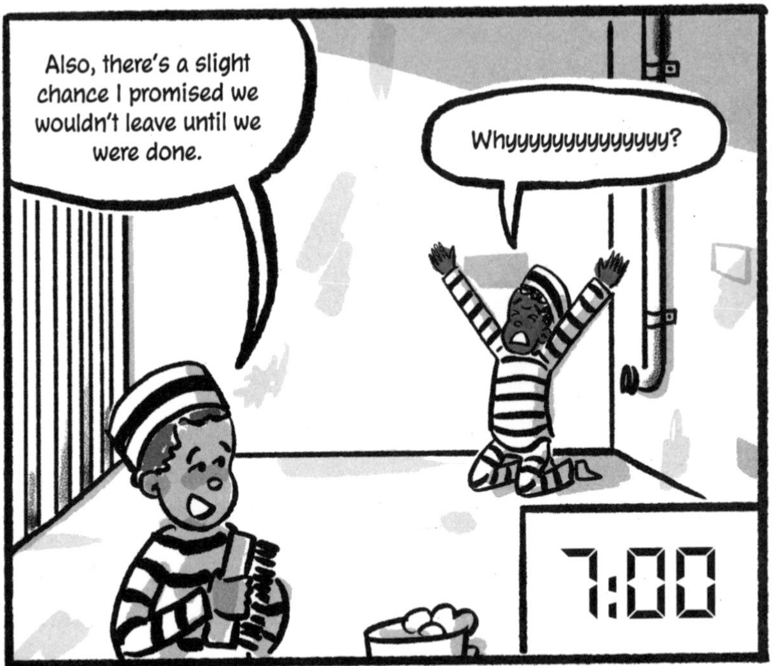
Also, there's a slight chance I promised we wouldn't leave until we were done.
Whyyyyyyyyyyyyyy?
7:00

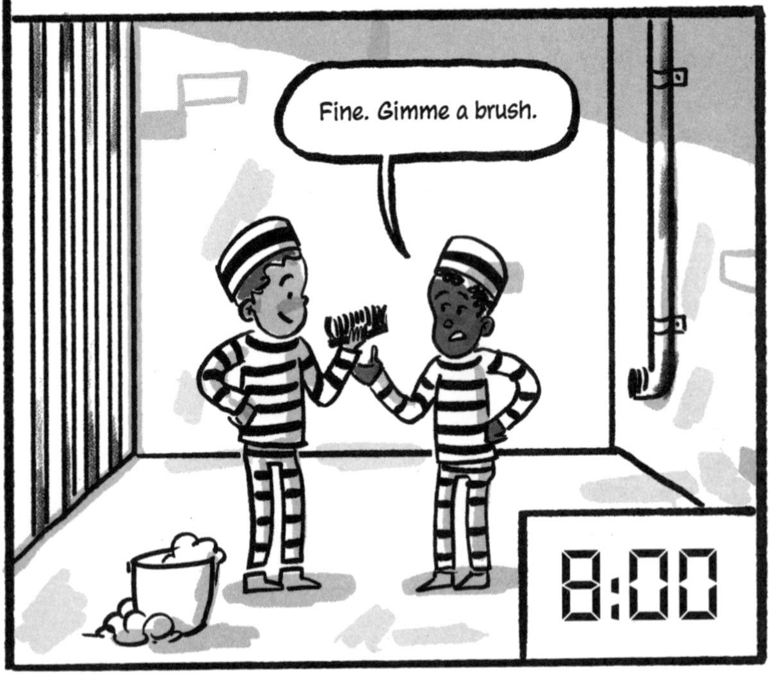
Fine. Gimme a brush.
8:00

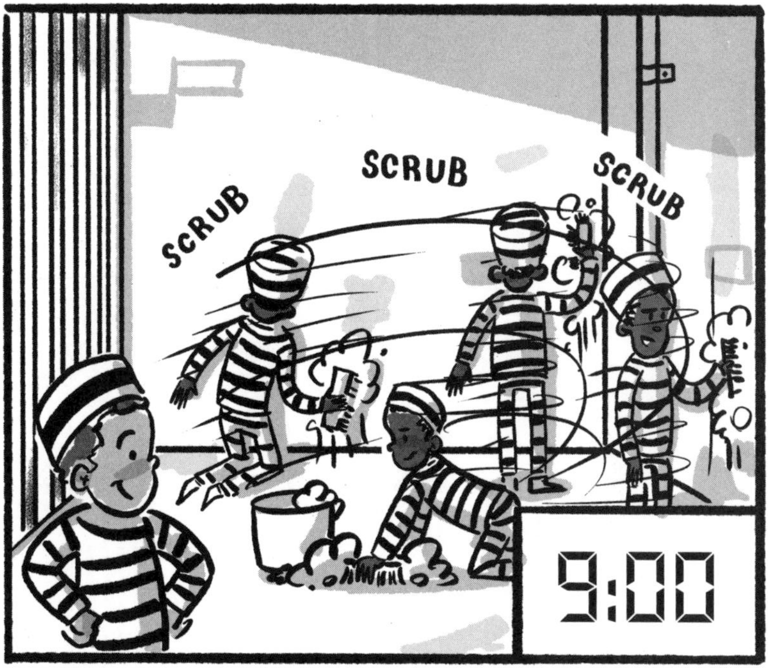
SCRUB
SCRUB
SCRUB
9:00

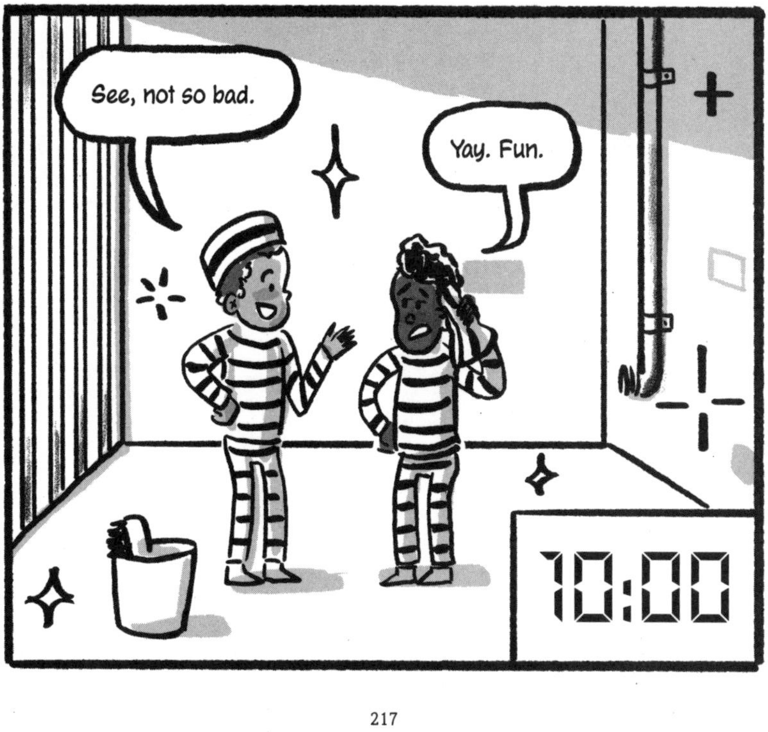
See, not so bad.
Yay. Fun.
10:00

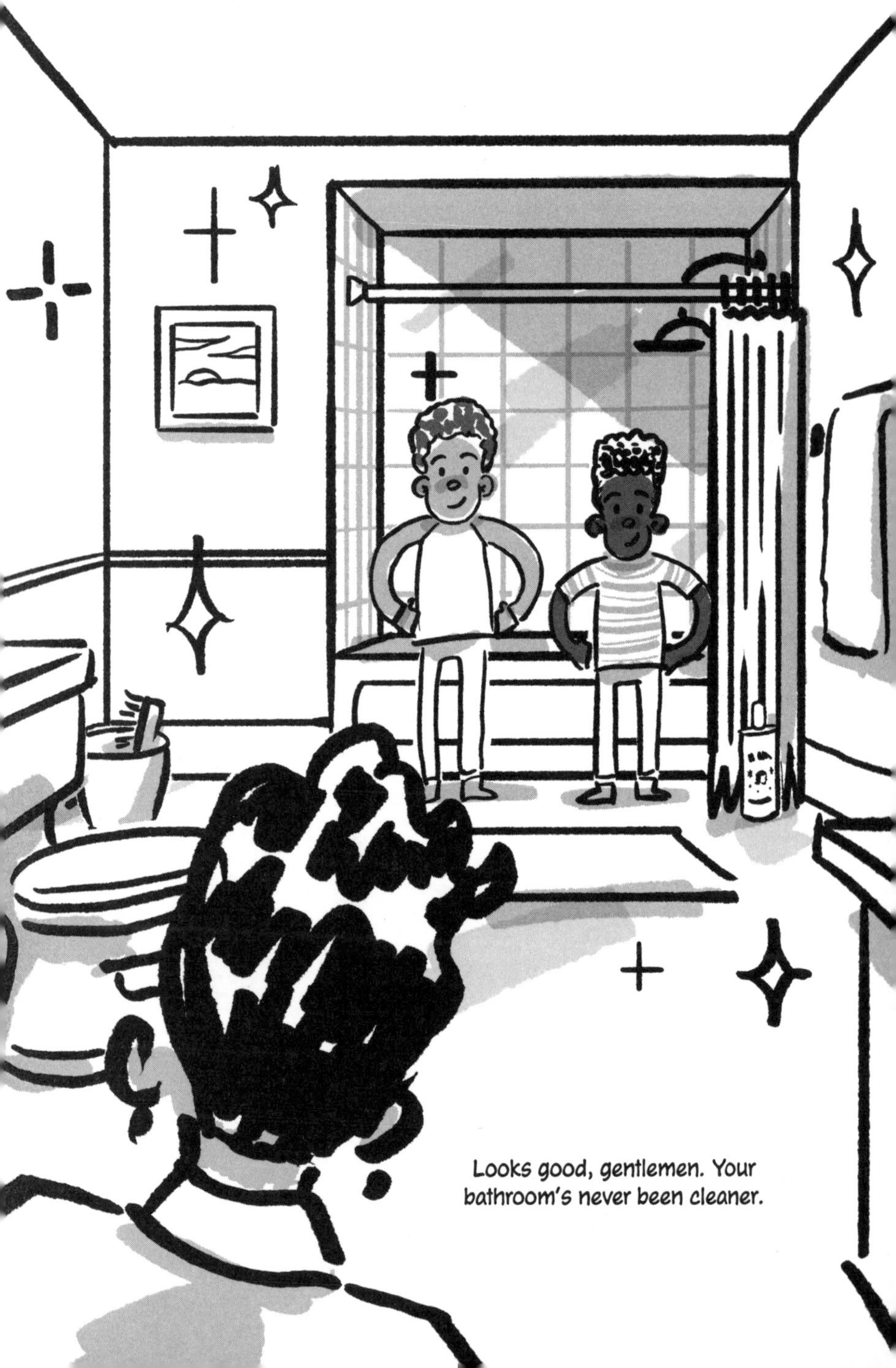
Looks good, gentlemen. Your bathroom's never been cleaner.

CHAPTER THIRTY-ONE

"WHEN THE BOYS TOLD US, I COULDN'T BELIEVE it! Who'da thought you'd been using Au Salon this whole time to clean the house?! And you say you add just a little bit of vinegar?"

Mrs. Dupré and the boys arrived in the kitchen to find Dr. Dupré and Ms. Joyce talking. He was holding an open bottle of Au Salon in one hand and pouring vinegar into it with the other.

"What you think? About that much?" asked Dr. Dupré, holding the bottles up for Ms. Joyce to see.

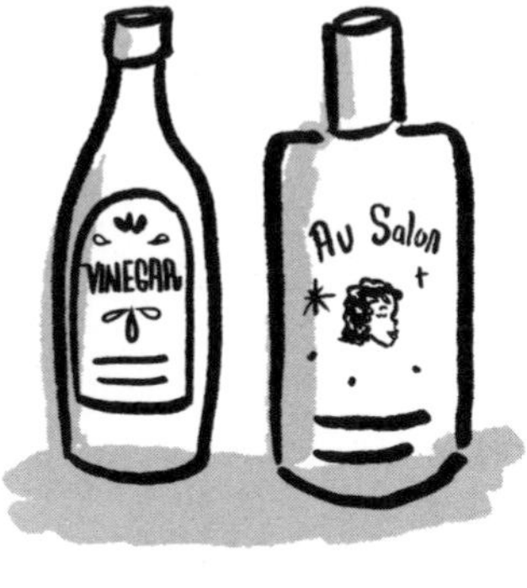
VINEGAR
Au Salon

"Mmm-hmmm. Just a little bit added to all 'em chemicals you got in there, and it do wonders," said Ms. Joyce.

There were several open Au Salon bottles on the counter. It looked like they'd been busy.

"I always carry a little vinegar with me in my pocketbook. Never know when you gon' need it. You can keep that bottle." She nodded at the bottle in Dr. Dupré's hand and then patted her purse under her arm. "I gots plenty more."

"Ahem." Mrs. Dupré cleared her throat to signal their presence.

"Ah, the prisoners have been released," said Dr. Dupré, setting down the bottles. "How'd it go, fellas?"

Link handed over the Au Salon bottle they'd used in the bathroom. "It worked great. Just like Ms. Joyce said it would."

"'Course it did," said Ms. Joyce, with a stern look on her face. She crossed her arms.

"Uh, boys," said Mrs. Dupré, nudging them from behind, "didn't you have something you wanted to say to Ms. Joyce?"

"Oh, yeah," said Link. "We're really sorry, Ms. Joyce."

"Yeah, sorry," said Hud.

"For the toilet paper and the water balloons," added Link, remembering their mom had said they should be specific about *why* they're apologizing.

"And for getting you fired," added Hud, following Link's lead.

Ms. Joyce's expression relaxed, and she chuckled. "Oh, that's fine." She waved a hand at Dr. and Mrs. Dupré. "Kids gon' be kids." Then she looked back at Link and Hud, her face stern again. "But next time, we gon' do better. Ain't that right?" She sucked her gold tooth.

The boys nodded.

"All right. I gots somethin' for you then." She unzipped her purse and reached around deep in its depths.

The boys looked at each other, a mix of confusion and anticipation on their faces.

"I don't mean to spoil 'em, now," she said to Mrs. Dupré as she ruffled through the contents of the purse. "That's if I can find 'em— *sigh*—Lord knows I could lose an elephant in here." She pulled her hand out and opened it, palm up, to reveal several items: an old tissue,

a clip-on earring, a penny, a nickel, a broken toothpick, some lint, and—"There they is!"—two peppermint candies. She set the purse down on the counter and picked out the peppermints, handing one to Link and the other to Hud. She put the rest of the things back in her purse and said, "Y'all just remember, Ms. Joyce ain't all vinegar. Sometimes, she's sugar." Then she smiled, her gold tooth gleaming.

The boys stared at the peppermints, lost for what to say. "Uh . . ."

"Ahem." Mrs. Dupré cleared her throat again. She glared at them in a way that told them everything they needed to hear without her having to say a word.

The boys looked back at Ms. Joyce. "Thank you."

"Oh, you welcome." She winked at them and smiled again.

"Well, uh, Ms. Joyce," interjected Dr. Dupré, "the boys aren't the only ones who need to say thank you."

"Oh, don't worry 'bout it, Doc," said Ms. Joyce. "You done kept me on my feet all these years. Least I can do is watch after your boys."

"No," said Dr. Dupré, "I mean, yes, thank you for that, but also for what you've done for Au Salon."

"Oh, that? I told you, that ain't nothin' but an old home remedy." She patted her purse. "That Au Salon was pretty strong to begin with. Wouldn't dare use it on my head—sorry, Doc—but with a little bit of vinegar, works great for cleanin' up 'round the house. And all that cocoa butter you got in there, you don't even smell it."

"Not just great, Ms. Joyce. It works better than anything I've ever seen before," said Dr. Dupré. He looked at Mrs. Dupré, excitement bubbling over. "It works better than any cleaning product you can buy from any store!"

"And you can do so much with it!" added Mrs. Dupré. "Laundry, carpet, floors, dishes—"

"Bathrooms!" said Hud.

Everyone laughed.

Link said, "It's like the greatest cleaning product of all time!"

"Yeah," said Hud, "it's the GOAT of cleaning products!"

"Ooh, I like that," said Dr. Dupré. "I can see it now." He held up his hand and moved it sideways like he was placing words in the air. "GOAT—Great On AnyThing!"

"Except hair, Doc," interjected Ms. Joyce.

"Oh, right, of course," said Dr. Dupré. He added an asterisk to the invisible sign only he could see.

Link and Hud looked at each other, a little confused. *Great on anything?*

"Um, dear," said Mrs. Dupré. "I don't think that's what the boys meant by—"

"Boss," Dr. Dupré said, still gazing up at his work, "y'all just gotta have a little vision."

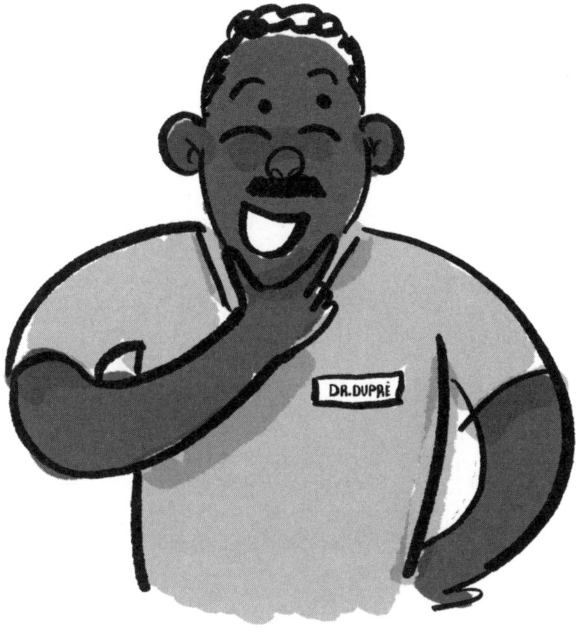
DR.DUPRÉ

CHAPTER THIRTY-TWO

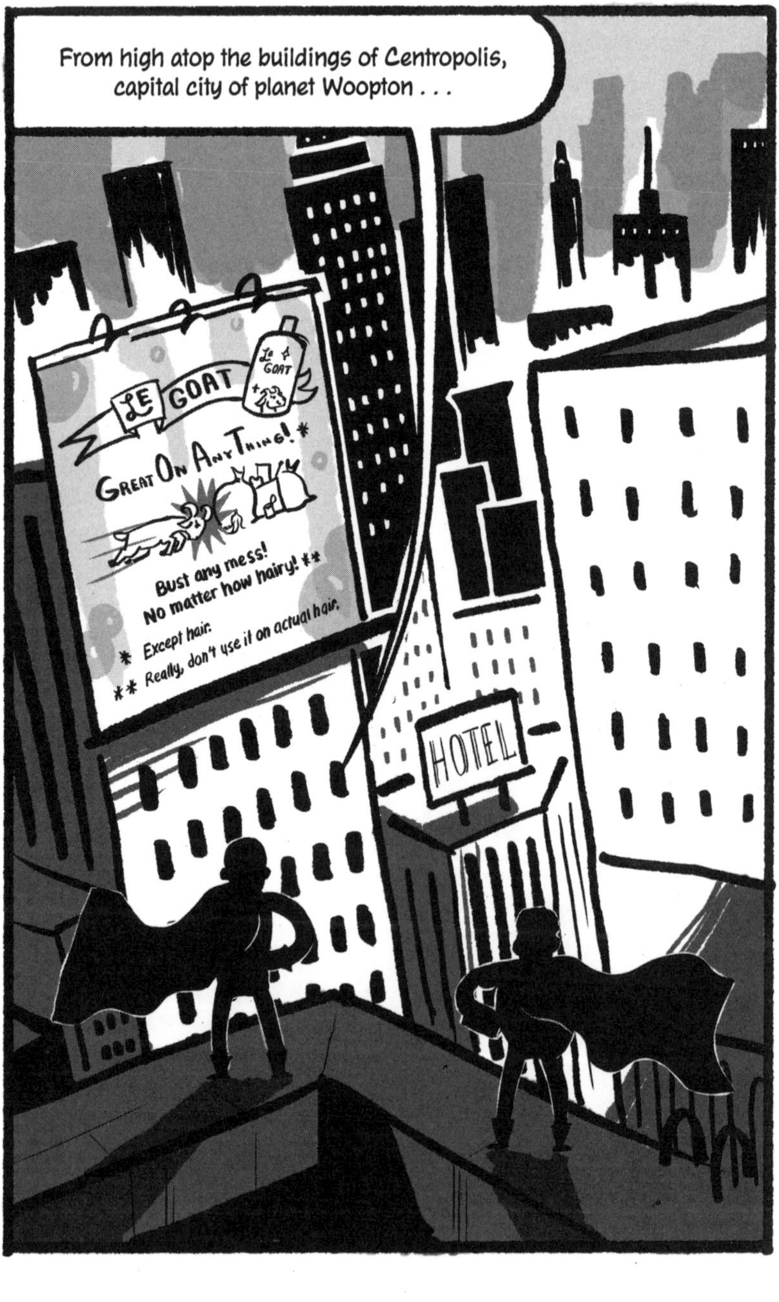

From high atop the buildings of Centropolis, capital city of planet Woopton . . .
LE GOAT
GREAT ON ANYTHING! *
Bust any mess! No matter how hairy! **
* Except hair.
** Really, don't use it on actual hair.
HOTEL

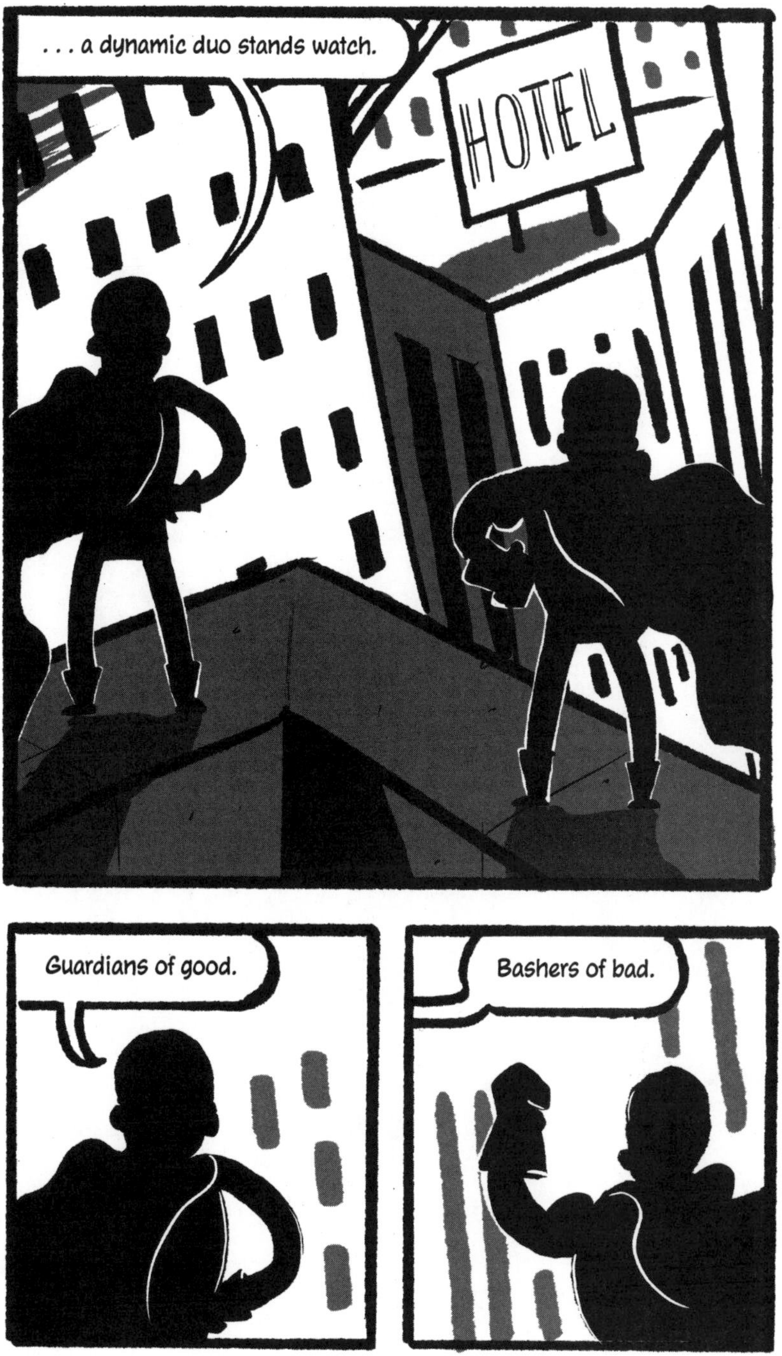
. . . a dynamic duo stands watch.
Guardians of good.
Bashers of bad.

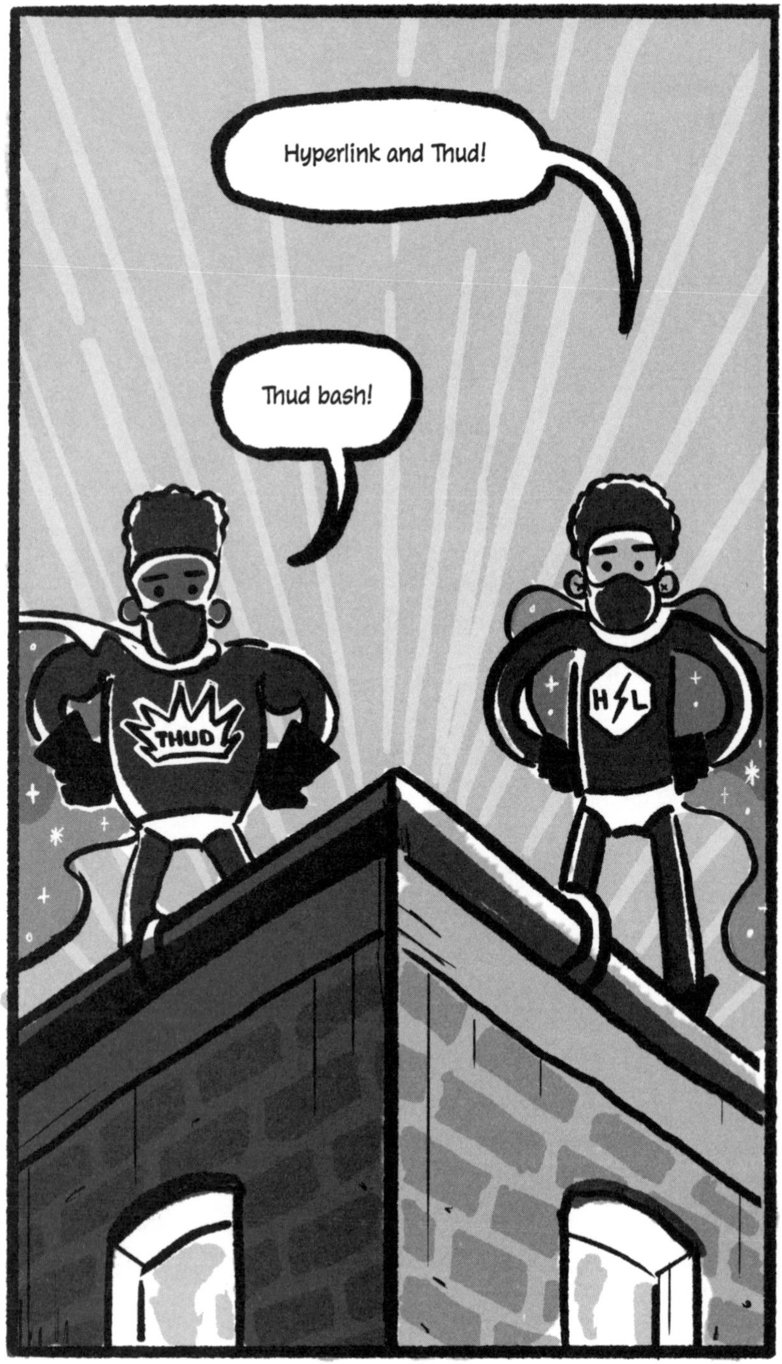
Hyperlink and Thud!
Thud bash!
THUD
H L

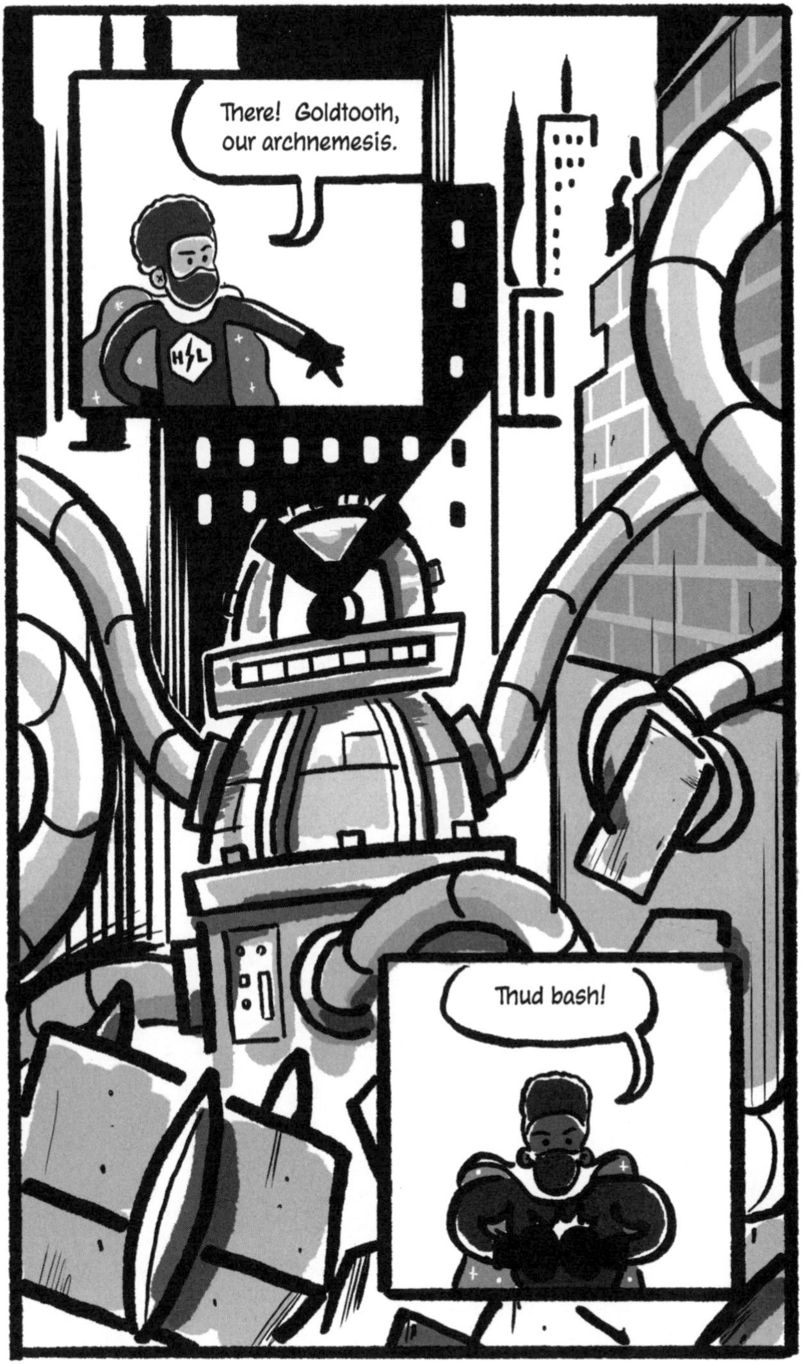
There! Goldtooth, our archnemesis.
Thud bash!

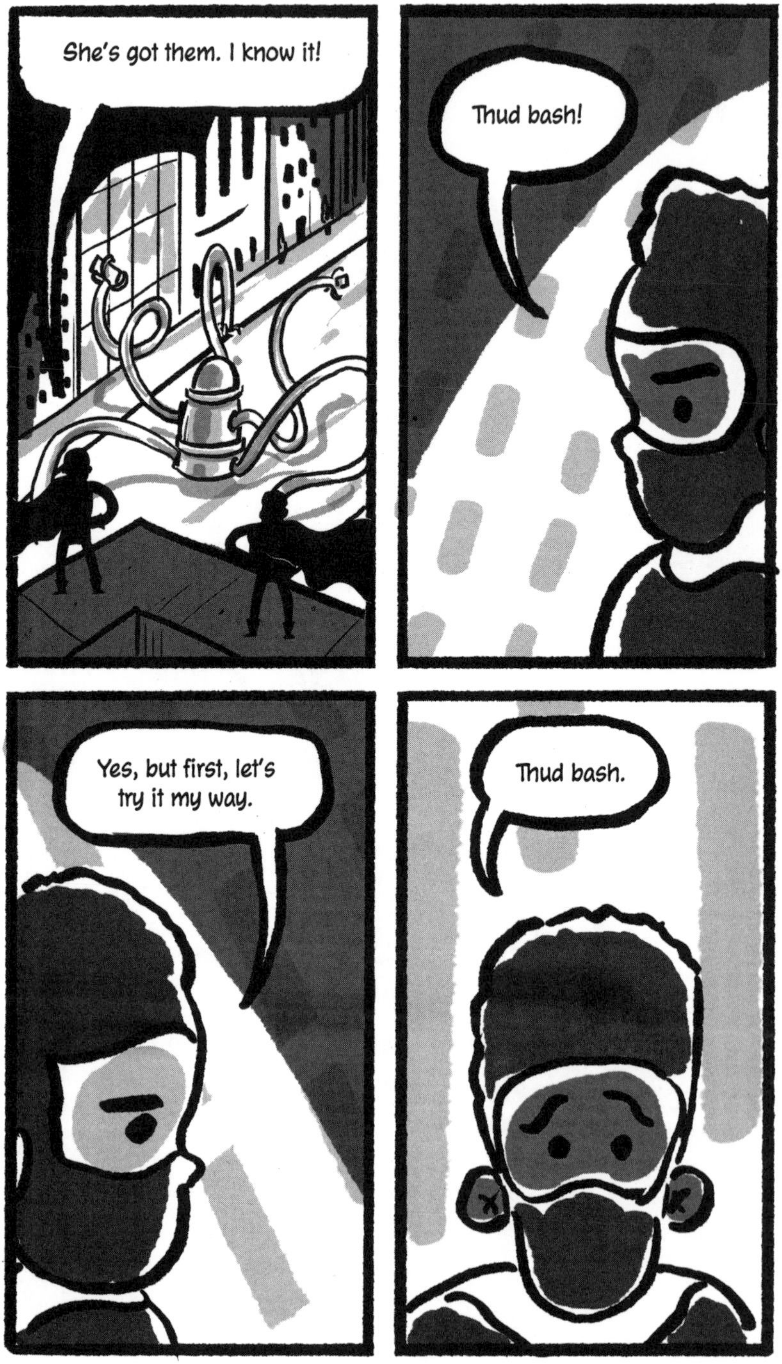
She's got them. I know it!
Thud bash!
Yes, but first, let's try it my way.
Thud bash.

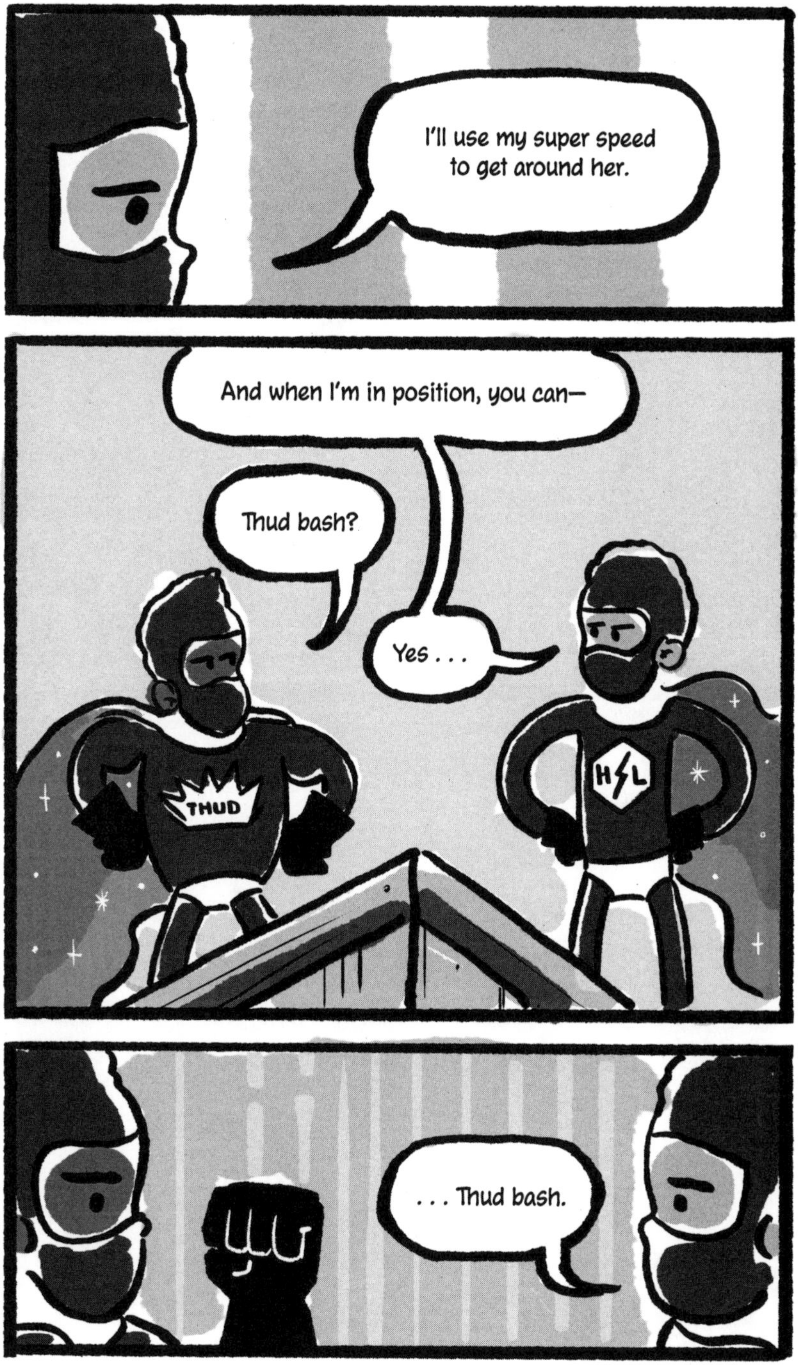
I'll use my super speed to get around her.
And when I'm in position, you can—
Thud bash?
Yes . . .
THUD
H L
. . . Thud bash.

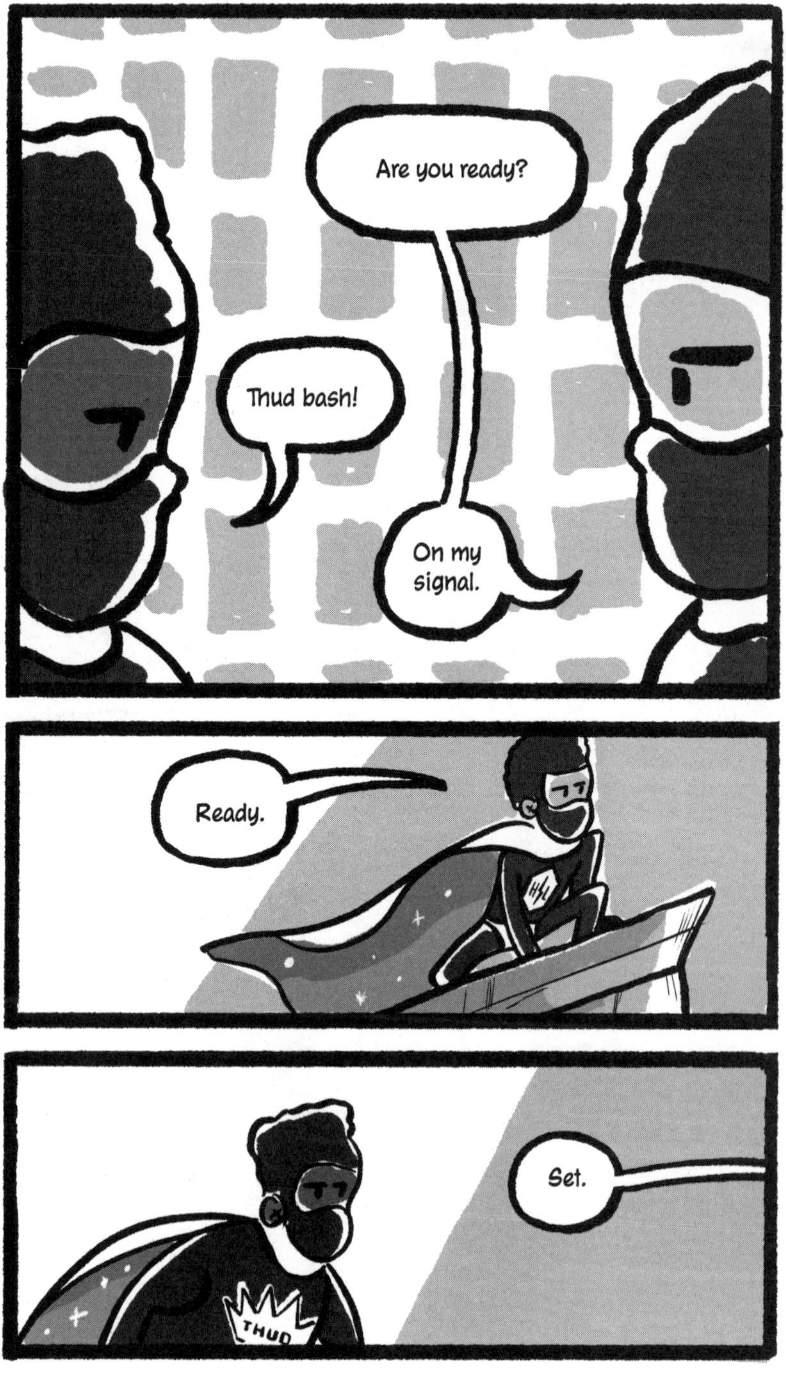
Are you ready?
Thud bash!
On my signal.
Ready.
Set.
THUD

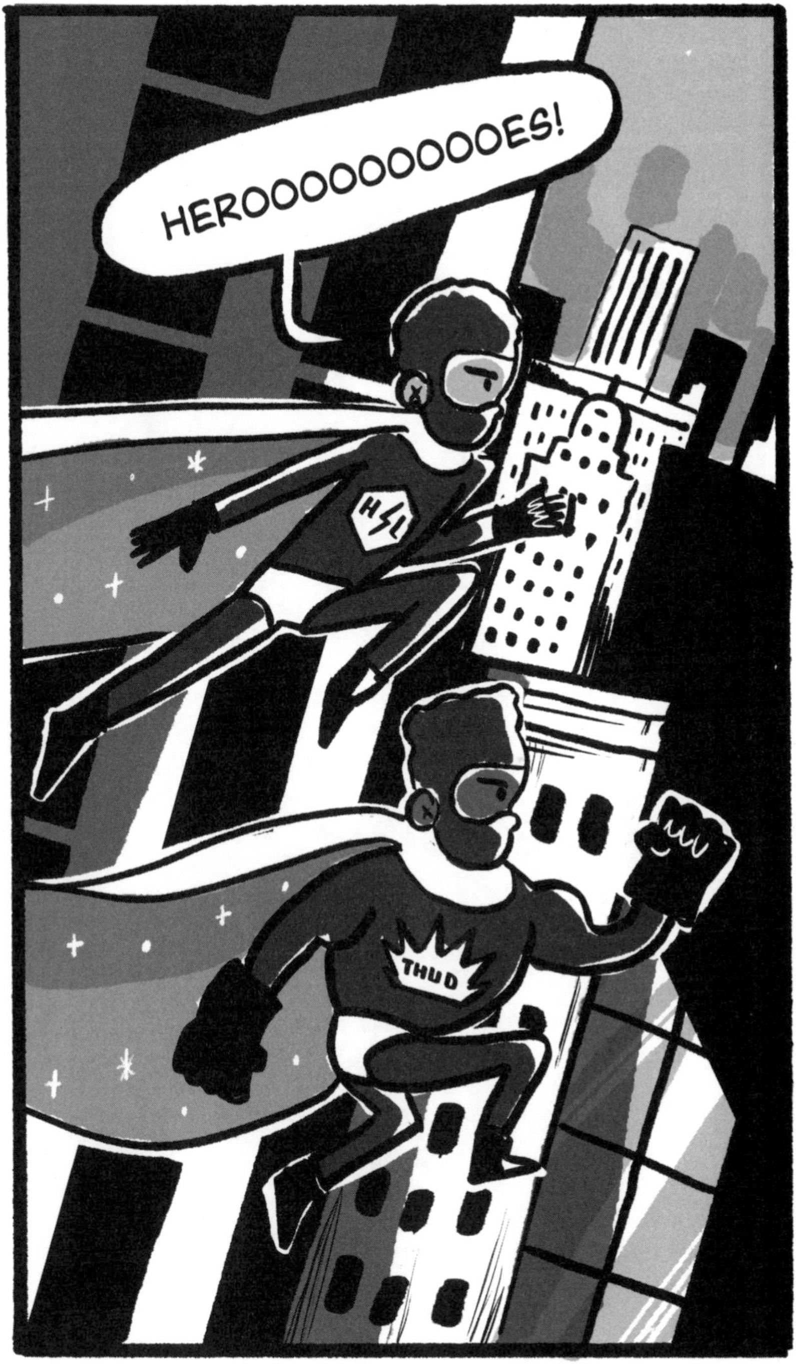
HEROOOOOOOOOOES!
HSL
THUD

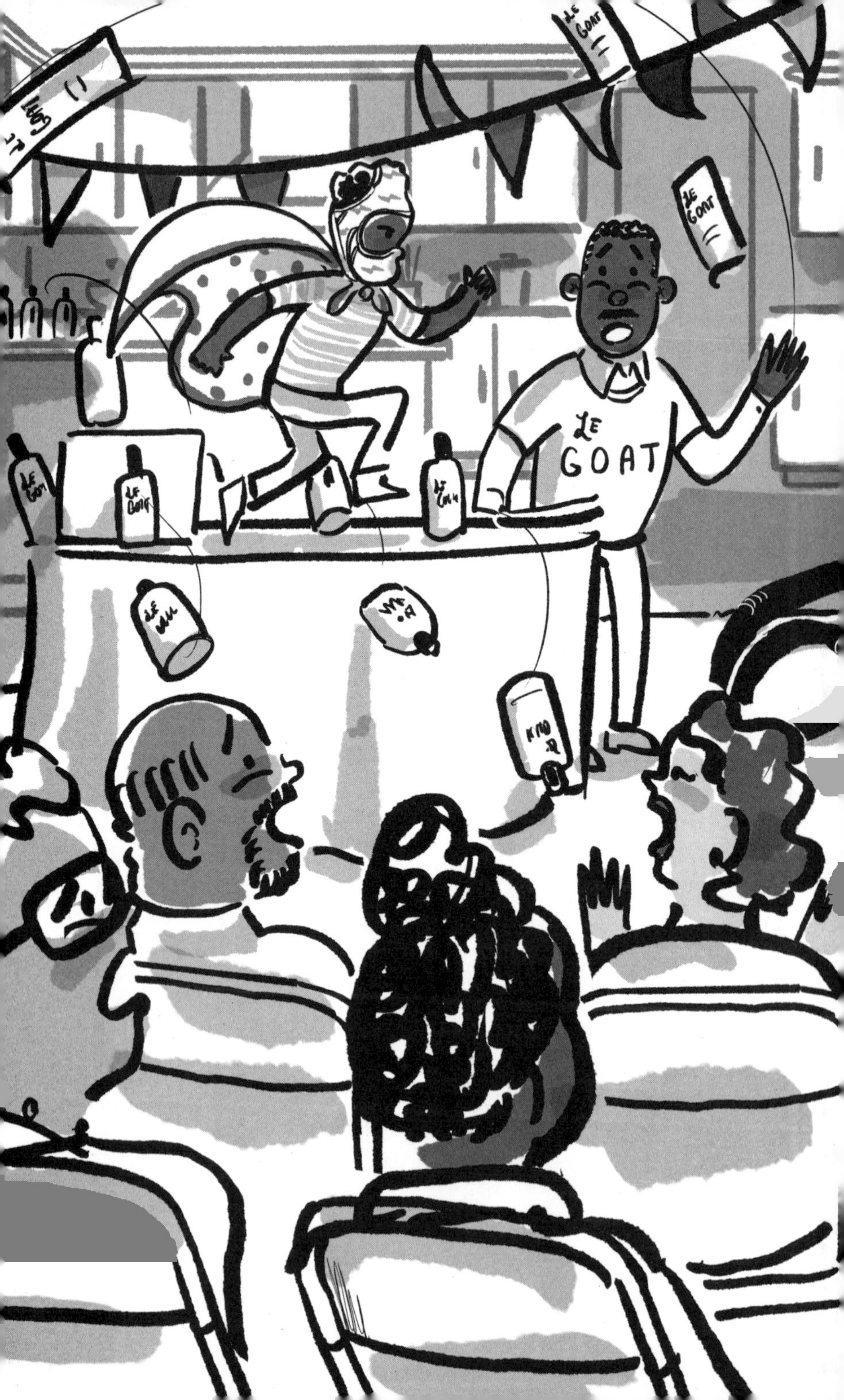
LE GOAT
LE GOAT
LE GOAT

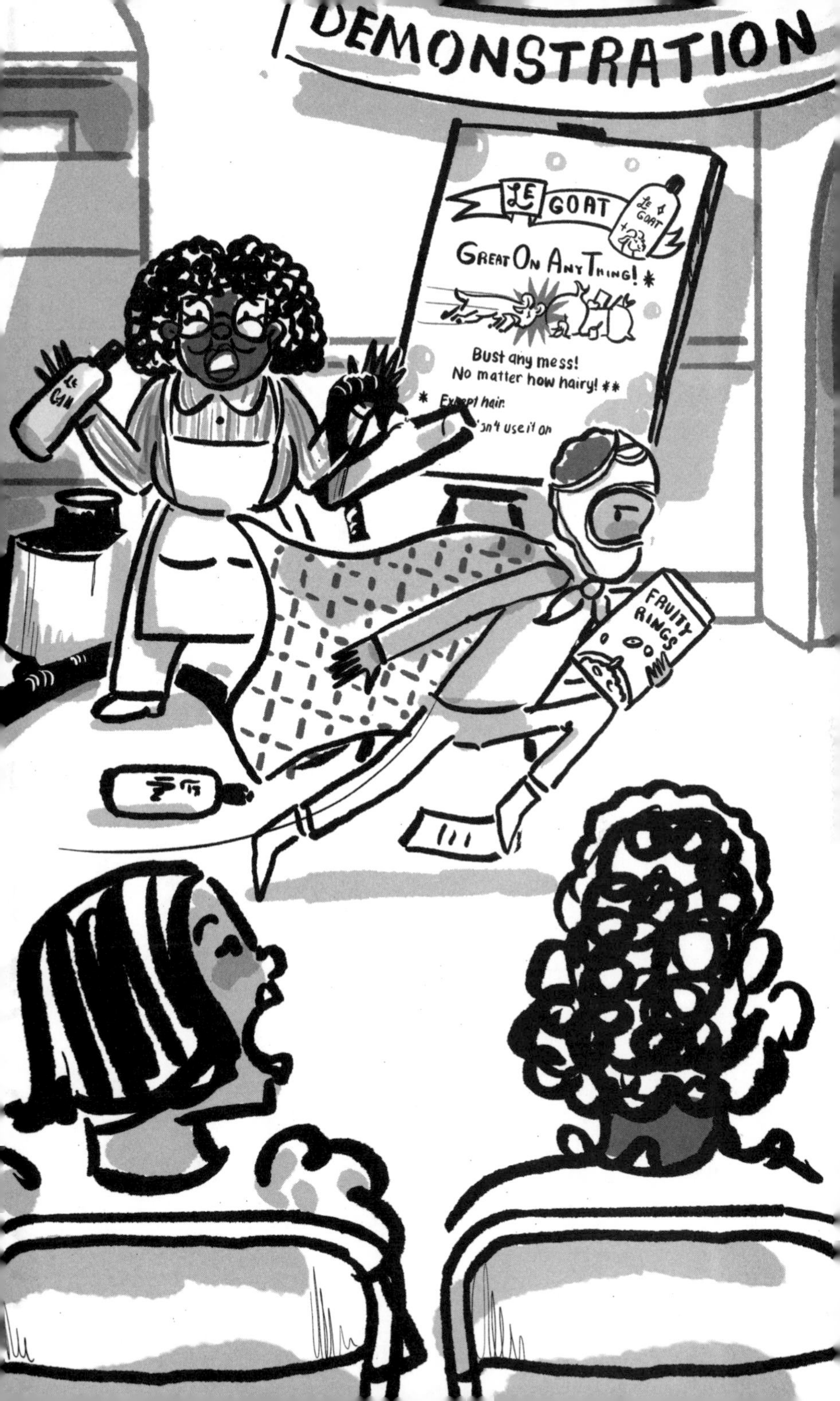
DEMONSTRATION
LE GOAT
LE GOAT
GREAT ON ANYTHING! *
Bust any mess!
No matter how hairy! **
* Except hair.
FRUITY RINGS

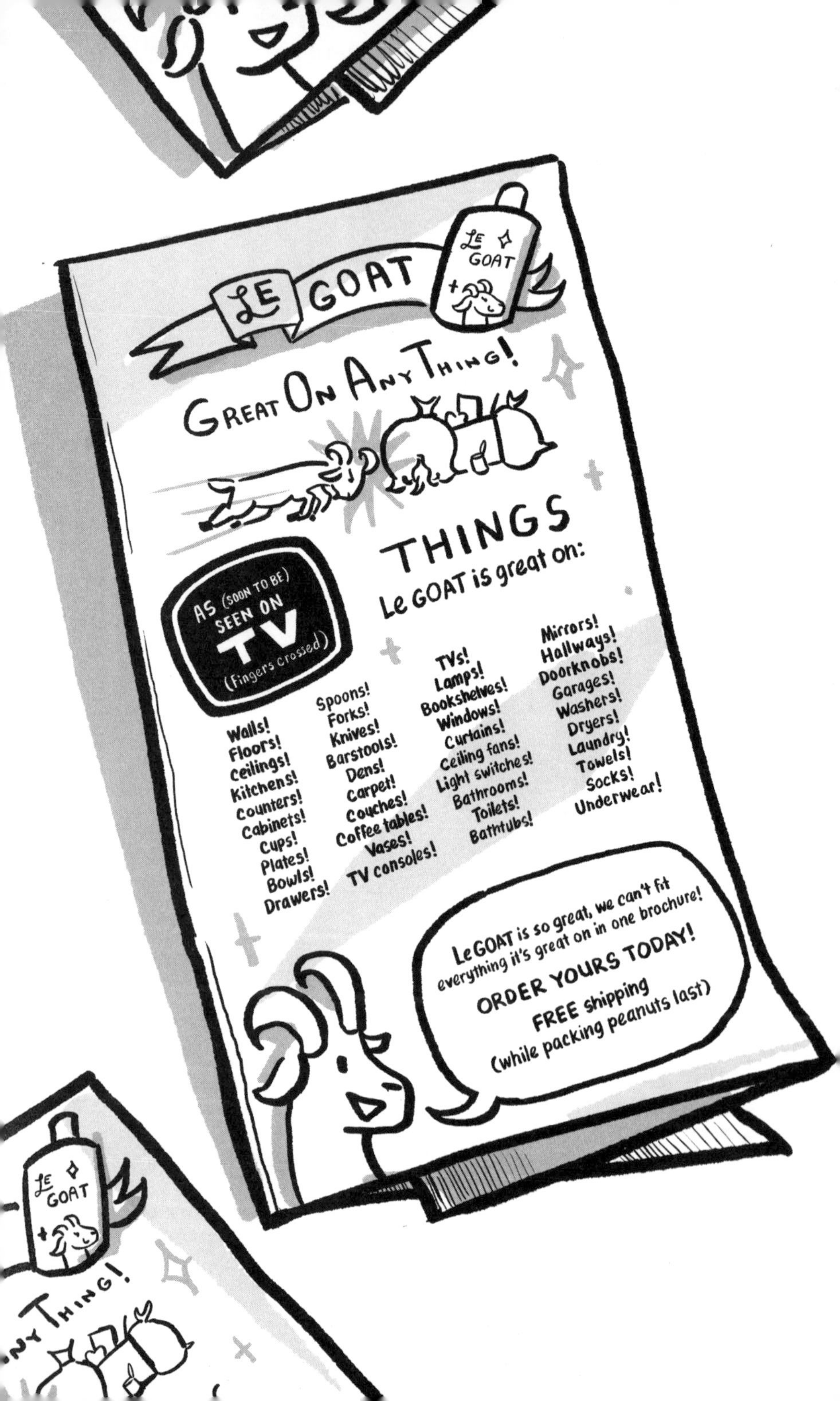

LE GOAT
LE GOAT
GREAT ON ANY THING!
THINGS
Le GOAT is great on:
AS (SOON TO BE) SEEN ON TV (Fingers crossed)
Walls!
Floors!
Ceilings!
Kitchens!
Counters!
Cabinets!
Cups!
Plates!
Bowls!
Drawers!
Spoons!
Forks!
Knives!
Barstools!
Dens!
Carpet!
Couches!
Coffee tables!
Vases!
TV consoles!
TVs!
Lamps!
Bookshelves!
Windows!
Curtains!
Ceiling fans!
Light switches!
Bathrooms!
Toilets!
Bathtubs!
Mirrors!
Hallways!
Doorknobs!
Garages!
Washers!
Dryers!
Laundry!
Towels!
Socks!
Underwear!
Le GOAT is so great, we can't fit everything it's great on in one brochure!
ORDER YOURS TODAY!
FREE shipping
(while packing peanuts last)
LE GOAT